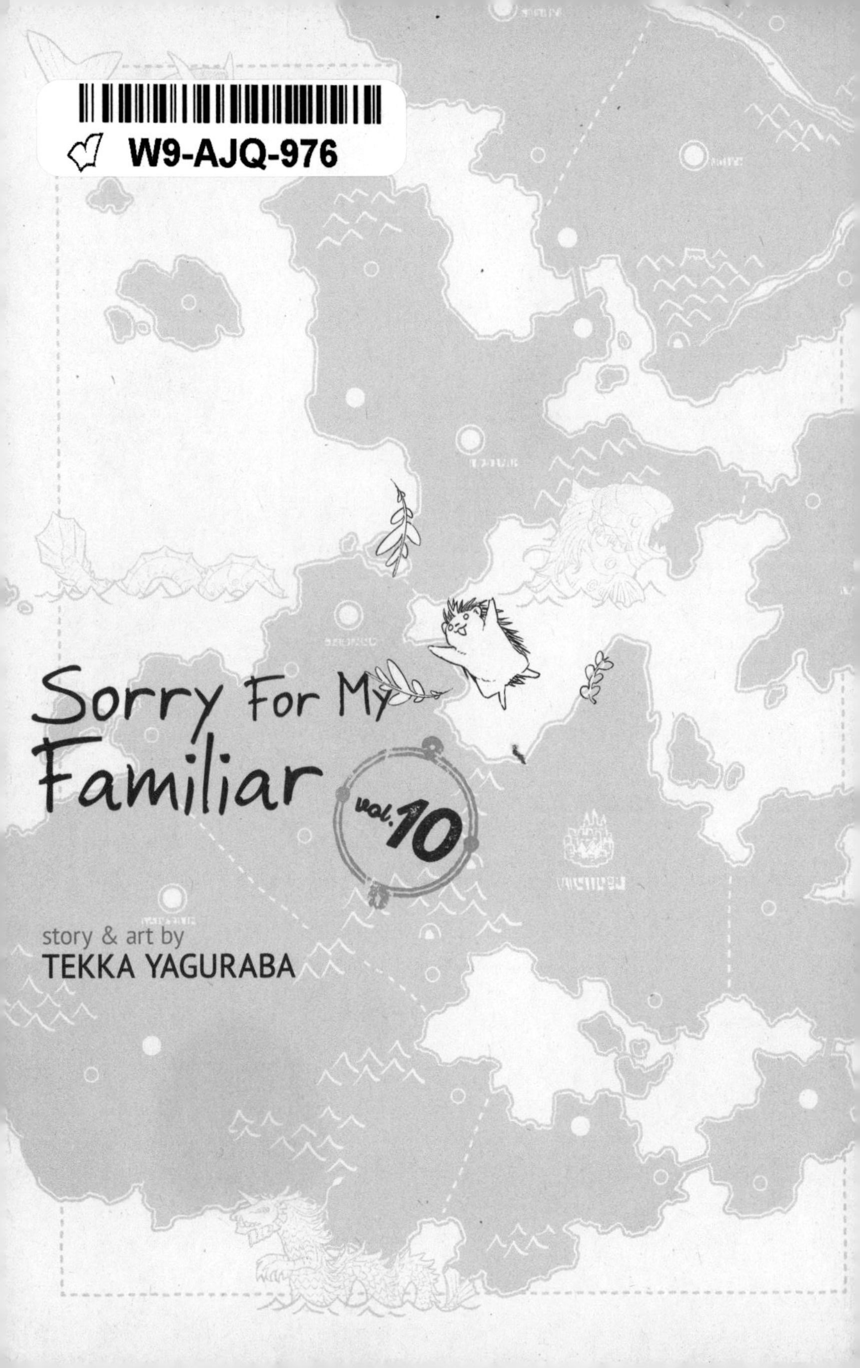

Sorry For My Familiar

vol. 10

story & art by
TEKKA YAGURABA

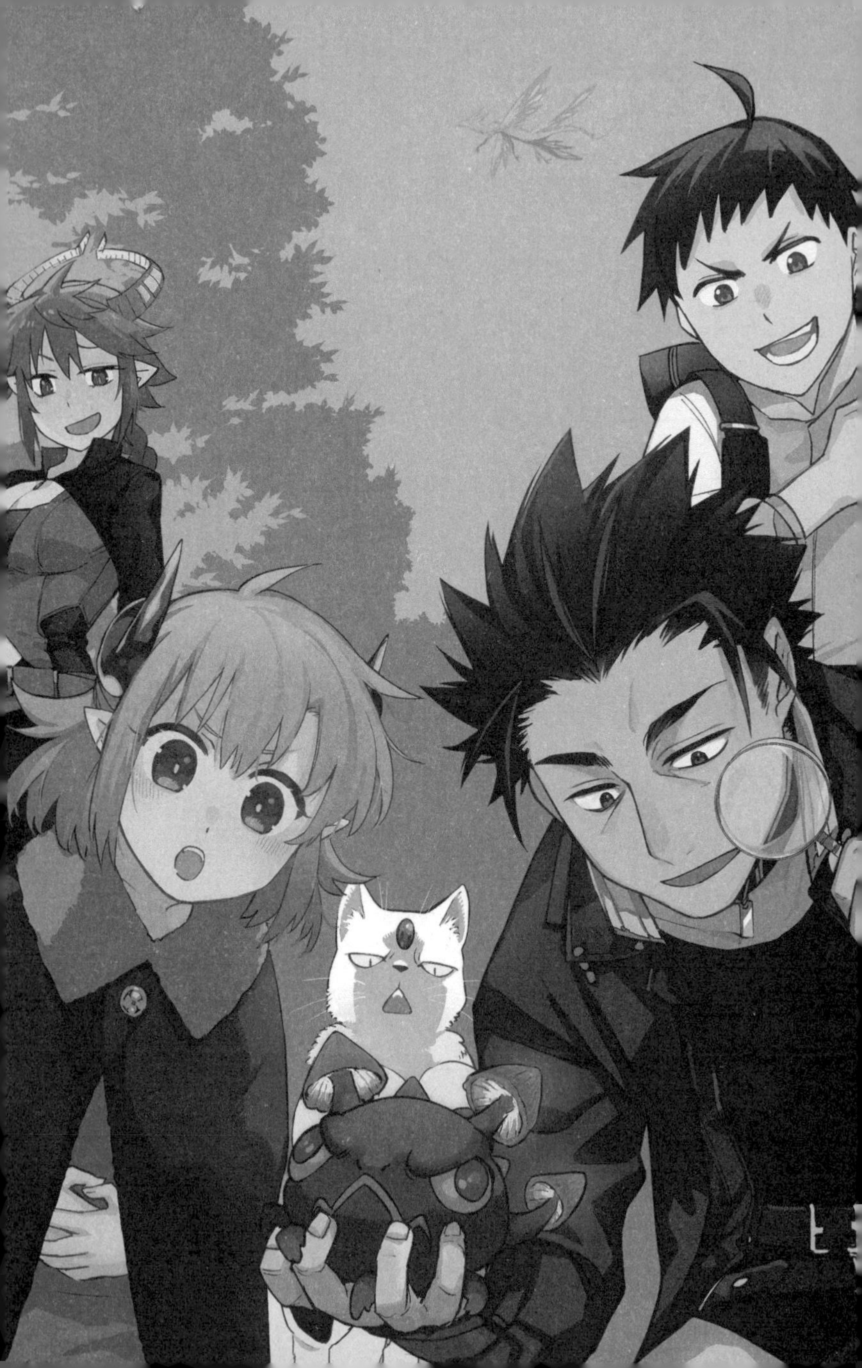

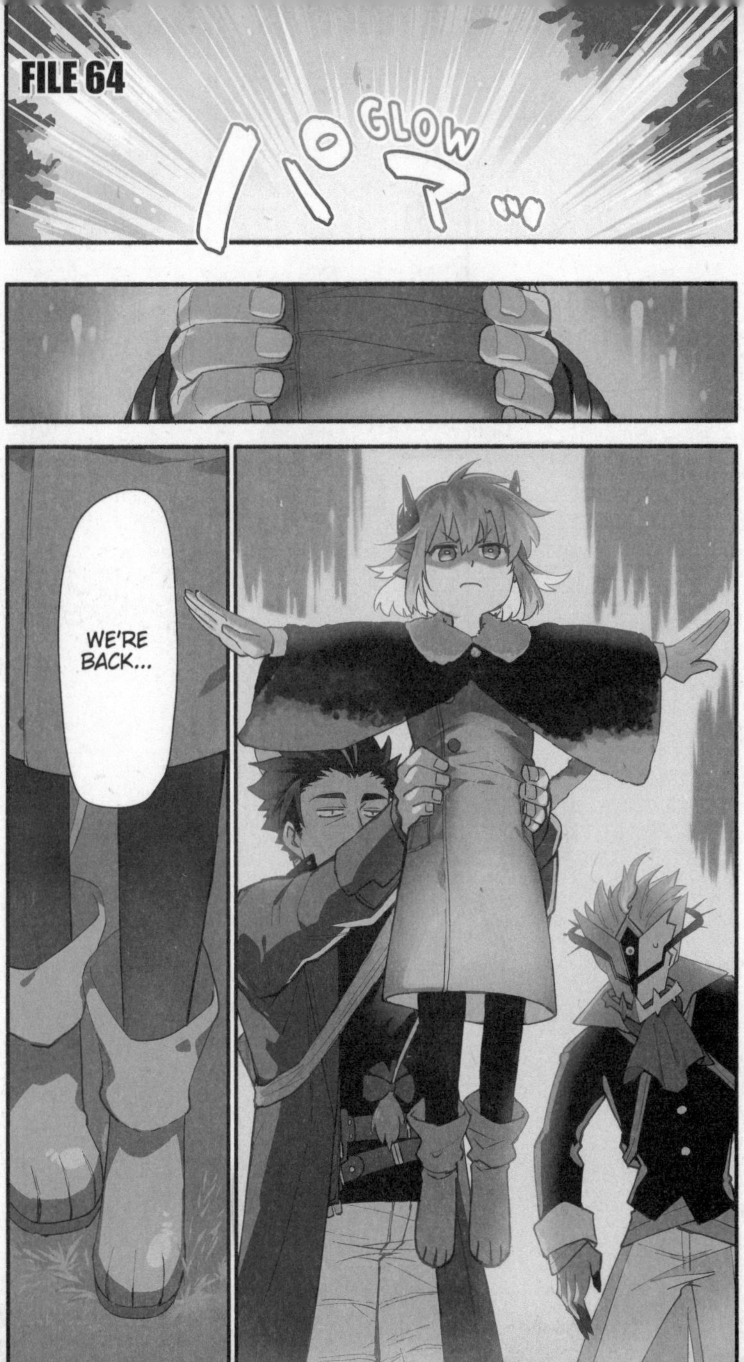
FILE 64
パァ…
GLOW
WE'RE BACK...

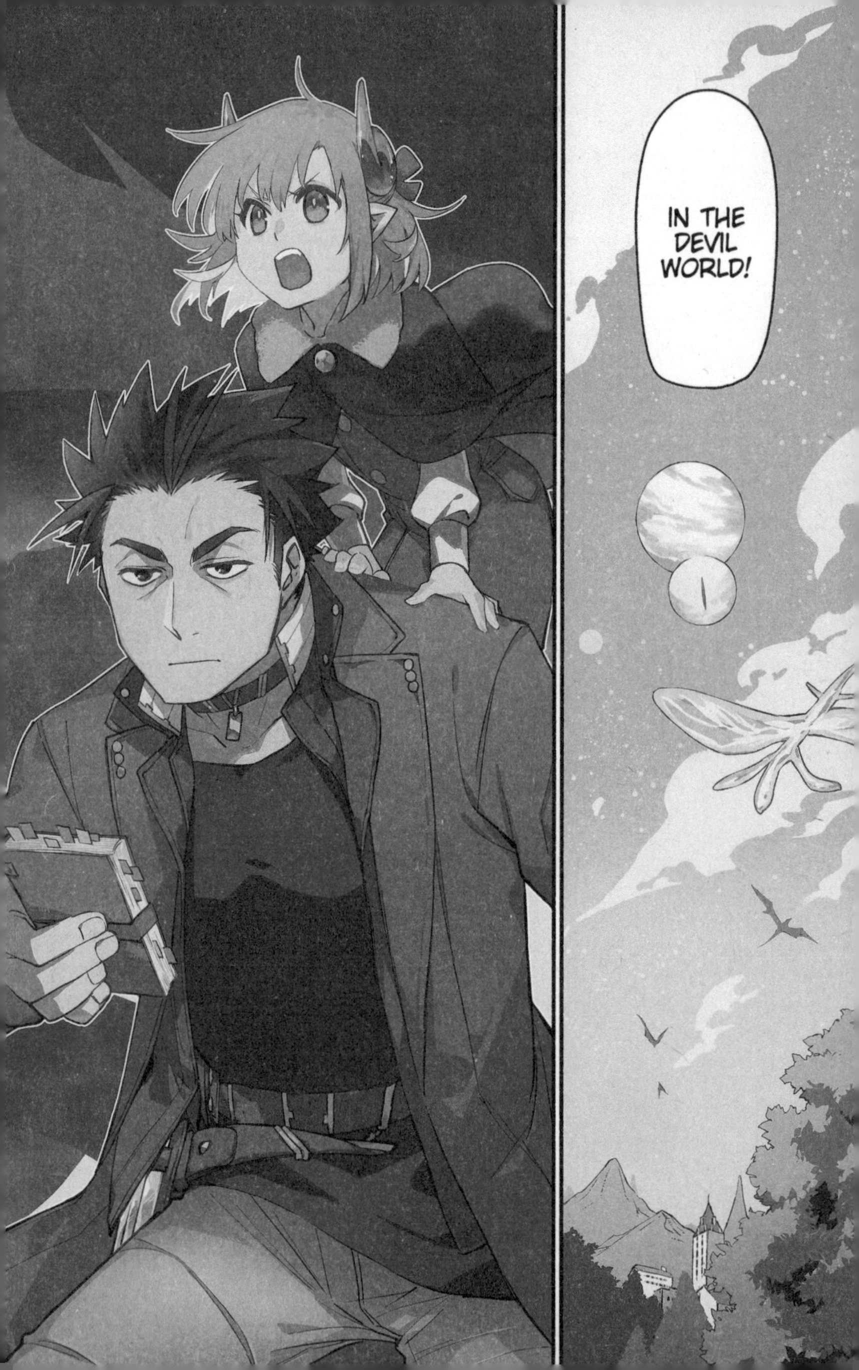
IN THE DEVIL WORLD!

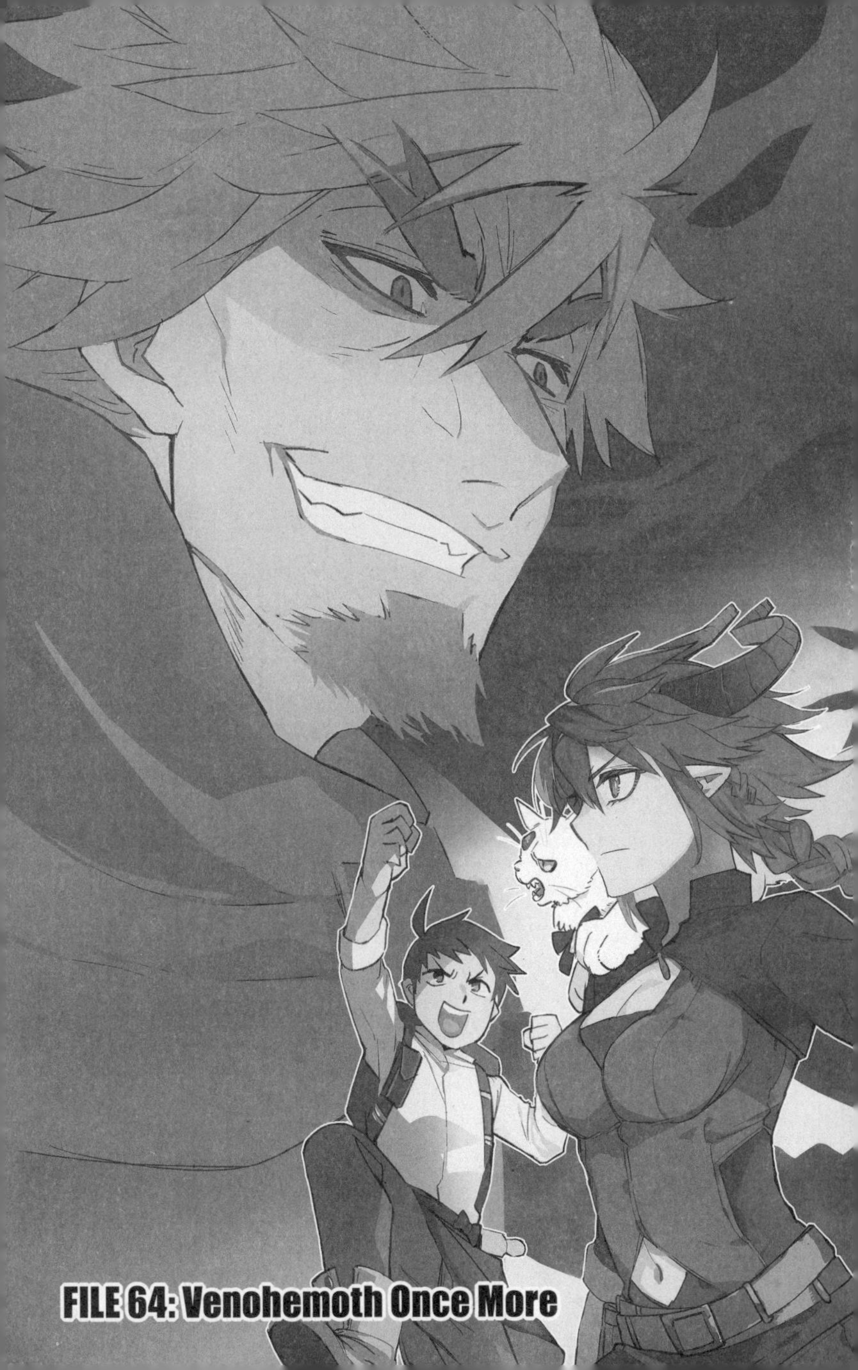

FILE 64: Venohemoth Once More

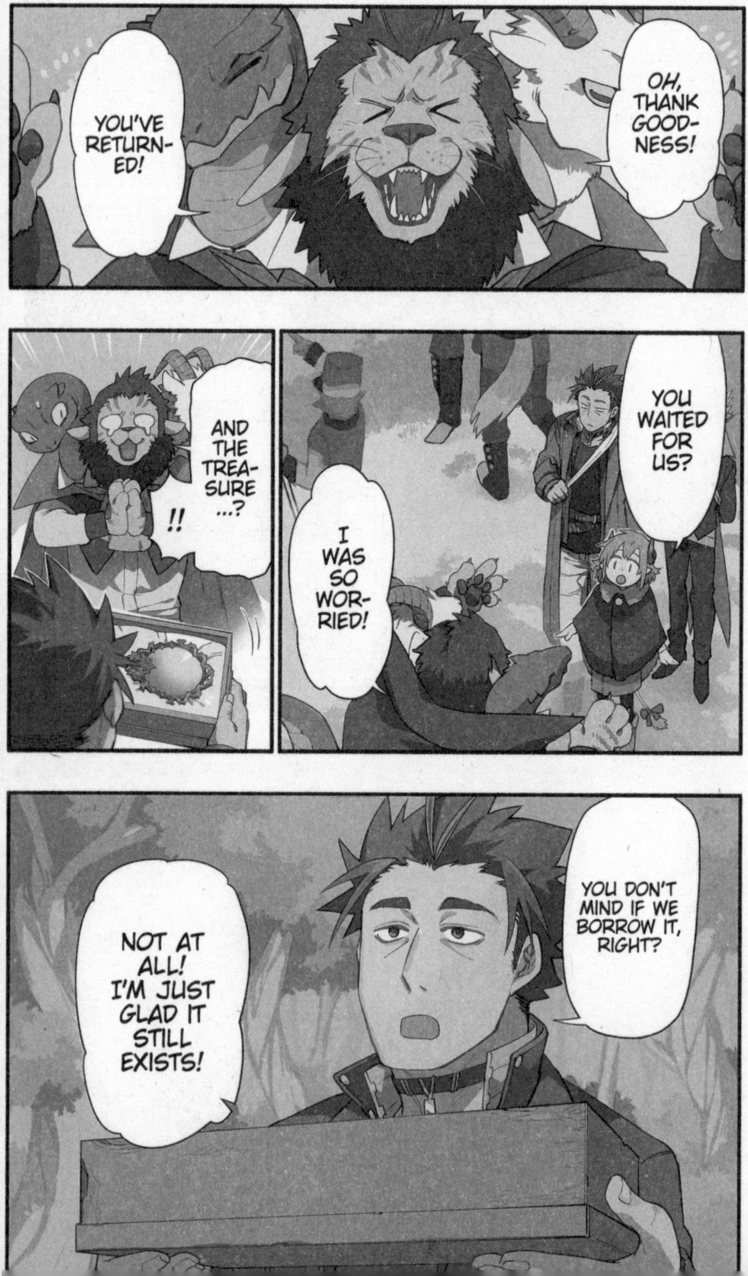
OH, THANK GOODNESS!
YOU'VE RETURNED!
YOU WAITED FOR US?
I WAS SO WORRIED!
AND THE TREASURE ...?
!!
YOU DON'T MIND IF WE BORROW IT, RIGHT?
NOT AT ALL! I'M JUST GLAD IT STILL EXISTS!

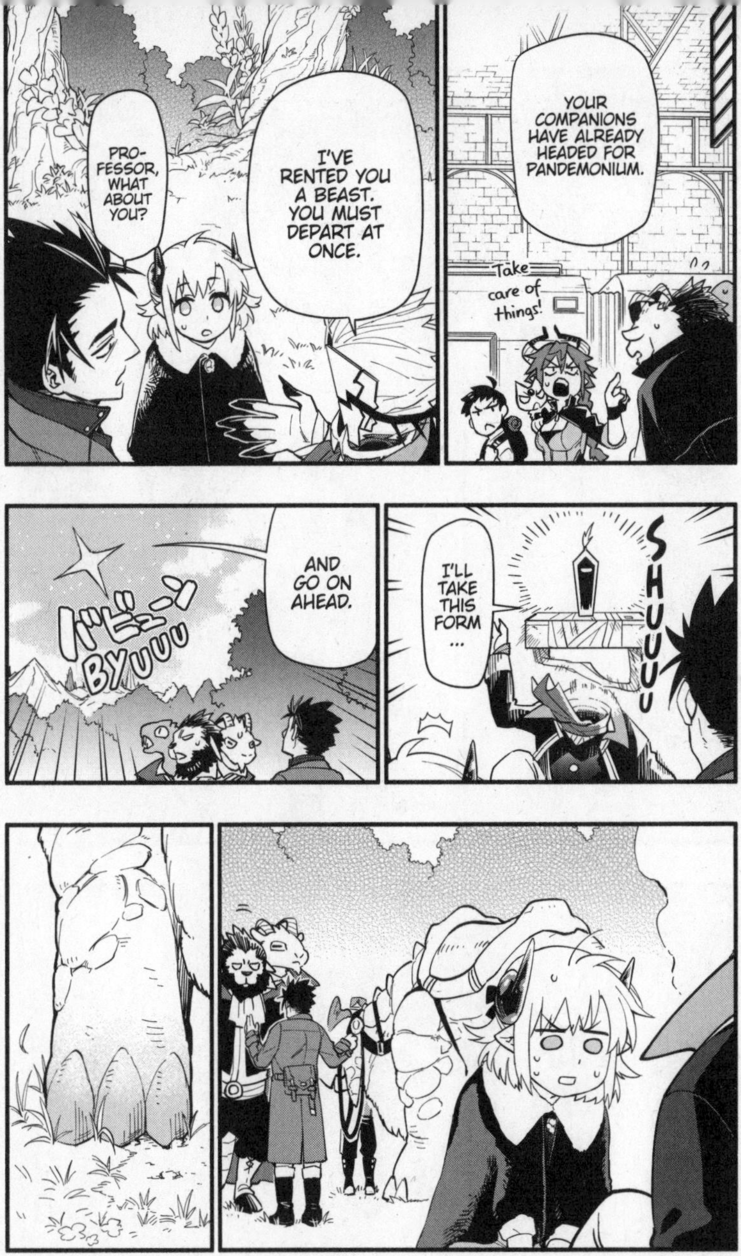
YOUR COMPANIONS HAVE ALREADY HEADED FOR PANDEMONIUM.
Take care of things!
I'VE RENTED YOU A BEAST. YOU MUST DEPART AT ONCE.
PRO-FESSOR, WHAT ABOUT YOU?
SHUUUUU
I'LL TAKE THIS FORM ...
AND GO ON AHEAD.
バビューン
BYUUU

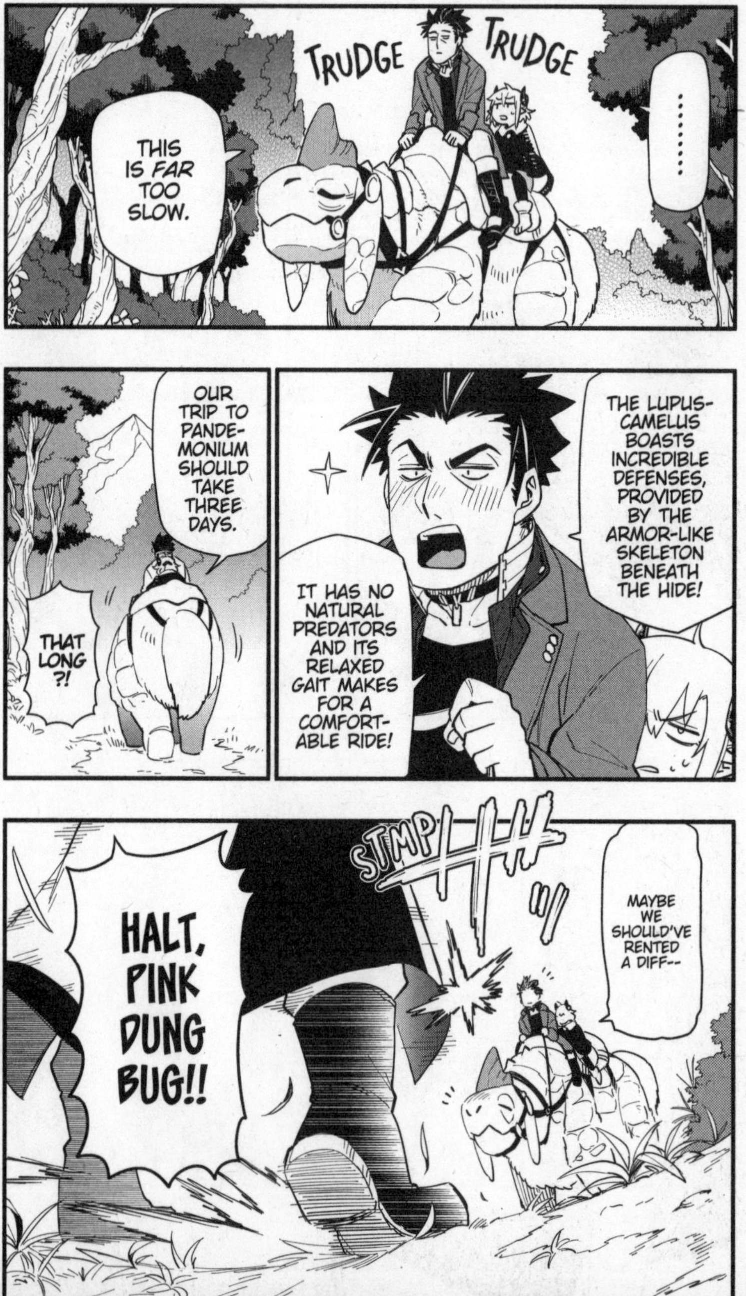

....
TRUDGE
TRUDGE
THIS IS FAR TOO SLOW.
THE LUPUS-CAMELUS BOASTS INCREDIBLE DEFENSES, PROVIDED BY THE ARMOR-LIKE SKELETON BENEATH THE HIDE!
IT HAS NO NATURAL PREDATORS AND ITS RELAXED GAIT MAKES FOR A COMFORTABLE RIDE!
OUR TRIP TO PANDEMONIUM SHOULD TAKE THREE DAYS.
THAT LONG?!
MAYBE WE SHOULD'VE RENTED A DIFF--
STMP
HALT, PINK DUNG BUG!!

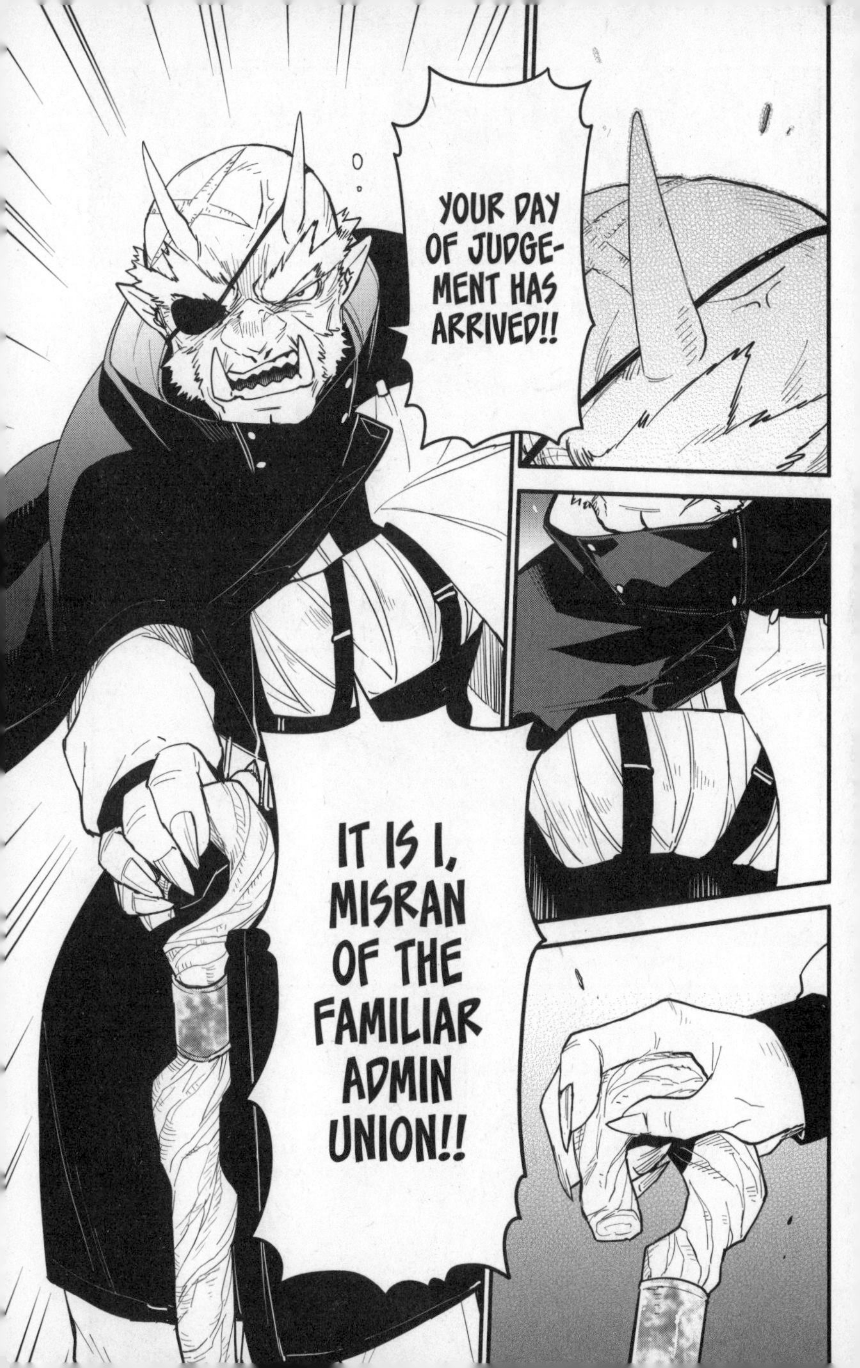
YOUR DAY OF JUDGE-MENT HAS ARRIVED!!
IT IS I, MISRAN OF THE FAMILIAR ADMIN UNION!!

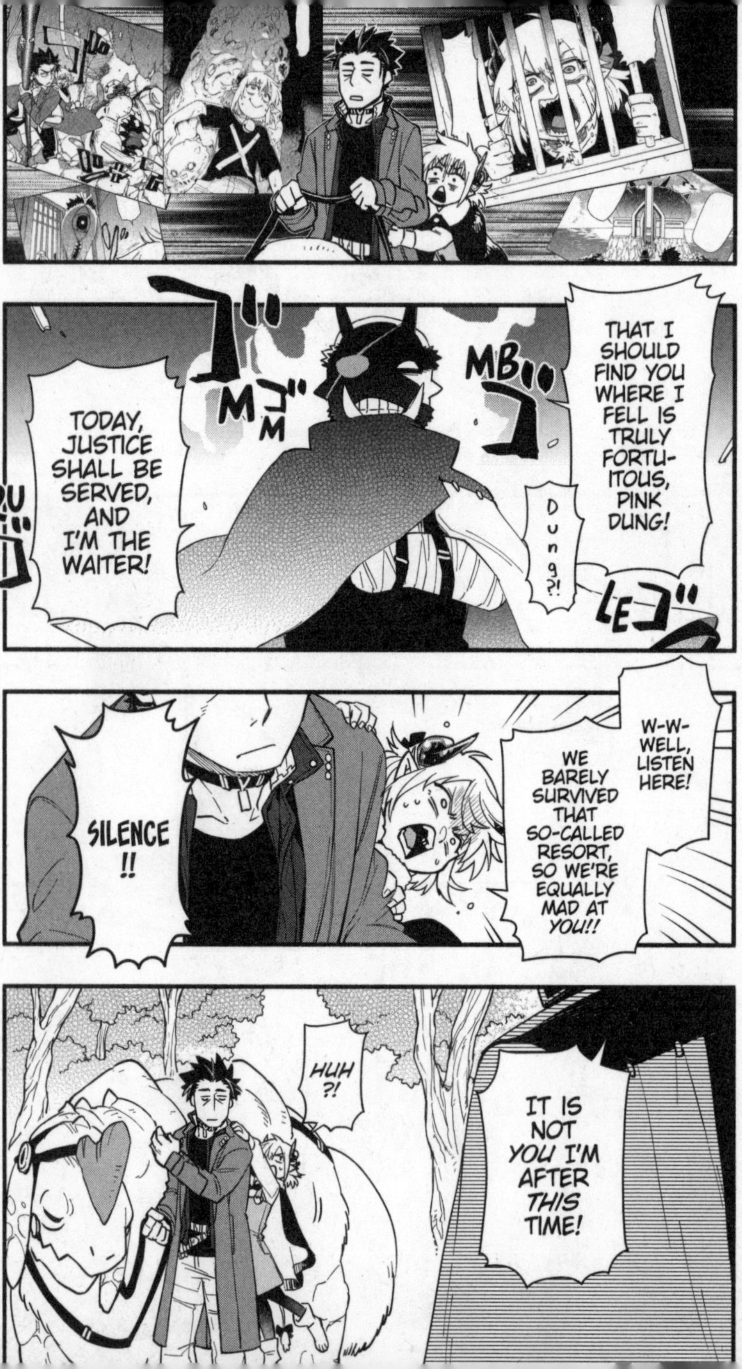

THAT I SHOULD FIND YOU WHERE I FELL IS TRULY FORTUITOUS, PINK DUNG!
Dung?!
TODAY, JUSTICE SHALL BE SERVED, AND I'M THE WAITER!
W-W-WELL, LISTEN HERE!
WE BARELY SURVIVED THAT SO-CALLED RESORT, SO WE'RE EQUALLY MAD AT YOU!!
SILENCE!!
IT IS NOT YOU I'M AFTER THIS TIME!
HUH?!

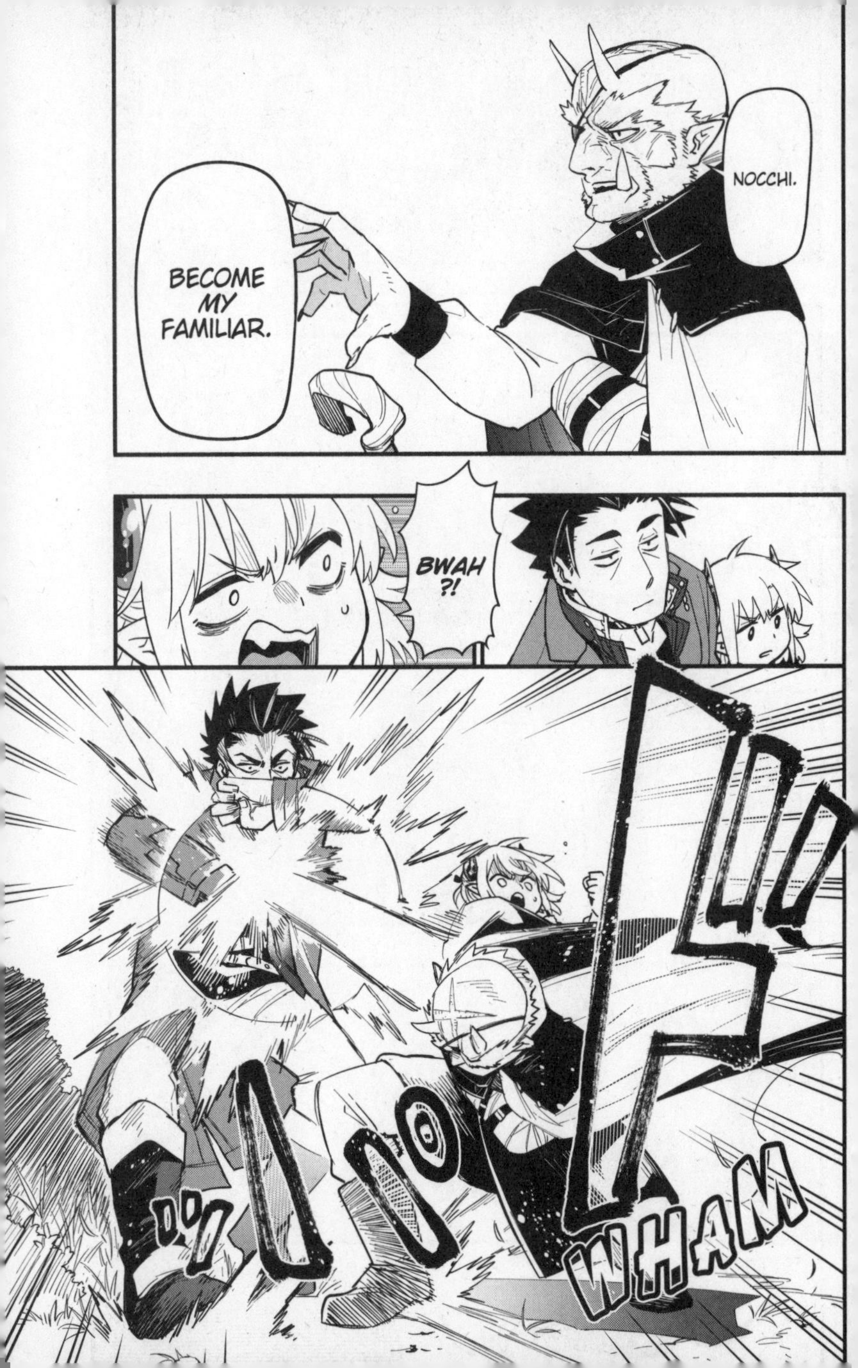
NOCCHI.
BECOME MY FAMILIAR.
BWAH ?!
DOOOOO
WHAM

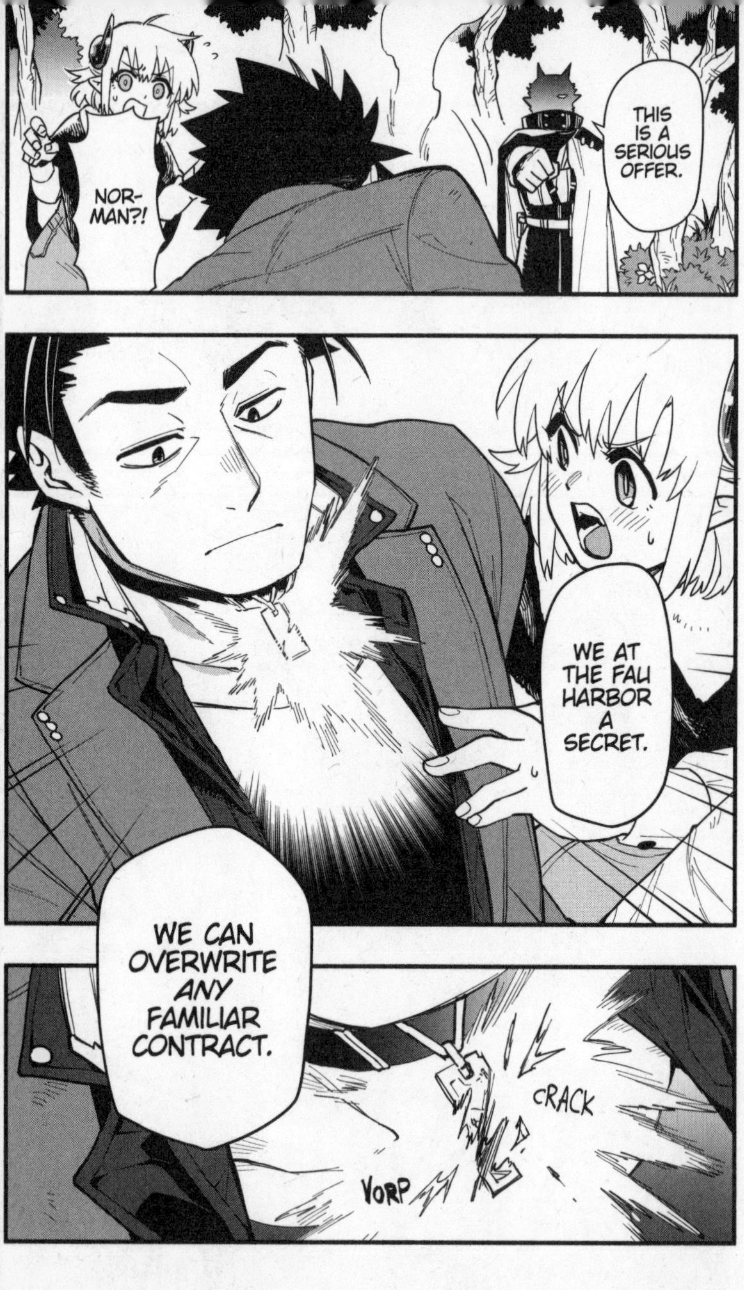
THIS IS A SERIOUS OFFER.
NOR-MAN?!
WE AT THE FAU HARBOR A SECRET.
WE CAN OVERWRITE *ANY* FAMILIAR CONTRACT.
CRACK
VORP

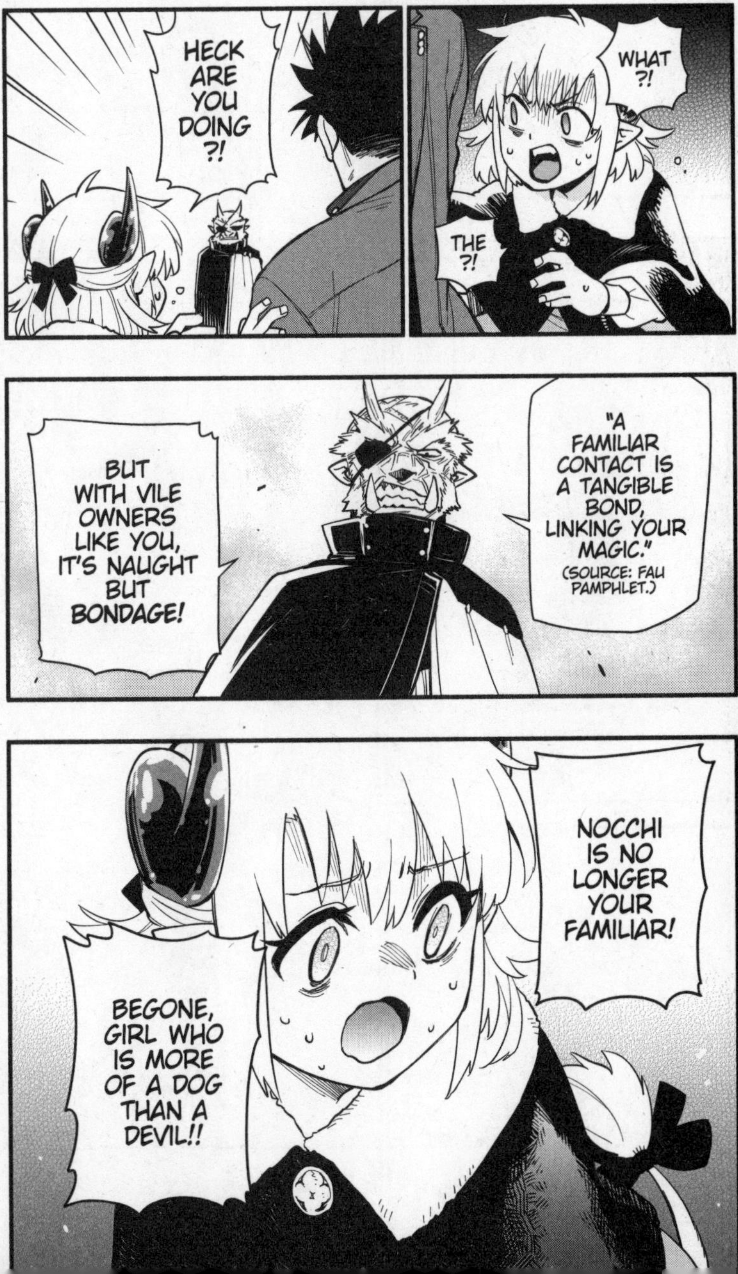
WHAT ?!
THE ?!
HECK ARE YOU DOING ?!
"A FAMILIAR CONTACT IS A TANGIBLE BOND, LINKING YOUR MAGIC."
(SOURCE: FAU PAMPHLET.)
BUT WITH VILE OWNERS LIKE YOU, IT'S NAUGHT BUT BONDAGE!
NOCCHI IS NO LONGER YOUR FAMILIAR!
BEGONE, GIRL WHO IS MORE OF A DOG THAN A DEVIL!!

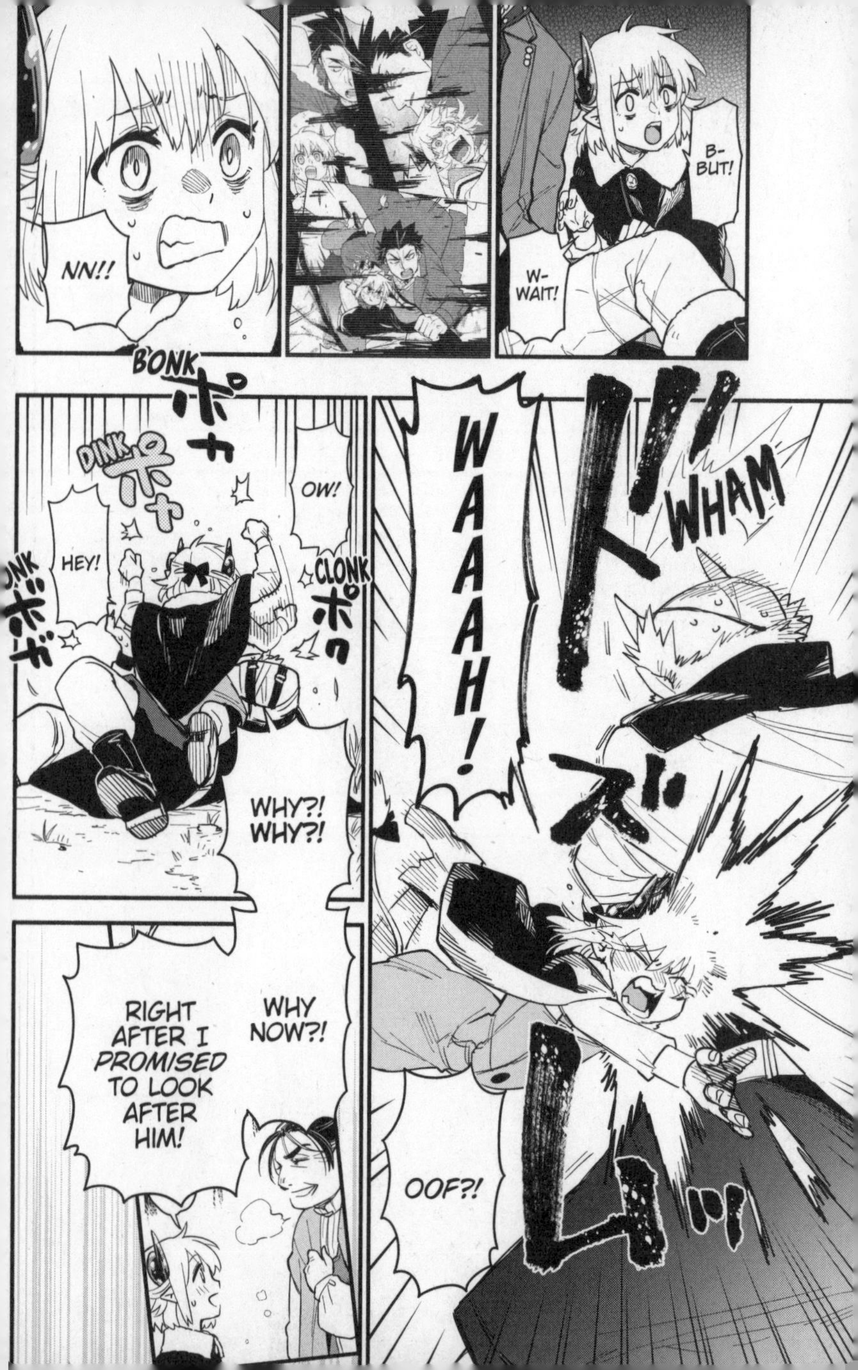
B-BUT!
W-WAIT!
NN!!
WHAM
WAAAAH!
OOF?!
BONK
DINK
OW!
HEY!
CLONK
ONK
WHY?! WHY?!
WHY NOW?!
RIGHT AFTER I PROMISED TO LOOK AFTER HIM!

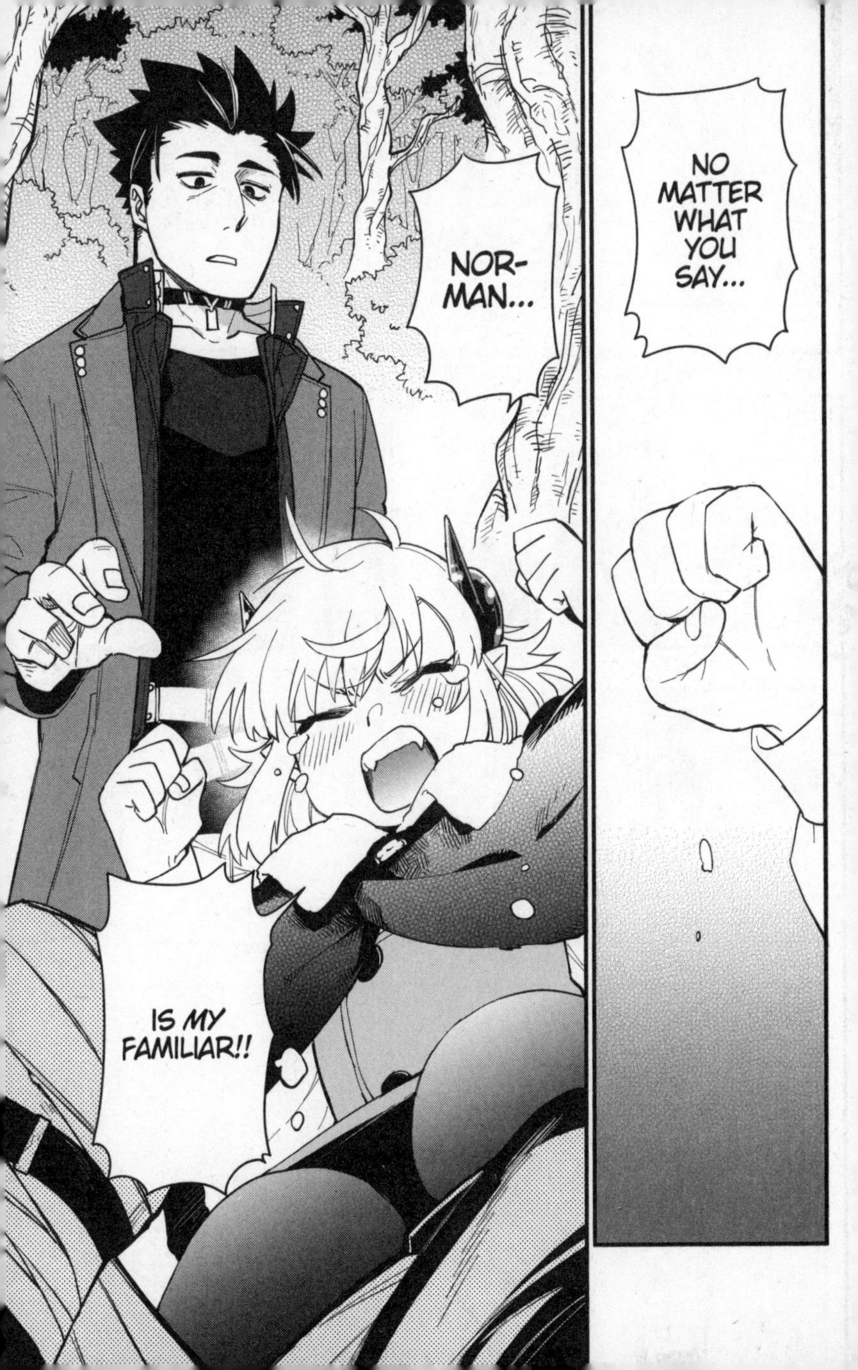
NO MATTER WHAT YOU SAY...
NOR-MAN...
IS MY FAMILIAR!!

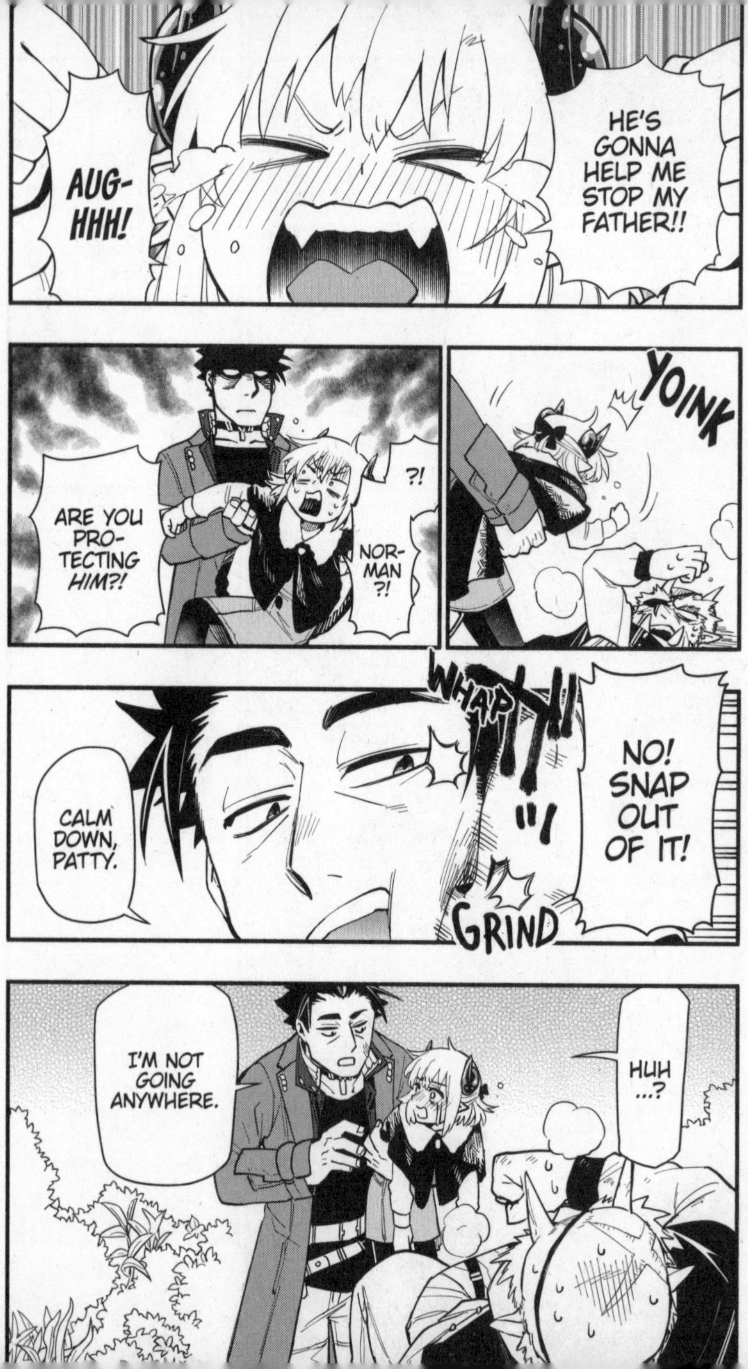
HE'S GONNA HELP ME STOP MY FATHER!!
AUGHHH!
YOINK
?!
NORMAN?!
ARE YOU PROTECTING HIM?!
WHAP
NO! SNAP OUT OF IT!
GRIND
CALM DOWN, PATTY.
HUH...?
I'M NOT GOING ANYWHERE.

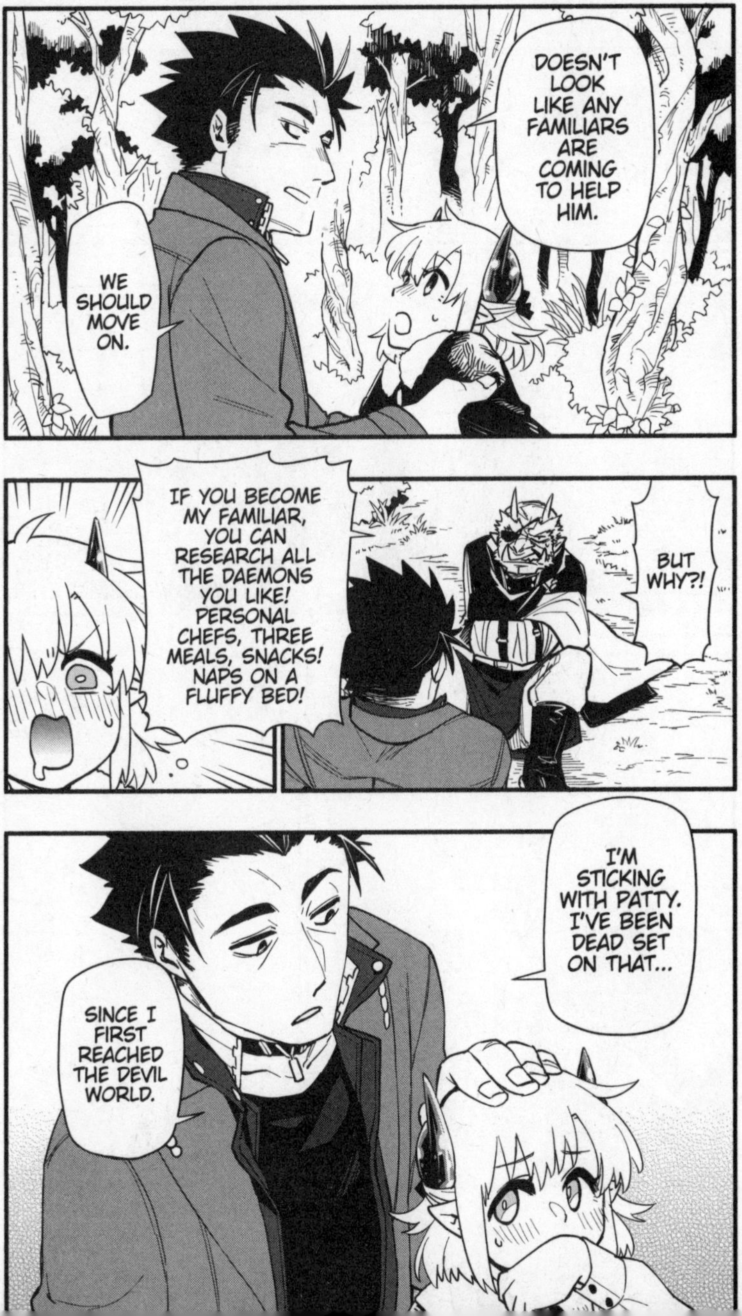
DOESN'T LOOK LIKE ANY FAMILIARS ARE COMING TO HELP HIM.
WE SHOULD MOVE ON.
BUT WHY?!
IF YOU BECOME MY FAMILIAR, YOU CAN RESEARCH ALL THE DAEMONS YOU LIKE! PERSONAL CHEFS, THREE MEALS, SNACKS! NAPS ON A FLUFFY BED!
I'M STICKING WITH PATTY. I'VE BEEN DEAD SET ON THAT...
SINCE I FIRST REACHED THE DEVIL WORLD.

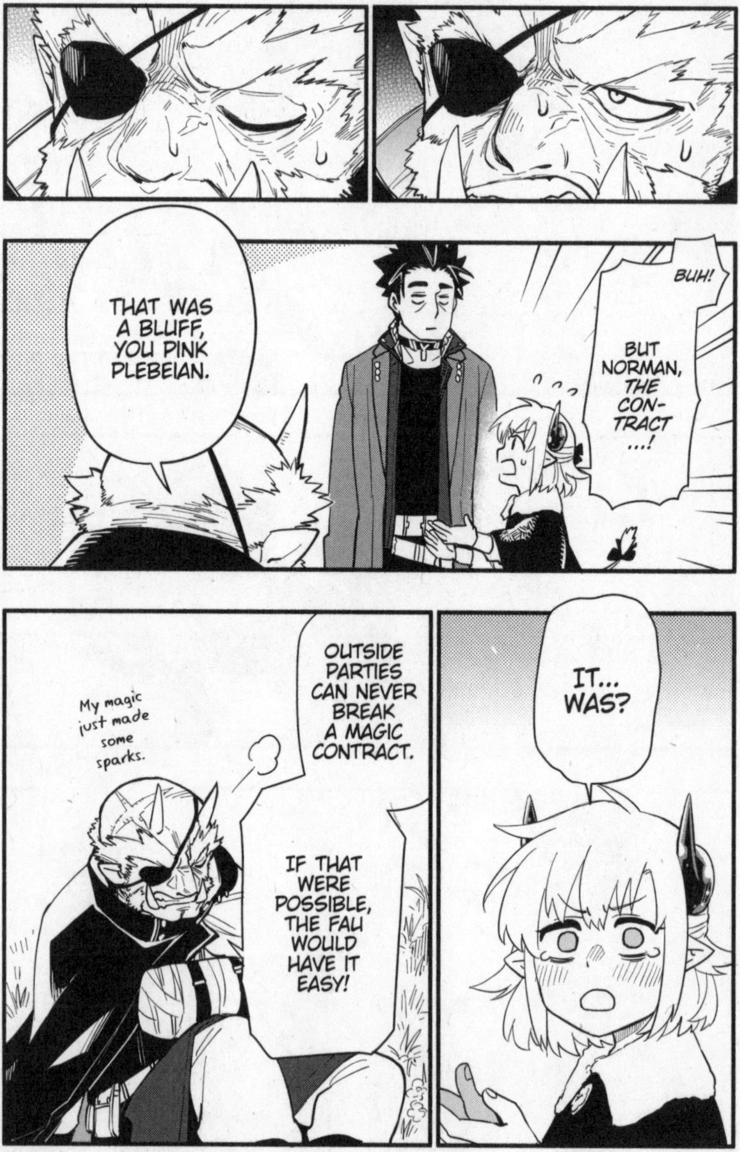
BUH!
BUT NORMAN, THE CON-TRACT ...!
THAT WAS A BLUFF, YOU PINK PLEBEIAN.
IT... WAS?
OUTSIDE PARTIES CAN NEVER BREAK A MAGIC CONTRACT.
IF THAT WERE POSSIBLE, THE FAU WOULD HAVE IT EASY!
My magic just made some sparks.

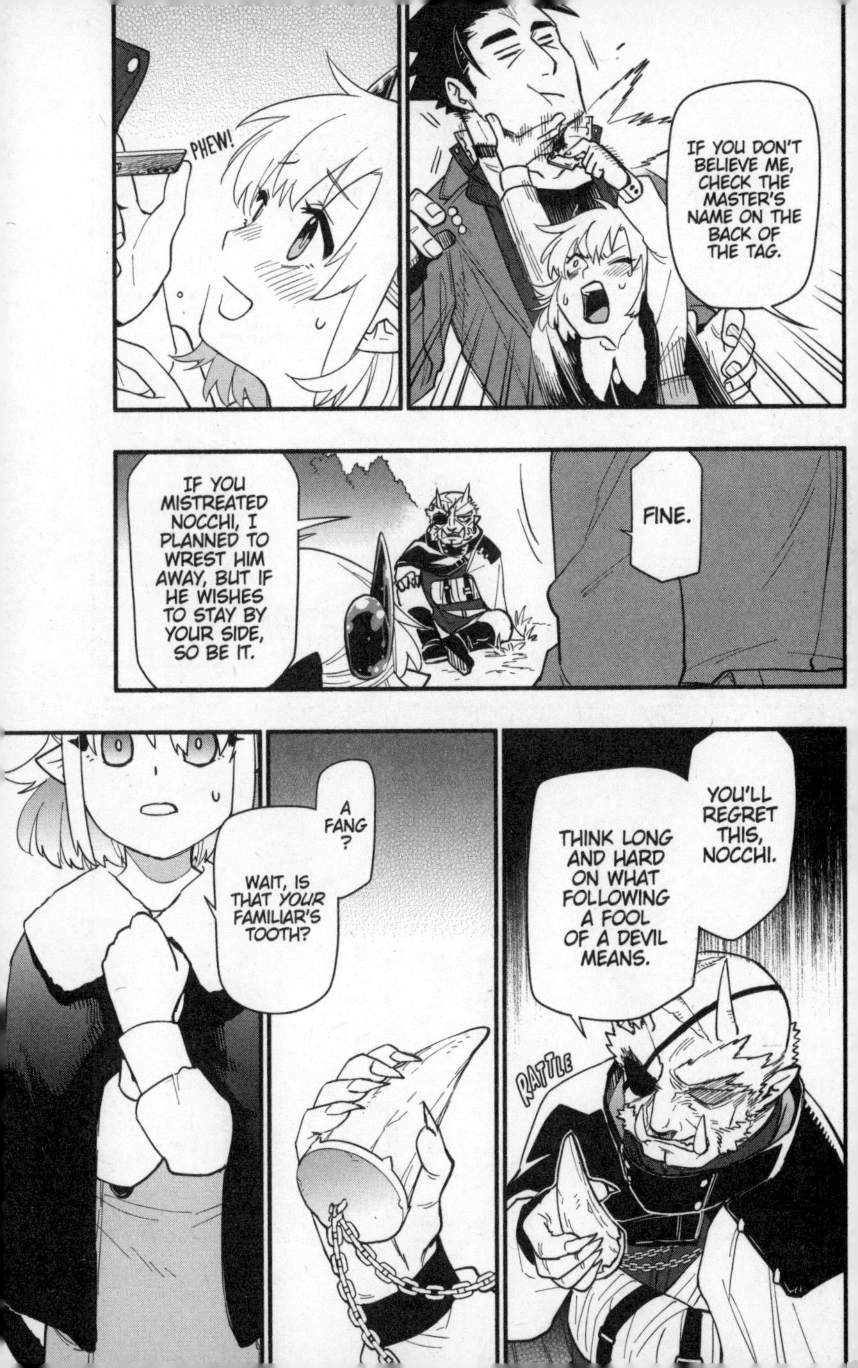
IF YOU DON'T BELIEVE ME, CHECK THE MASTER'S NAME ON THE BACK OF THE TAG.
PHEW!
FINE.
IF YOU MISTREATED NOCCHI, I PLANNED TO WREST HIM AWAY, BUT IF HE WISHES TO STAY BY YOUR SIDE, SO BE IT.
YOU'LL REGRET THIS, NOCCHI.
THINK LONG AND HARD ON WHAT FOLLOWING A FOOL OF A DEVIL MEANS.
RATTLE
A FANG?
WAIT, IS THAT *YOUR* FAMILIAR'S TOOTH?

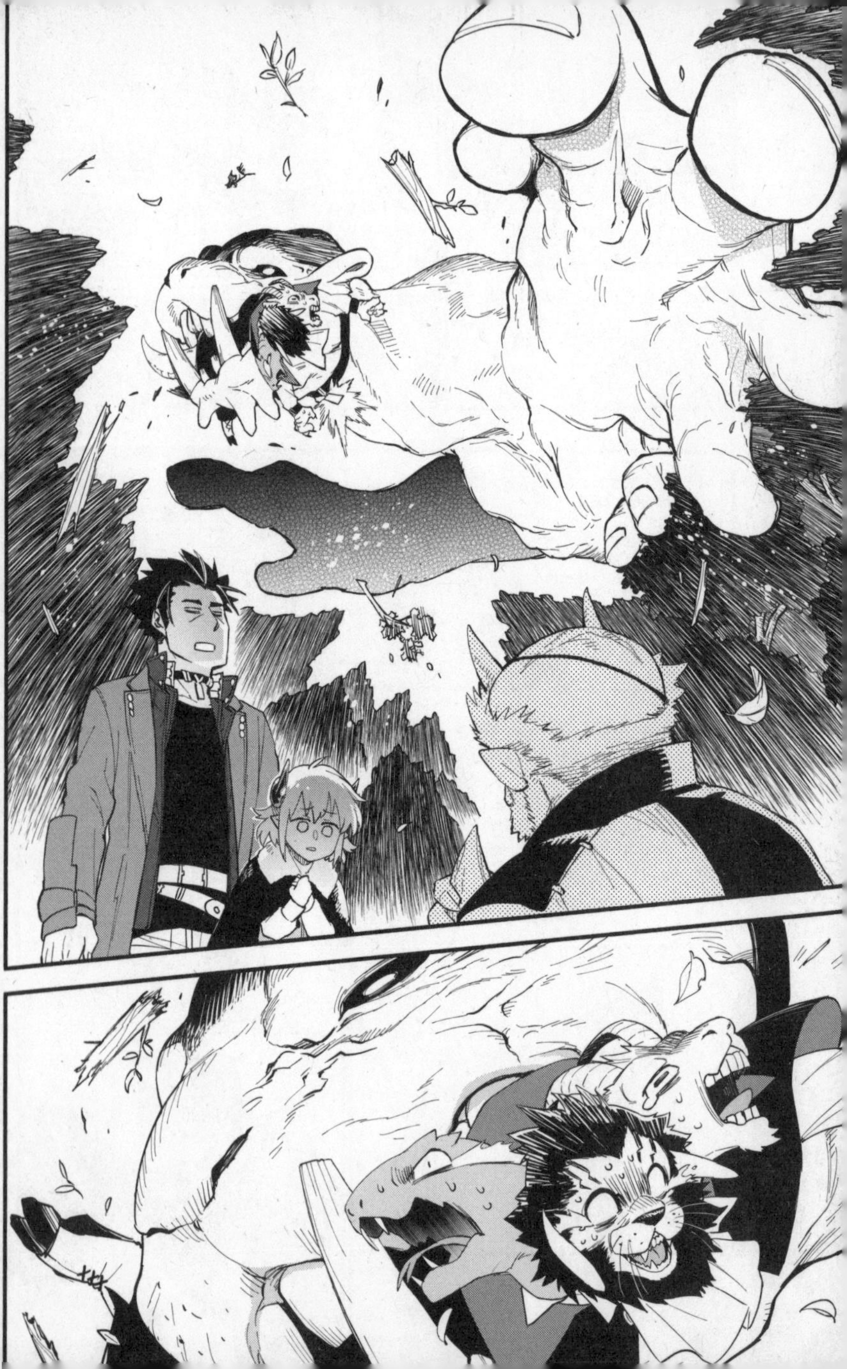

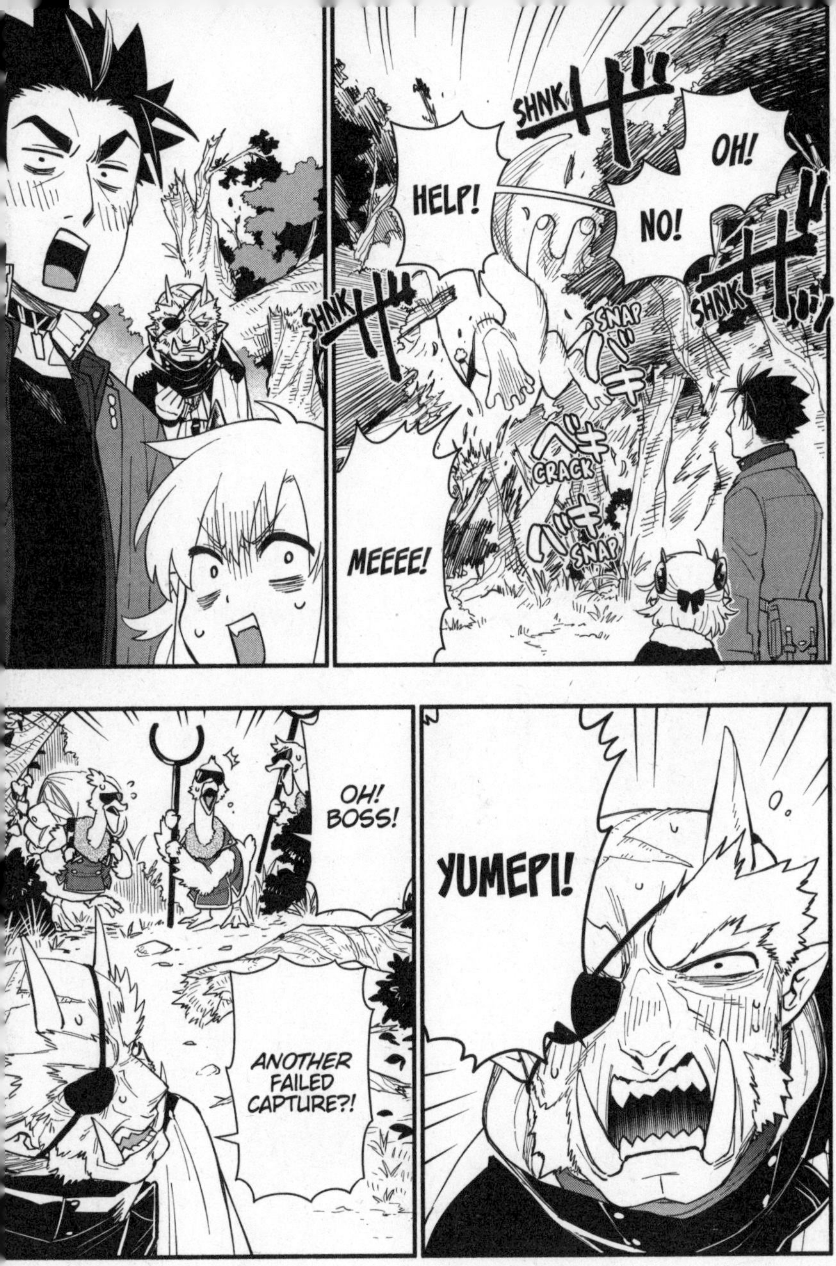
SHNK
OH! NO!
SHNK
HELP! MEEEE!
SHNK
SNAP
CRACK
SNAP
YUMEPI!
OH! BOSS!
ANOTHER FAILED CAPTURE?!

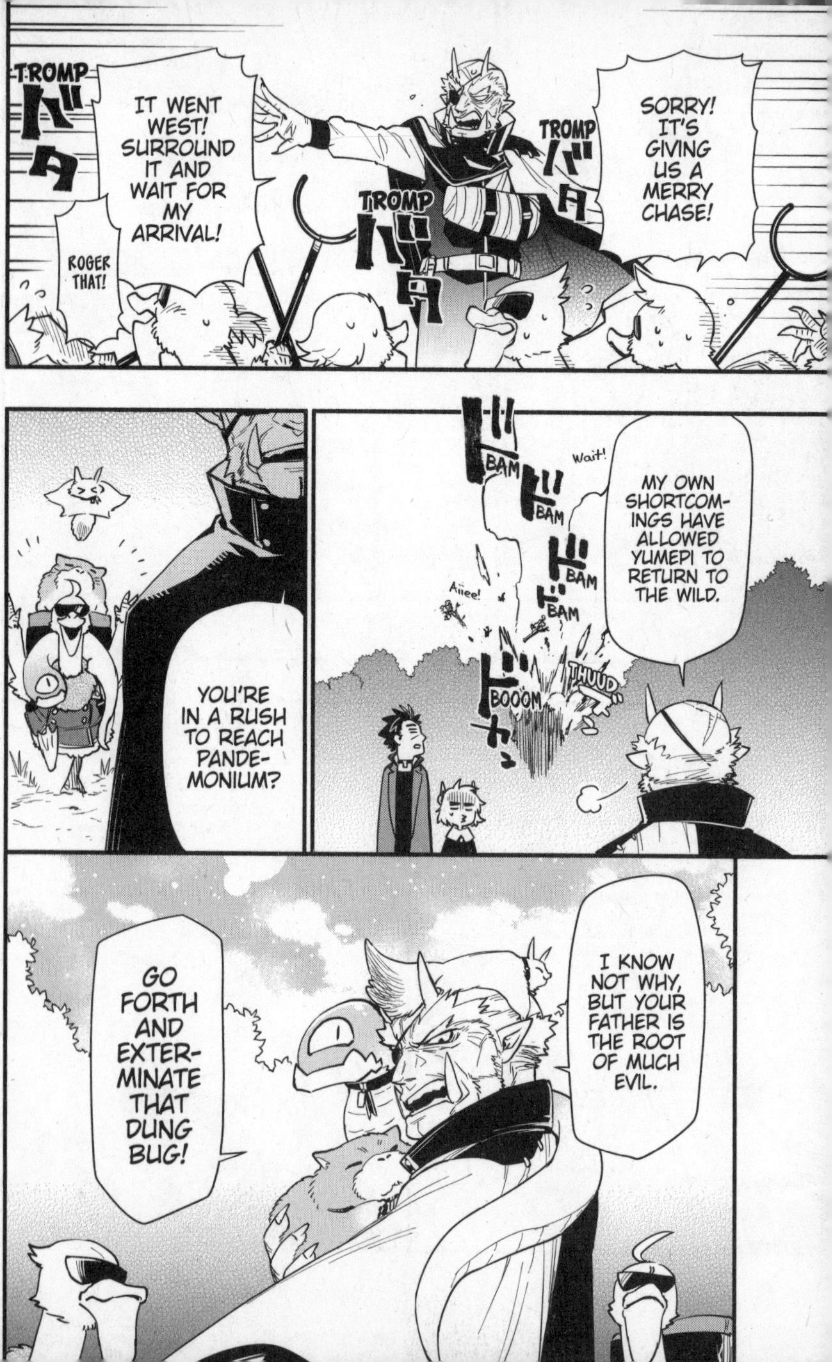
SORRY! IT'S GIVING US A MERRY CHASE!
TROMP
TROMP
IT WENT WEST! SURROUND IT AND WAIT FOR MY ARRIVAL!
TROMP
ROGER THAT!
BAM
BAM
BAM
BAM
Wait!
MY OWN SHORTCOMINGS HAVE ALLOWED YUMEPI TO RETURN TO THE WILD.
Aiiee!
THUUD
BOOOM
YOU'RE IN A RUSH TO REACH PANDEMONIUM?
I KNOW NOT WHY, BUT YOUR FATHER IS THE ROOT OF MUCH EVIL.
GO FORTH AND EXTERMINATE THAT DUNG BUG!

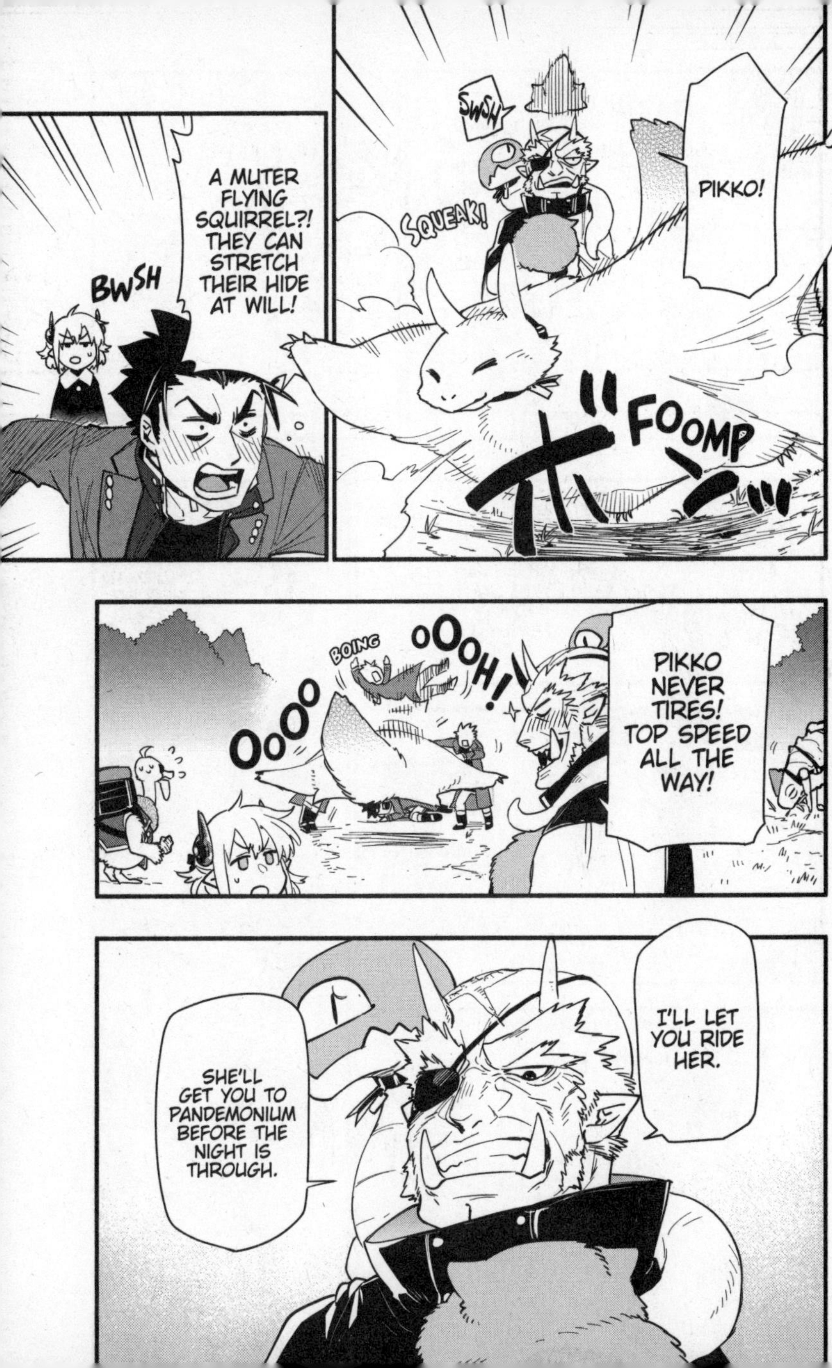
PIKKO!
SWSH
SQUEAK!
FOOMP
ボンッ
A MUTER FLYING SQUIRREL?! THEY CAN STRETCH THEIR HIDE AT WILL!
BWSH
PIKKO NEVER TIRES! TOP SPEED ALL THE WAY!
OOOH!
BOING
OOOO
I'LL LET YOU RIDE HER.
SHE'LL GET YOU TO PANDEMONIUM BEFORE THE NIGHT IS THROUGH.

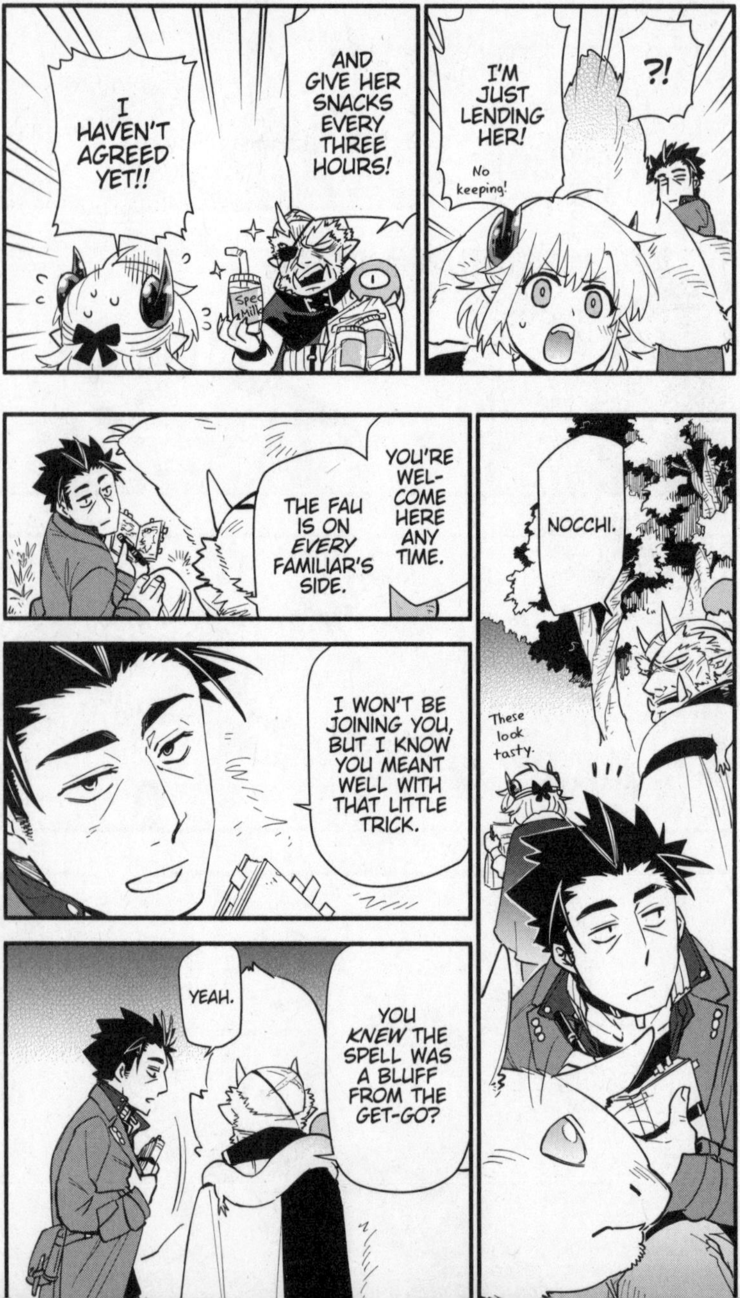
?!
I'M JUST LENDING HER!
No keeping!
AND GIVE HER SNACKS EVERY THREE HOURS!
I HAVEN'T AGREED YET!!
NOCCHI.
These look tasty.
!!!
YOU'RE WEL-COME HERE ANY TIME.
THE FAU IS ON *EVERY* FAMILIAR'S SIDE.
I WON'T BE JOINING YOU, BUT I KNOW YOU MEANT WELL WITH THAT LITTLE TRICK.
YOU *KNEW* THE SPELL WAS A BLUFF FROM THE GET-GO?
YEAH.

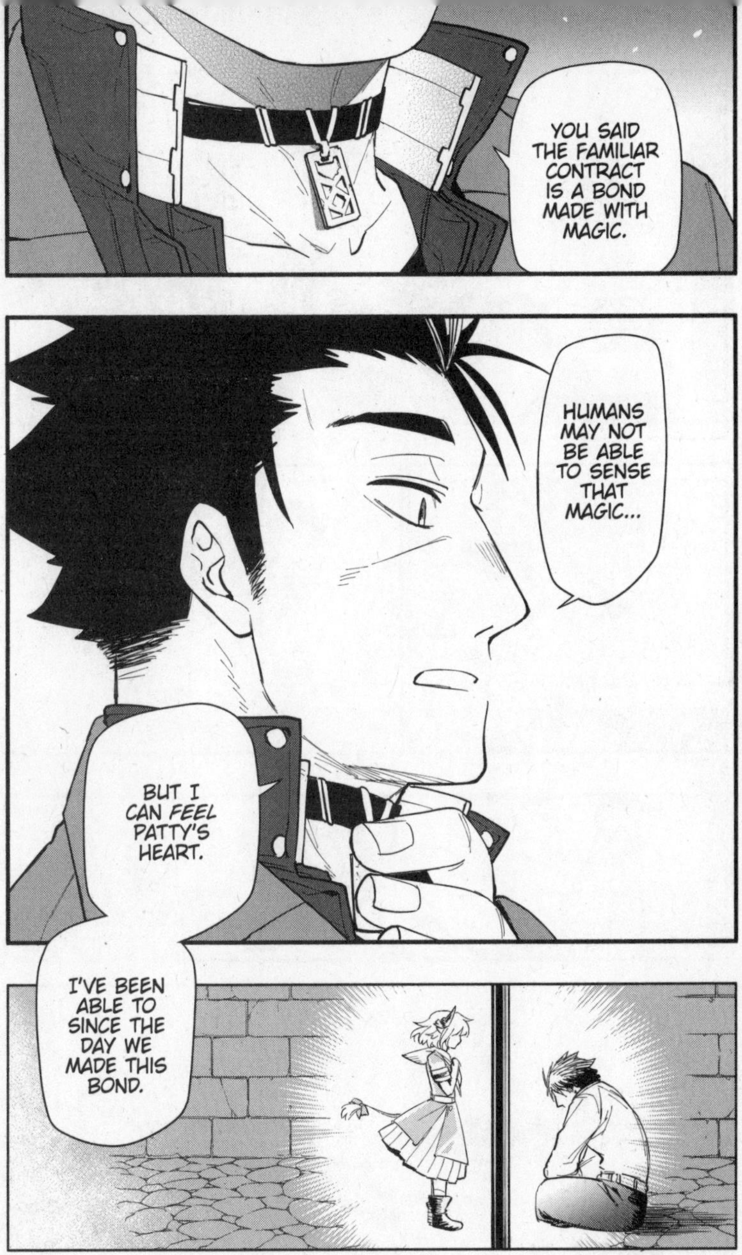
YOU SAID THE FAMILIAR CONTRACT IS A BOND MADE WITH MAGIC.
HUMANS MAY NOT BE ABLE TO SENSE THAT MAGIC...
BUT I CAN *FEEL* PATTY'S HEART.
I'VE BEEN ABLE TO SINCE THE DAY WE MADE THIS BOND.

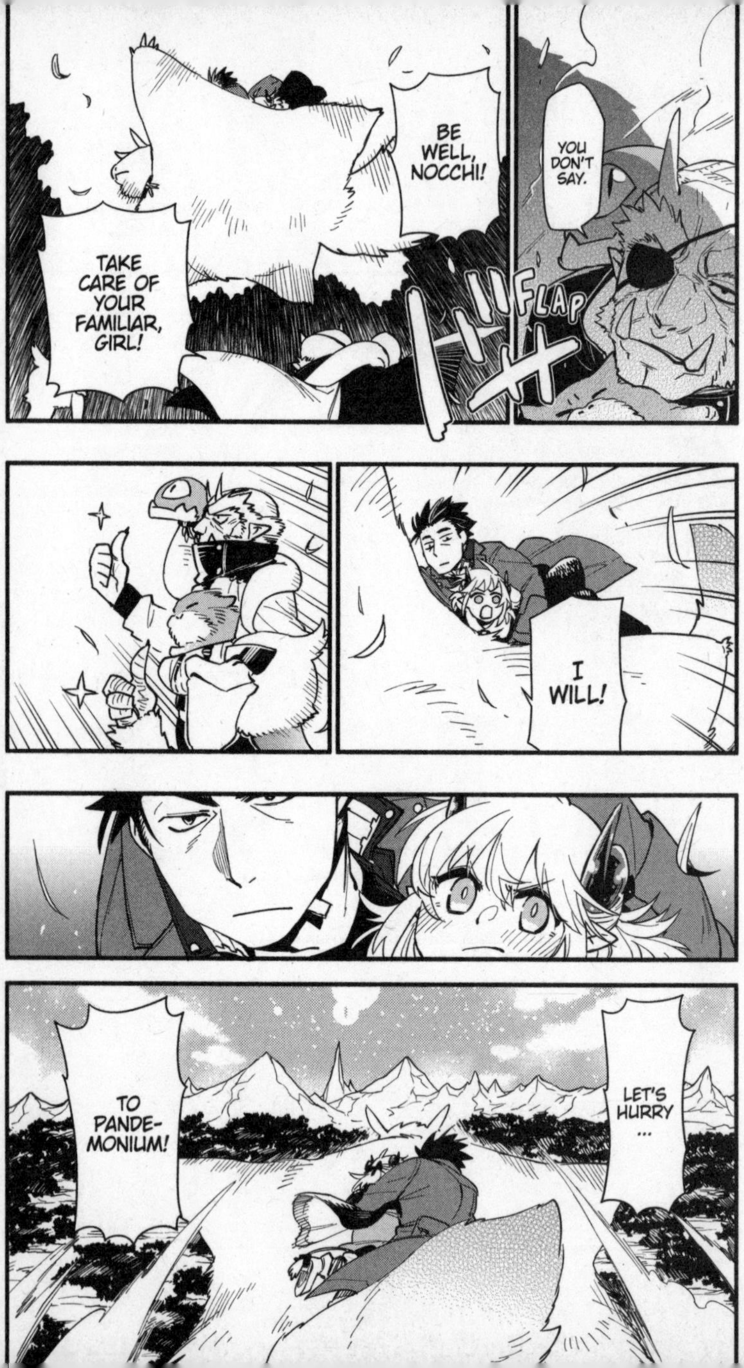
YOU DON'T SAY.
FLAP
BE WELL, NOCCHI!
TAKE CARE OF YOUR FAMILIAR, GIRL!
I WILL!
LET'S HURRY ...
TO PANDE-MONIUM!

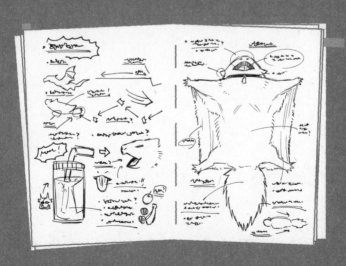

Sorry For My Familiar

FILE 65

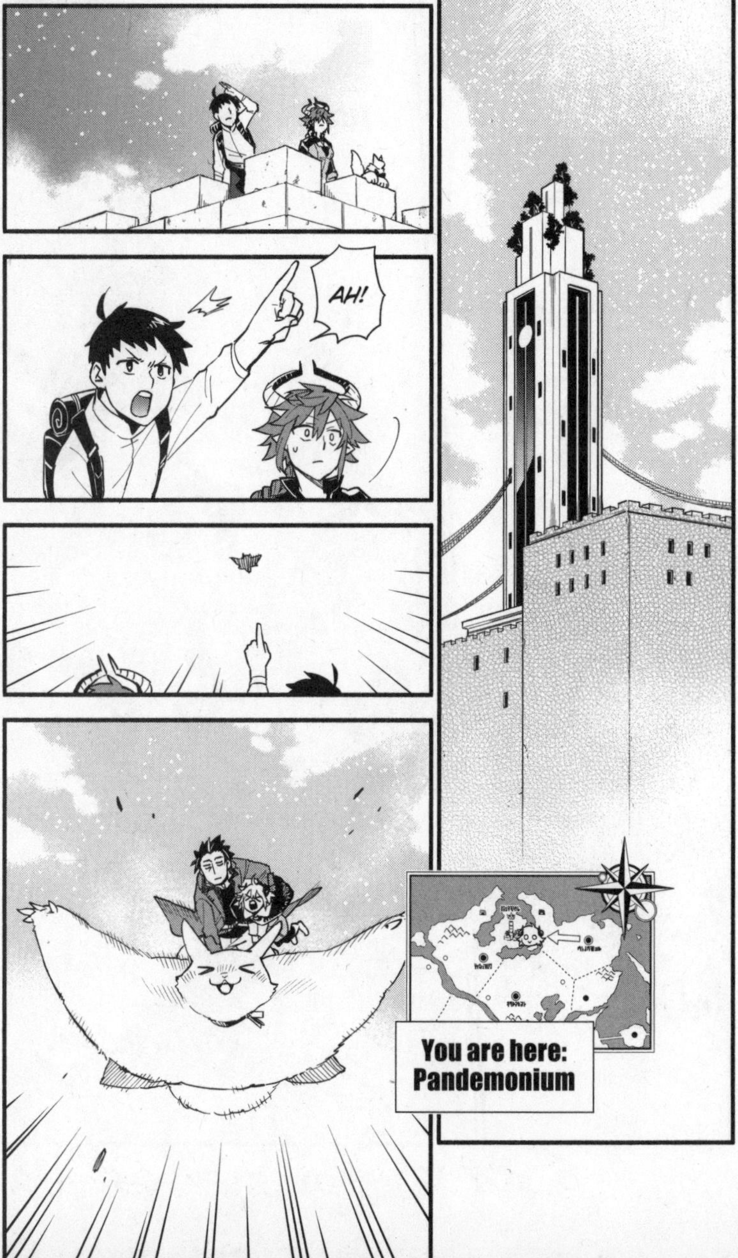
You are here:
Pandemonium
AH!

FILE 65: Royal Capital: Pandemonium ⑨

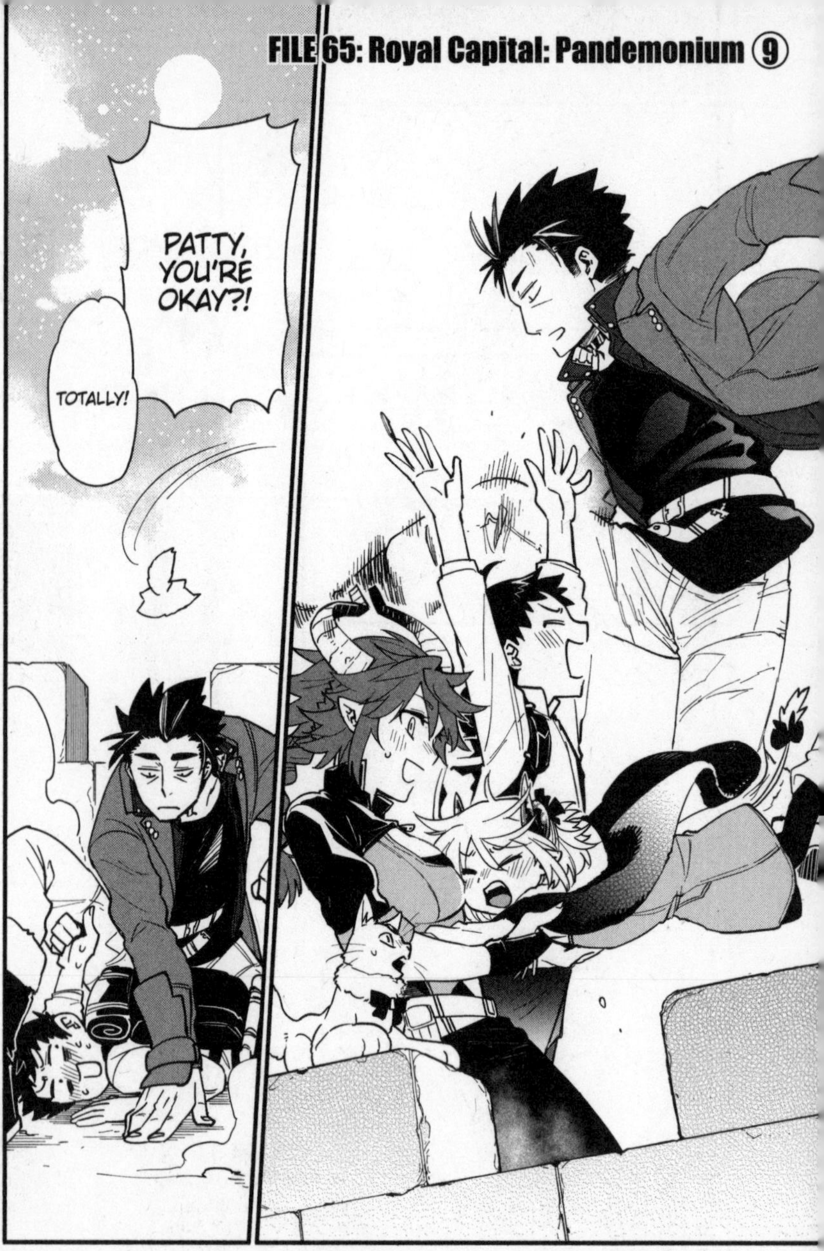
PATTY, YOU'RE OKAY?!
TOTALLY!

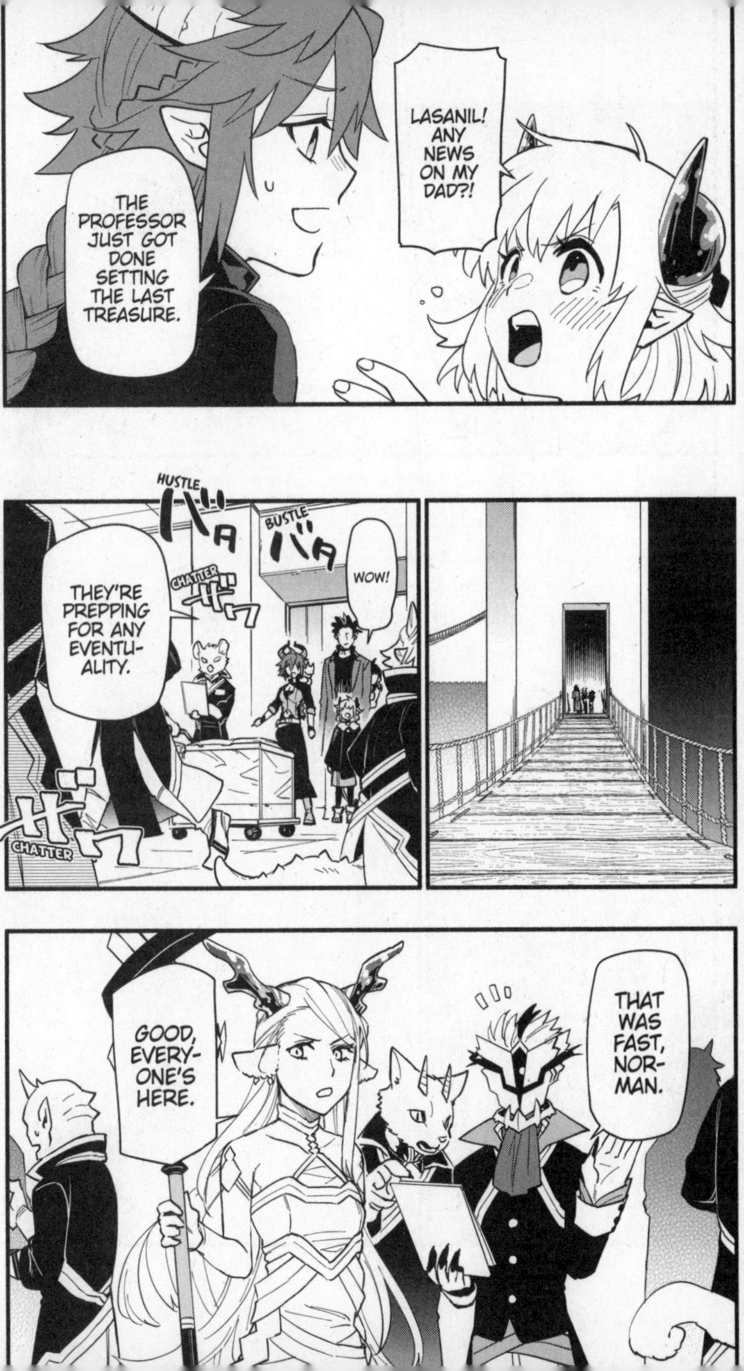
LASANIL! ANY NEWS ON MY DAD?!
THE PROFESSOR JUST GOT DONE SETTING THE LAST TREASURE.
WOW!
BUSTLE バタ
HUSTLE バタ
THEY'RE PREPPING FOR ANY EVENTU-ALITY.
CHATTER ザワ
CHATTER ザワ
THAT WAS FAST, NOR-MAN.
GOOD, EVERY-ONE'S HERE.

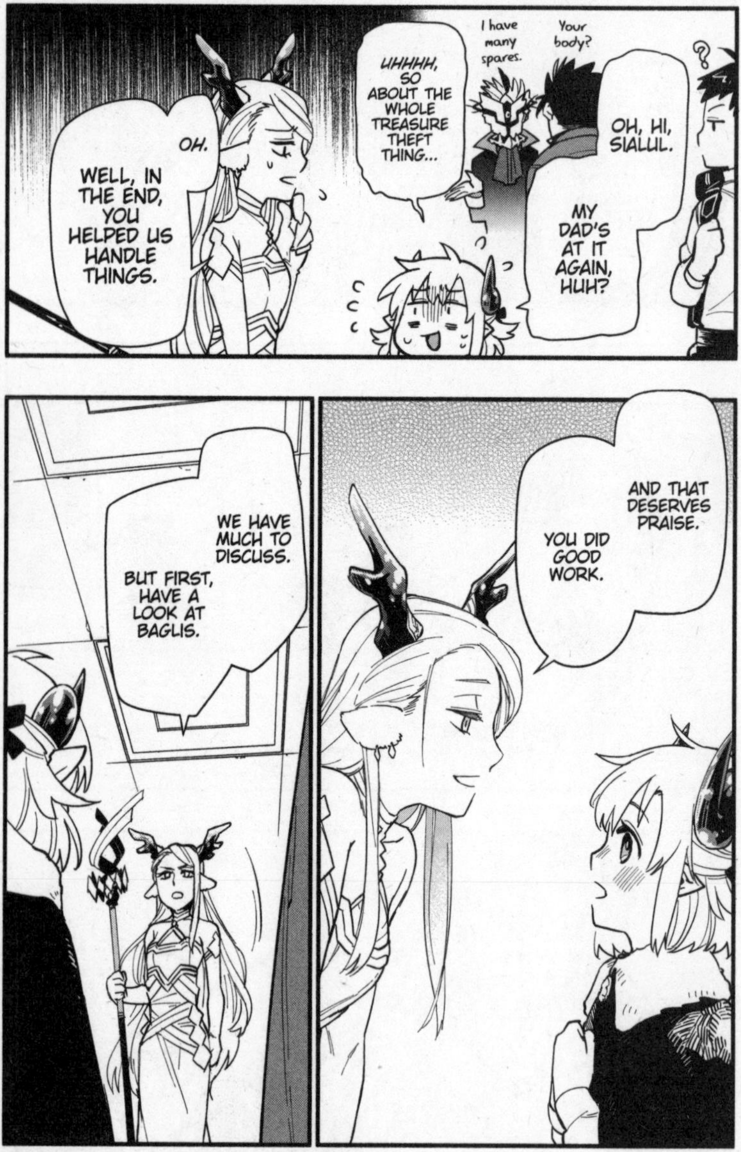
OH, HI, SIALUL.
MY DAD'S AT IT AGAIN, HUH?
Your body?
I have many spares.
UHHHH, SO ABOUT THE WHOLE TREASURE THEFT THING...
OH.
WELL, IN THE END, YOU HELPED US HANDLE THINGS.
AND THAT DESERVES PRAISE.
YOU DID GOOD WORK.
WE HAVE MUCH TO DISCUSS.
BUT FIRST, HAVE A LOOK AT BAGLIS.

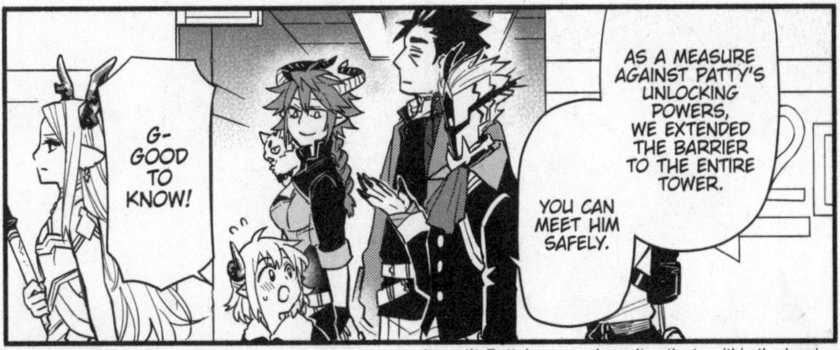
AS A MEASURE AGAINST PATTY'S UNLOCKING POWERS, WE EXTENDED THE BARRIER TO THE ENTIRE TOWER.
YOU CAN MEET HIM SAFELY.
G-GOOD TO KNOW!

※ *Patty's power doesn't activate within the barrier.*

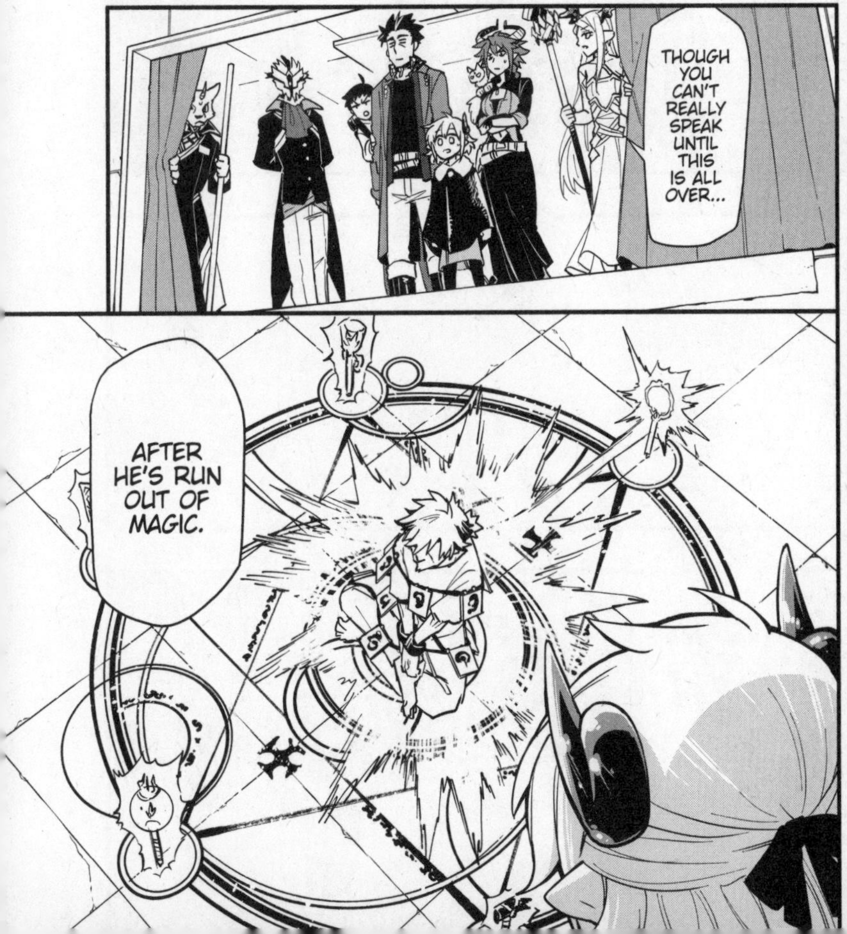
THOUGH YOU CAN'T REALLY SPEAK UNTIL THIS IS ALL OVER...
AFTER HE'S RUN OUT OF MAGIC.

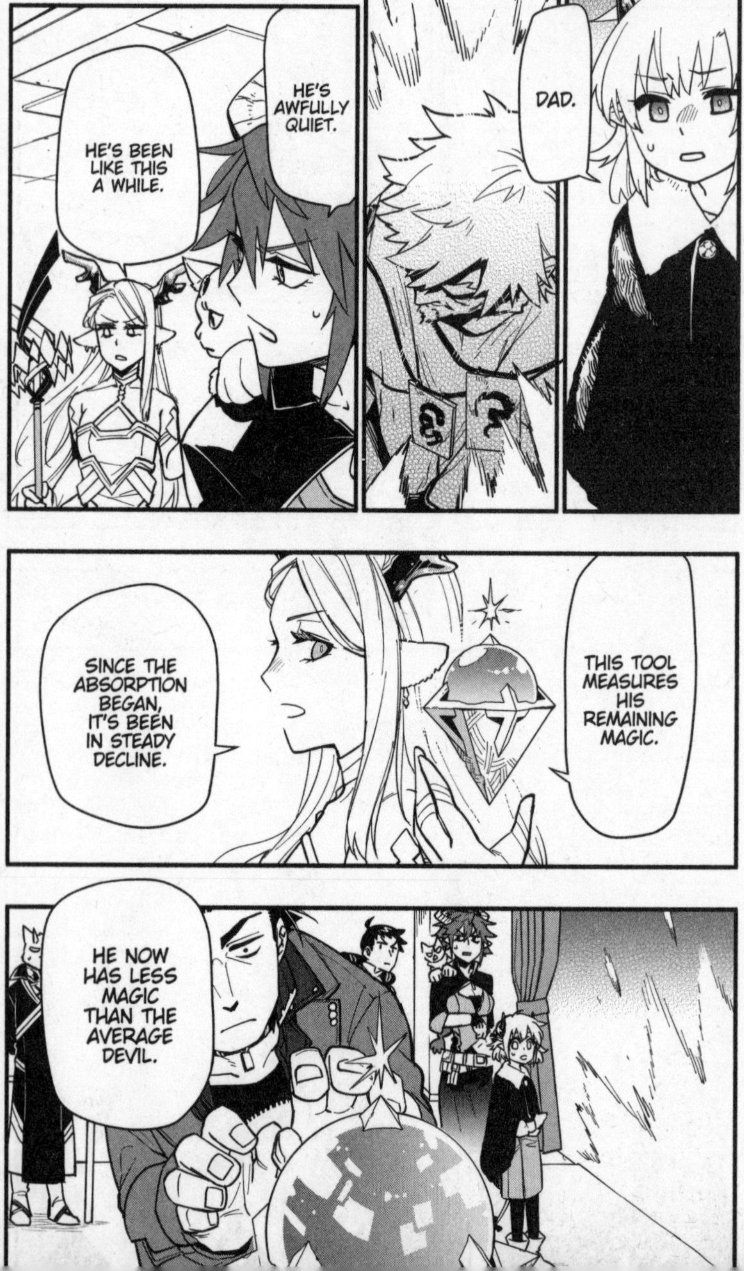
DAD.
HE'S AWFULLY QUIET.
HE'S BEEN LIKE THIS A WHILE.
THIS TOOL MEASURES HIS REMAINING MAGIC.
SINCE THE ABSORPTION BEGAN, IT'S BEEN IN STEADY DECLINE.
HE NOW HAS LESS MAGIC THAN THE AVERAGE DEVIL.

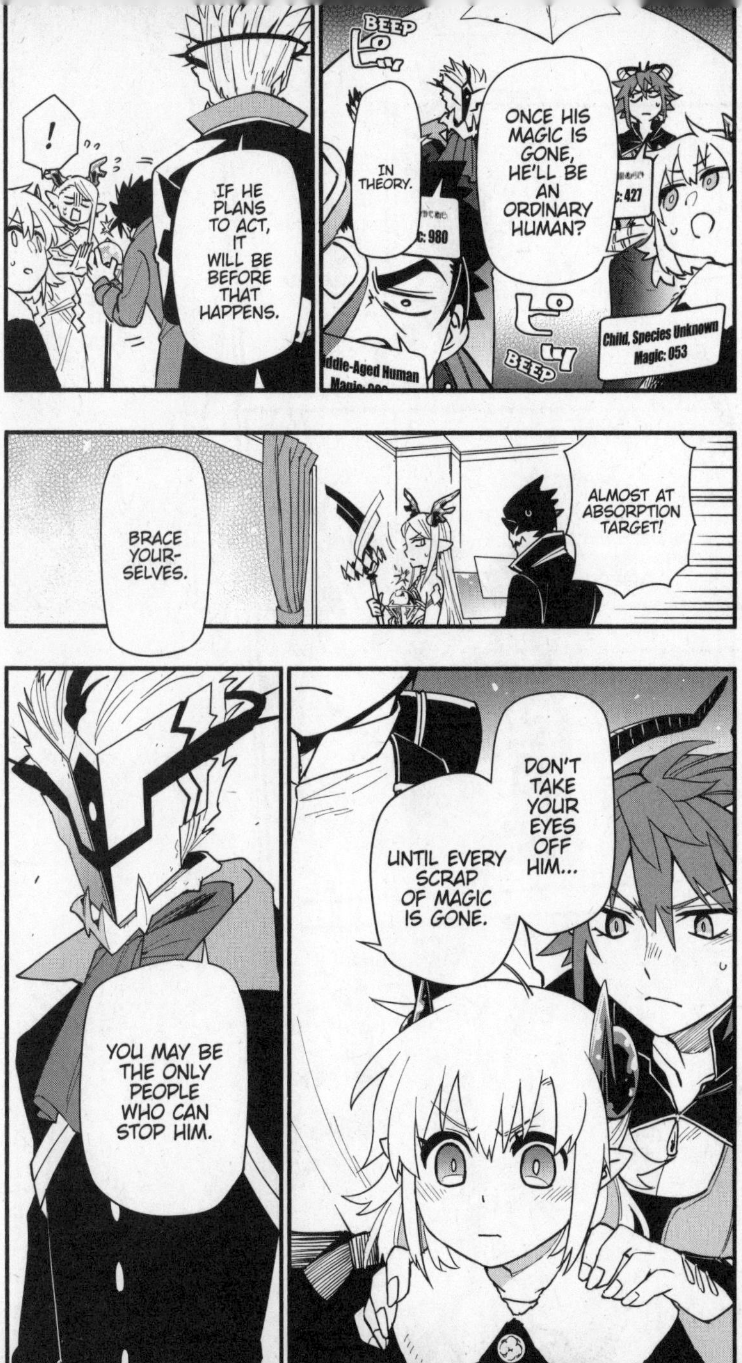
BEEP
ピロッ
ONCE HIS MAGIC IS GONE, HE'LL BE AN ORDINARY HUMAN?
c: 427
IN THEORY.
c: 980
ピッ
BEEP
Child, Species Unknown Magic: 053
!
IF HE PLANS TO ACT, IT WILL BE BEFORE THAT HAPPENS.
ALMOST AT ABSORPTION TARGET!
BRACE YOUR-SELVES.
DON'T TAKE YOUR EYES OFF HIM...
UNTIL EVERY SCRAP OF MAGIC IS GONE.
YOU MAY BE THE ONLY PEOPLE WHO CAN STOP HIM.

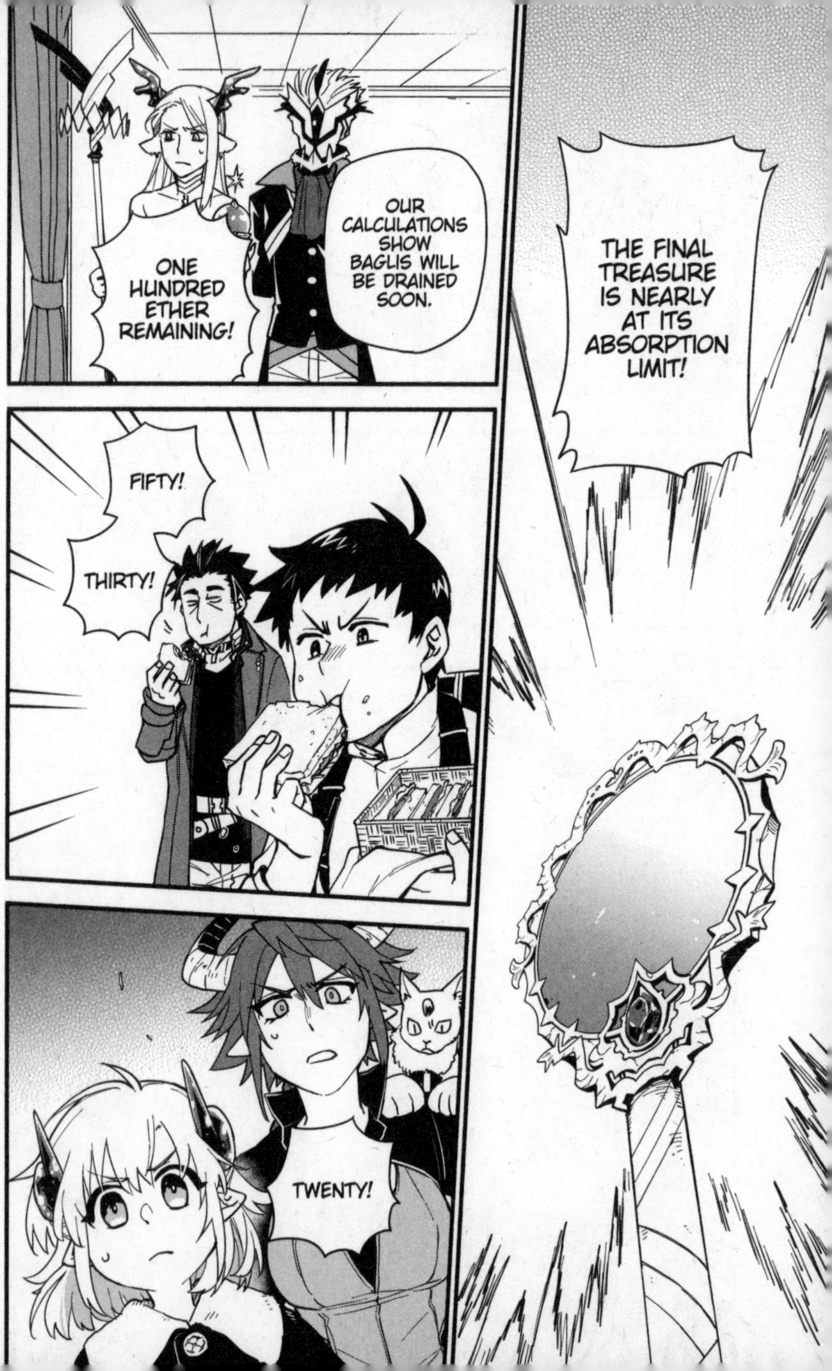
THE FINAL TREASURE IS NEARLY AT ITS ABSORPTION LIMIT!
OUR CALCULATIONS SHOW BAGLIS WILL BE DRAINED SOON.
ONE HUNDRED ETHER REMAINING!
FIFTY!
THIRTY!
TWENTY!

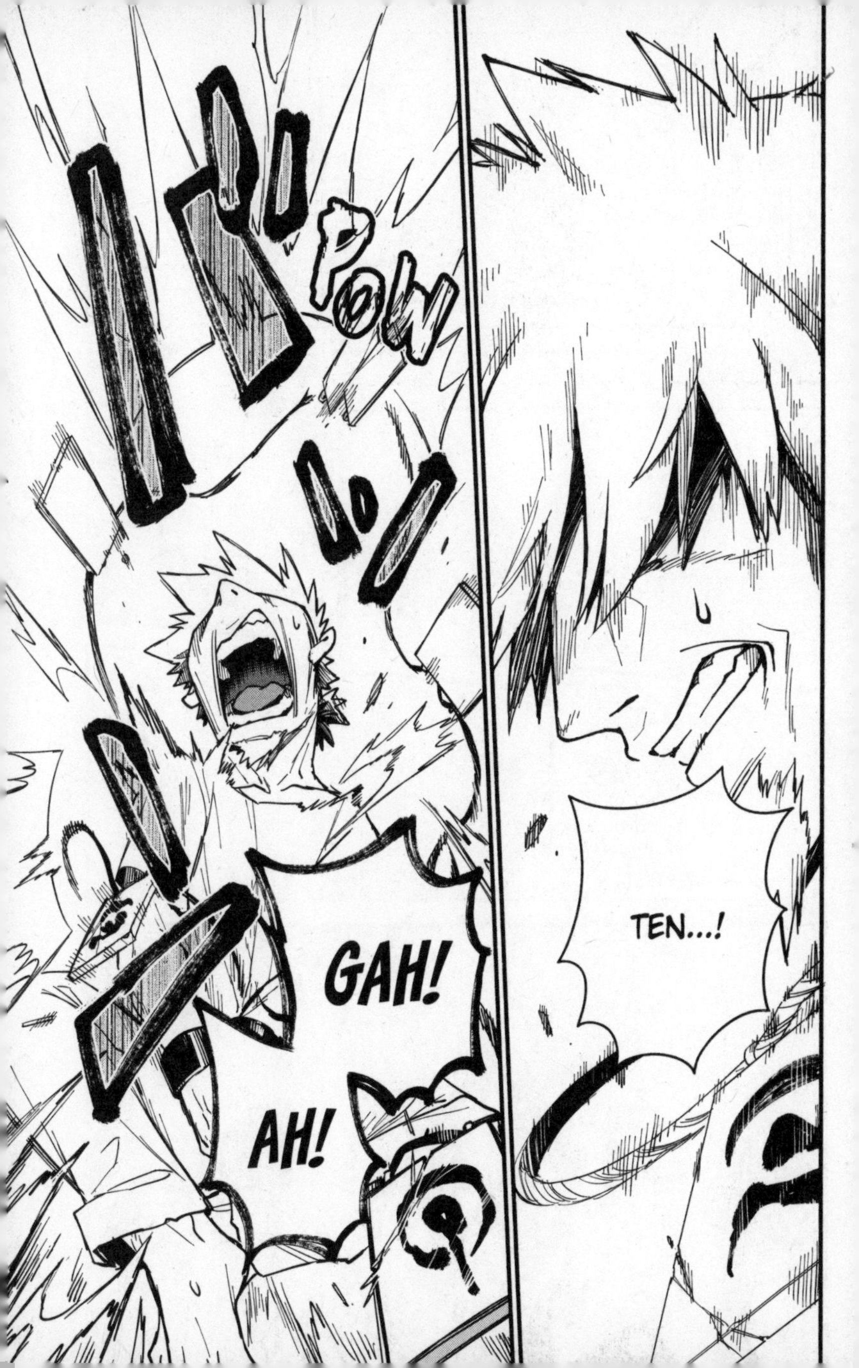
TEN...!
POW
GAH!
AH!

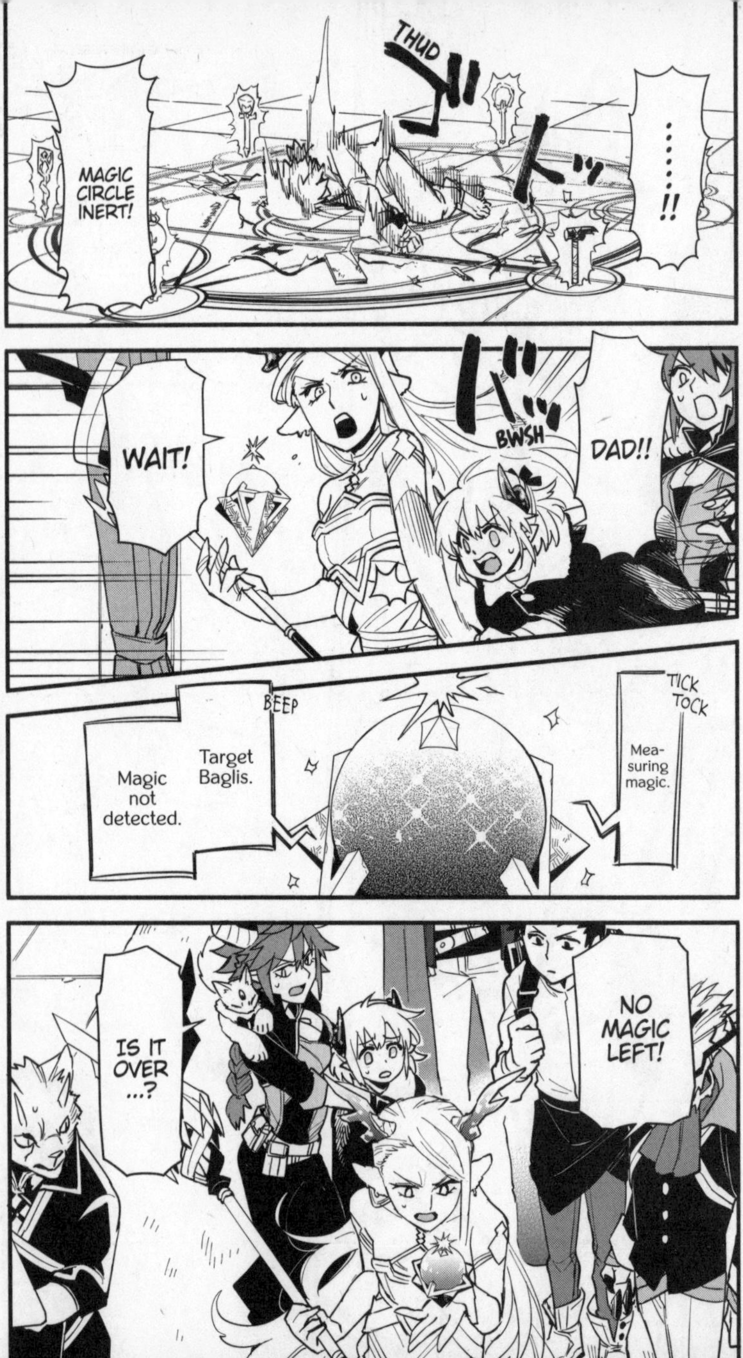
......!!
THUD
MAGIC CIRCLE INERT!
DAD!!
BWSH
WAIT!
TICK TOCK
Mea-suring magic.
BEEP
Target Baglis.
Magic not detected.
NO MAGIC LEFT!
IS IT OVER ...?

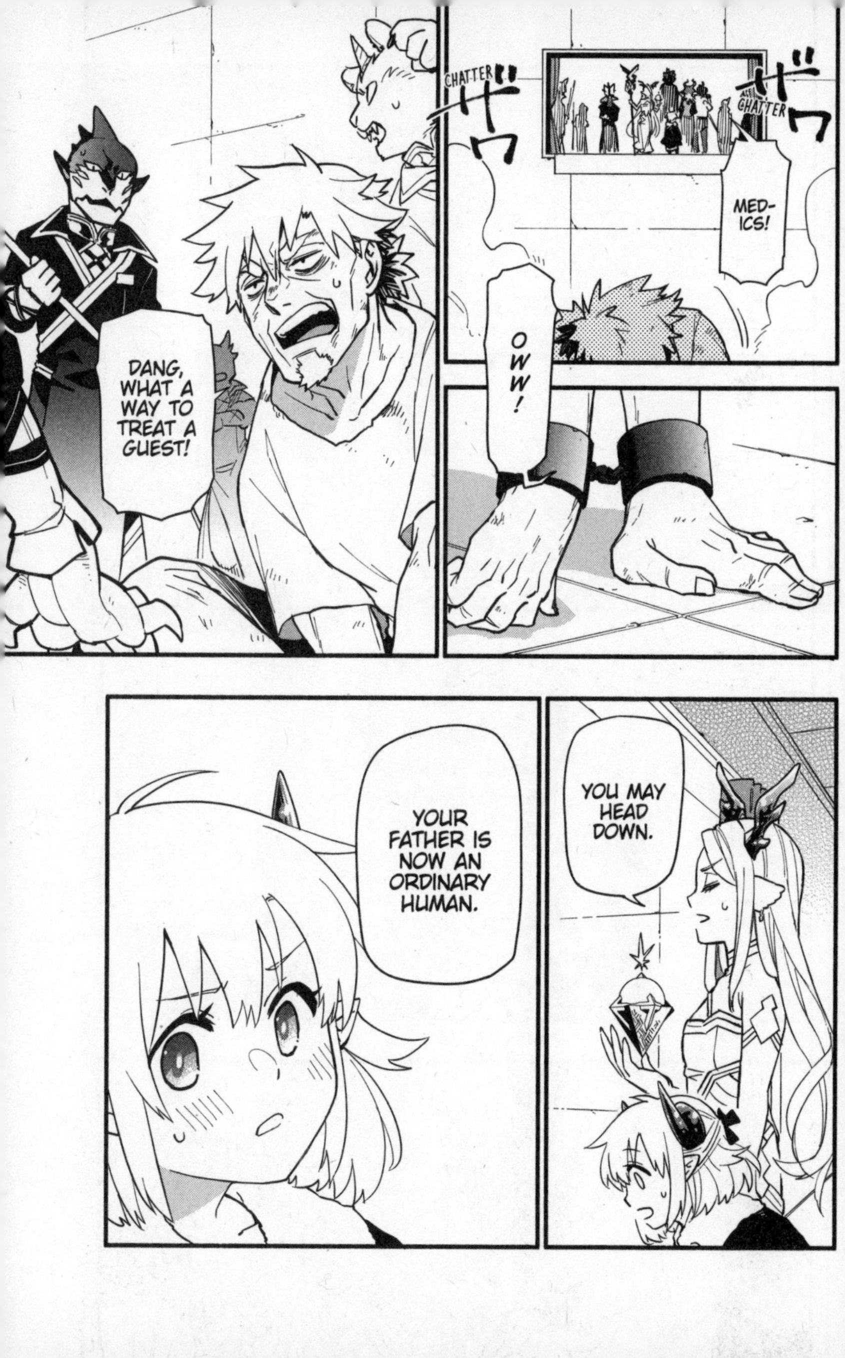
CHATTER
ザワ
MED-ICS!
CHATTER
ザワ
OWW!
DANG, WHAT A WAY TO TREAT A GUEST!
YOU MAY HEAD DOWN.
YOUR FATHER IS NOW AN ORDINARY HUMAN.

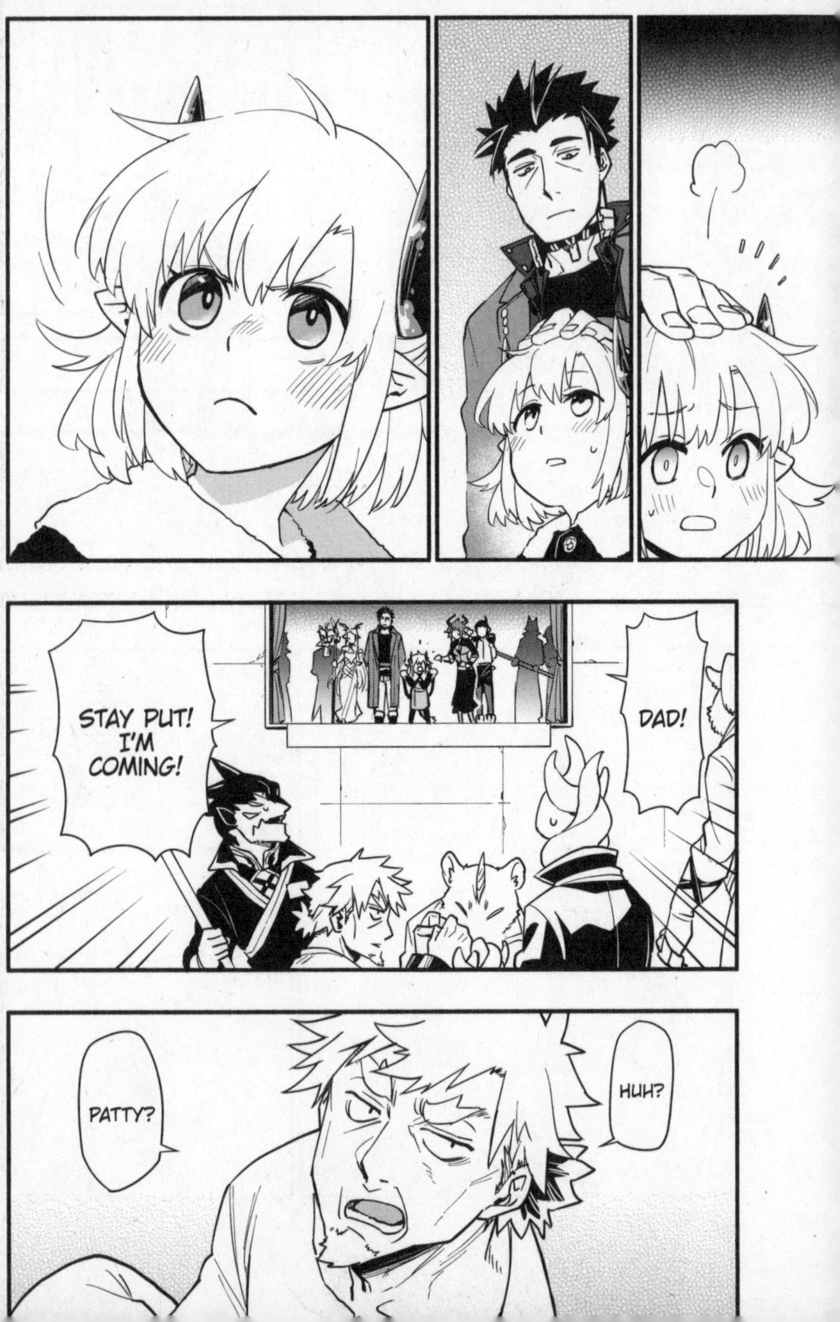
DAD!
STAY PUT! I'M COMING!
HUH?
PATTY?

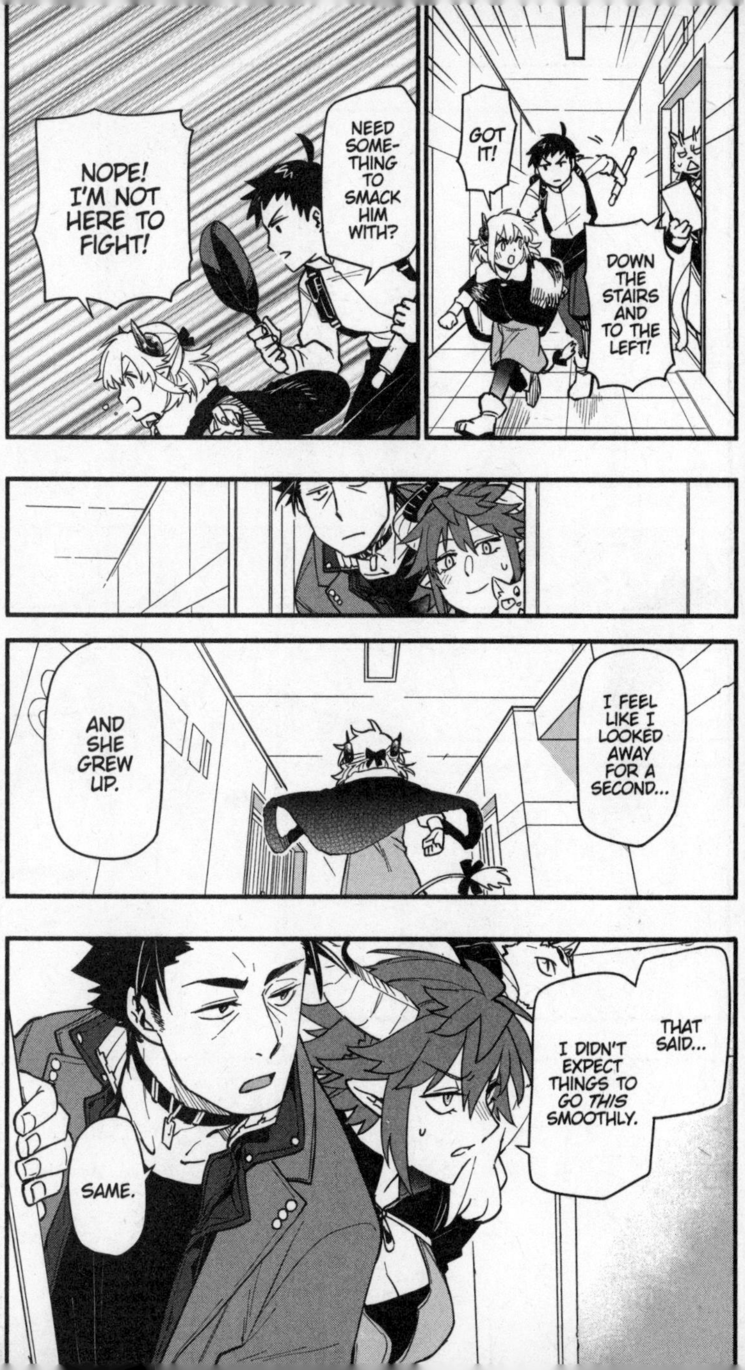

DOWN THE STAIRS AND TO THE LEFT!
GOT IT!
NEED SOME-THING TO SMACK HIM WITH?
NOPE! I'M NOT HERE TO FIGHT!
I FEEL LIKE I LOOKED AWAY FOR A SECOND...
AND SHE GREW UP.
THAT SAID...
I DIDN'T EXPECT THINGS TO GO *THIS* SMOOTHLY.
SAME.

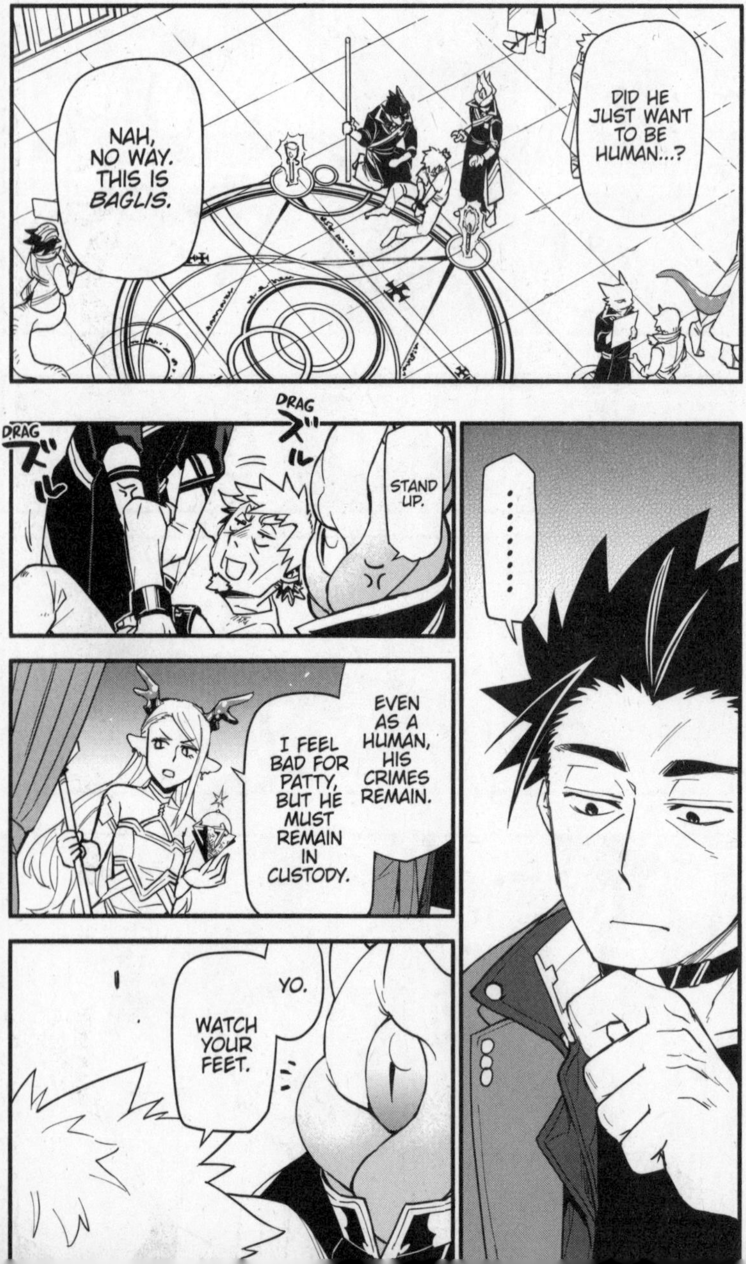
DID HE JUST WANT TO BE HUMAN...?
NAH, NO WAY. THIS IS BAGLIS.
....
DRAG ズル
STAND UP.
DRAG ズル
EVEN AS A HUMAN, HIS CRIMES REMAIN.
I FEEL BAD FOR PATTY, BUT HE MUST REMAIN IN CUSTODY.
YO.
WATCH YOUR FEET.

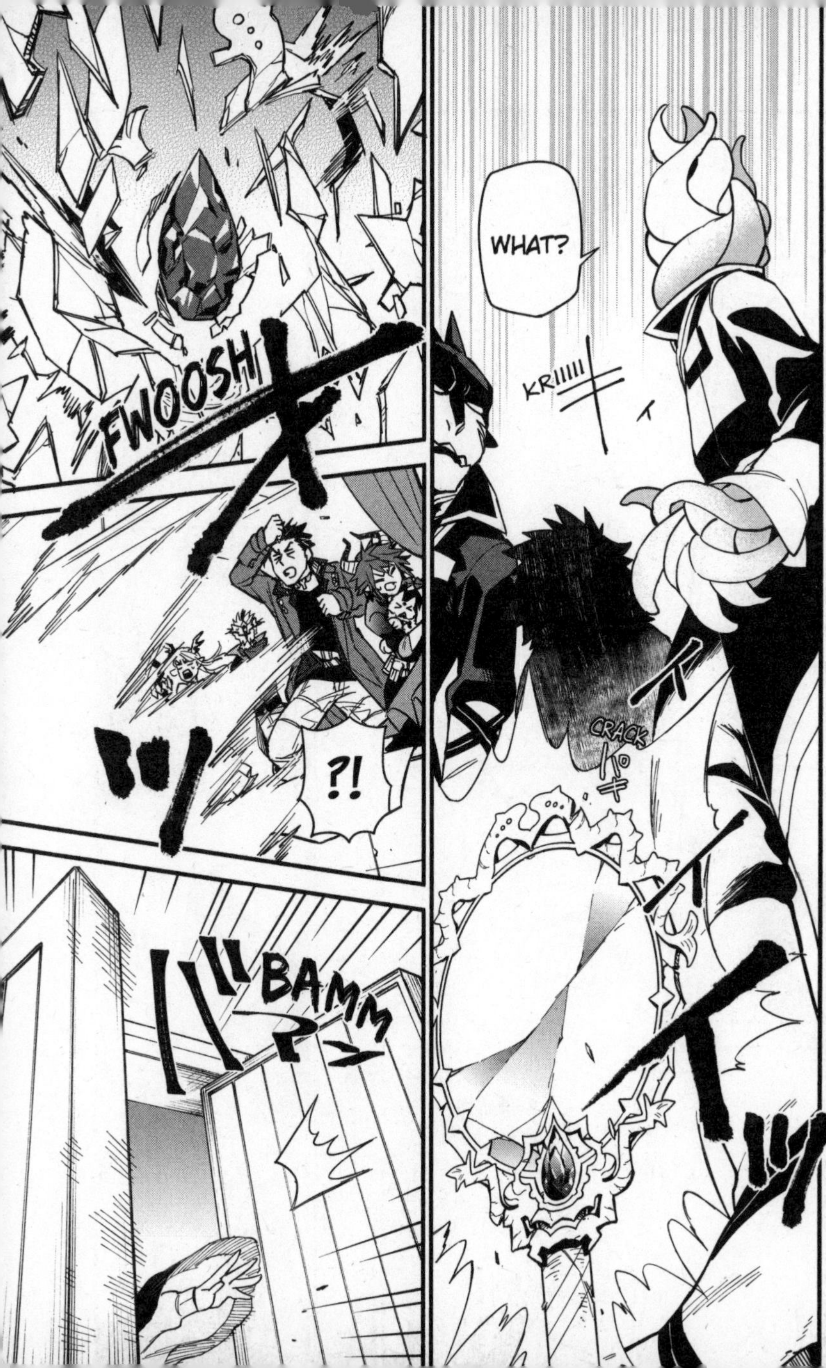
WHAT?
KRIIIII
CRACK
パキ
FWOOSH
?!
BAMM

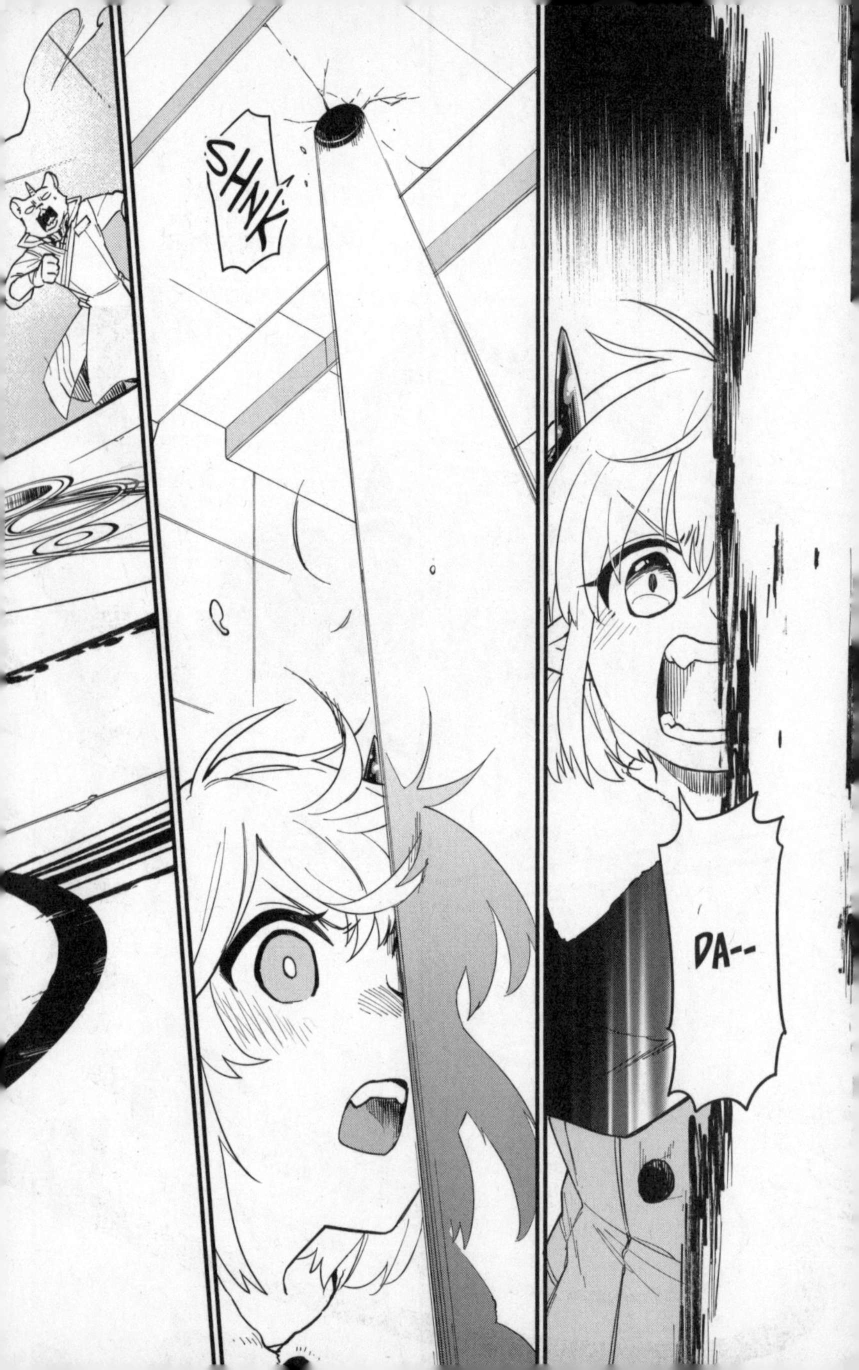
DA--
SHNK

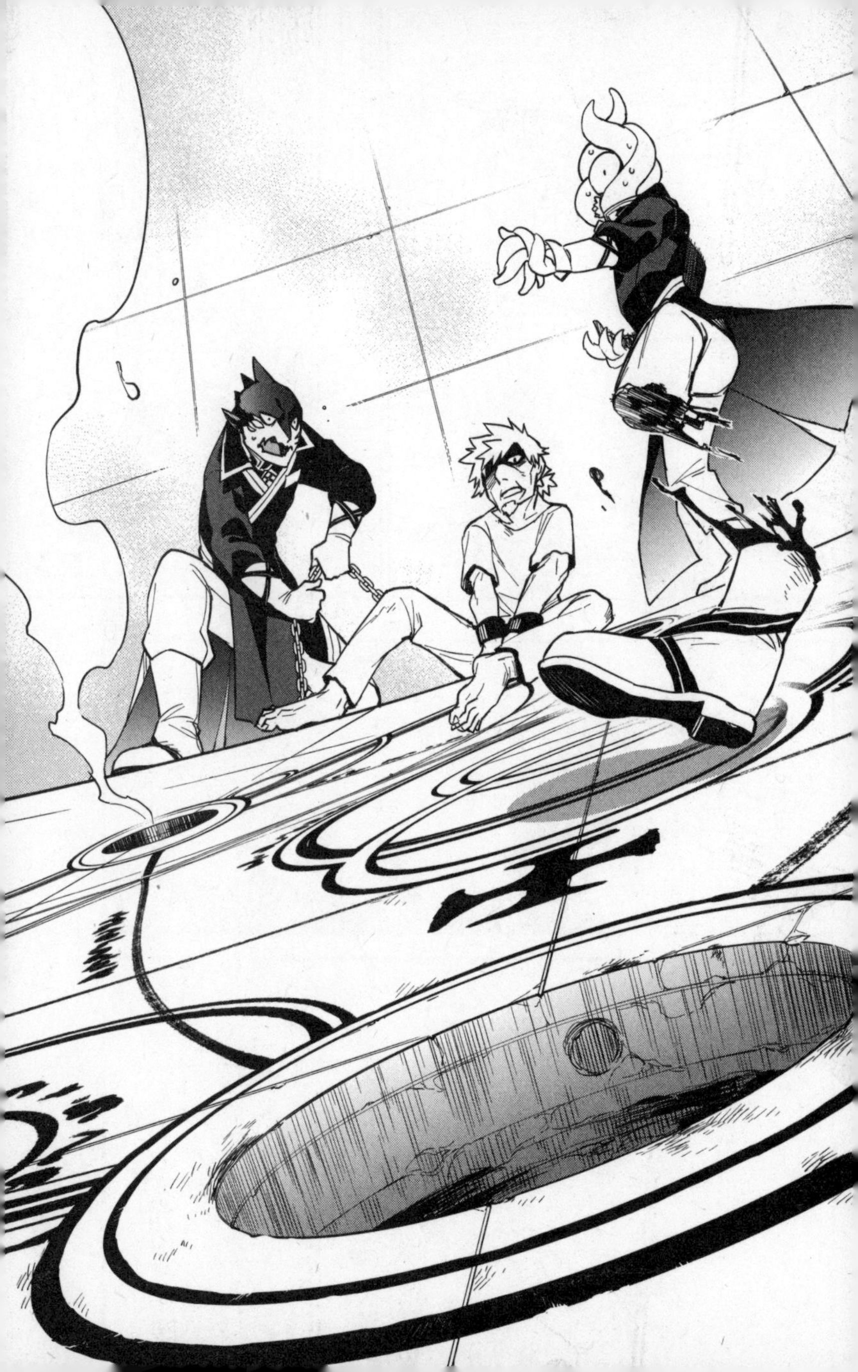

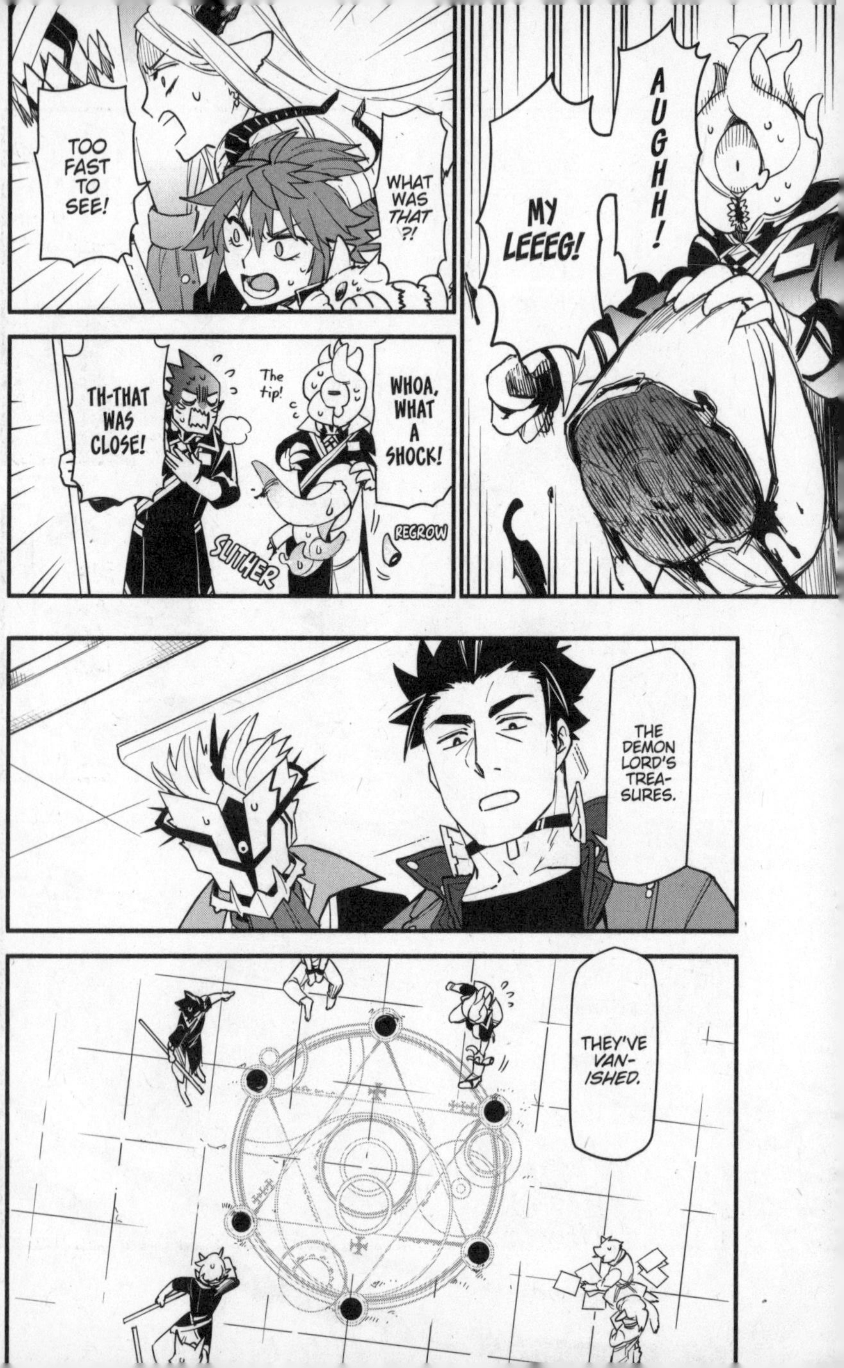
AUGHH!
MY LEEEG!
WHAT WAS THAT?!
TOO FAST TO SEE!
WHOA, WHAT A SHOCK!
The tip!
TH-THAT WAS CLOSE!
REGROW
SLITHER
THE DEMON LORD'S TREASURES.
THEY'VE VANISHED.

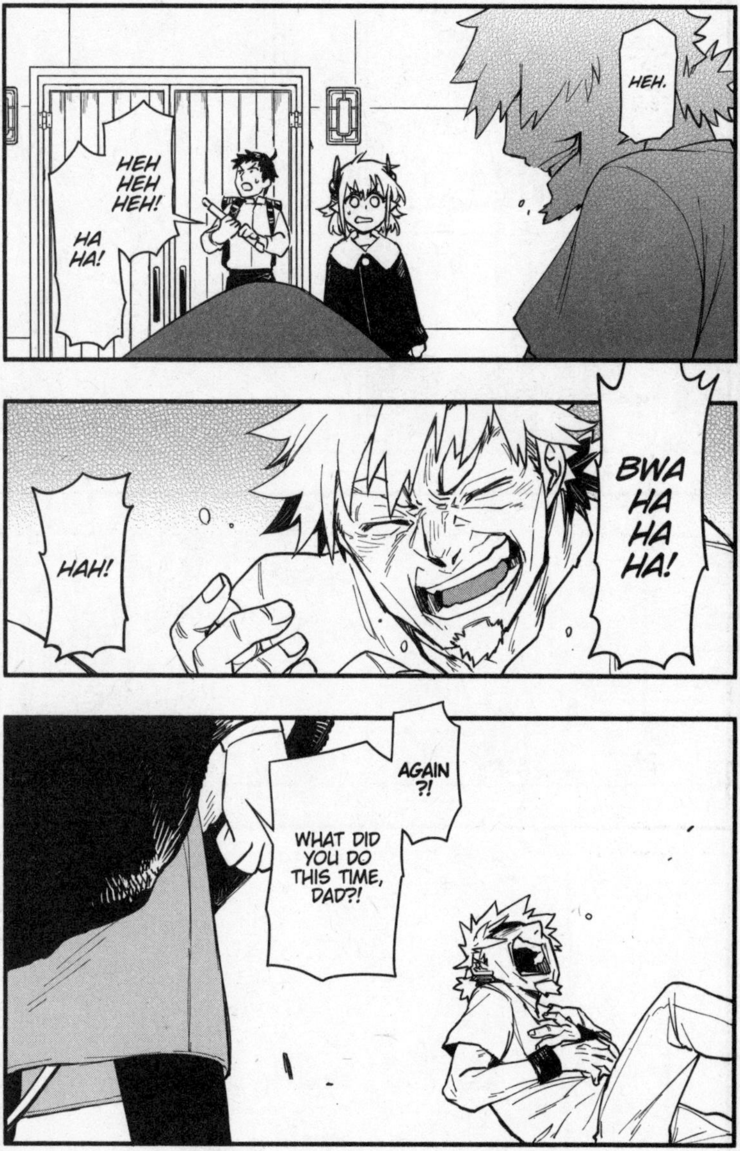
HEH.
HEH HEH HEH!
HA HA!
BWA HA HA HA!
HAH!
AGAIN?!
WHAT DID YOU DO THIS TIME, DAD?!

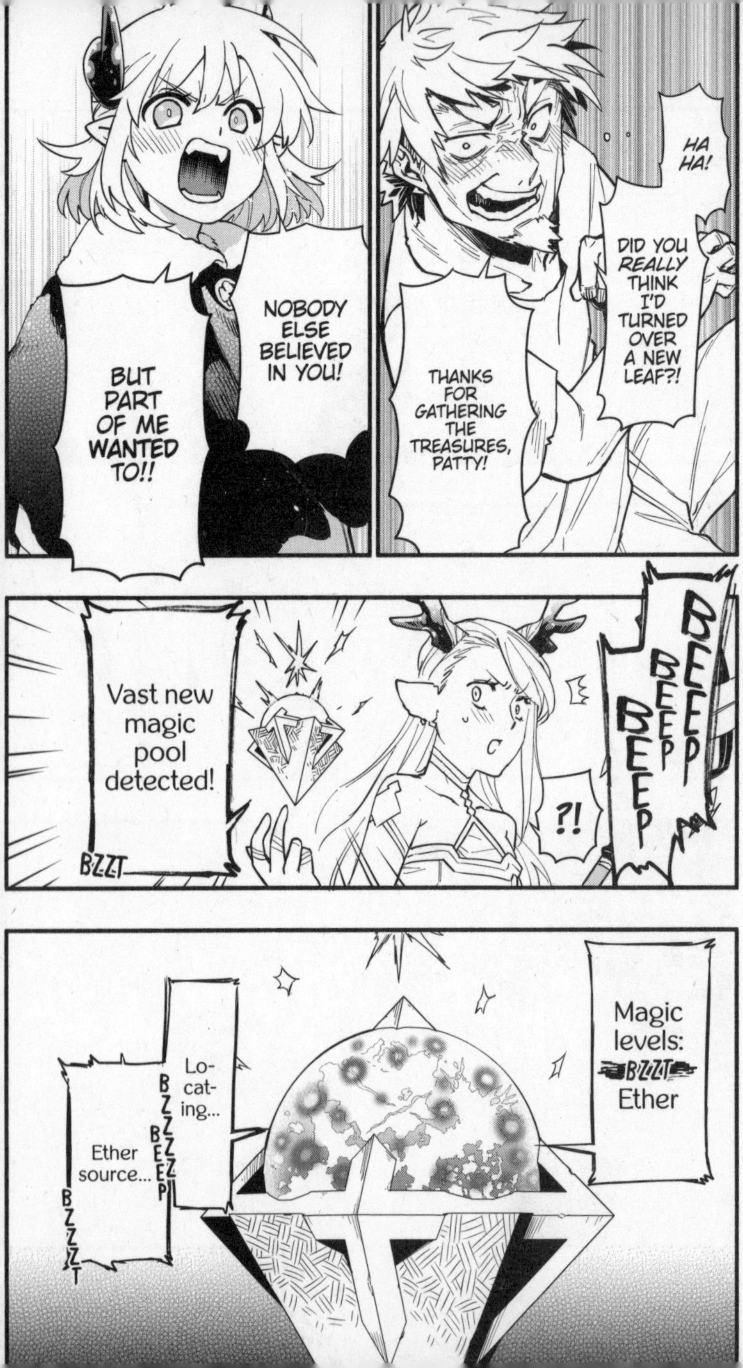
HA HA!
DID YOU REALLY THINK I'D TURNED OVER A NEW LEAF?!
THANKS FOR GATHERING THE TREASURES, PATTY!
NOBODY ELSE BELIEVED IN YOU!
BUT PART OF ME WANTED TO!!
BEEP BEEP BEEP
?!
Vast new magic pool detected!
BZZT
Magic levels: BZZT Ether
Lo-cating...
BZZZ
BEEP
Ether source...
BZZZT

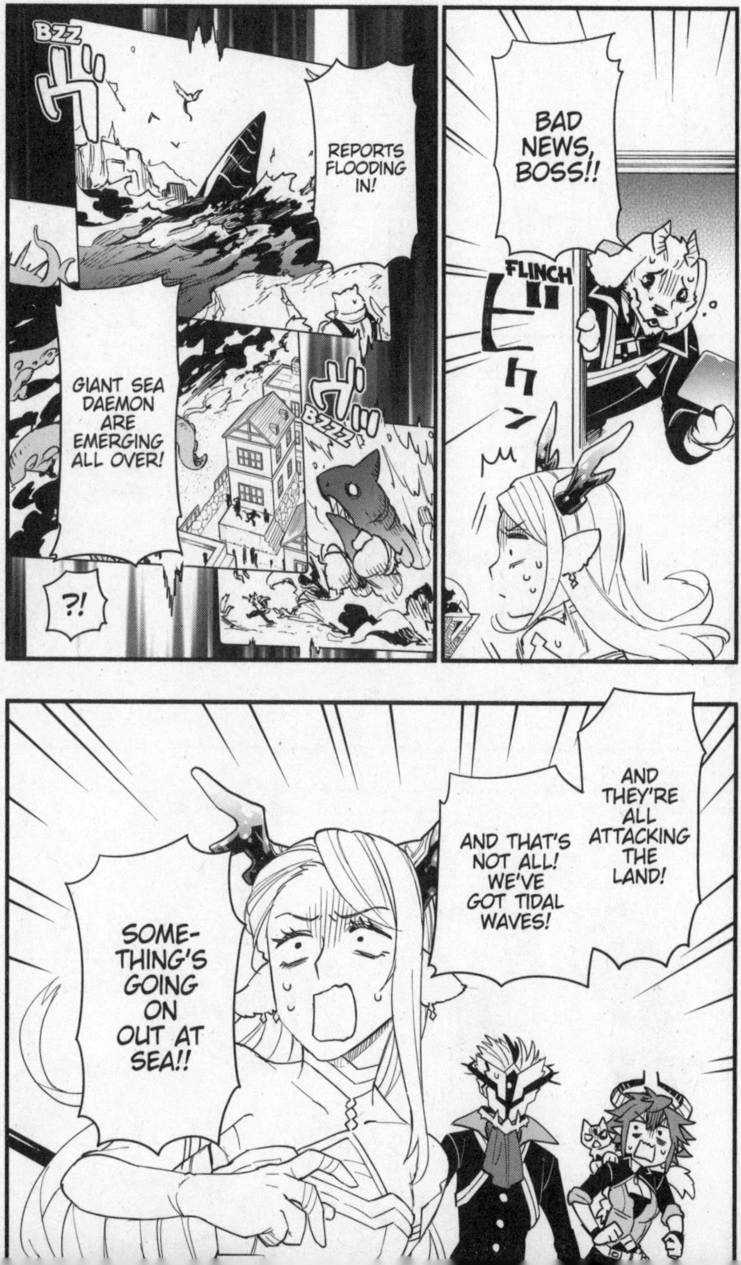
BAD NEWS, BOSS!!
FLINCH
REPORTS FLOODING IN!
BZZ
BZZZ
GIANT SEA DAEMON ARE EMERGING ALL OVER!
?!
AND THEY'RE ALL ATTACKING THE LAND!
AND THAT'S NOT ALL! WE'VE GOT TIDAL WAVES!
SOME-THING'S GOING ON OUT AT SEA!!

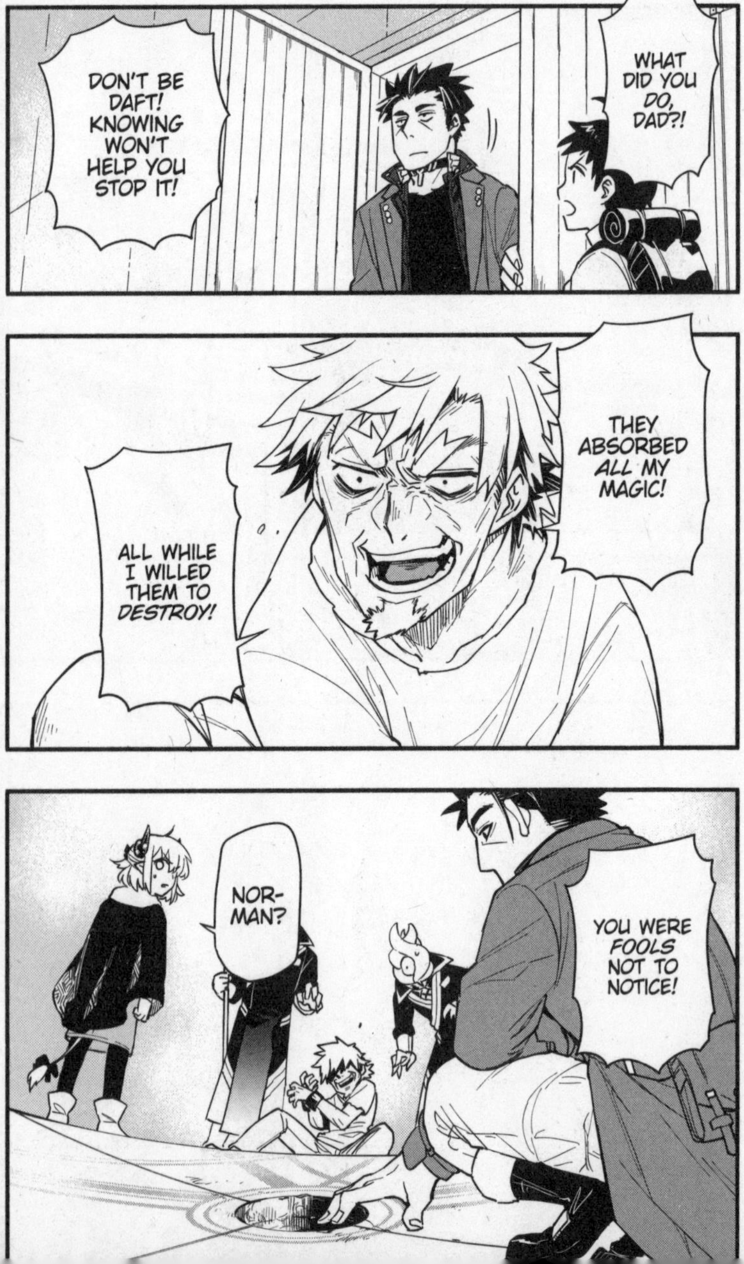
WHAT DID YOU *DO*, DAD?!
DON'T BE DAFT! KNOWING WON'T HELP YOU STOP IT!
THEY ABSORBED *ALL* MY MAGIC!
ALL WHILE I WILLED THEM TO *DESTROY!*
YOU WERE *FOOLS* NOT TO NOTICE!
NOR-MAN?

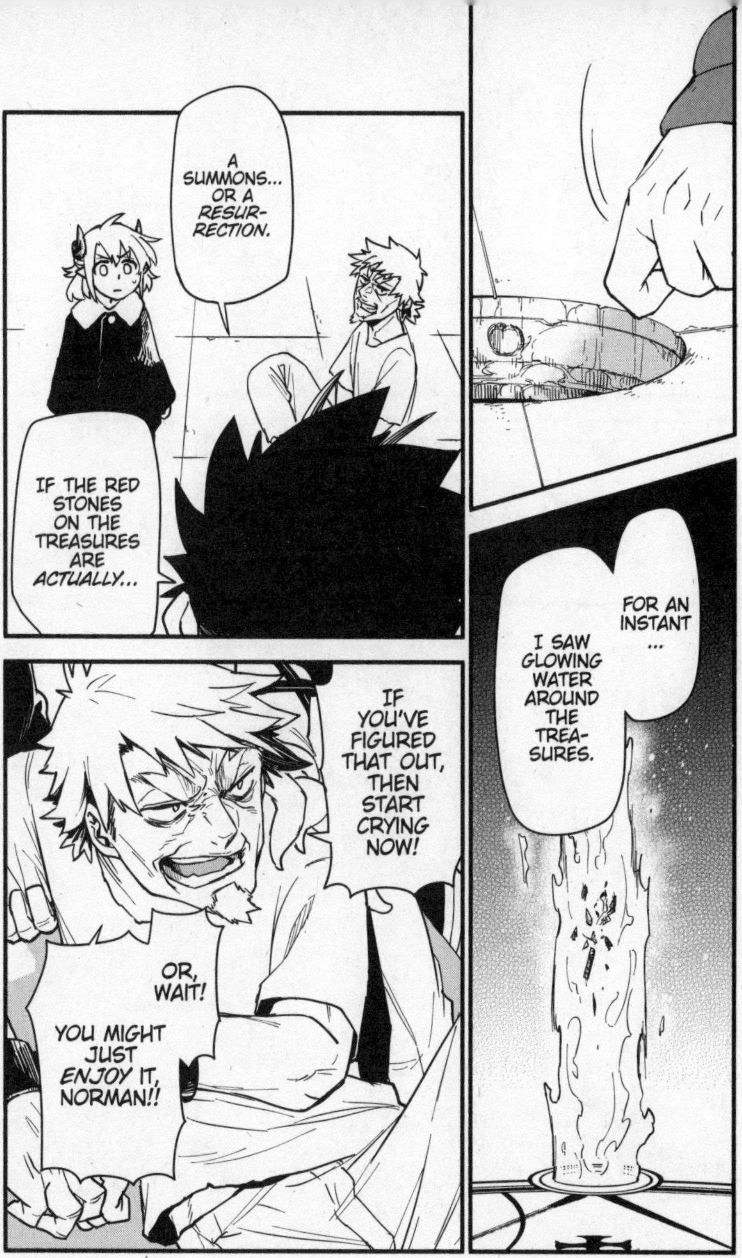
A SUMMONS... OR A *RESURRECTION.*
IF THE RED STONES ON THE TREASURES ARE *ACTUALLY...*
FOR AN INSTANT ...
I SAW GLOWING WATER AROUND THE TREASURES.
IF YOU'VE FIGURED THAT OUT, THEN START CRYING NOW!
OR, WAIT!
YOU MIGHT JUST *ENJOY* IT, NORMAN!!

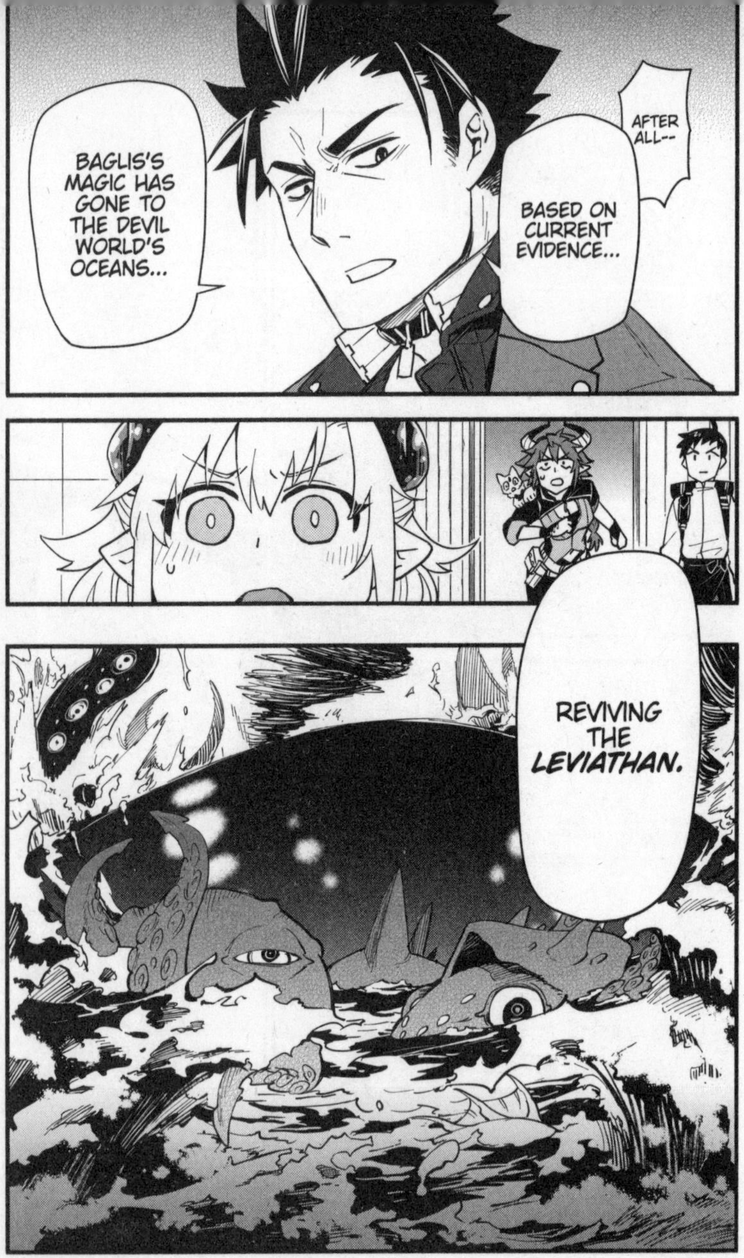
AFTER ALL--
BASED ON CURRENT EVIDENCE...
BAGLIS'S MAGIC HAS GONE TO THE DEVIL WORLD'S OCEANS...
REVIVING THE *LEVIATHAN.*

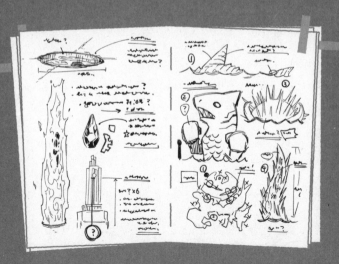

Sorry For My Familiar

FILE 66

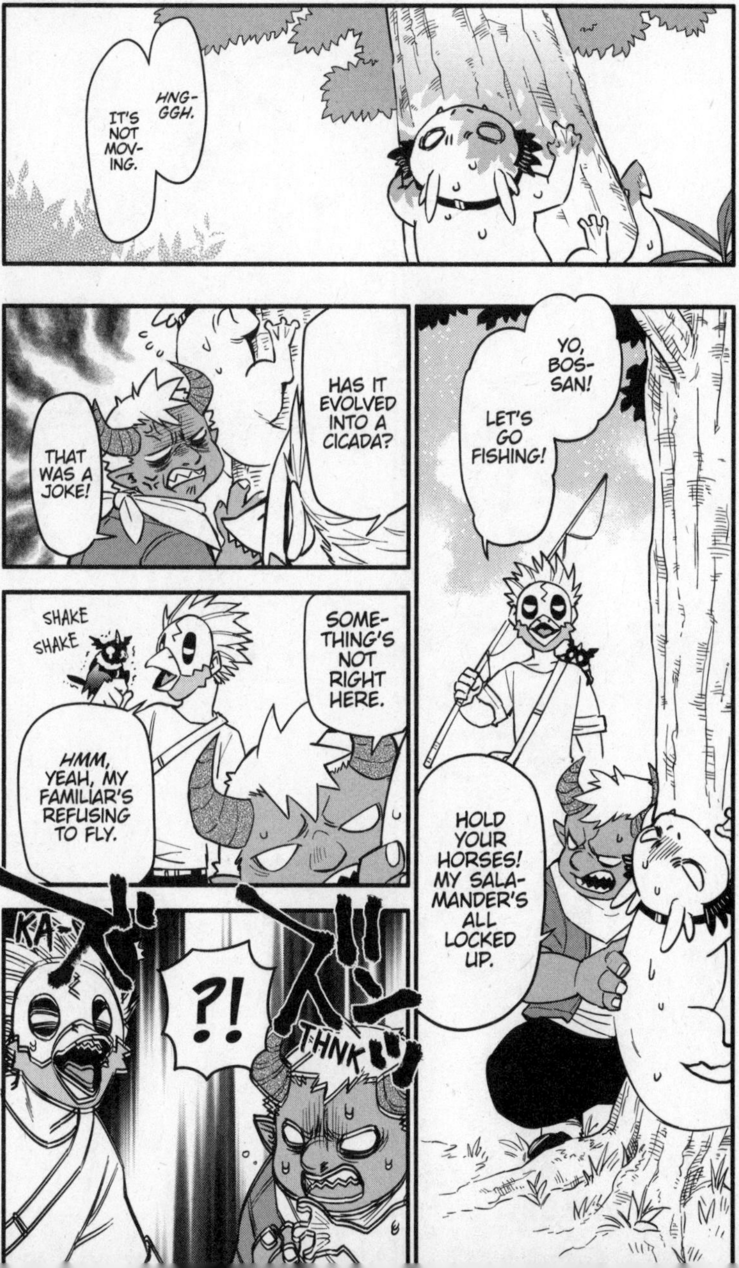
HNG-GGH.
IT'S NOT MOVING.
YO, BOS-SAN!
LET'S GO FISHING!
HOLD YOUR HORSES! MY SALAMANDER'S ALL LOCKED UP.
HAS IT EVOLVED INTO A CICADA?
THAT WAS A JOKE!
SOMETHING'S NOT RIGHT HERE.
SHAKE SHAKE
HMM, YEAH, MY FAMILIAR'S REFUSING TO FLY.
KA-
?!
THNK

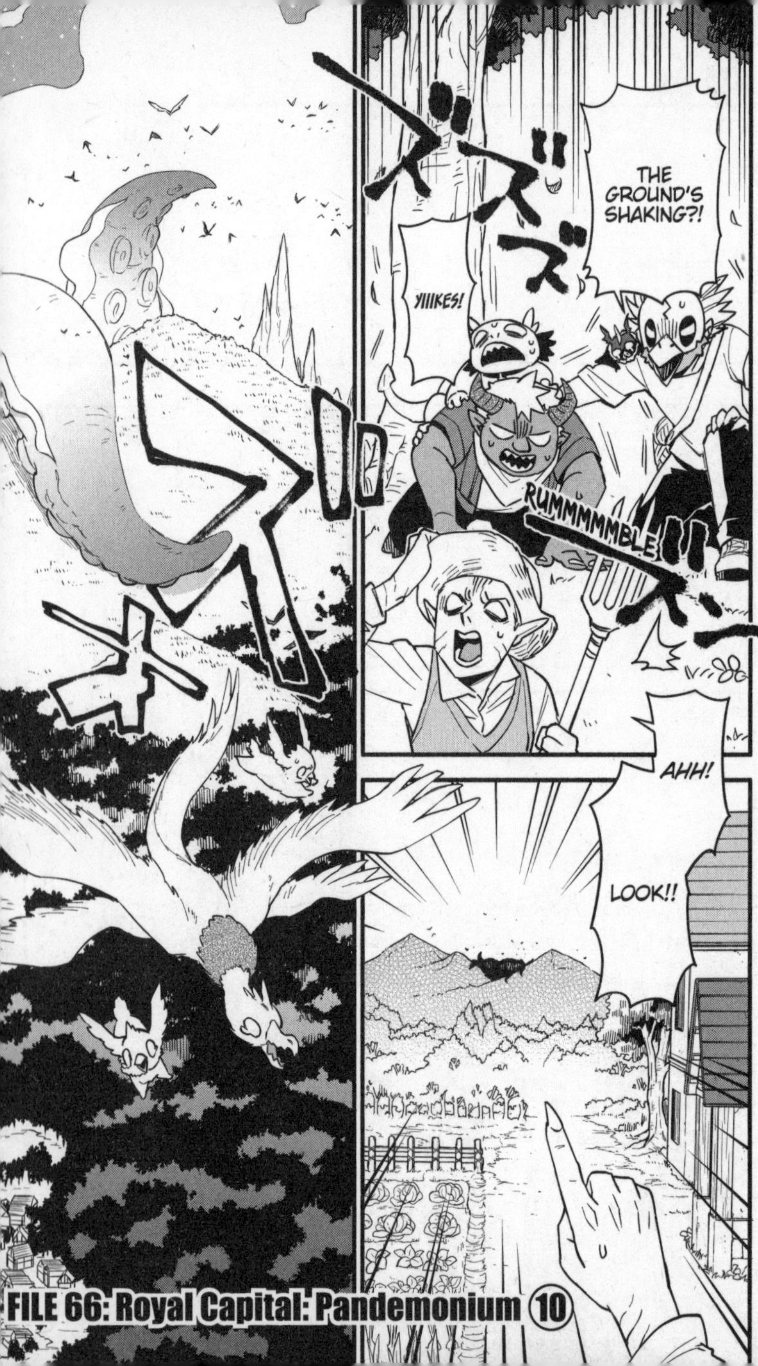
THE GROUND'S SHAKING?!
YIIIKES!
RUMMMMMBLE
AHH!
LOOK!!
FILE 66: Royal Capital: Pandemonium 10

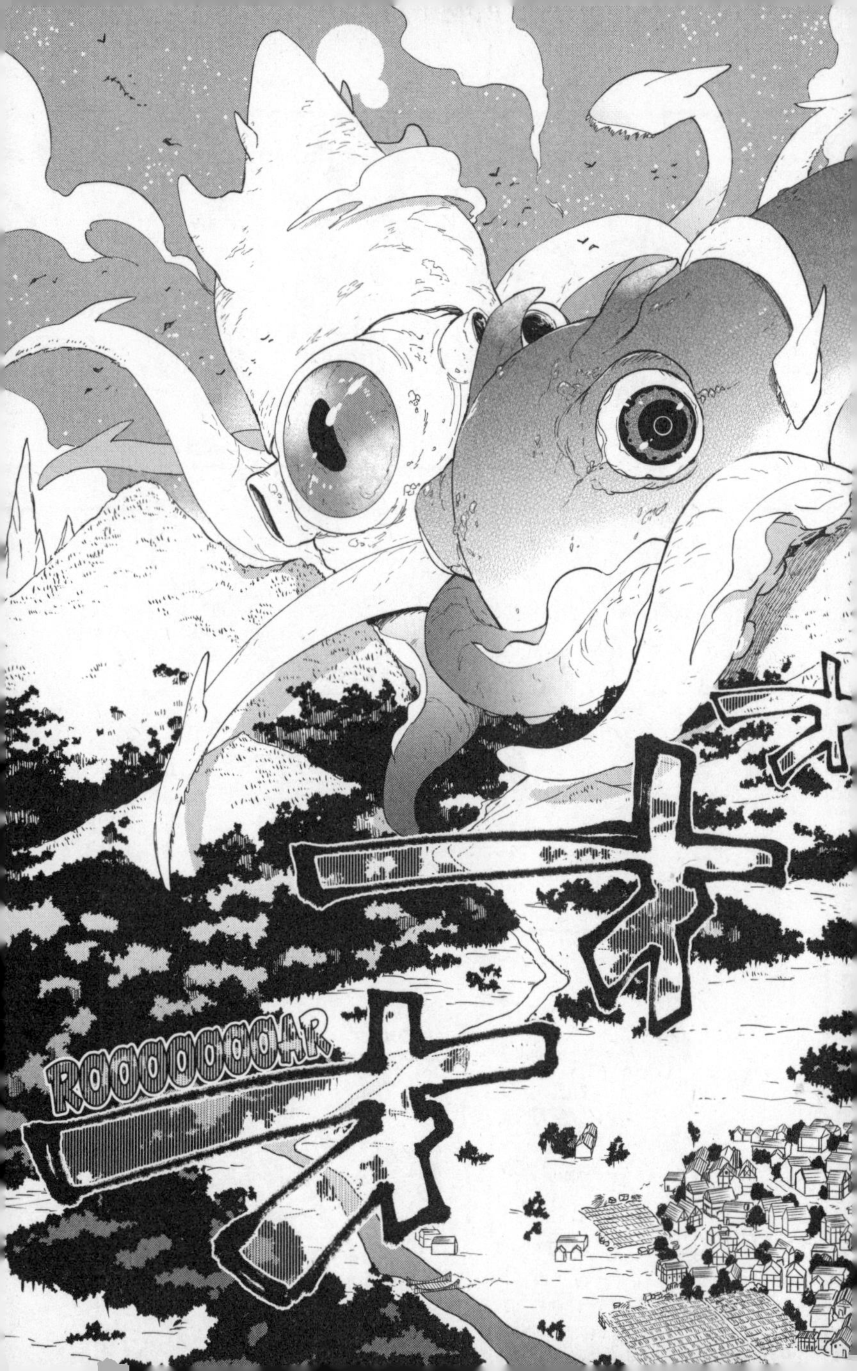
ROOOOOOOAR

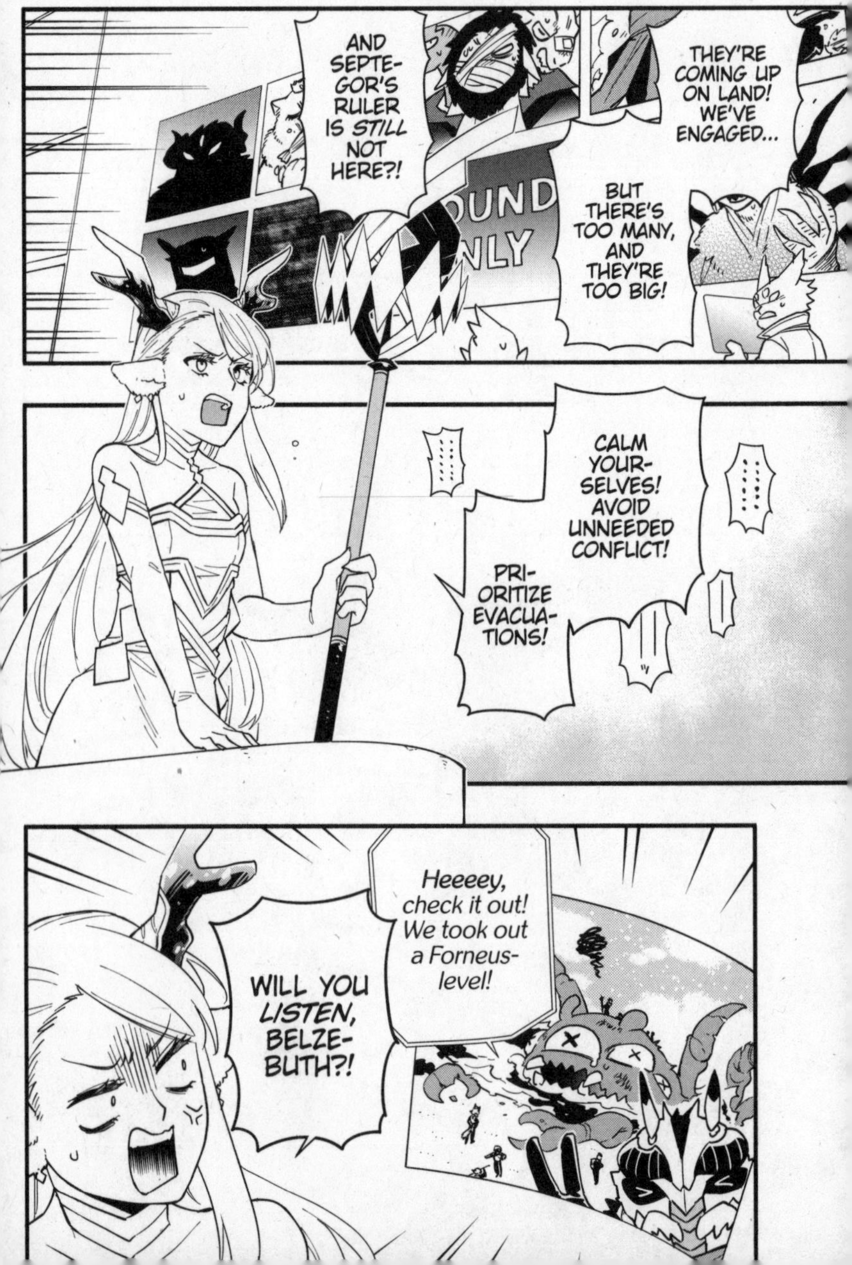
THEY'RE COMING UP ON LAND! WE'VE ENGAGED...
BUT THERE'S TOO MANY, AND THEY'RE TOO BIG!
AND SEPTEGOR'S RULER IS STILL NOT HERE?!
CALM YOURSELVES! AVOID UNNEEDED CONFLICT!
PRIORITIZE EVACUATIONS!
Heeeey, check it out! We took out a Forneus-level!
WILL YOU LISTEN, BELZEBUTH?!

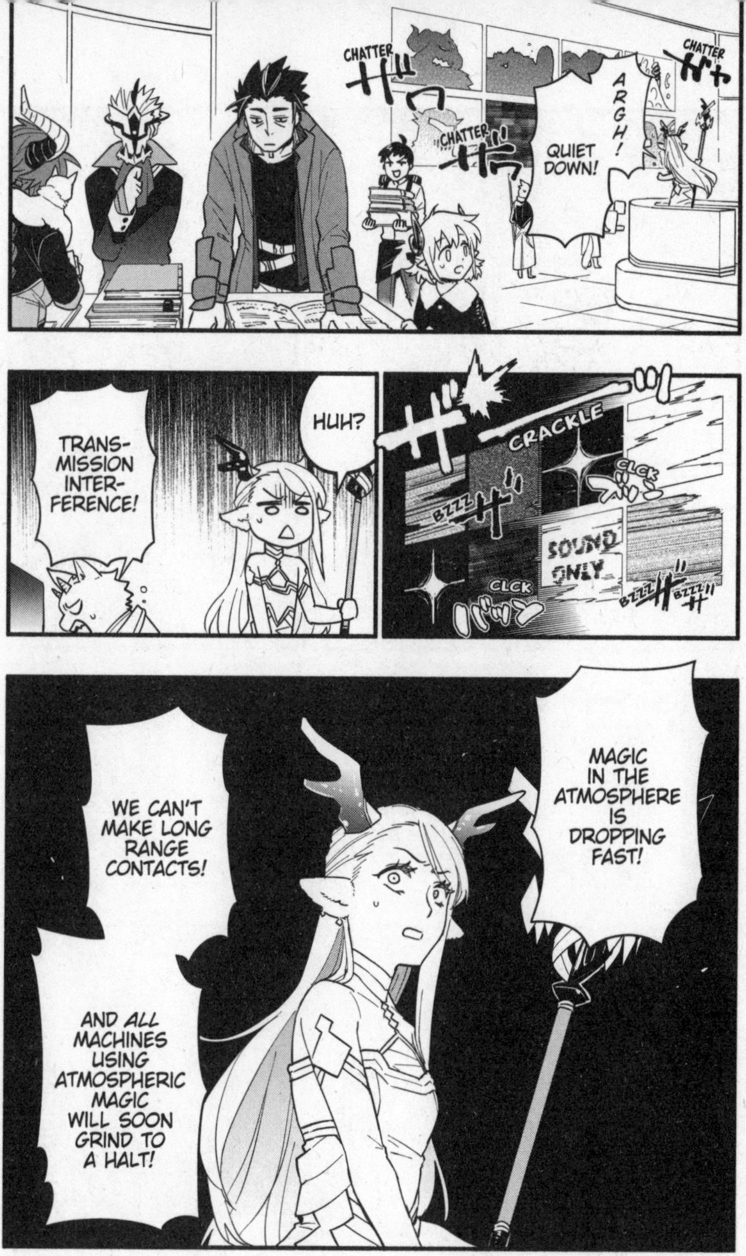
CHATTER
ARGH!
QUIET DOWN!
CHATTER
CHATTER
CRACKLE
CLCK
BZZZ
SOUND ONLY
BZZZ
BZZZ
CLCK
HUH?
TRANSMISSION INTERFERENCE!
MAGIC IN THE ATMOSPHERE IS DROPPING FAST!
WE CAN'T MAKE LONG RANGE CONTACTS!
AND ALL MACHINES USING ATMOSPHERIC MAGIC WILL SOON GRIND TO A HALT!

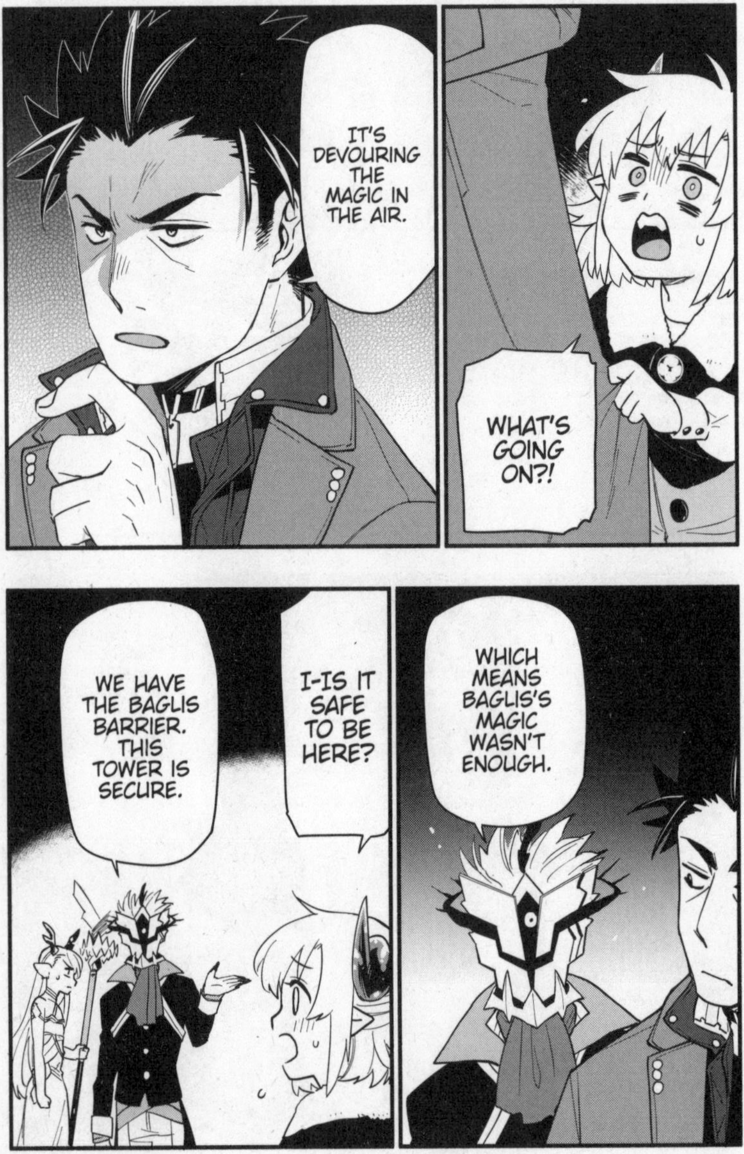
WHAT'S GOING ON?!
IT'S DEVOURING THE MAGIC IN THE AIR.
WHICH MEANS BAGLIS'S MAGIC WASN'T ENOUGH.
I-IS IT SAFE TO BE HERE?
WE HAVE THE BAGLIS BARRIER. THIS TOWER IS SECURE.

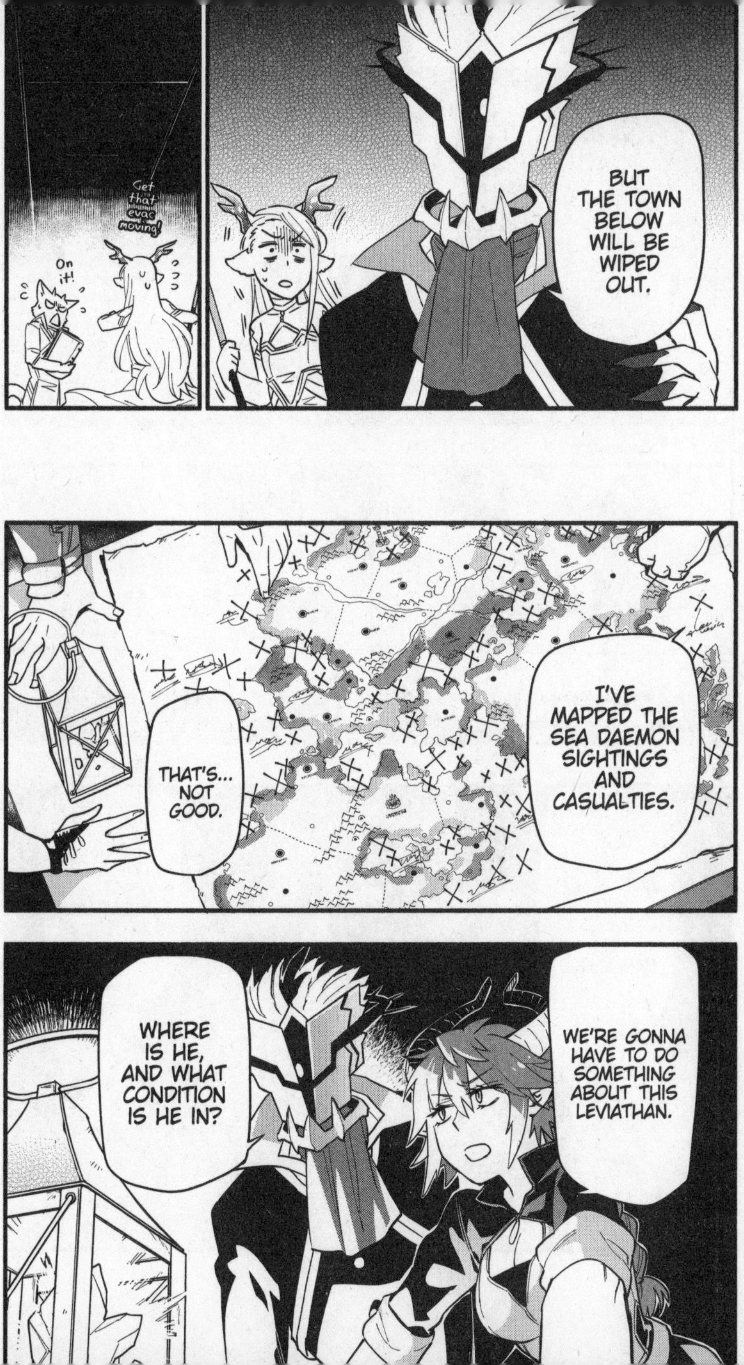
BUT THE TOWN BELOW WILL BE WIPED OUT.
Get that evac moving!
On it!
I'VE MAPPED THE SEA DAEMON SIGHTINGS AND CASUALTIES.
THAT'S... NOT GOOD.
WE'RE GONNA HAVE TO DO SOMETHING ABOUT THIS LEVIATHAN.
WHERE IS HE, AND WHAT CONDITION IS HE IN?

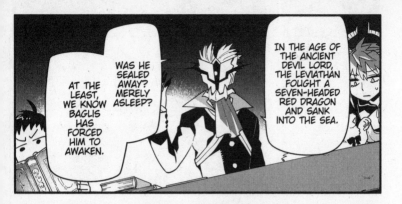

IN THE AGE OF THE ANCIENT DEVIL LORD, THE LEVIATHAN FOUGHT A SEVEN-HEADED RED DRAGON AND SANK INTO THE SEA.
WAS HE SEALED AWAY? MERELY ASLEEP?
AT THE LEAST, WE KNOW BAGLIS HAS FORCED HIM TO AWAKEN.
SO DAD *MUST* KNOW MORE.
PER-HAPS.
BUT HE HASN'T SAID A WORD SINCE.
NO REPORTS OF LEVIATHAN SIGHTINGS?
NO. ALL AREAS ARE BUSY WITH REGULAR SEA DAEMONS.

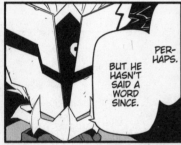

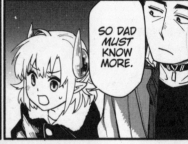

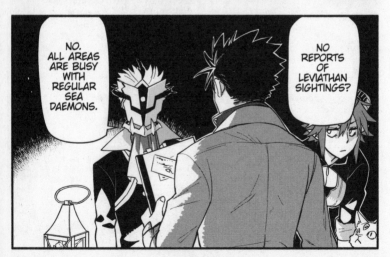

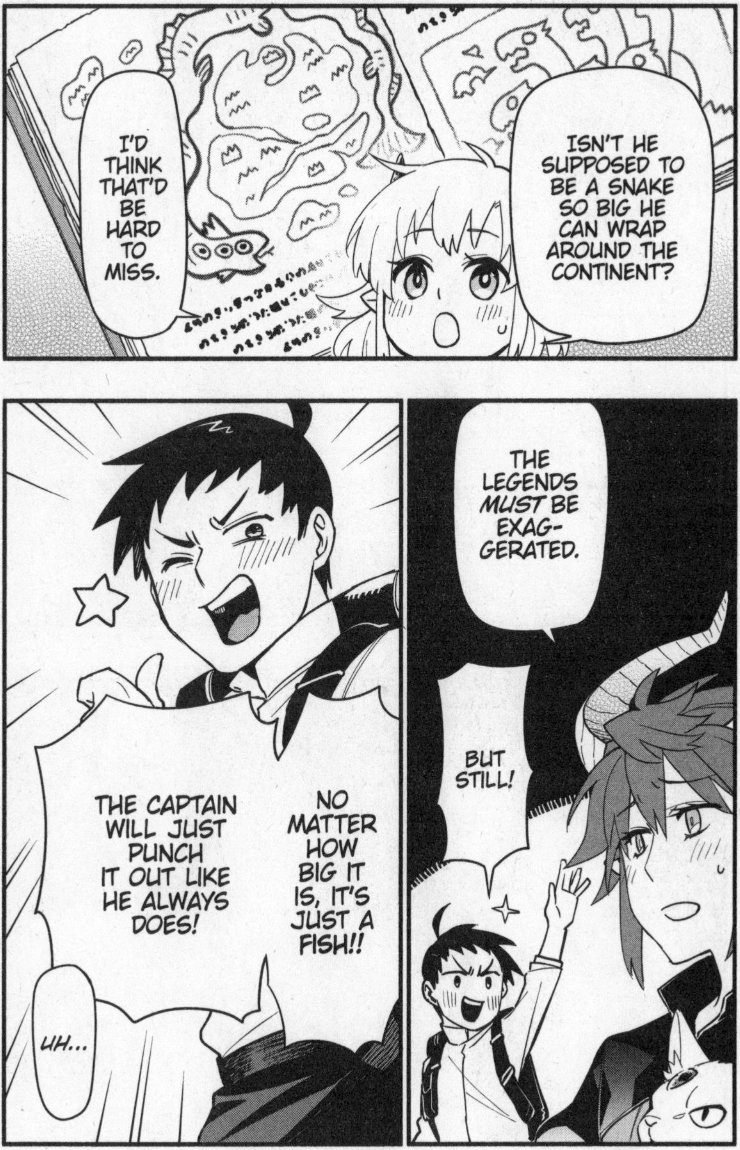
ISN'T HE SUPPOSED TO BE A SNAKE SO BIG HE CAN WRAP AROUND THE CONTINENT?
I'D THINK THAT'D BE HARD TO MISS.
THE LEGENDS *MUST* BE EXAG-GERATED.
BUT STILL!
NO MATTER HOW BIG IT IS, IT'S JUST A FISH!!
THE CAPTAIN WILL JUST PUNCH IT OUT LIKE HE ALWAYS DOES!
UH...

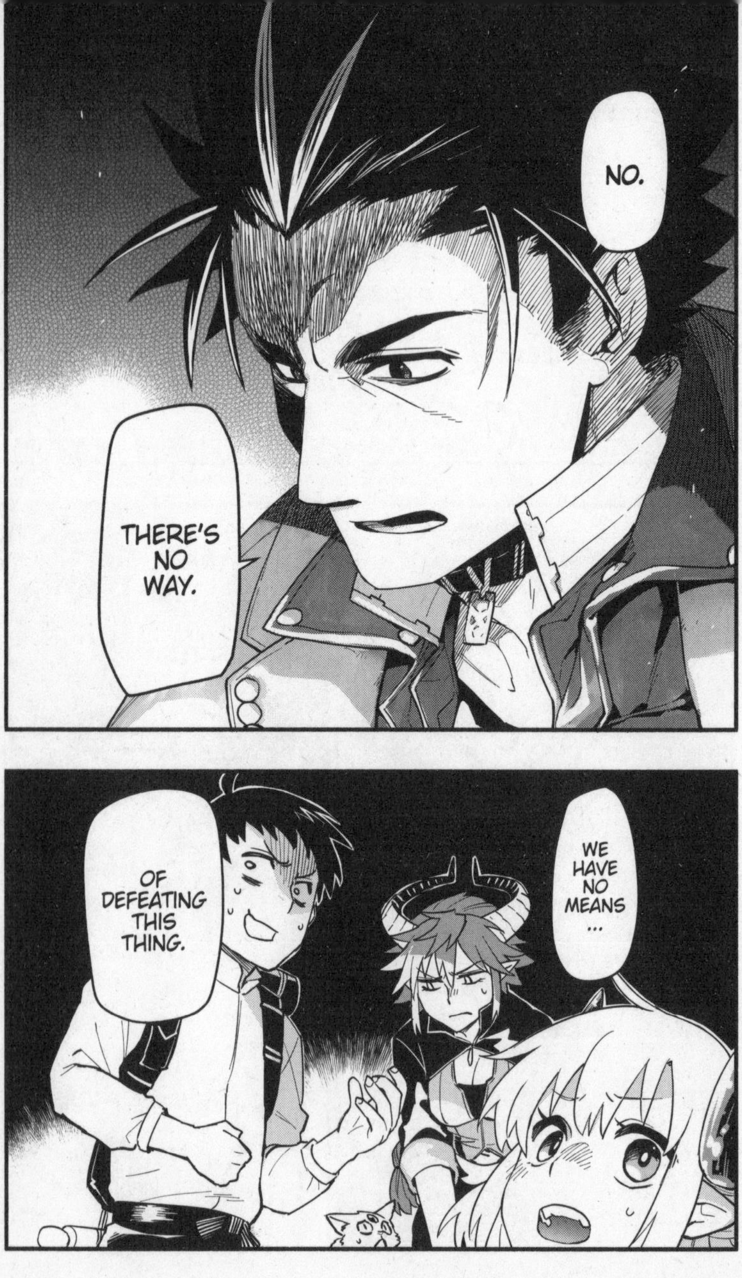
NO.
THERE'S NO WAY.
WE HAVE NO MEANS ...
OF DEFEATING THIS THING.

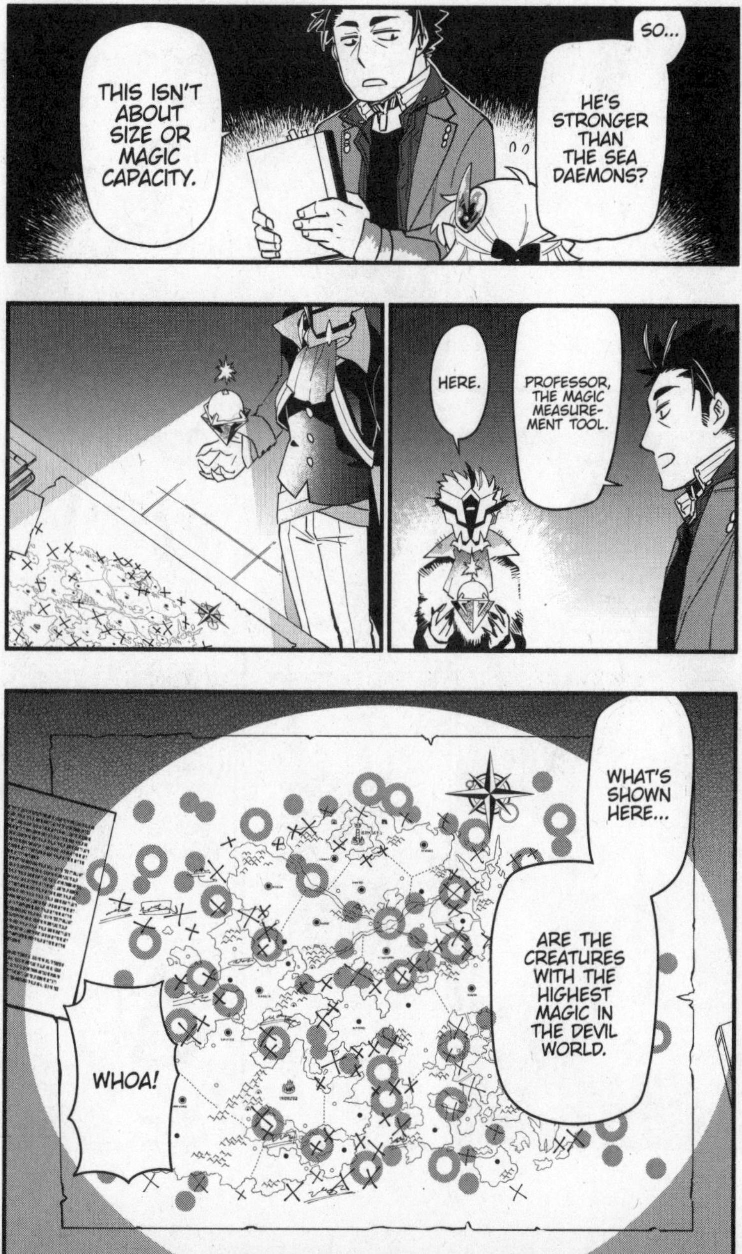
SO...
HE'S STRONGER THAN THE SEA DAEMONS?
THIS ISN'T ABOUT SIZE OR MAGIC CAPACITY.
PROFESSOR, THE MAGIC MEASUREMENT TOOL.
HERE.
WHAT'S SHOWN HERE...
ARE THE CREATURES WITH THE HIGHEST MAGIC IN THE DEVIL WORLD.
WHOA!

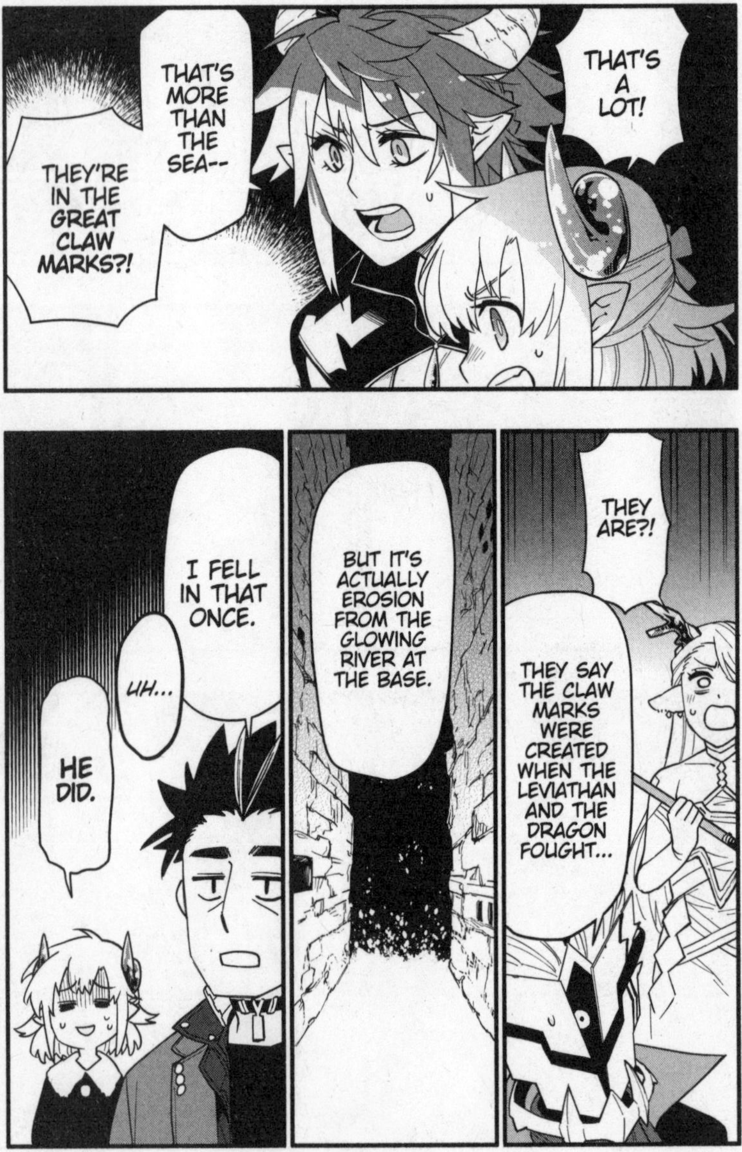
THAT'S A LOT!
THAT'S MORE THAN THE SEA--
THEY'RE IN THE GREAT CLAW MARKS?!
THEY ARE?!
THEY SAY THE CLAW MARKS WERE CREATED WHEN THE LEVIATHAN AND THE DRAGON FOUGHT...
BUT IT'S ACTUALLY EROSION FROM THE GLOWING RIVER AT THE BASE.
I FELL IN THAT ONCE.
UH...
HE DID.

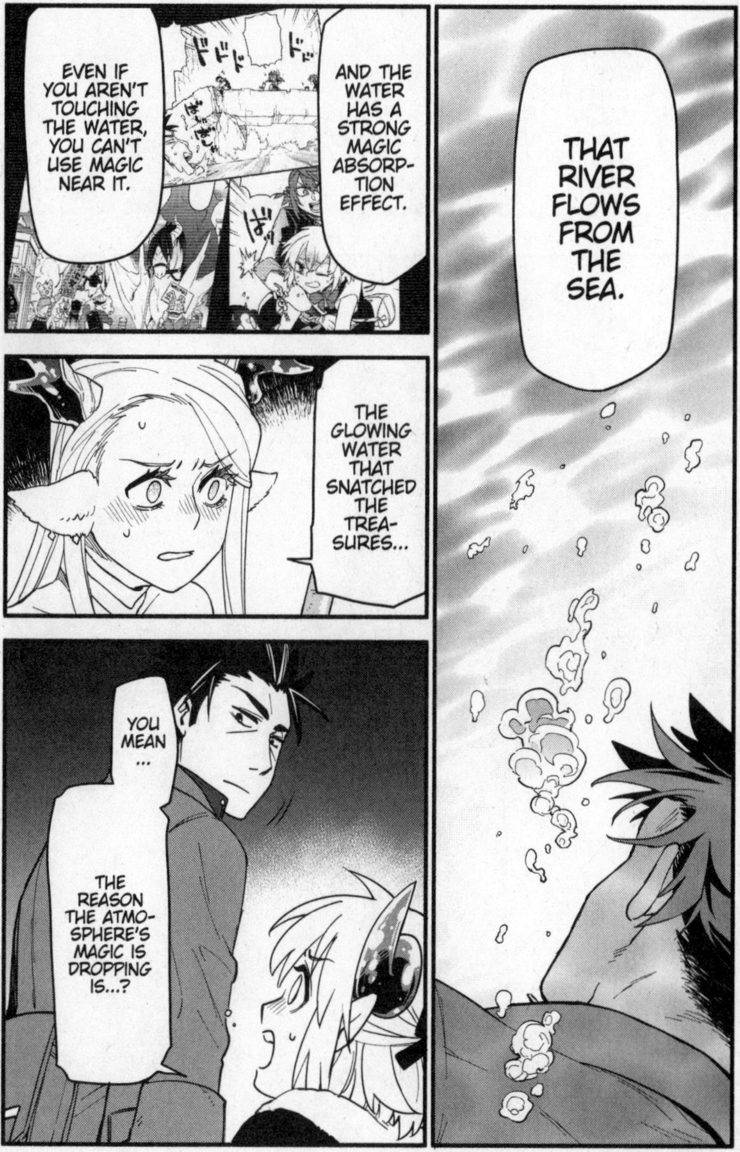
THAT RIVER FLOWS FROM THE SEA.
AND THE WATER HAS A STRONG MAGIC ABSORPTION EFFECT.
EVEN IF YOU AREN'T TOUCHING THE WATER, YOU CAN'T USE MAGIC NEAR IT.
THE GLOWING WATER THAT SNATCHED THE TREASURES...
YOU MEAN ...
THE REASON THE ATMOSPHERE'S MAGIC IS DROPPING IS...?

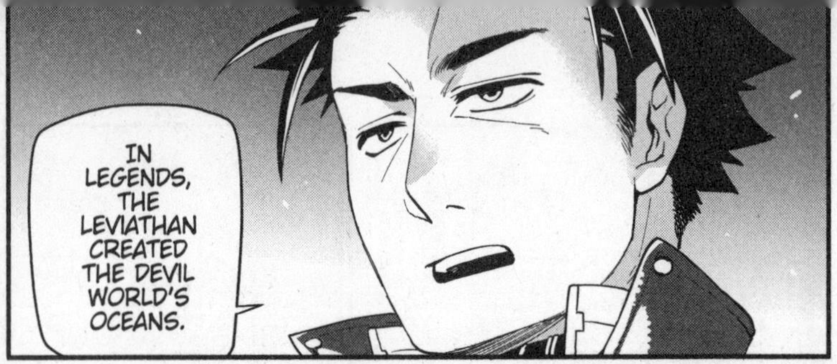
IN LEGENDS, THE LEVIATHAN CREATED THE DEVIL WORLD'S OCEANS.
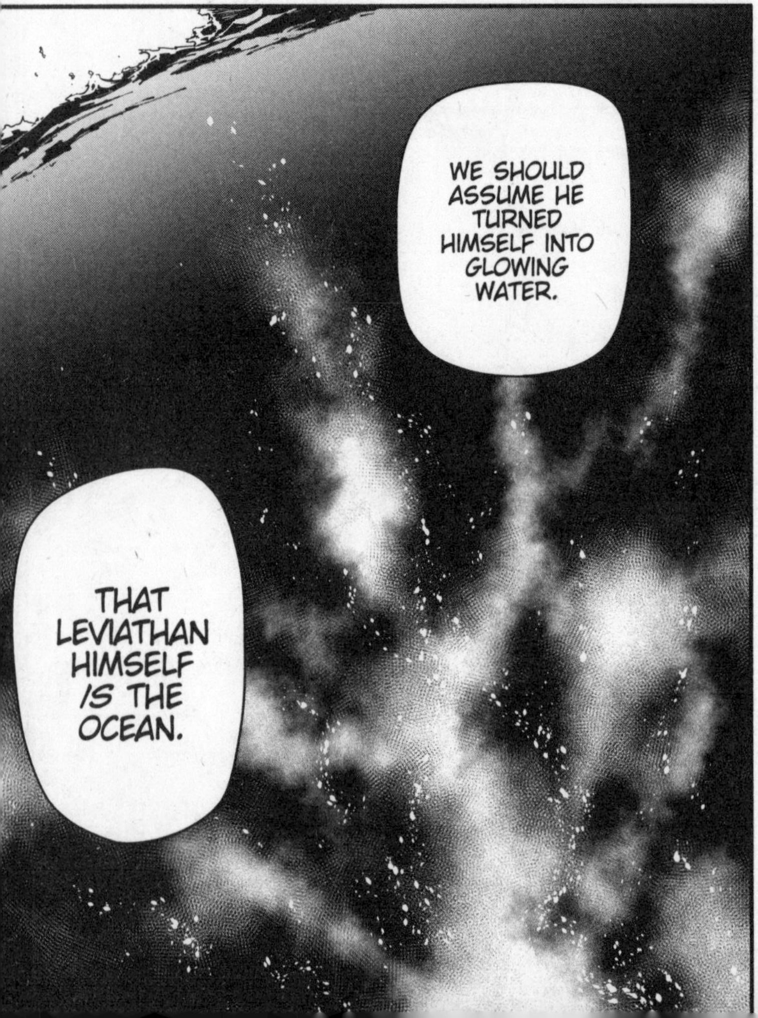
WE SHOULD ASSUME HE TURNED HIMSELF INTO GLOWING WATER.
THAT LEVIATHAN HIMSELF *IS* THE OCEAN.

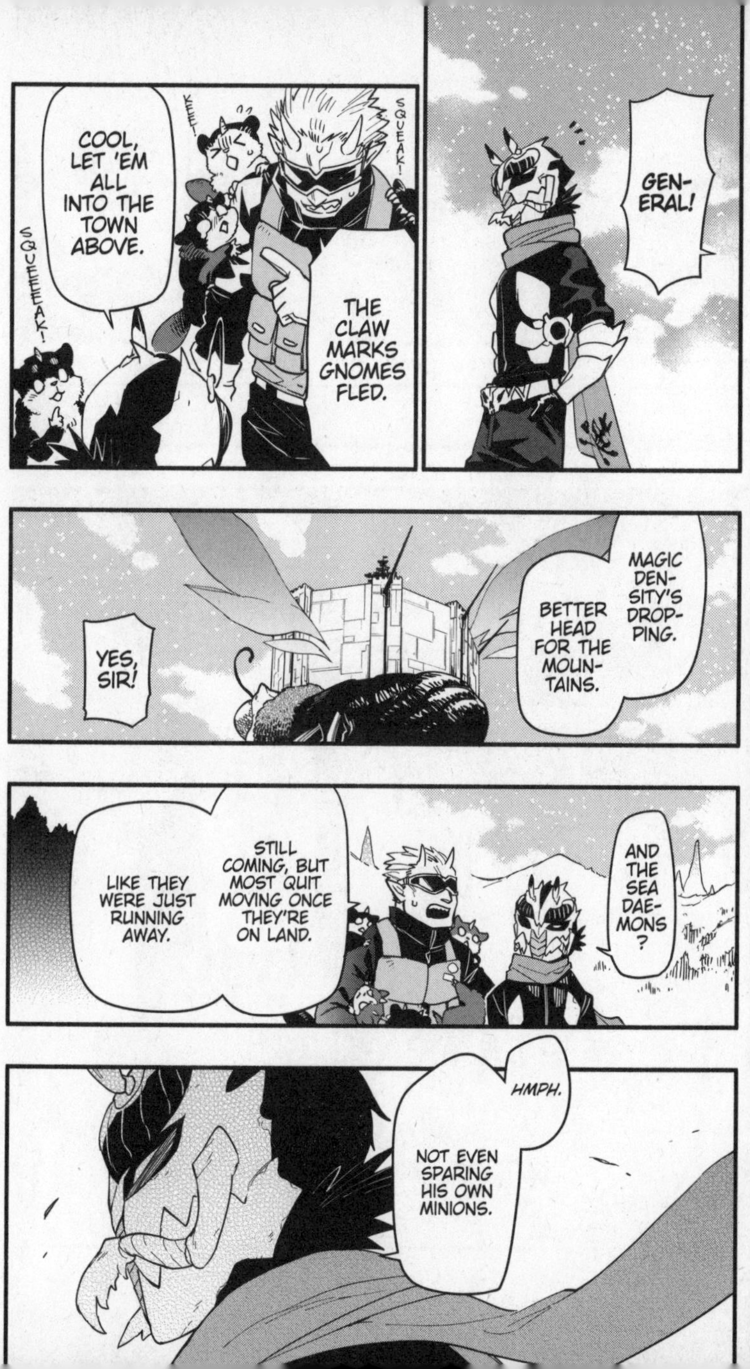
GEN-ERAL!
SQUEAK!
KEE!
THE CLAW MARKS GNOMES FLED.
COOL, LET 'EM ALL INTO THE TOWN ABOVE.
SQUEEEAK!
MAGIC DEN-SITY'S DROP-PING.
BETTER HEAD FOR THE MOUN-TAINS.
YES, SIR!
AND THE SEA DAE-MONS?
STILL COMING, BUT MOST QUIT MOVING ONCE THEY'RE ON LAND.
LIKE THEY WERE JUST RUNNING AWAY.
HMPH.
NOT EVEN SPARING HIS OWN MINIONS.

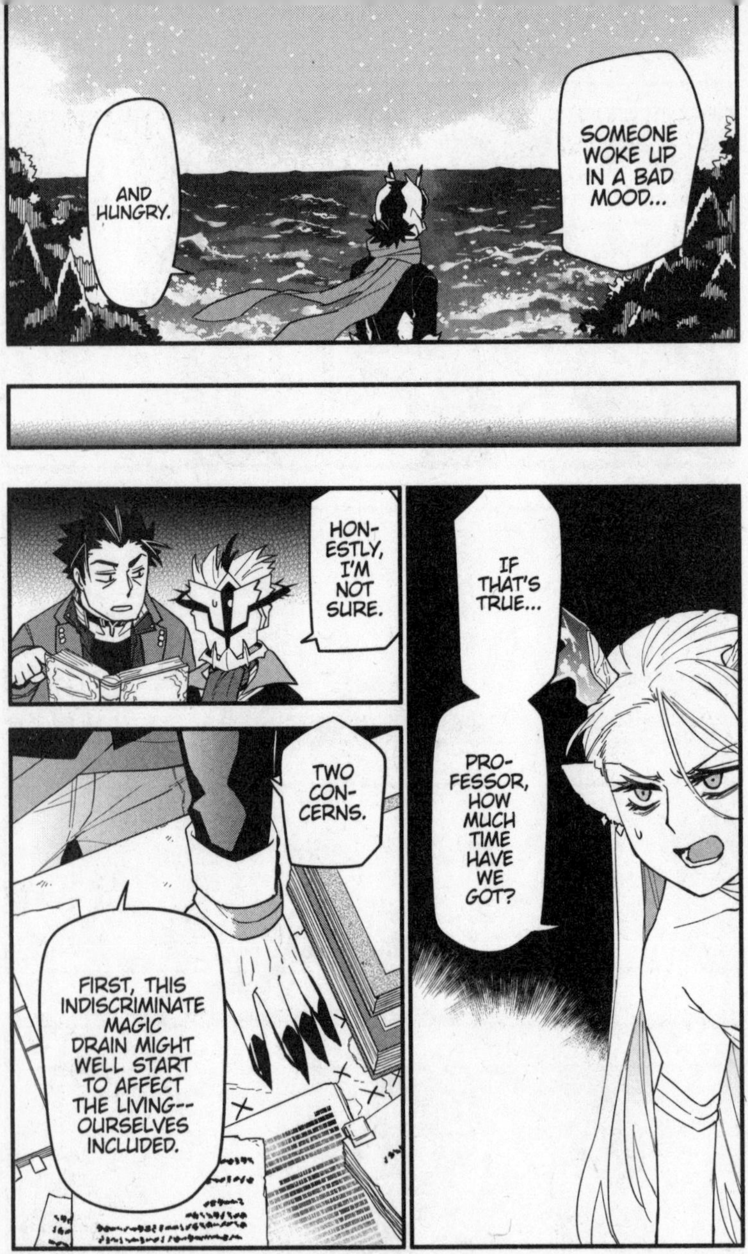
SOMEONE WOKE UP IN A BAD MOOD...
AND HUNGRY.
IF THAT'S TRUE...
PROFESSOR, HOW MUCH TIME HAVE WE GOT?
HONESTLY, I'M NOT SURE.
TWO CONCERNS.
FIRST, THIS INDISCRIMINATE MAGIC DRAIN MIGHT WELL START TO AFFECT THE LIVING--OURSELVES INCLUDED.

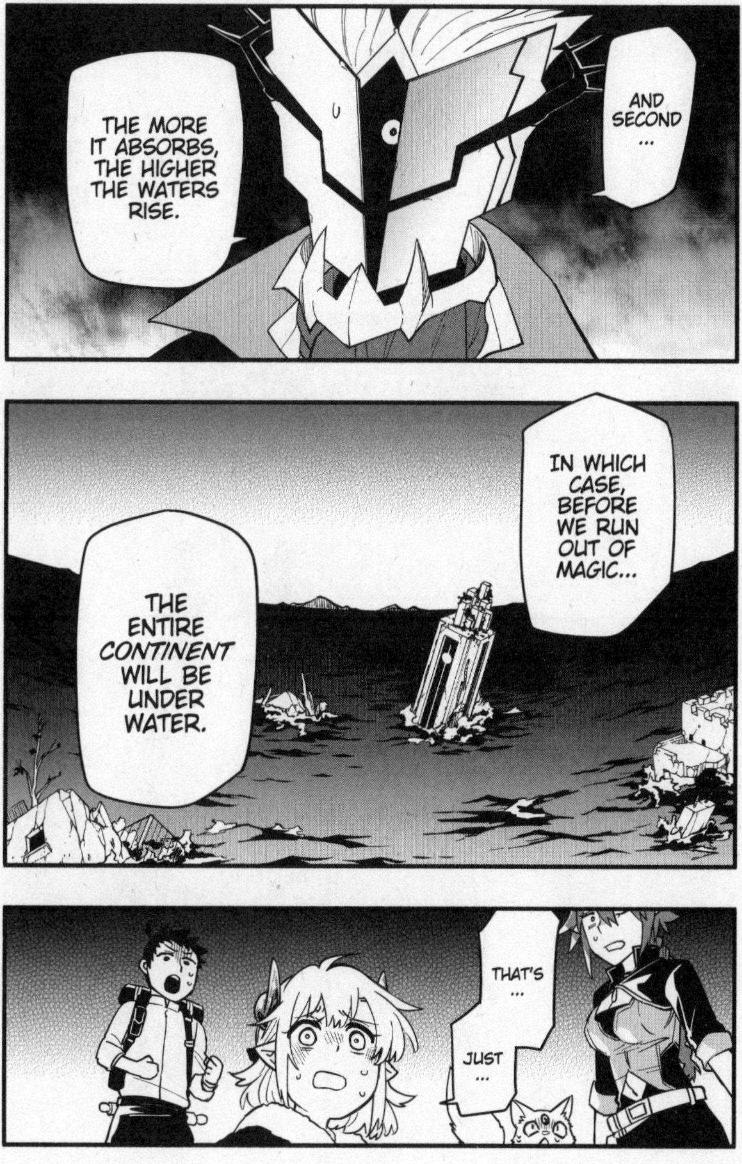
AND SECOND ...
THE MORE IT ABSORBS, THE HIGHER THE WATERS RISE.
IN WHICH CASE, BEFORE WE RUN OUT OF MAGIC...
THE ENTIRE *CONTINENT* WILL BE UNDER WATER.
THAT'S ...
JUST ...

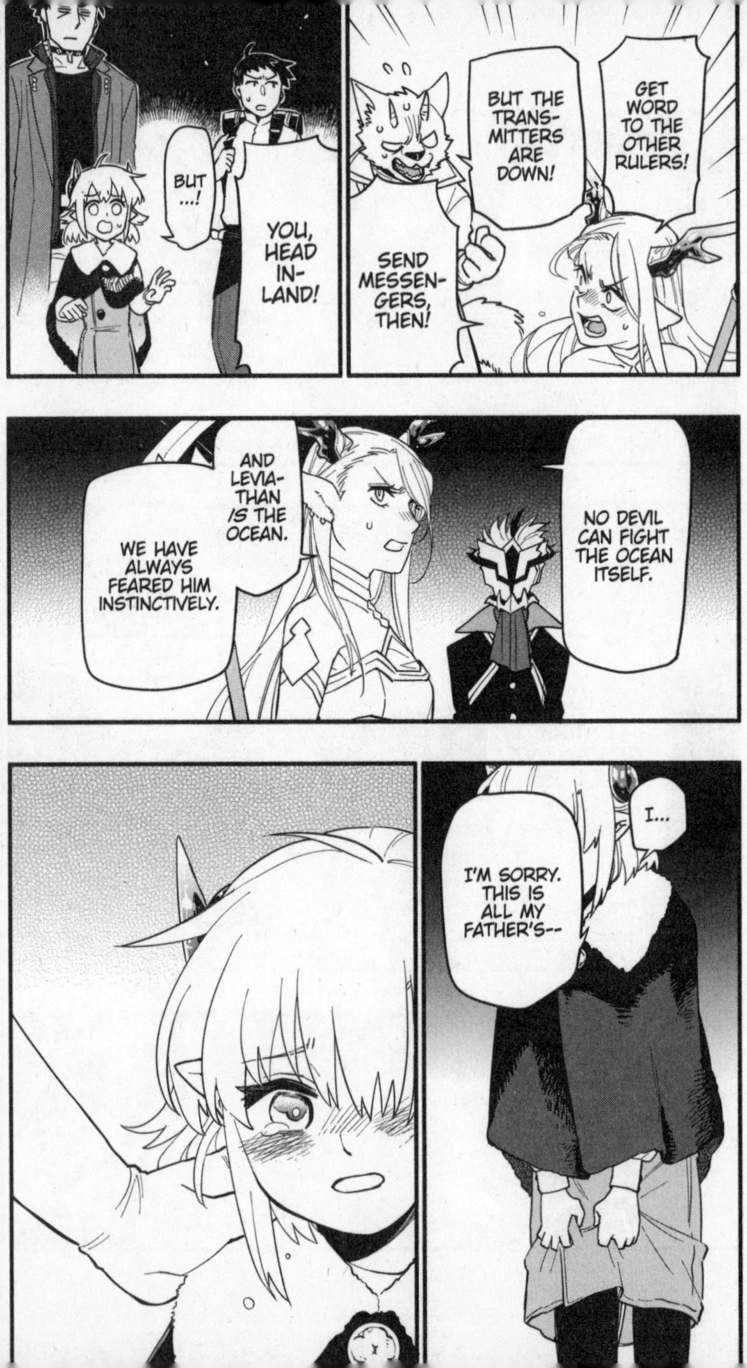
GET WORD TO THE OTHER RULERS!
BUT THE TRANSMITTERS ARE DOWN!
SEND MESSENGERS, THEN!
YOU, HEAD INLAND!
BUT ...!
NO DEVIL CAN FIGHT THE OCEAN ITSELF.
AND LEVIATHAN IS THE OCEAN.
WE HAVE ALWAYS FEARED HIM INSTINCTIVELY.
I...
I'M SORRY. THIS IS ALL MY FATHER'S--

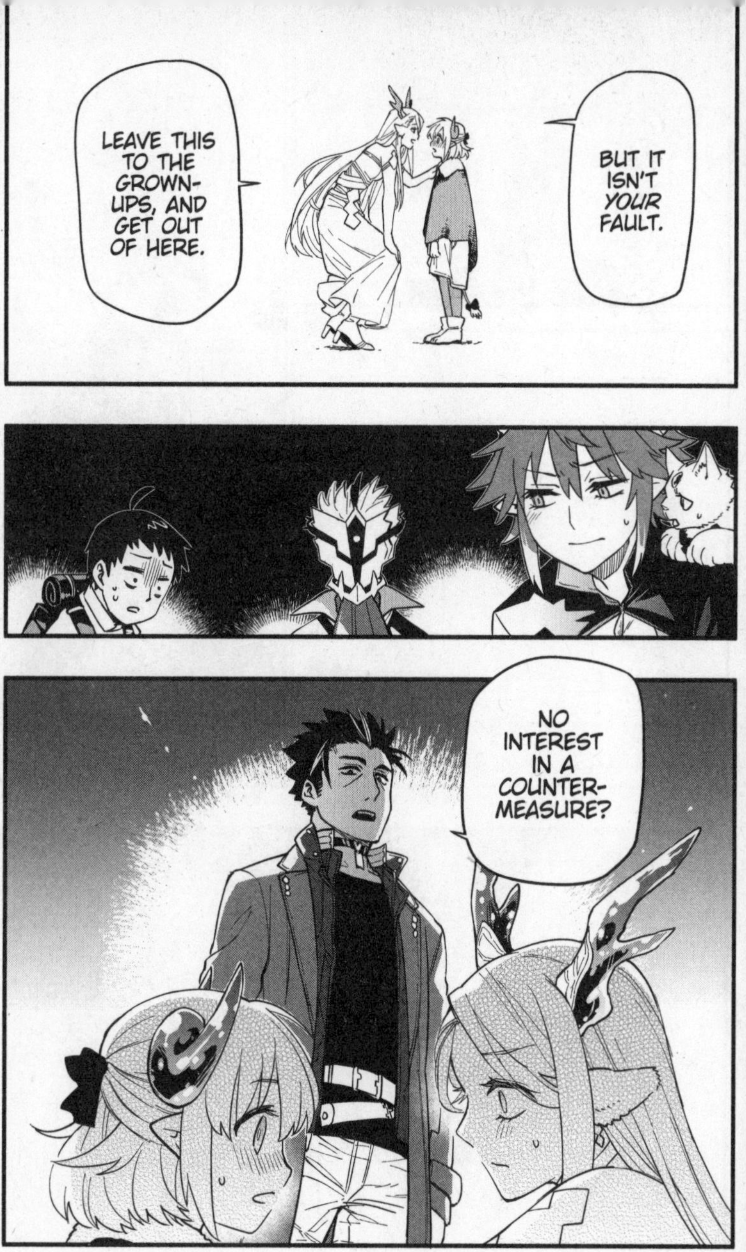
BUT IT ISN'T *YOUR* FAULT.
LEAVE THIS TO THE GROWN-UPS, AND GET OUT OF HERE.
NO INTEREST IN A COUNTER-MEASURE?

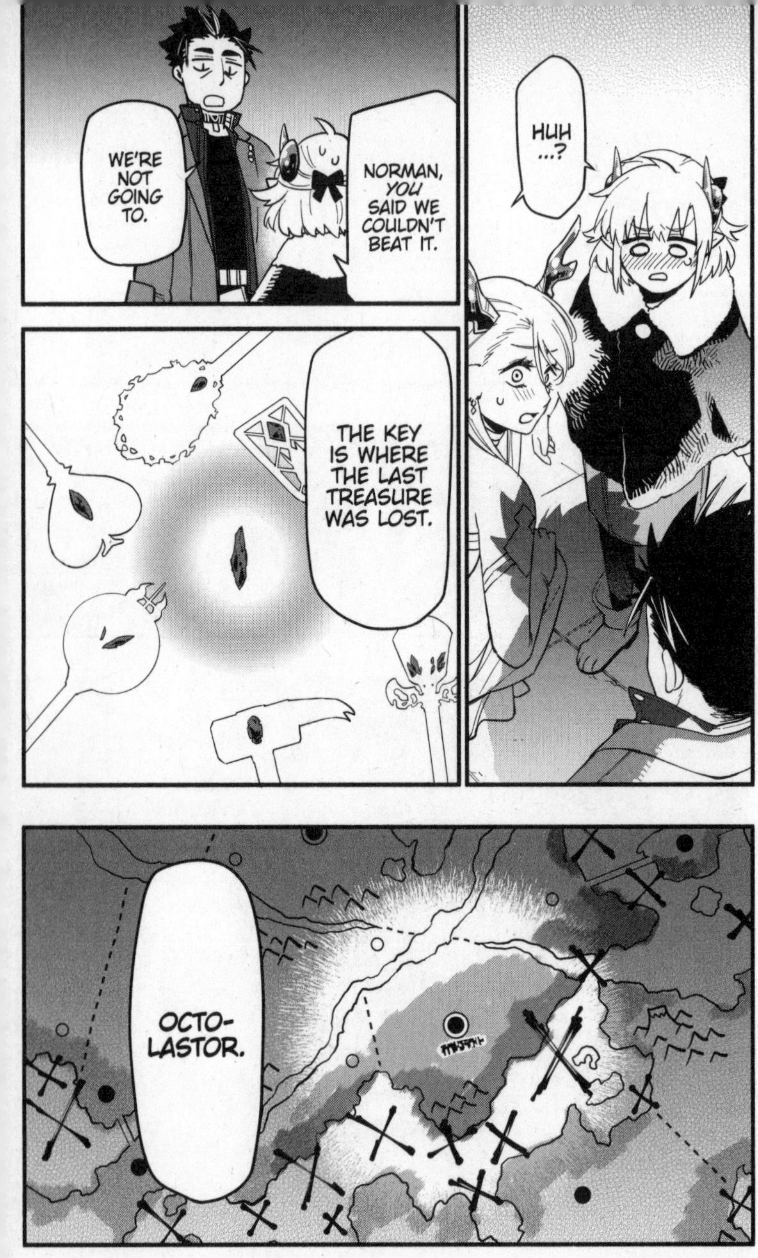
HUH ...?
NORMAN, *YOU* SAID WE COULDN'T BEAT IT.
WE'RE NOT GOING TO.
THE KEY IS WHERE THE LAST TREASURE WAS LOST.
OCTO-LASTOR.

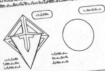

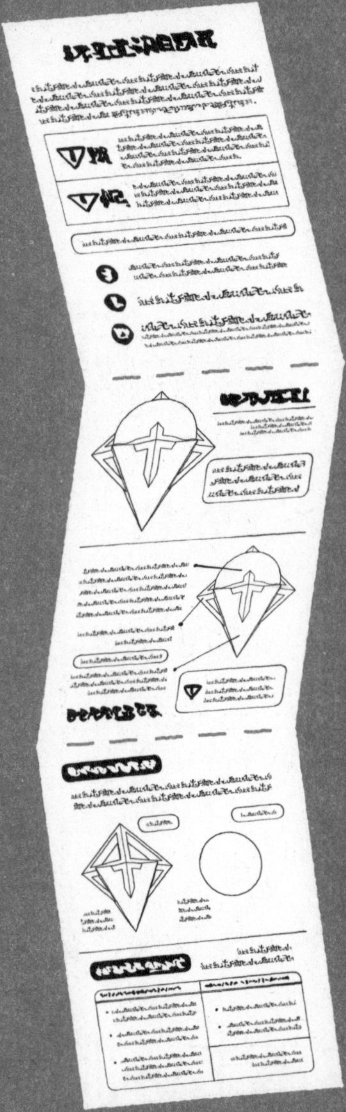

Sorry For My Familiar

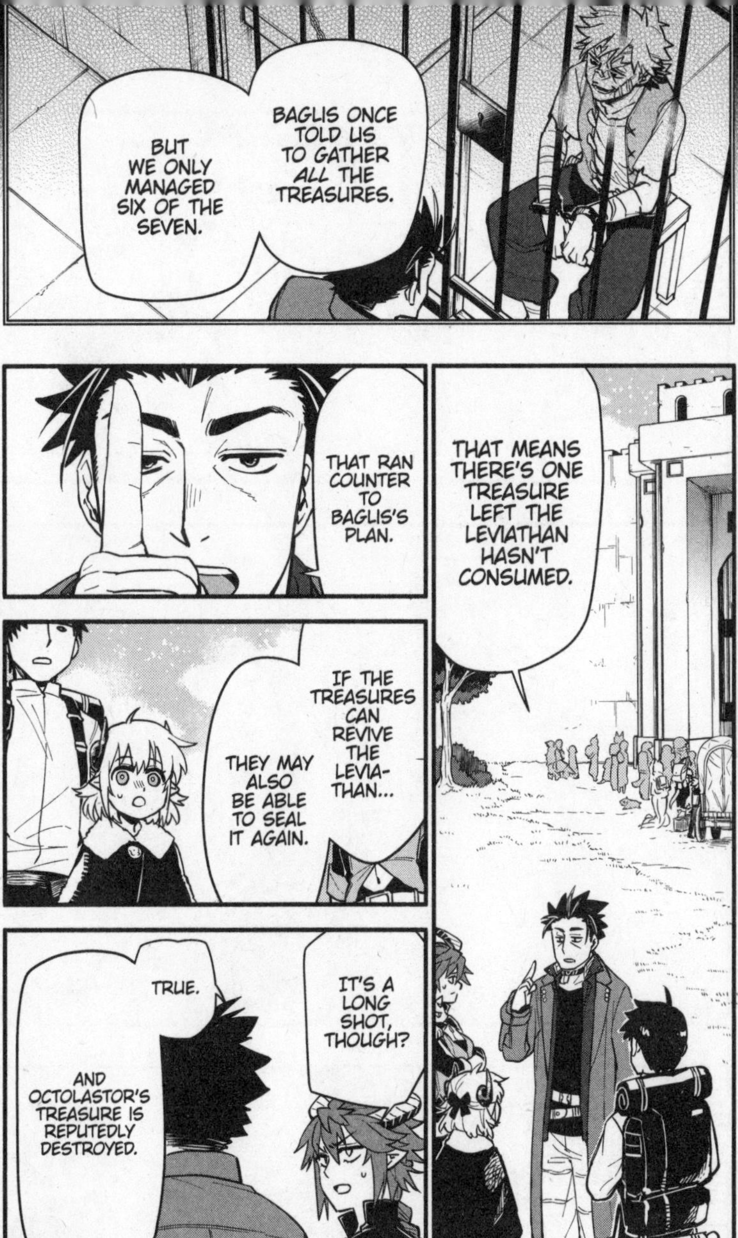
BAGLIS ONCE TOLD US TO GATHER ALL THE TREASURES.
BUT WE ONLY MANAGED SIX OF THE SEVEN.
THAT MEANS THERE'S ONE TREASURE LEFT THE LEVIATHAN HASN'T CONSUMED.
THAT RAN COUNTER TO BAGLIS'S PLAN.
IF THE TREASURES CAN REVIVE THE LEVIA-THAN...
THEY MAY ALSO BE ABLE TO SEAL IT AGAIN.
IT'S A LONG SHOT, THOUGH?
TRUE.
AND OCTOLASTOR'S TREASURE IS REPUTEDLY DESTROYED.

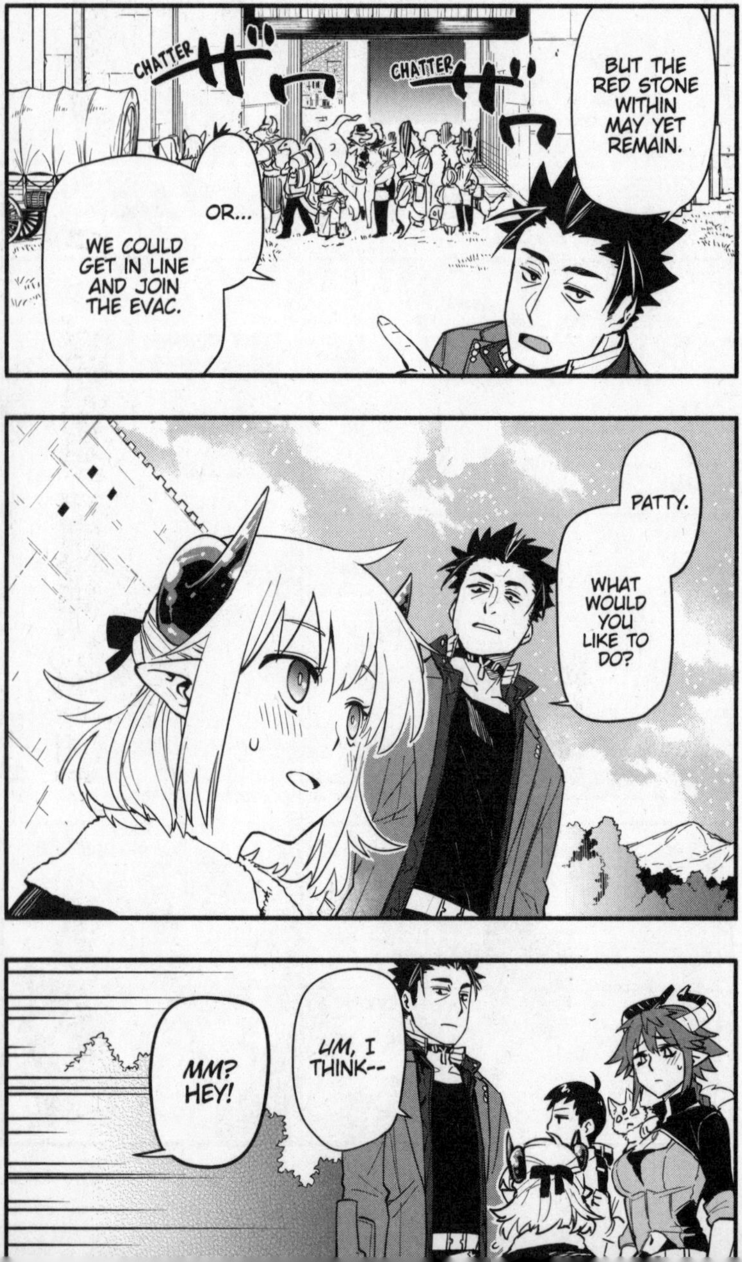
BUT THE RED STONE WITHIN MAY YET REMAIN.
CHATTER
CHATTER
OR...
WE COULD GET IN LINE AND JOIN THE EVAC.
PATTY.
WHAT WOULD YOU LIKE TO DO?
UM, I THINK--
MM? HEY!

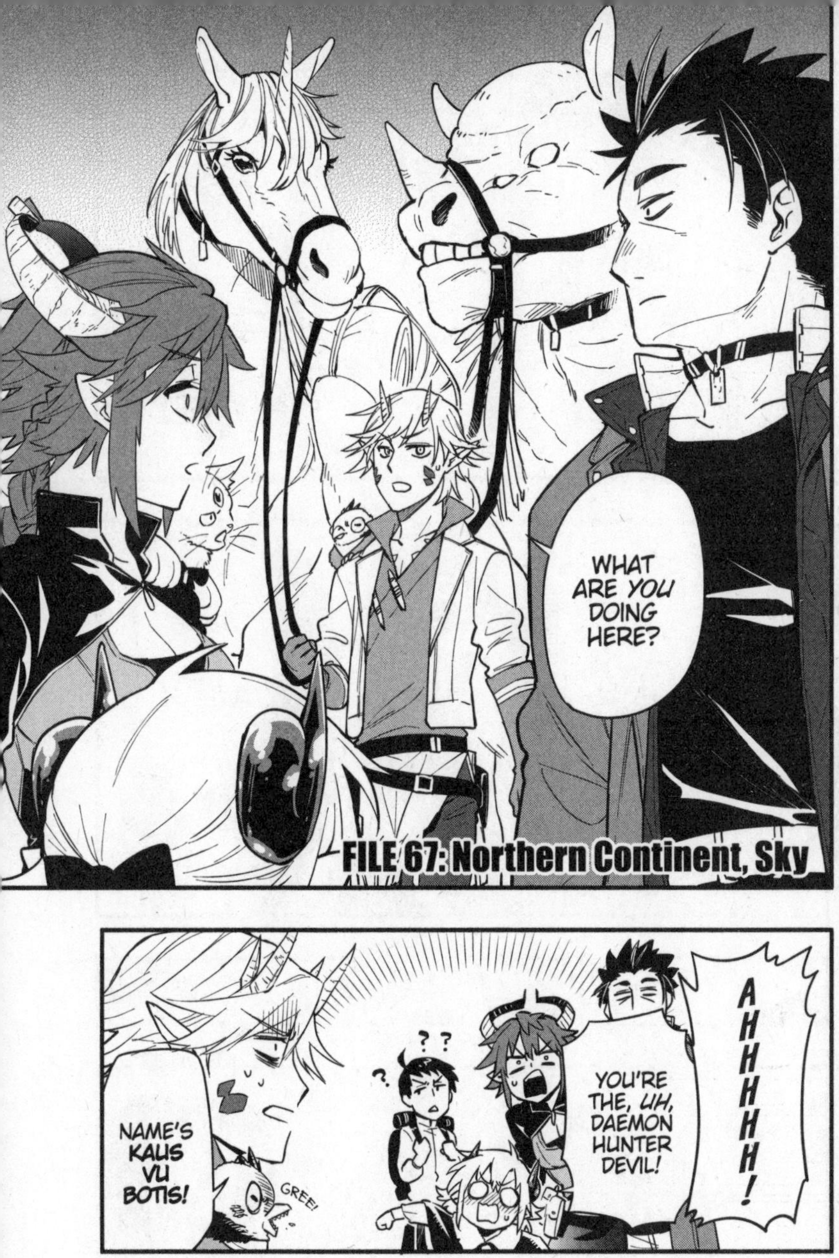
WHAT ARE YOU DOING HERE?
FILE 67: Northern Continent, Sky
AHHHHHH!
YOU'RE THE, UH, DAEMON HUNTER DEVIL!
GREE!
NAME'S KAUS VU BOTIS!

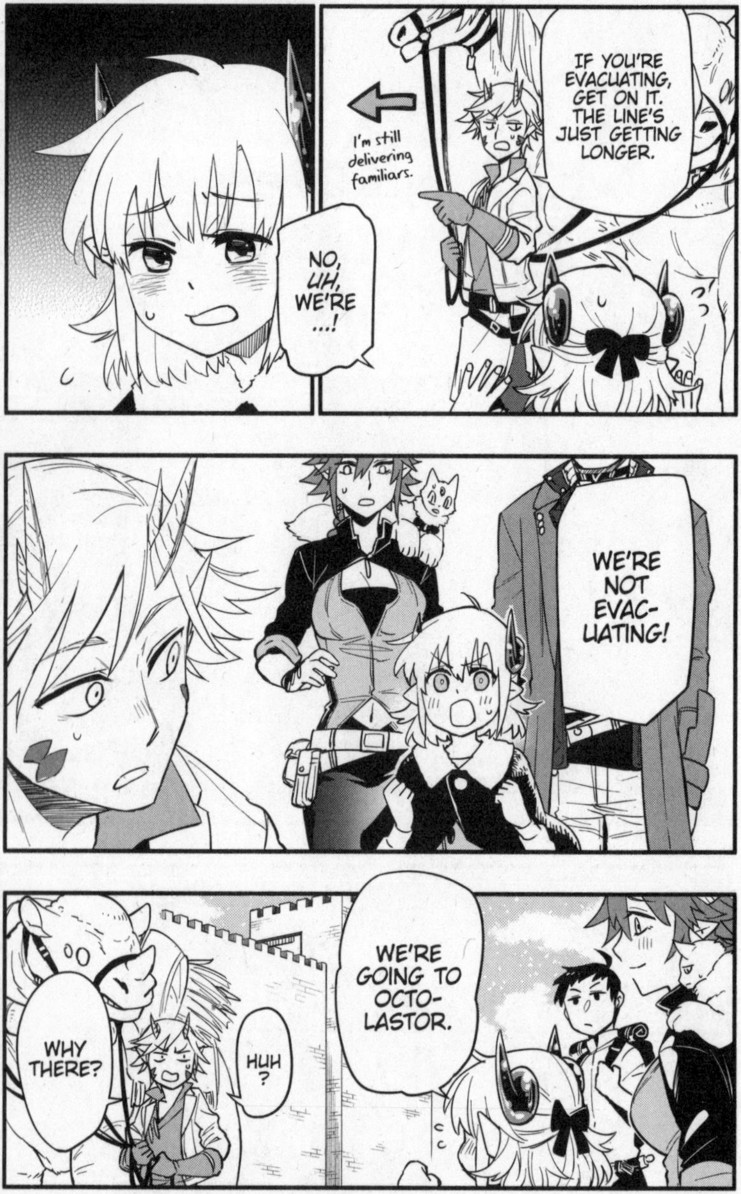
IF YOU'RE EVACUATING, GET ON IT. THE LINE'S JUST GETTING LONGER.
I'm still delivering familiars.
NO, UH, WE'RE ...!
WE'RE NOT EVAC-UATING!
WE'RE GOING TO OCTO-LASTOR.
HUH?
WHY THERE?

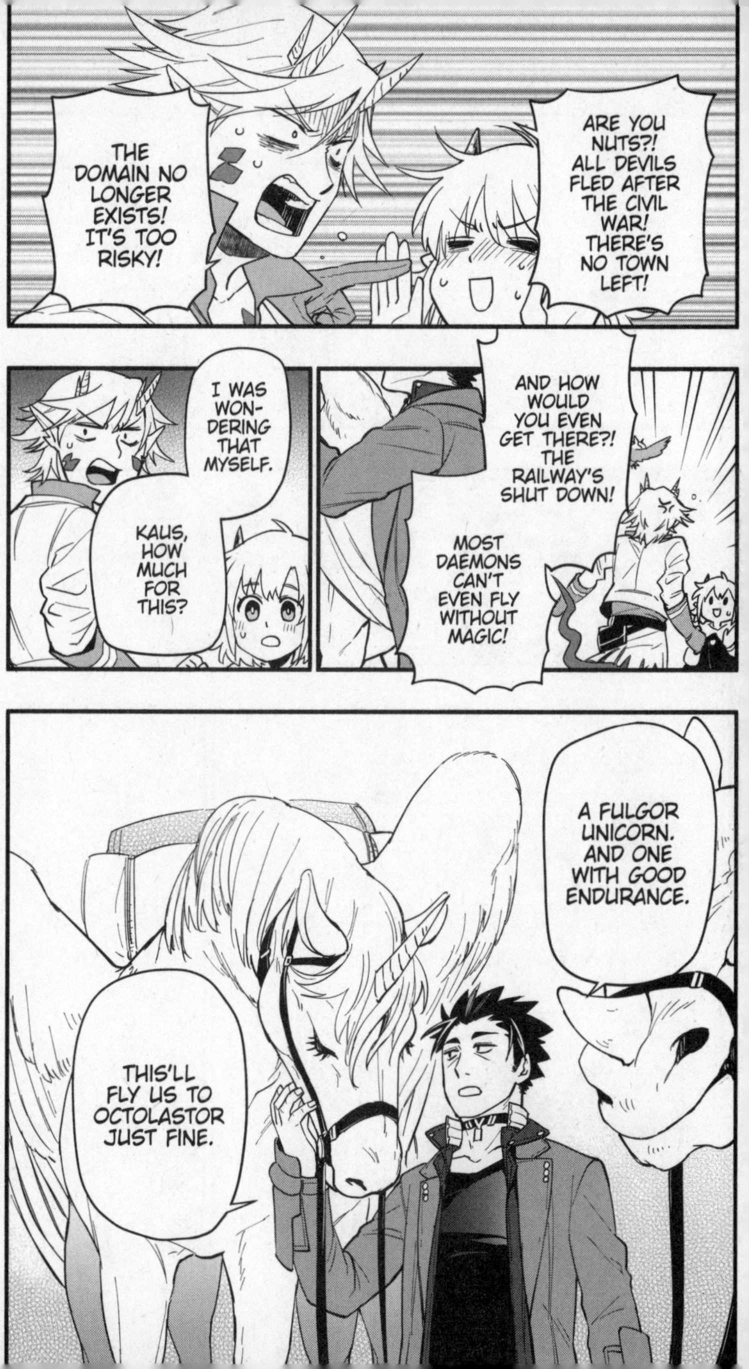
ARE YOU NUTS?! ALL DEVILS FLED AFTER THE CIVIL WAR! THERE'S NO TOWN LEFT!
THE DOMAIN NO LONGER EXISTS! IT'S TOO RISKY!
AND HOW WOULD YOU EVEN GET THERE?! THE RAILWAY'S SHUT DOWN!
MOST DAEMONS CAN'T EVEN FLY WITHOUT MAGIC!
I WAS WON-DERING THAT MYSELF.
KAUS, HOW MUCH FOR THIS?
A FULGOR UNICORN. AND ONE WITH GOOD ENDURANCE.
THIS'LL FLY US TO OCTOLASTOR JUST FINE.

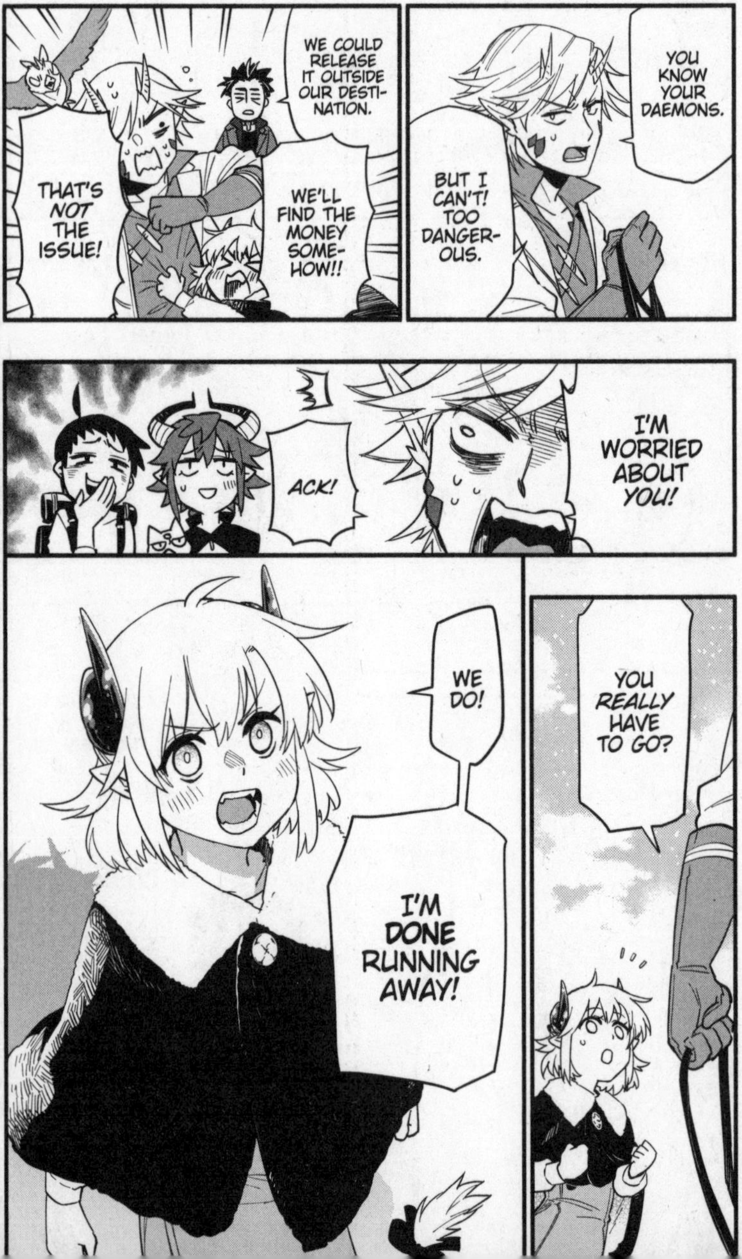
YOU KNOW YOUR DAEMONS.
BUT I CAN'T! TOO DANGEROUS.
WE COULD RELEASE IT OUTSIDE OUR DESTINATION.
WE'LL FIND THE MONEY SOMEHOW!!
THAT'S *NOT* THE ISSUE!
I'M WORRIED ABOUT *YOU!*
ACK!
YOU *REALLY* HAVE TO GO?
WE DO!
I'M DONE RUNNING AWAY!

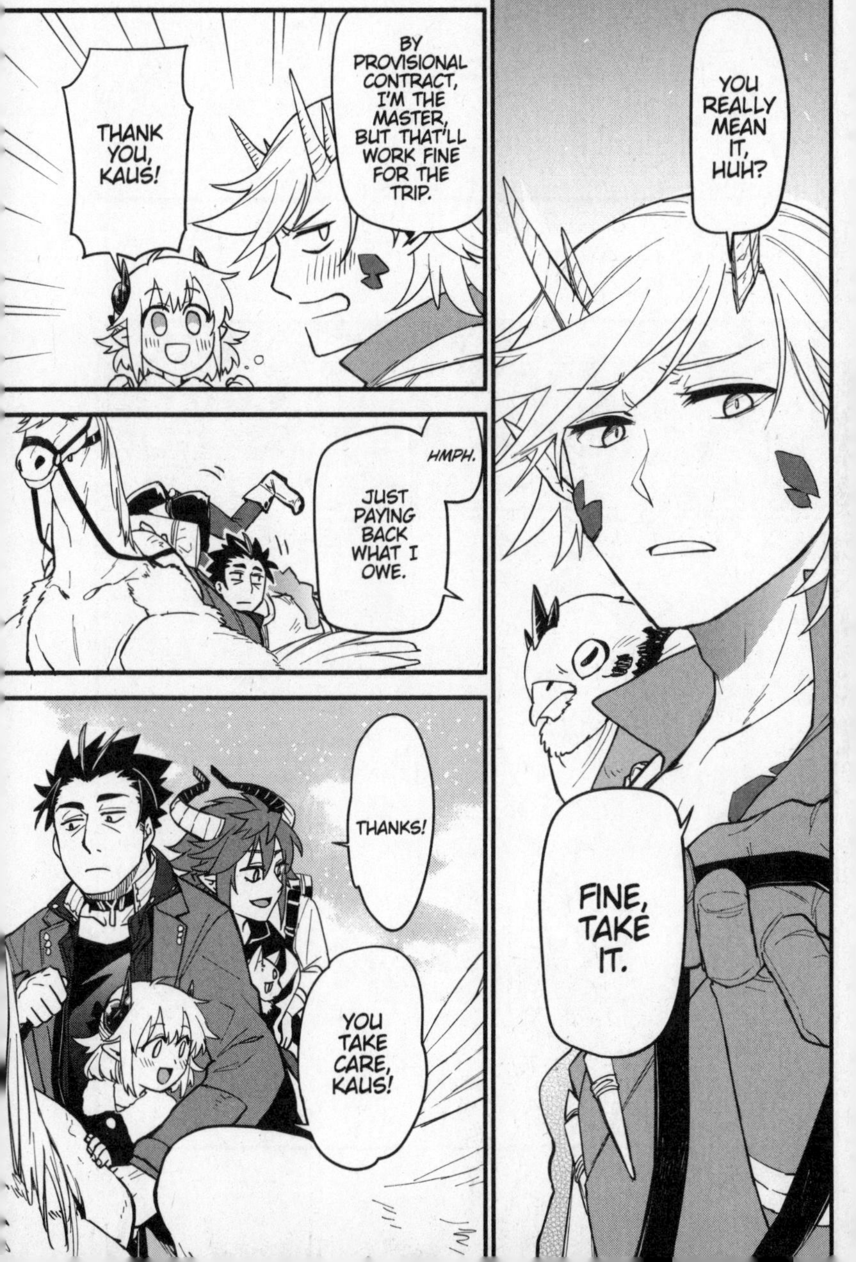
YOU REALLY MEAN IT, HUH?
FINE, TAKE IT.
BY PROVISIONAL CONTRACT, I'M THE MASTER, BUT THAT'LL WORK FINE FOR THE TRIP.
THANK YOU, KAUS!
HMPH.
JUST PAYING BACK WHAT I OWE.
THANKS!
YOU TAKE CARE, KAUS!

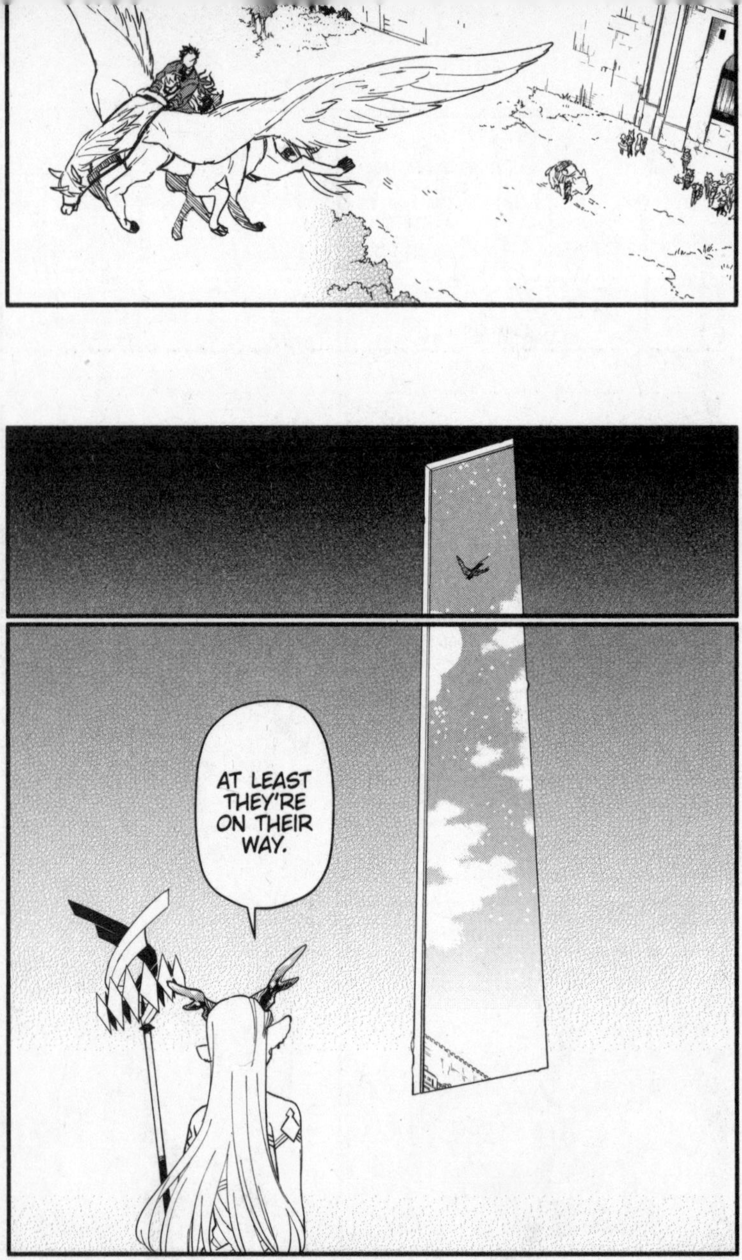
AT LEAST THEY'RE ON THEIR WAY.

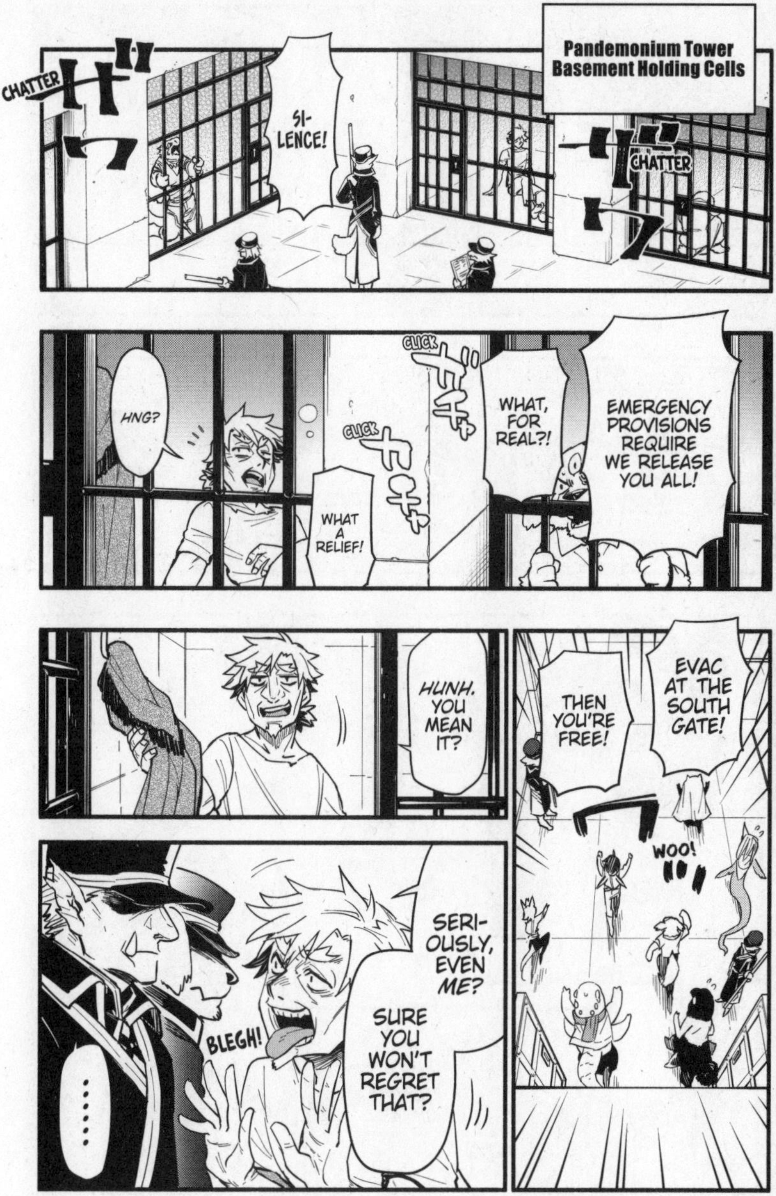
Pandemonium Tower Basement Holding Cells
CHATTER
SI-LENCE!
CHATTER
EMERGENCY PROVISIONS REQUIRE WE RELEASE YOU ALL!
WHAT, FOR REAL?!
CLICK
CLICK
WHAT A RELIEF!
HNG?
EVAC AT THE SOUTH GATE!
THEN YOU'RE FREE!
WOO!
HUNH. YOU MEAN IT?
SERI-OUSLY, EVEN ME?
SURE YOU WON'T REGRET THAT?
BLEGH!
......

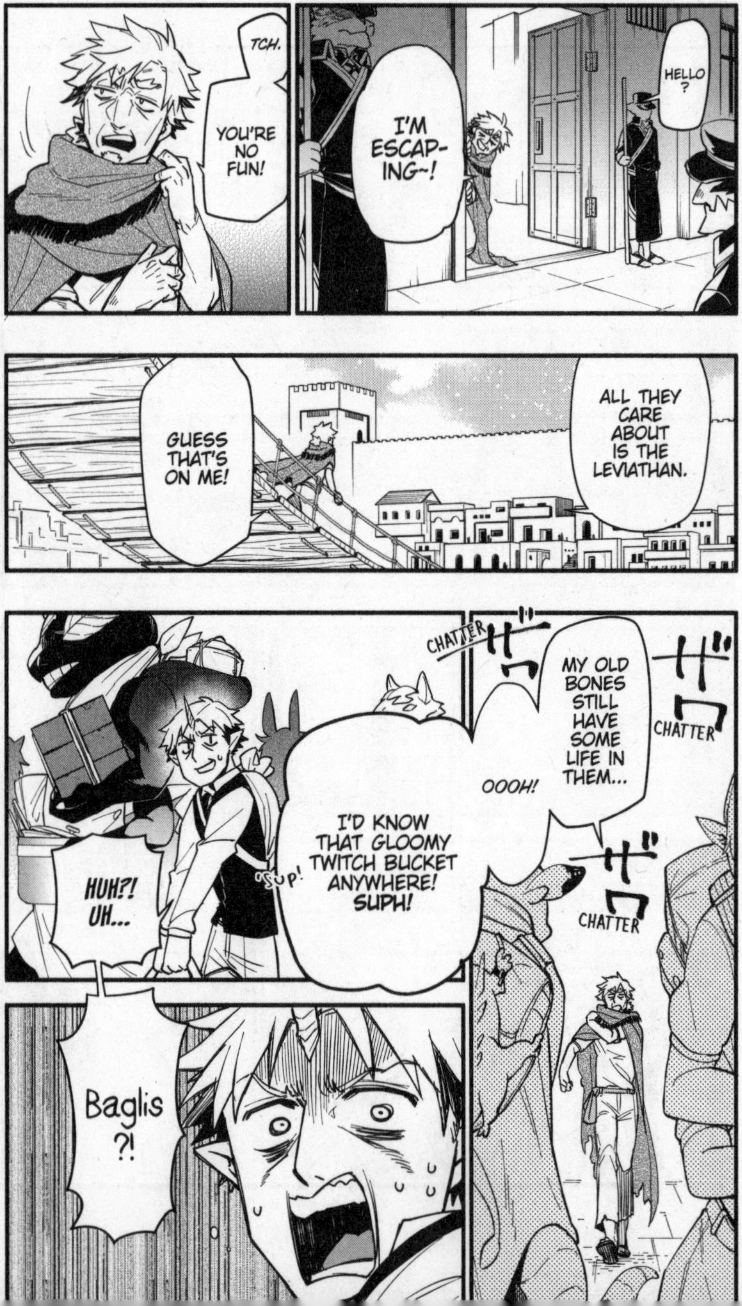
HELLO?
I'M ESCAPING~!
TCH.
YOU'RE NO FUN!
ALL THEY CARE ABOUT IS THE LEVIATHAN.
GUESS THAT'S ON ME!
ザワ CHATTER
MY OLD BONES STILL HAVE SOME LIFE IN THEM...
ザワ CHATTER
OOOH!
ザワ CHATTER
I'D KNOW THAT GLOOMY TWITCH BUCKET ANYWHERE! SUPH!
'SUP!
HUH?! UH...
Baglis?!

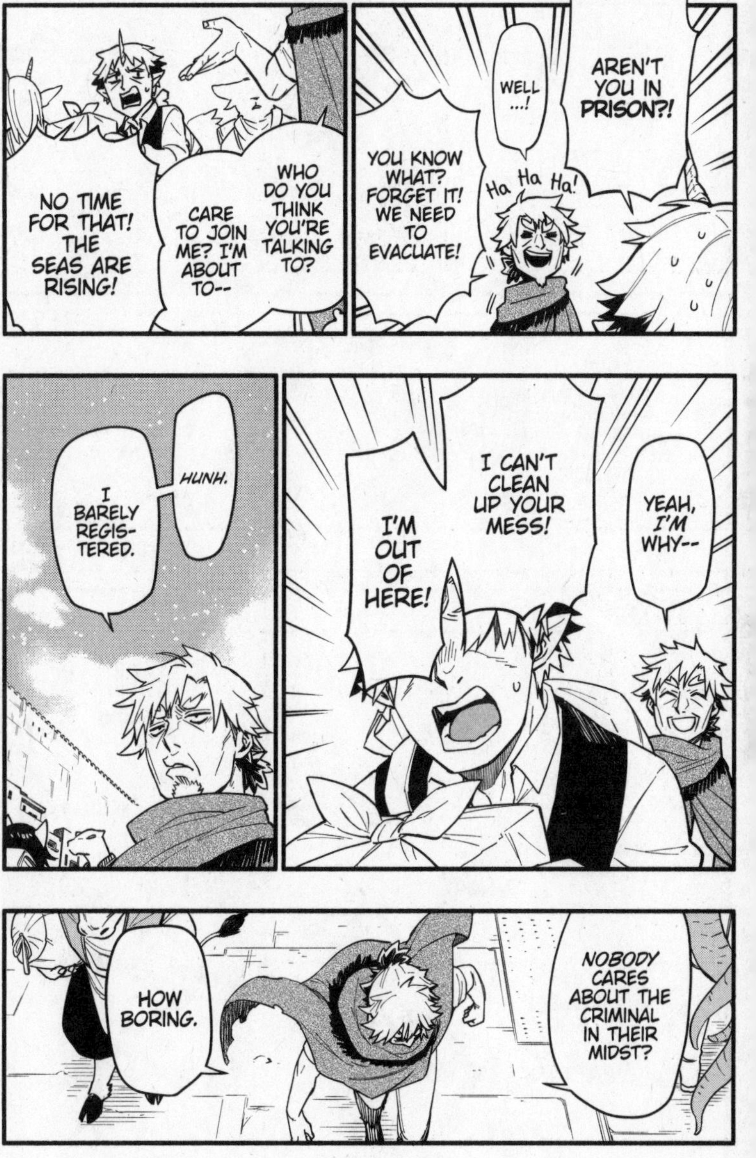
AREN'T YOU IN PRISON?!
WELL ...!
Ha Ha Ha!
YOU KNOW WHAT? FORGET IT! WE NEED TO EVACUATE!
WHO DO YOU THINK YOU'RE TALKING TO?
CARE TO JOIN ME? I'M ABOUT TO--
NO TIME FOR THAT! THE SEAS ARE RISING!
YEAH, I'M WHY--
I CAN'T CLEAN UP YOUR MESS!
I'M OUT OF HERE!
HUNH.
I BARELY REGIS-TERED.
NOBODY CARES ABOUT THE CRIMINAL IN THEIR MIDST?
HOW BORING.

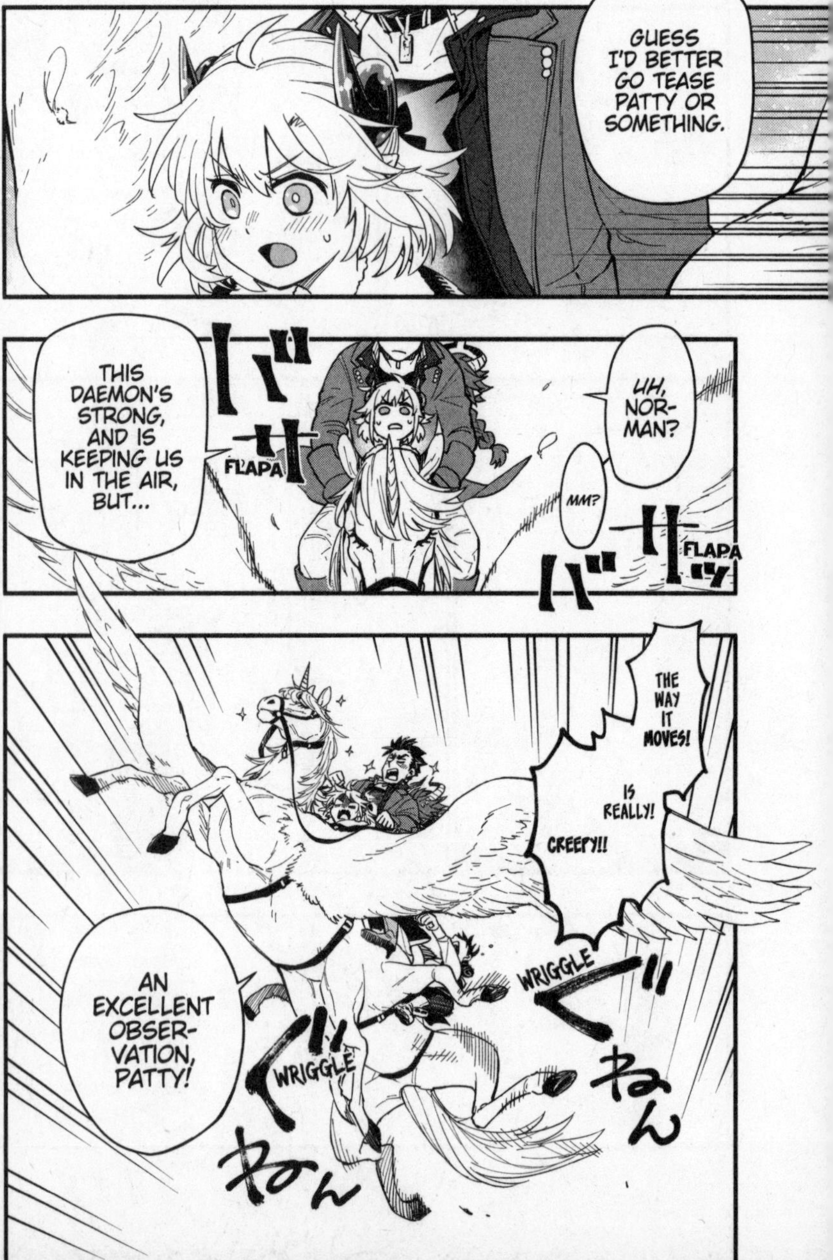
GUESS I'D BETTER GO TEASE PATTY OR SOMETHING.
UH, NOR-MAN?
MM?
FLAPA
THIS DAEMON'S STRONG, AND IS KEEPING US IN THE AIR, BUT...
FLAPA
THE WAY IT MOVES!
IS REALLY!
CREEPY!!
WRIGGLE
AN EXCELLENT OBSER-VATION, PATTY!
WRIGGLE

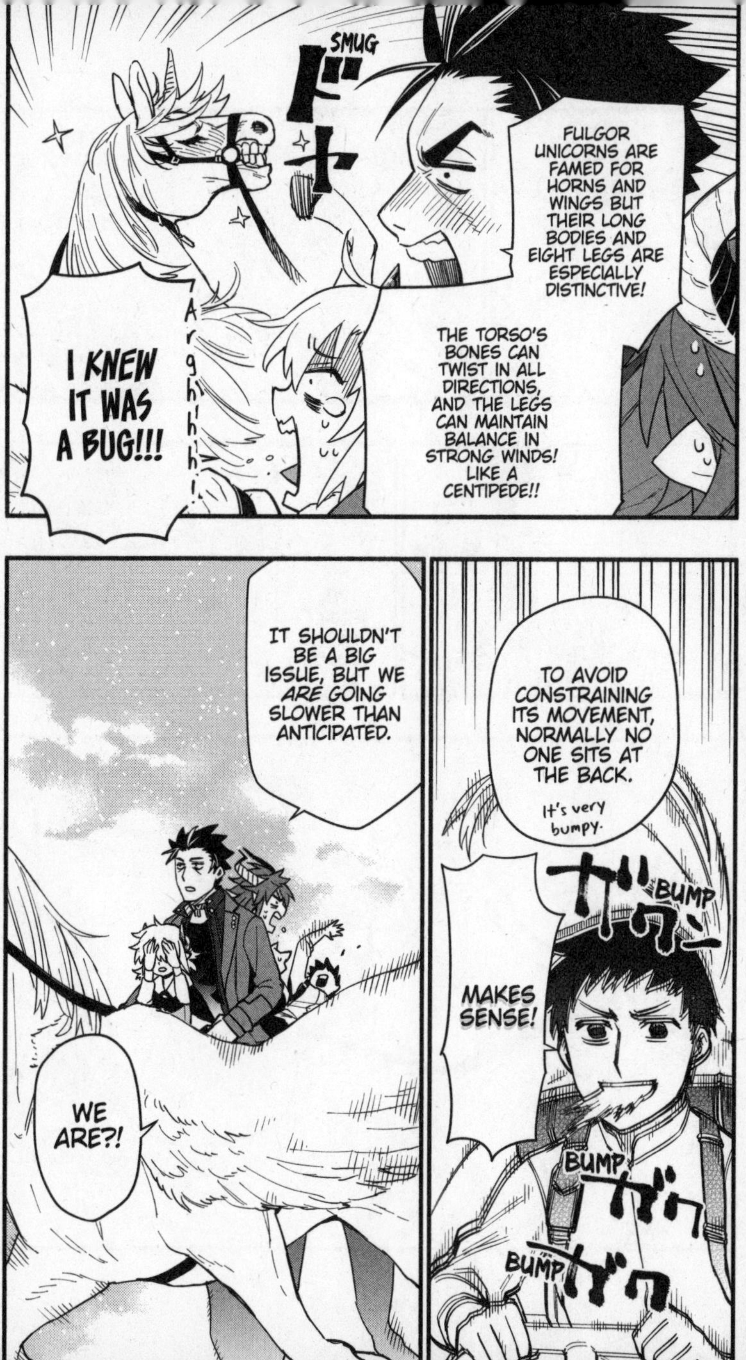
SMUG
ドヤ
FULGOR UNICORNS ARE FAMED FOR HORNS AND WINGS BUT THEIR LONG BODIES AND EIGHT LEGS ARE ESPECIALLY DISTINCTIVE!
THE TORSO'S BONES CAN TWIST IN ALL DIRECTIONS, AND THE LEGS CAN MAINTAIN BALANCE IN STRONG WINDS! LIKE A CENTIPEDE!!
Arghhh!
I KNEW IT WAS A BUG!!!
TO AVOID CONSTRAINING ITS MOVEMENT, NORMALLY NO ONE SITS AT THE BACK.
It's very bumpy.
BUMP
ガクン
MAKES SENSE!
BUMP
ガク
BUMP
ガク
IT SHOULDN'T BE A BIG ISSUE, BUT WE *ARE* GOING SLOWER THAN ANTICIPATED.
WE ARE?!

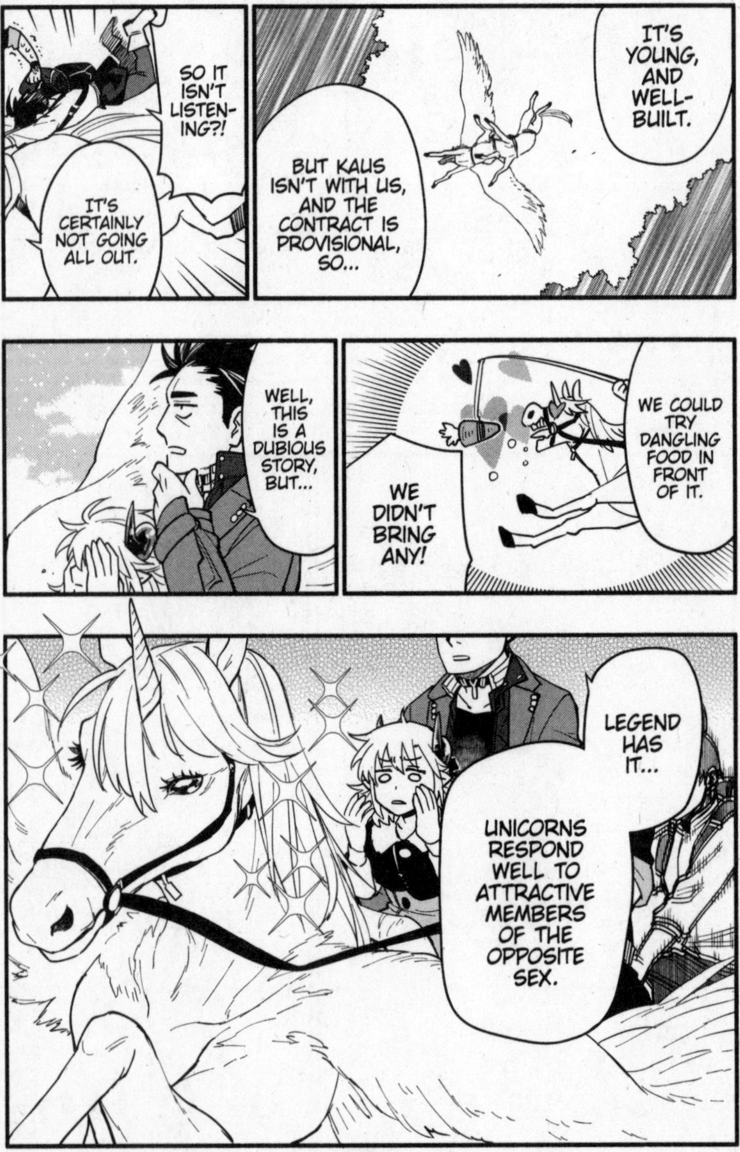
IT'S YOUNG, AND WELL-BUILT.
BUT KAUS ISN'T WITH US, AND THE CONTRACT IS PROVISIONAL, SO...
SO IT ISN'T LISTENING?!
IT'S CERTAINLY NOT GOING ALL OUT.
WE COULD TRY DANGLING FOOD IN FRONT OF IT.
WE DIDN'T BRING ANY!
WELL, THIS IS A DUBIOUS STORY, BUT...
LEGEND HAS IT...
UNICORNS RESPOND WELL TO ATTRACTIVE MEMBERS OF THE OPPOSITE SEX.

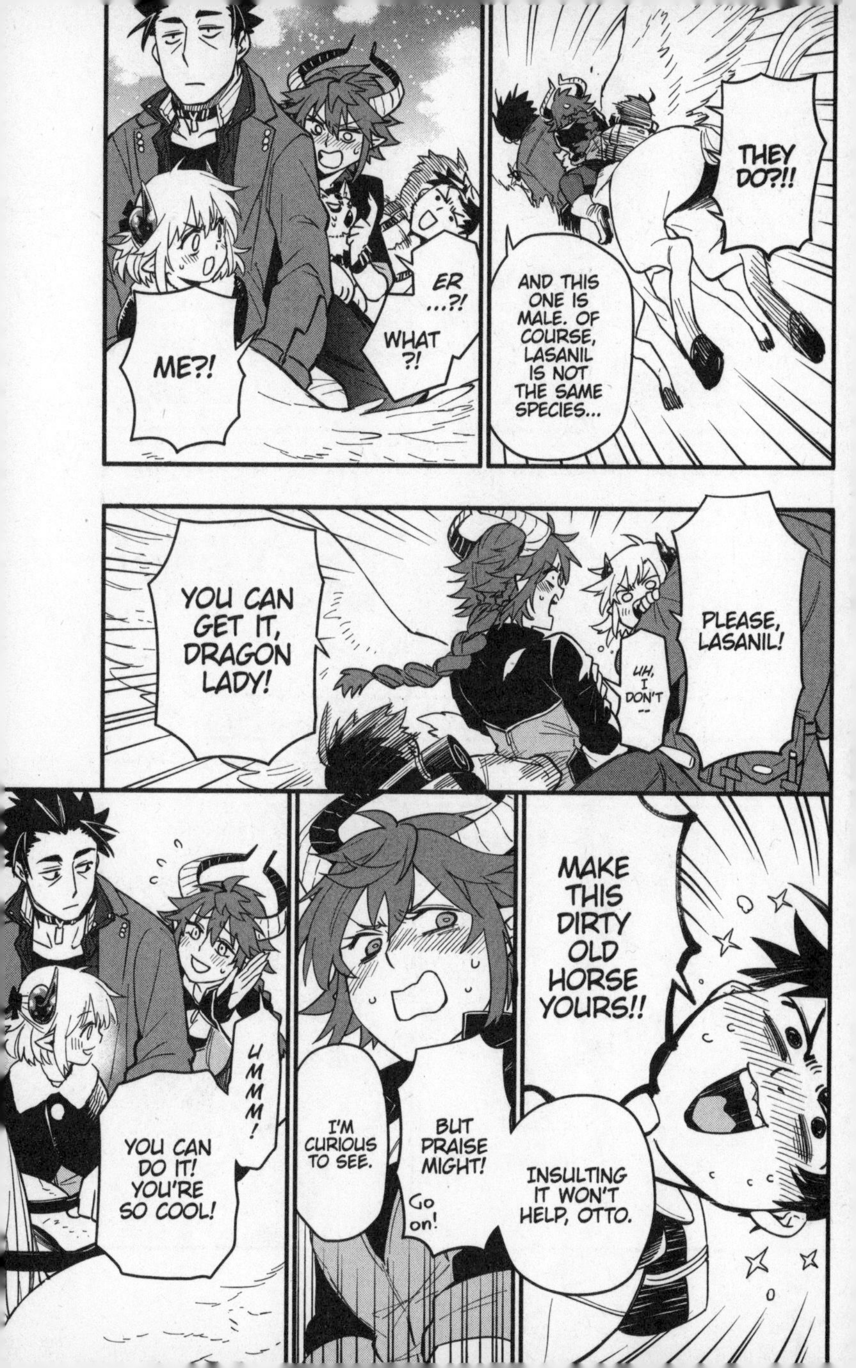
THEY DO?!!
AND THIS ONE IS MALE. OF COURSE, LASANIL IS NOT THE SAME SPECIES...
ER ...?!
WHAT ?!
ME?!
PLEASE, LASANIL!
UH, I DON'T --
YOU CAN GET IT, DRAGON LADY!
MAKE THIS DIRTY OLD HORSE YOURS!!
INSULTING IT WON'T HELP, OTTO.
BUT PRAISE MIGHT!
I'M CURIOUS TO SEE.
Go on!
UMMMM!
YOU CAN DO IT! YOU'RE SO COOL!

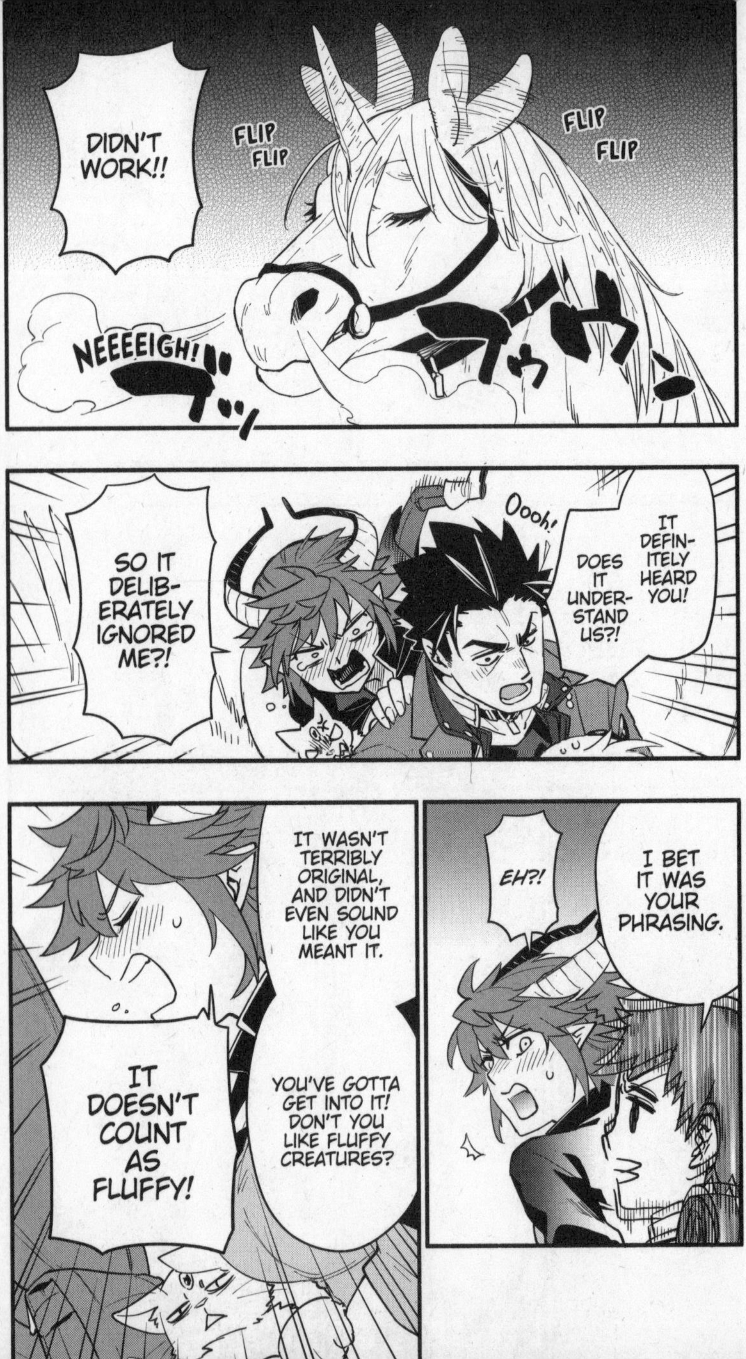
FLIP FLIP
FLIP FLIP
DIDN'T WORK!!
NEEEEIGH!
IT DEFIN-ITELY HEARD YOU!
DOES IT UNDER-STAND US?!
Oooh!
SO IT DELIB-ERATELY IGNORED ME?!
I BET IT WAS YOUR PHRASING.
EH?!
IT WASN'T TERRIBLY ORIGINAL, AND DIDN'T EVEN SOUND LIKE YOU MEANT IT.
YOU'VE GOTTA GET INTO IT! DON'T YOU LIKE FLUFFY CREATURES?
IT DOESN'T COUNT AS FLUFFY!

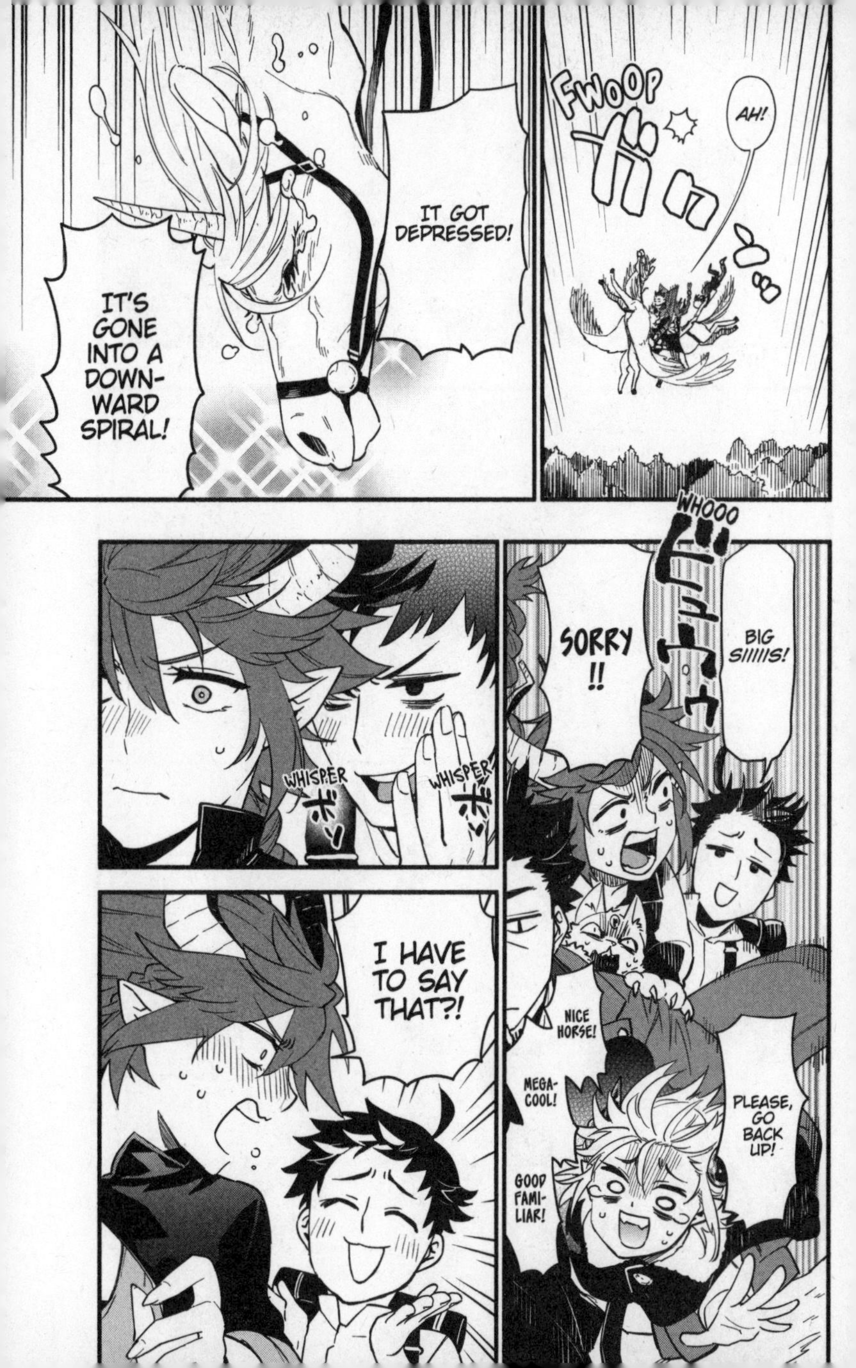
FWOOP
AH!
IT GOT DEPRESSED!
IT'S GONE INTO A DOWNWARD SPIRAL!
WHOOO
BIG SIIIIIS!
SORRY!!
NICE HORSE!
MEGA-COOL!
PLEASE, GO BACK UP!
GOOD FAMILIAR!
WHISPER
WHISPER
I HAVE TO SAY THAT?!

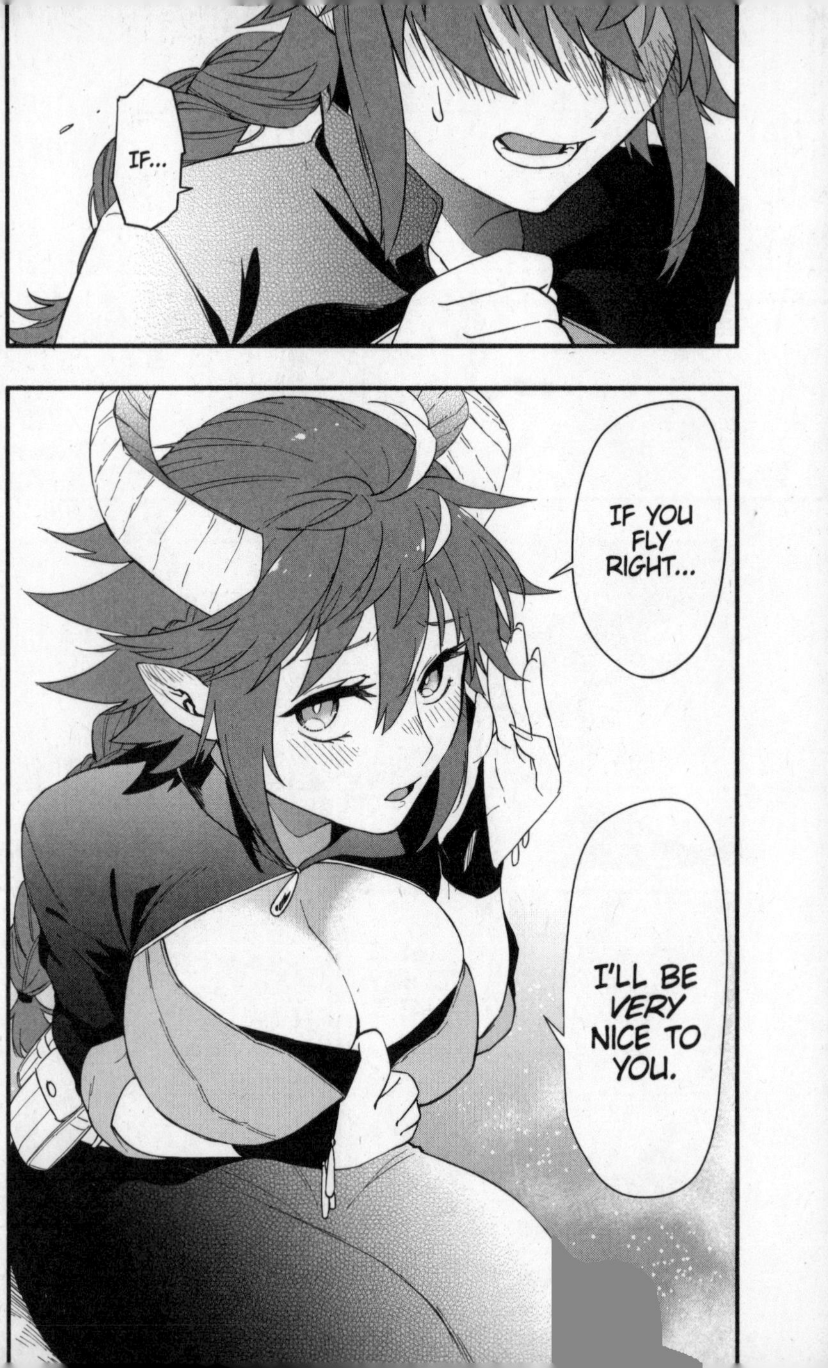
IF...
IF YOU FLY RIGHT...
I'LL BE *VERY* NICE TO YOU.

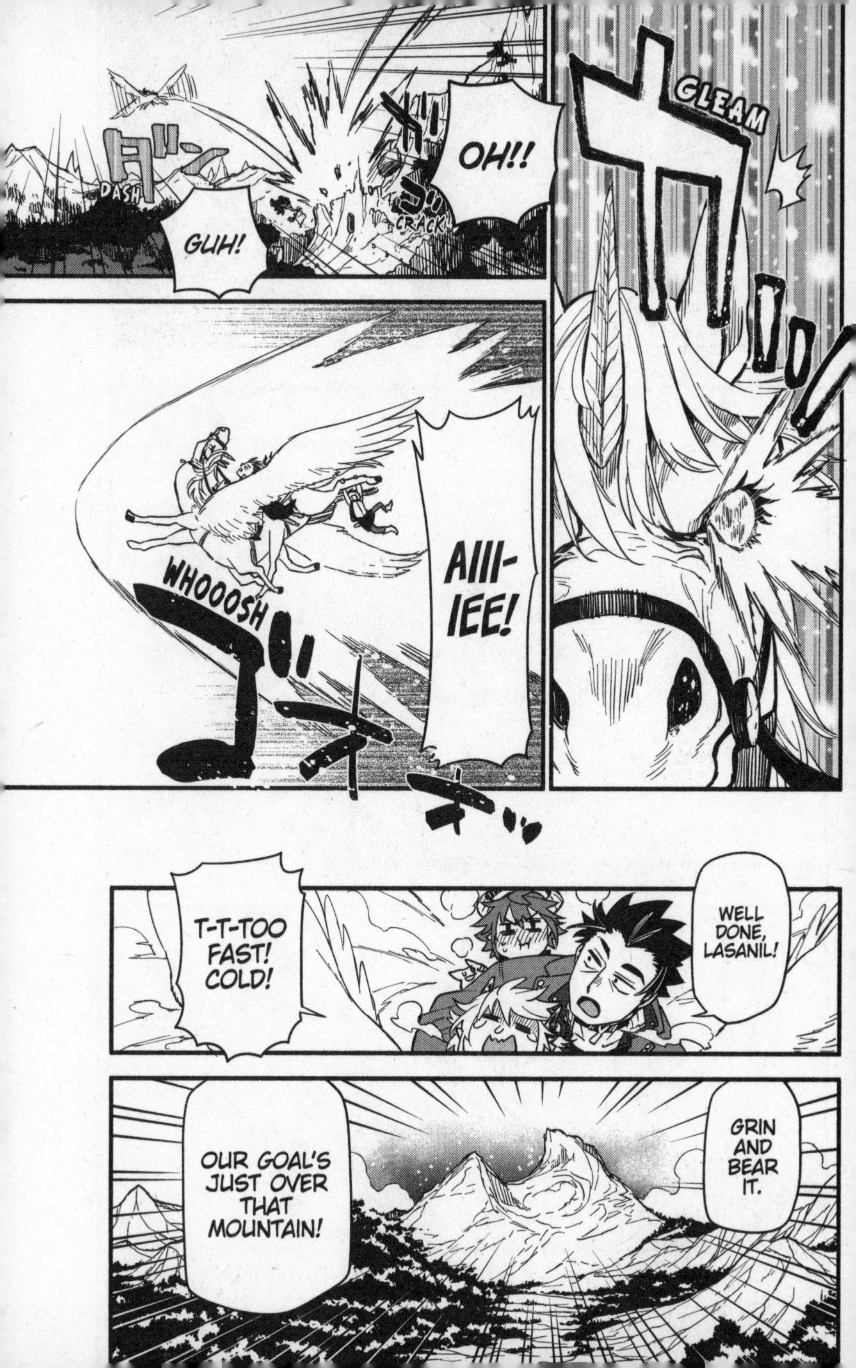
GLEAM
OH!!
CRACK
DASH
GUH!
AIIII-IEE!
WHOOOSH
WELL DONE, LASANIL!
T-T-TOO FAST! COLD!
GRIN AND BEAR IT.
OUR GOAL'S JUST OVER THAT MOUNTAIN!

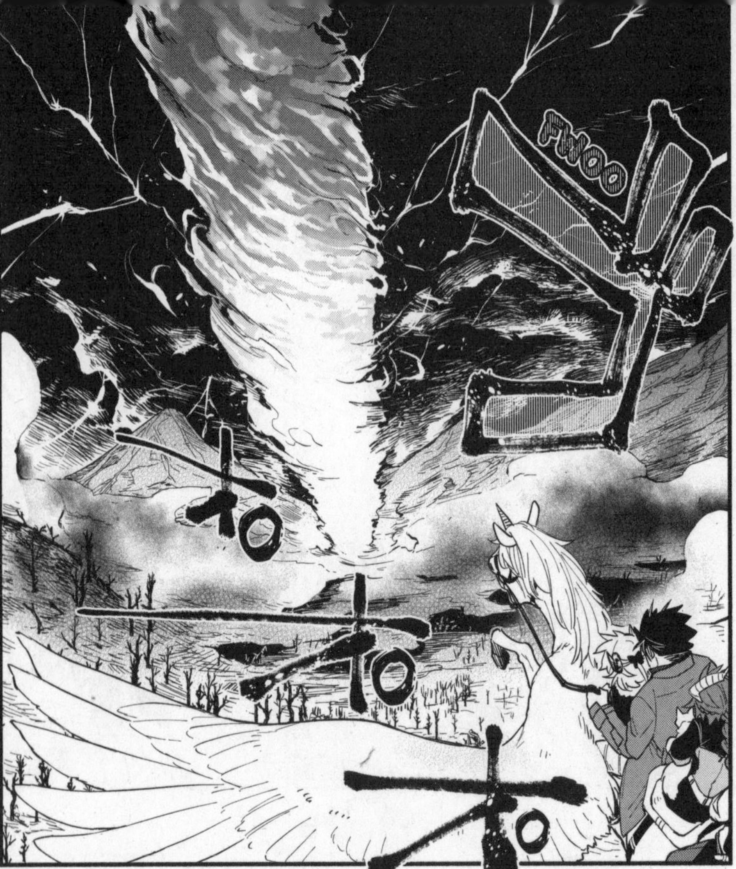
FWOO

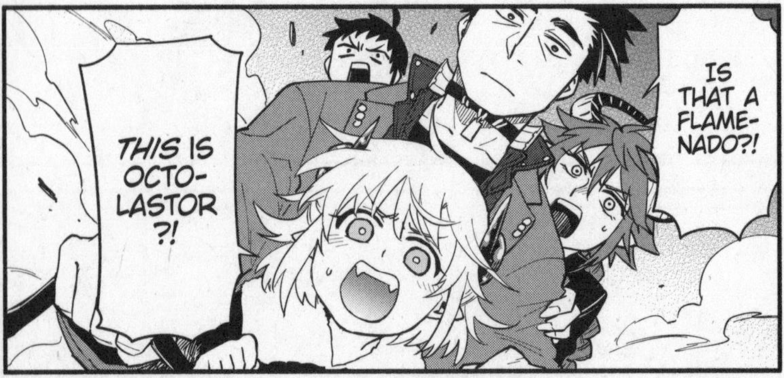
IS THAT A FLAMENADO?!
THIS IS OCTOLASTOR?!

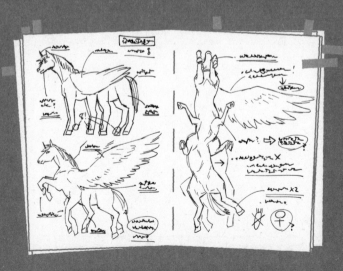

Sorry For My Familiar

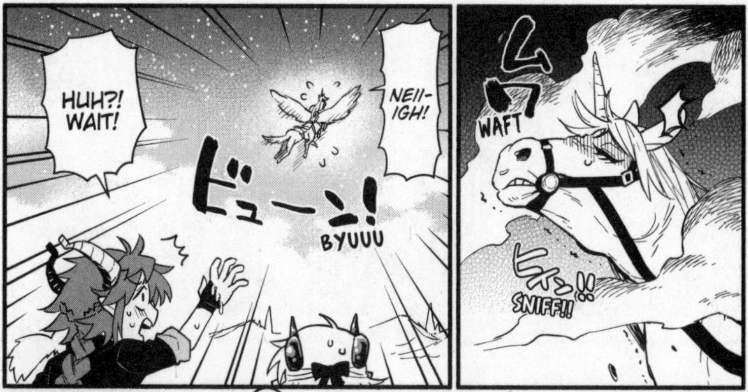
WAFT
SNIFF!!
NEII-IGH!
HUH?! WAIT!
BYUUU

FILE 68: Octolastor ①

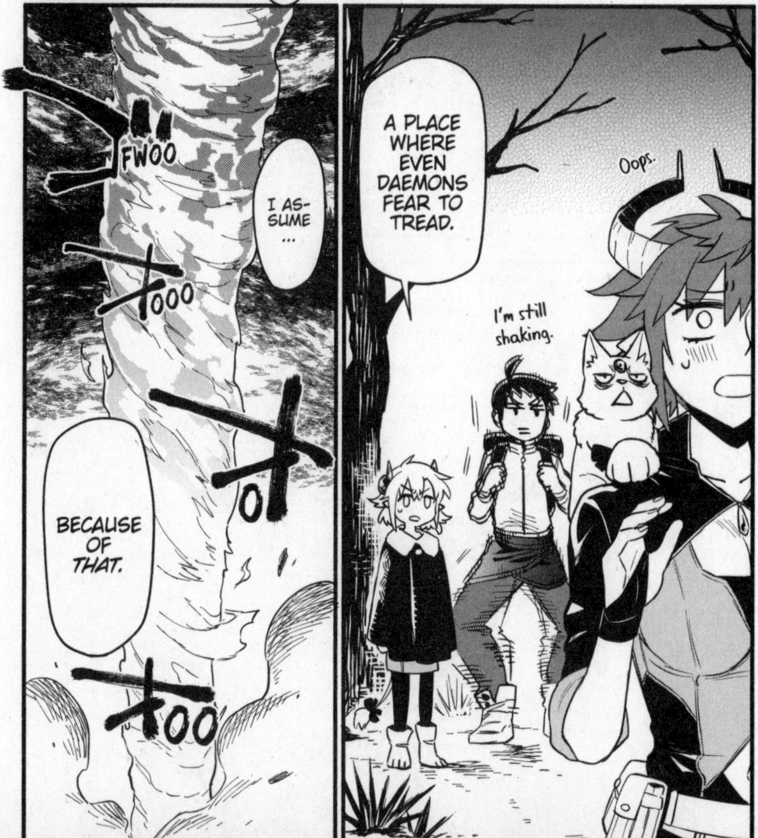
Oops.
A PLACE WHERE EVEN DAEMONS FEAR TO TREAD.
I'm still shaking.
I AS-SUME ...
FWOO
HOOO
O
BECAUSE OF THAT.
HOO

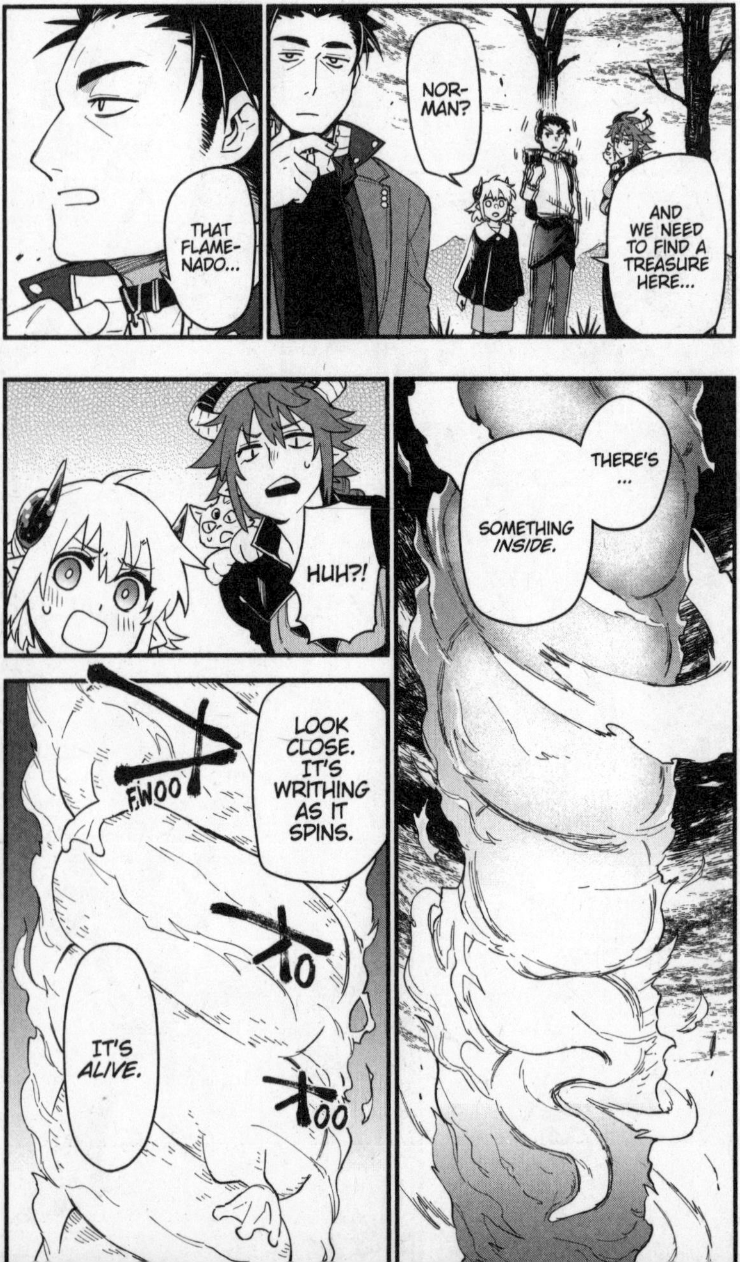
NOR-MAN?
AND WE NEED TO FIND A TREASURE HERE...
THAT FLAMENADO...
THERE'S ...
SOMETHING *INSIDE.*
HUH?!
LOOK CLOSE. IT'S WRITHING AS IT SPINS.
FWOO
IT'S *ALIVE.*

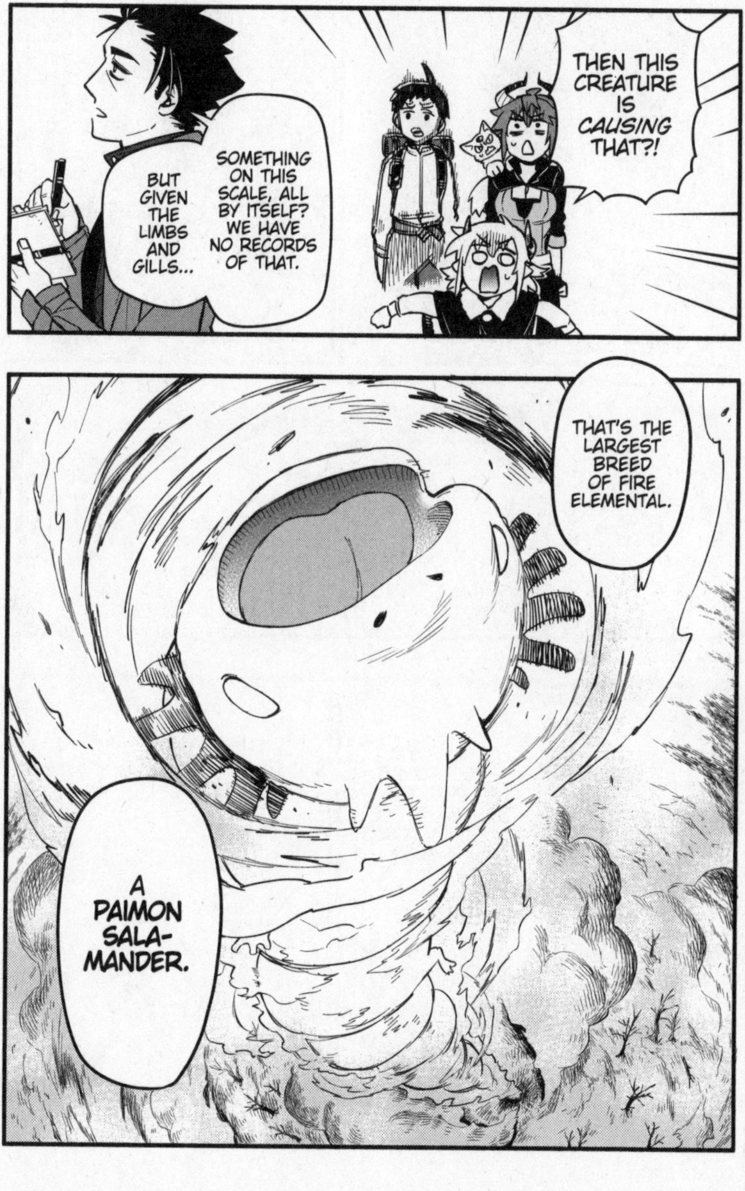
THEN THIS CREATURE IS *CAUSING* THAT?!
SOMETHING ON THIS SCALE, ALL BY ITSELF? WE HAVE NO RECORDS OF THAT.
BUT GIVEN THE LIMBS AND GILLS...
THAT'S THE LARGEST BREED OF FIRE ELEMENTAL.
A PAIMON SALA-MANDER.

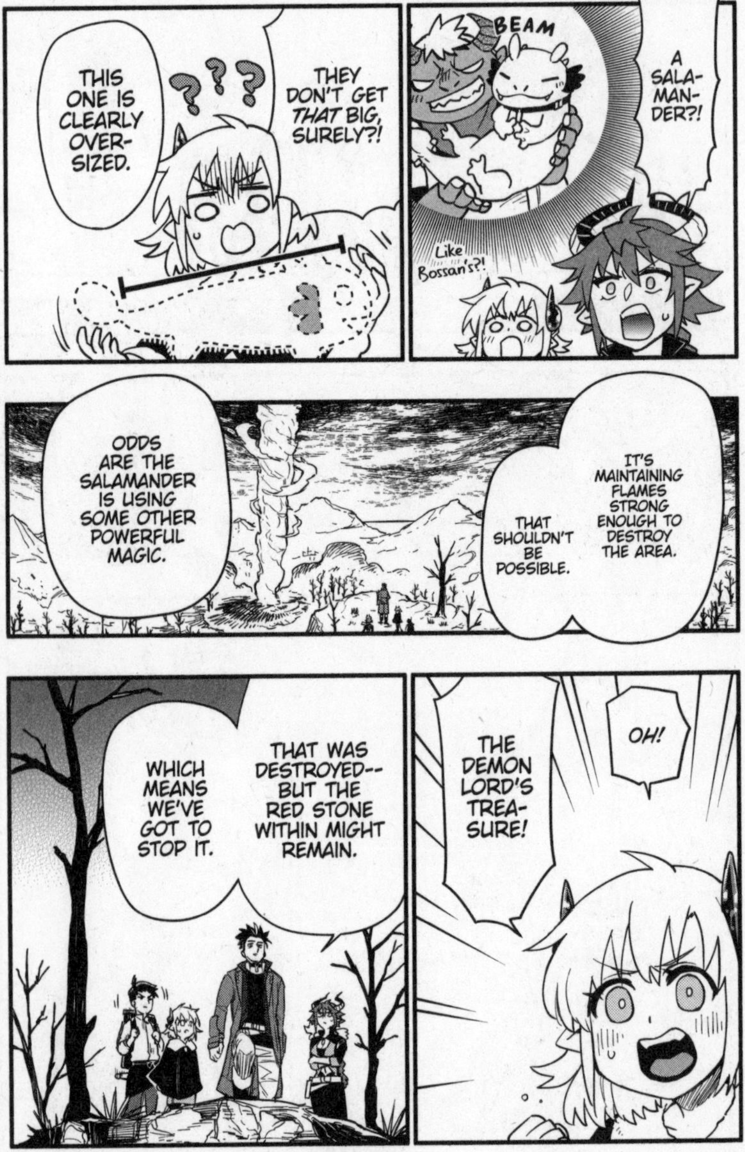
A SALAMANDER?!
BEAM
Like Bossan's?!
THEY DON'T GET *THAT* BIG, SURELY?!
???
THIS ONE IS CLEARLY OVERSIZED.
IT'S MAINTAINING FLAMES STRONG ENOUGH TO DESTROY THE AREA.
THAT SHOULDN'T BE POSSIBLE.
ODDS ARE THE SALAMANDER IS USING SOME OTHER POWERFUL MAGIC.
OH!
THE DEMON LORD'S TREASURE!
THAT WAS DESTROYED-- BUT THE RED STONE WITHIN MIGHT REMAIN.
WHICH MEANS WE'VE GOT TO STOP IT.

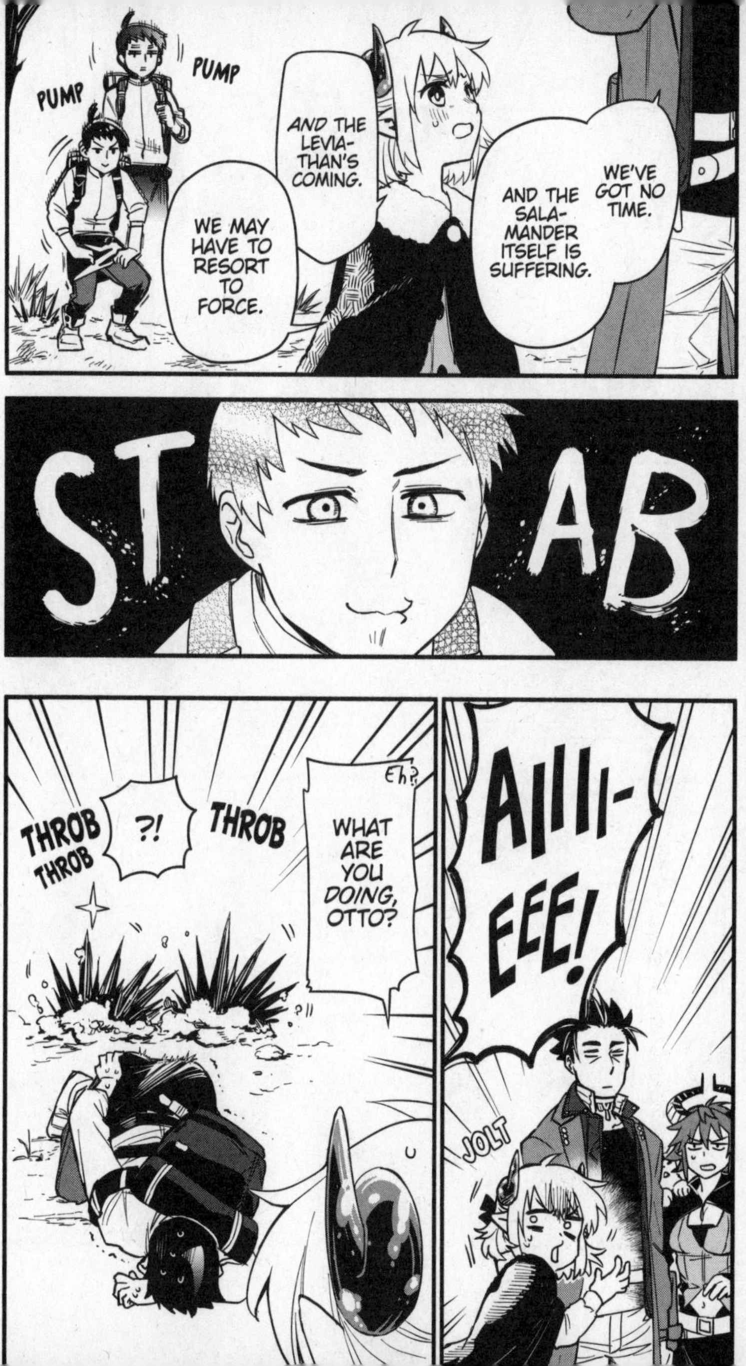
WE'VE GOT NO TIME.
AND THE SALA-MANDER ITSELF IS SUFFERING.
AND THE LEVIA-THAN'S COMING.
WE MAY HAVE TO RESORT TO FORCE.
PUMP
PUMP
ST AB
AIIII-EEE!
JOLT
Eh?
WHAT ARE YOU DOING, OTTO?
THROB
?!
THROB THROB
?!

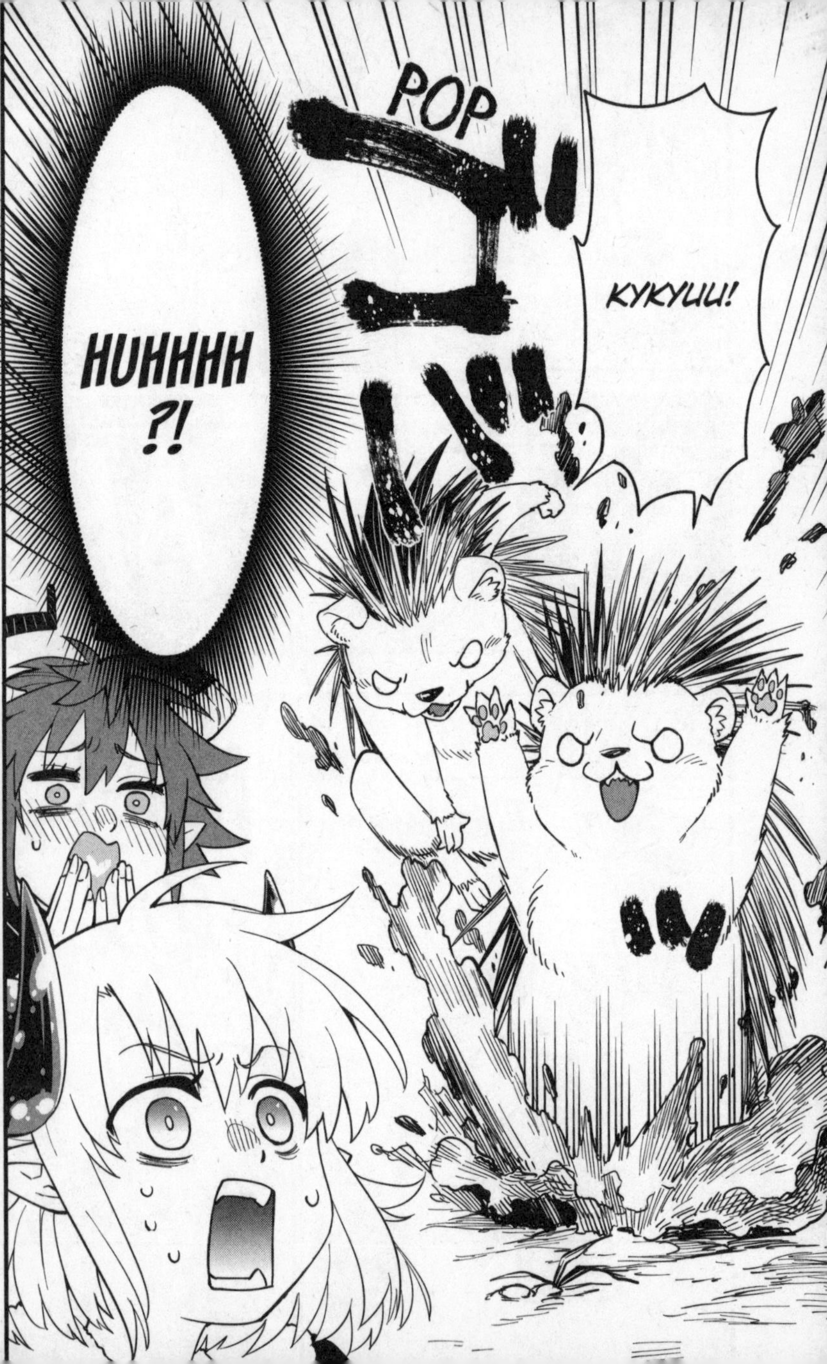
KYKYUU!
POP
HUHHHH ?!

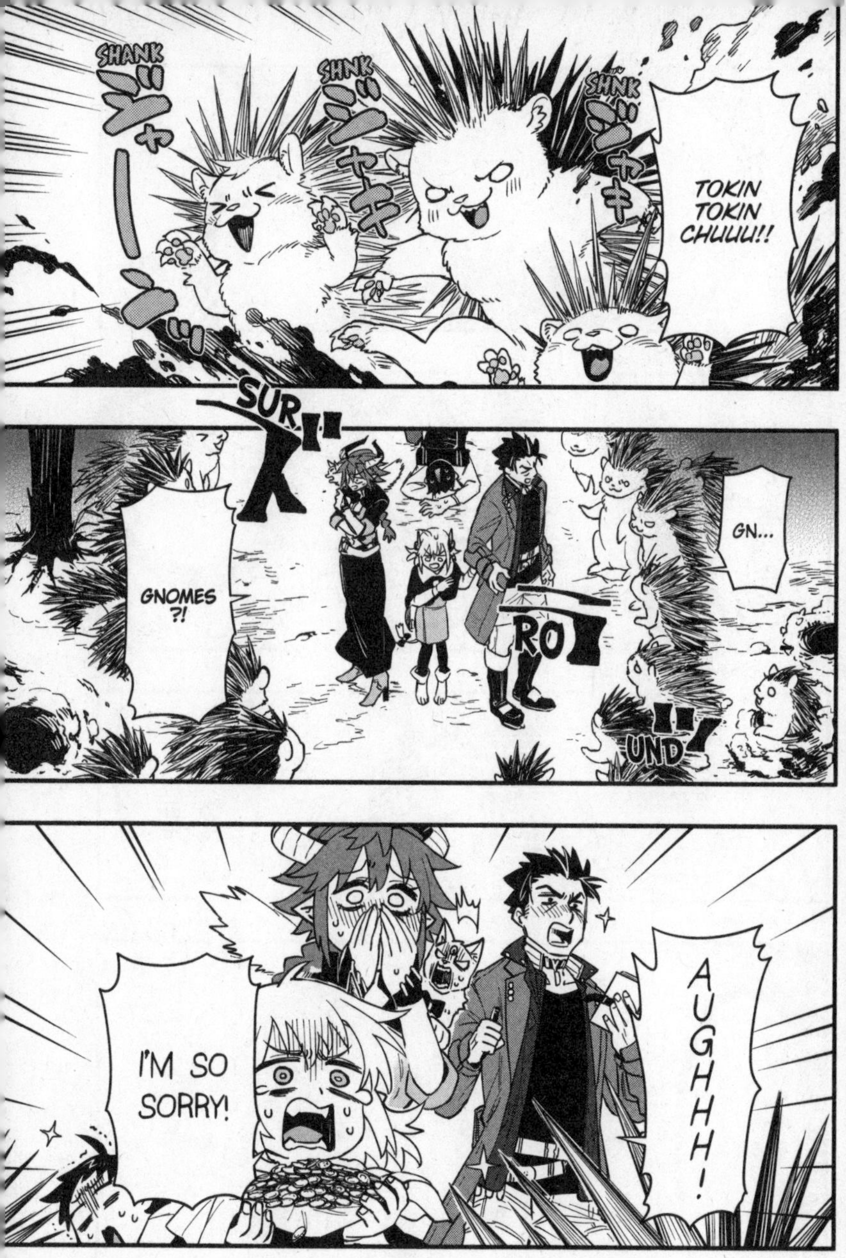
TOKIN TOKIN CHUUU!!
SHNK
SHNK
SHANK
GN...
SUR
RO
UND
GNOMES ?!
AUGHHH!
I'M SO SORRY!

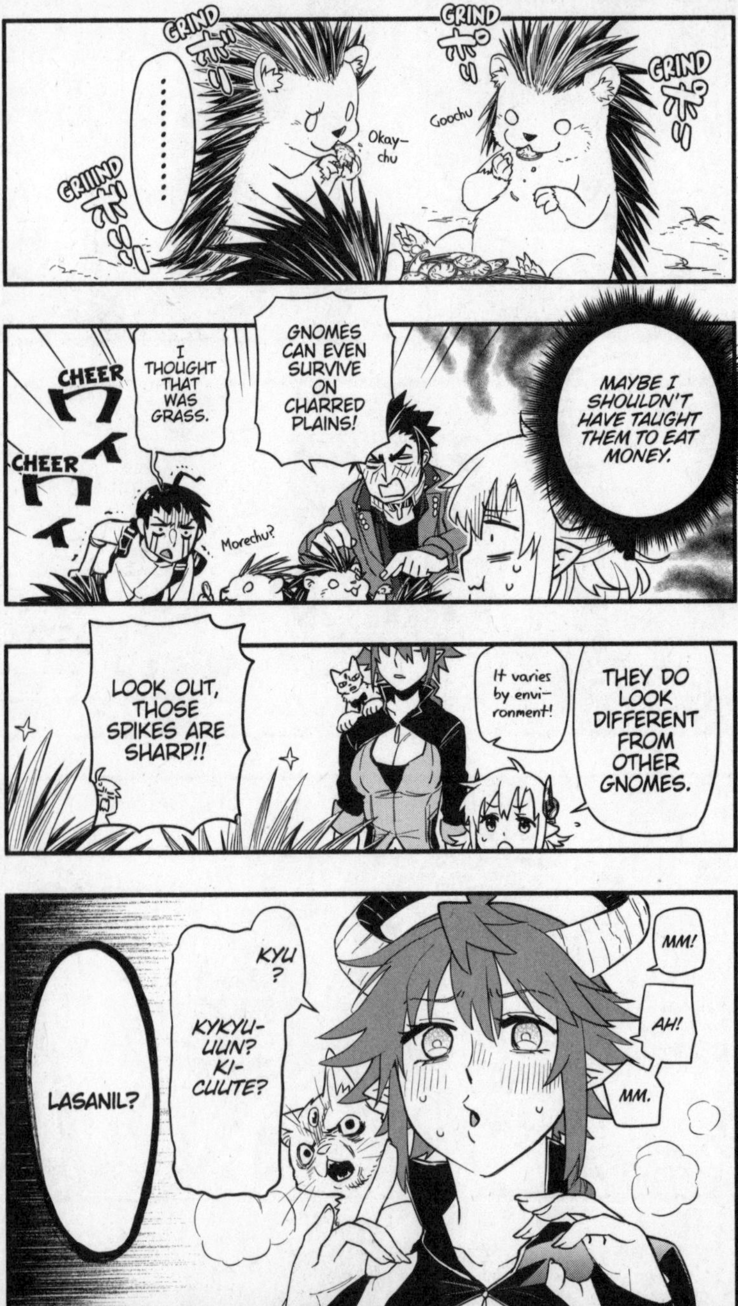
GRIND
Goochu
GRIND
Okay-chu
......
GRIND
GRIIIND
MAYBE I SHOULDN'T HAVE TAUGHT THEM TO EAT MONEY.
GNOMES CAN EVEN SURVIVE ON CHARRED PLAINS!
I THOUGHT THAT WAS GRASS.
Morechu?
CHEER
CHEER
THEY DO LOOK DIFFERENT FROM OTHER GNOMES.
It varies by envi-ronment!
LOOK OUT, THOSE SPIKES ARE SHARP!!
MM!
AH!
MM.
KYU?
KYKYU-UUN? KI-CUUTE?
LASANIL?

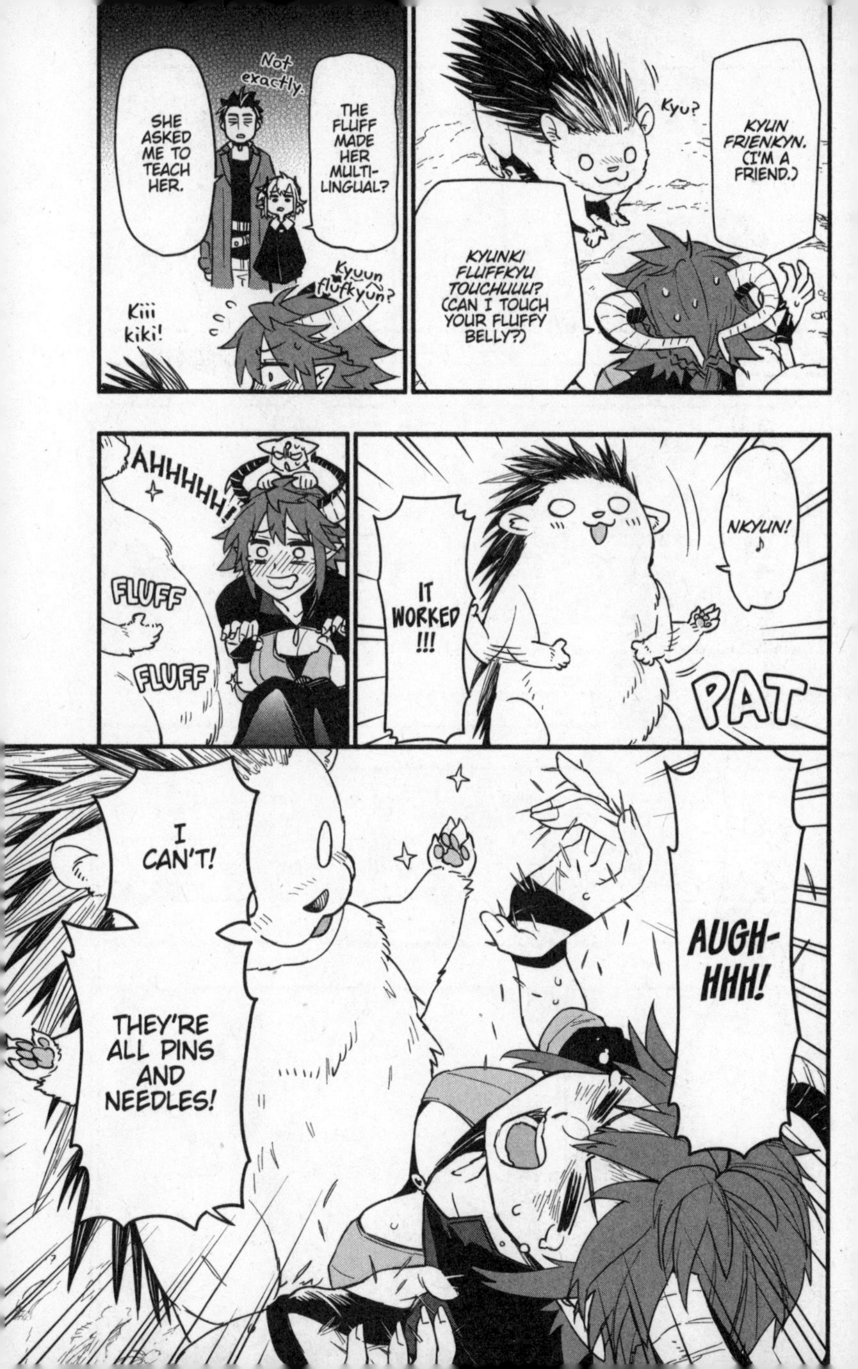
Kyu?
KYUN FRIENKYN. (I'M A FRIEND.)
KYUNKI FLUFFKYU TOUCHUUU? (CAN I TOUCH YOUR FLUFFY BELLY?)
THE FLUFF MADE HER MULTI-LINGUAL?
Not exactly.
SHE ASKED ME TO TEACH HER.
Kyuun flufkyun?
Kiii kiki!
NKYUN! ♪
PAT
IT WORKED!!!
AHHHHHH!
FLUFF
FLUFF
AUGH-HHH!
I CAN'T!
THEY'RE ALL PINS AND NEEDLES!

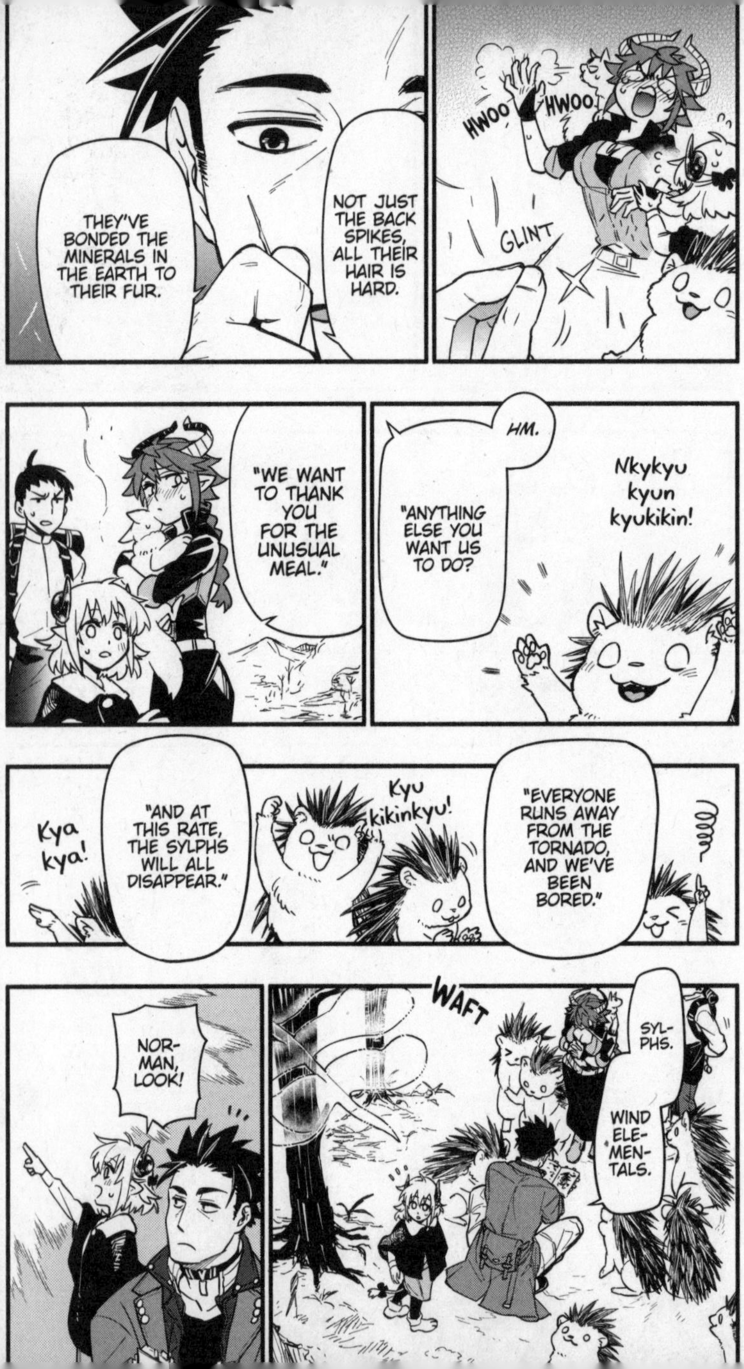
HWOO
HWOO
GLINT
NOT JUST THE BACK SPIKES, ALL THEIR HAIR IS HARD.
THEY'VE BONDED THE MINERALS IN THE EARTH TO THEIR FUR.
HM.
Nkykyu kyun kyukikin!
"ANYTHING ELSE YOU WANT US TO DO?
"WE WANT TO THANK YOU FOR THE UNUSUAL MEAL."
"EVERYONE RUNS AWAY FROM THE TORNADO, AND WE'VE BEEN BORED."
Kyu kikinkyu!
"AND AT THIS RATE, THE SYLPHS WILL ALL DISAPPEAR."
Kya kya!
WAFT
SYL-PHS.
WIND ELE-MEN-TALS.
NOR-MAN, LOOK!

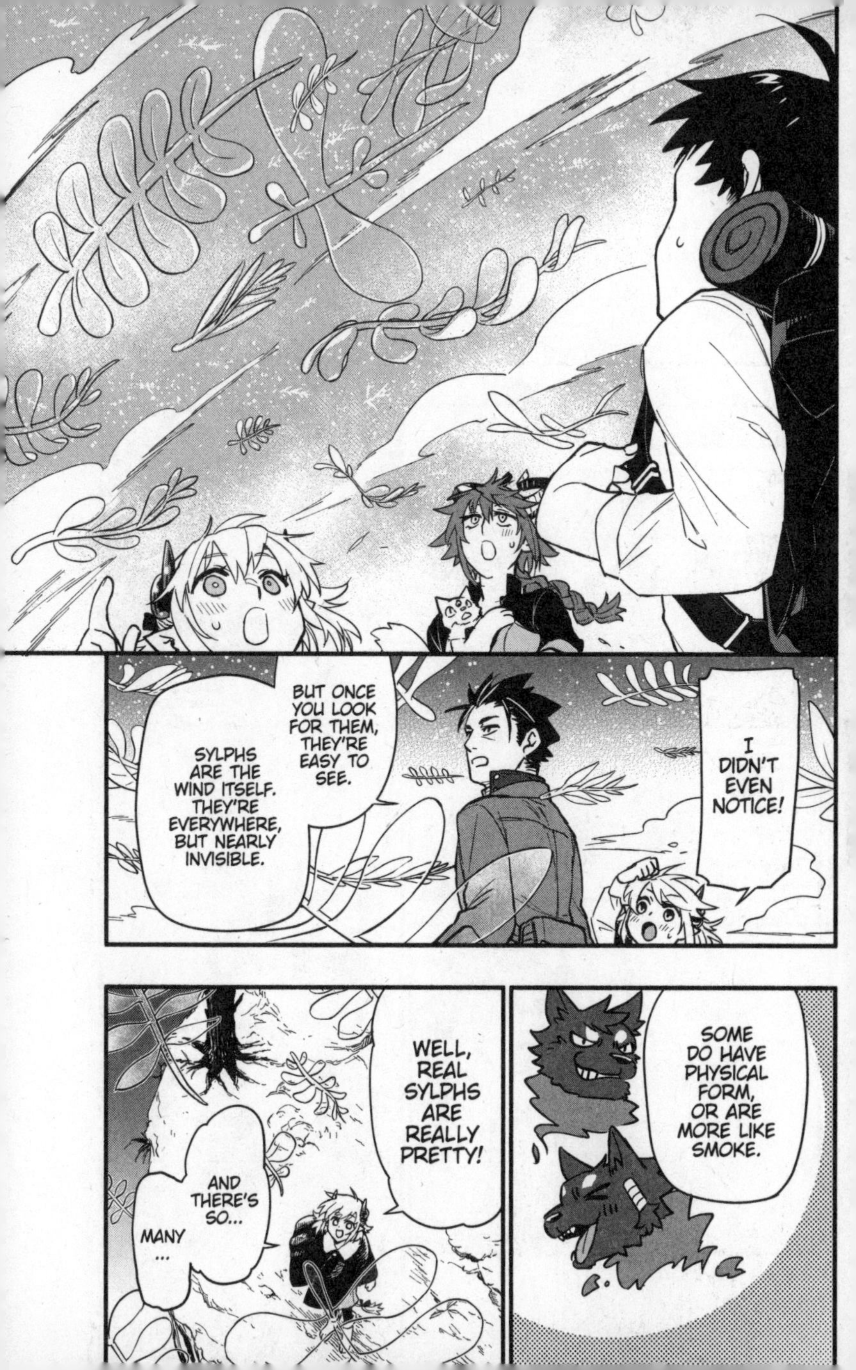
I DIDN'T EVEN NOTICE!
SYLPHS ARE THE WIND ITSELF. THEY'RE EVERYWHERE, BUT NEARLY INVISIBLE.
BUT ONCE YOU LOOK FOR THEM, THEY'RE EASY TO SEE.
SOME DO HAVE PHYSICAL FORM, OR ARE MORE LIKE SMOKE.
WELL, REAL SYLPHS ARE REALLY PRETTY!
AND THERE'S SO...
MANY ...

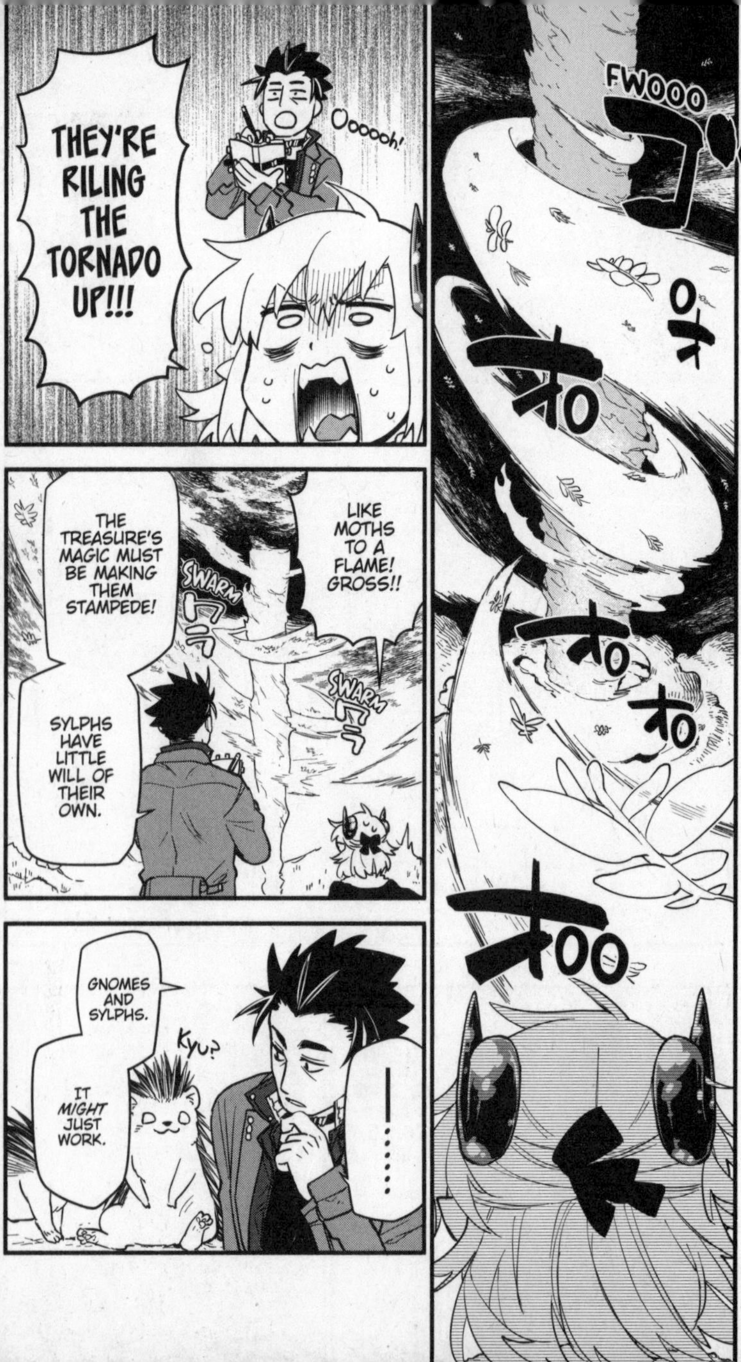
FWOOO
THEY'RE RILING THE TORNADO UP!!!
Oooooh!
LIKE MOTHS TO A FLAME! GROSS!!
SWARM
SWARM
THE TREASURE'S MAGIC MUST BE MAKING THEM STAMPEDE!
SYLPHS HAVE LITTLE WILL OF THEIR OWN.
......
GNOMES AND SYLPHS.
Kyu?
IT *MIGHT* JUST WORK.

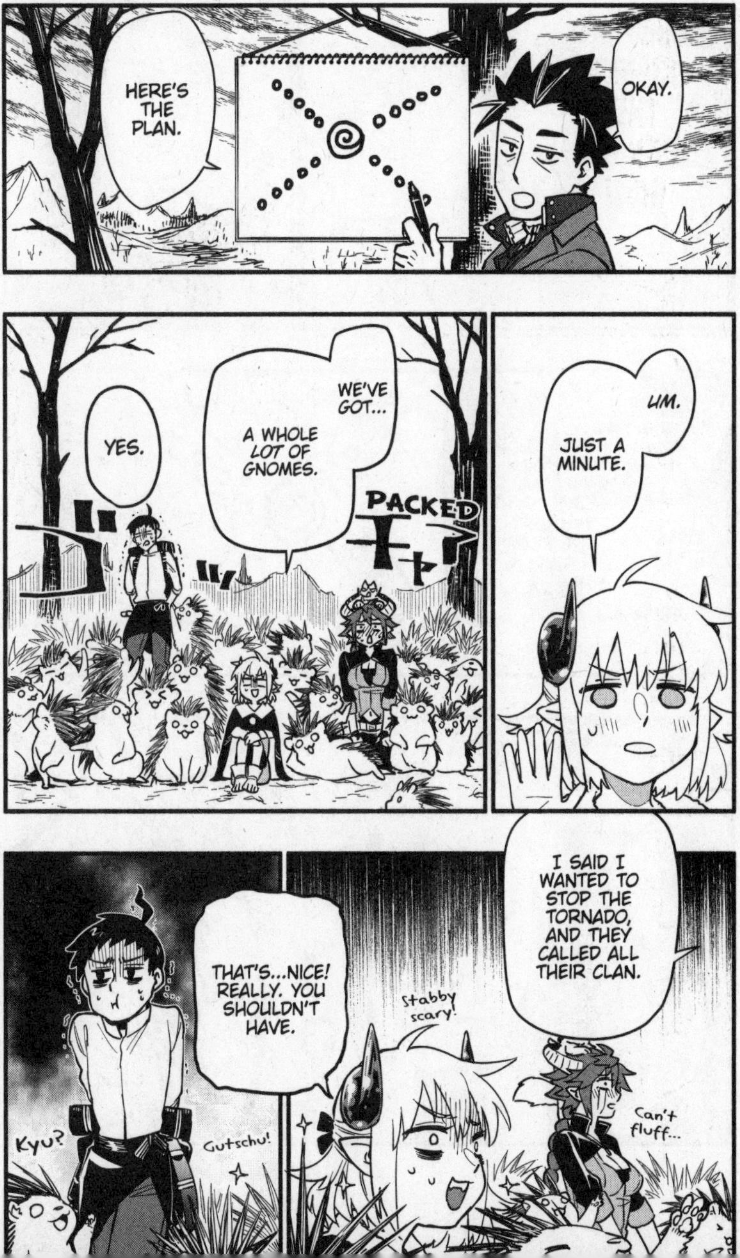

OKAY.
HERE'S THE PLAN.
UM.
JUST A MINUTE.
WE'VE GOT...
A WHOLE LOT OF GNOMES.
PACKED
YES.
I SAID I WANTED TO STOP THE TORNADO, AND THEY CALLED ALL THEIR CLAN.
Stabby scary!
Can't fluff...
THAT'S...NICE! REALLY. YOU SHOULDN'T HAVE.
Gutschu!
Kyu?

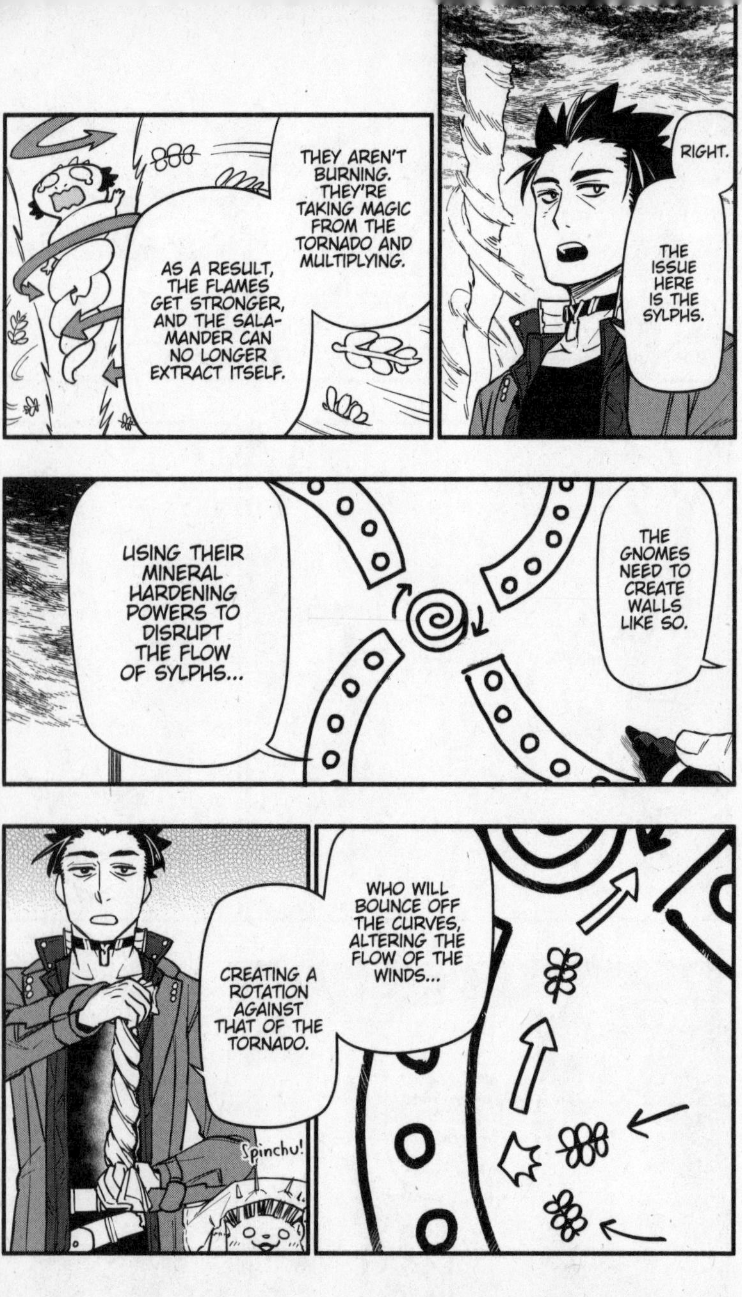
RIGHT.
THE ISSUE HERE IS THE SYLPHS.
THEY AREN'T BURNING. THEY'RE TAKING MAGIC FROM THE TORNADO AND MULTIPLYING.
AS A RESULT, THE FLAMES GET STRONGER, AND THE SALA-MANDER CAN NO LONGER EXTRACT ITSELF.
THE GNOMES NEED TO CREATE WALLS LIKE SO.
USING THEIR MINERAL HARDENING POWERS TO DISRUPT THE FLOW OF SYLPHS...
WHO WILL BOUNCE OFF THE CURVES, ALTERING THE FLOW OF THE WINDS...
CREATING A ROTATION AGAINST THAT OF THE TORNADO.
Spinchu!

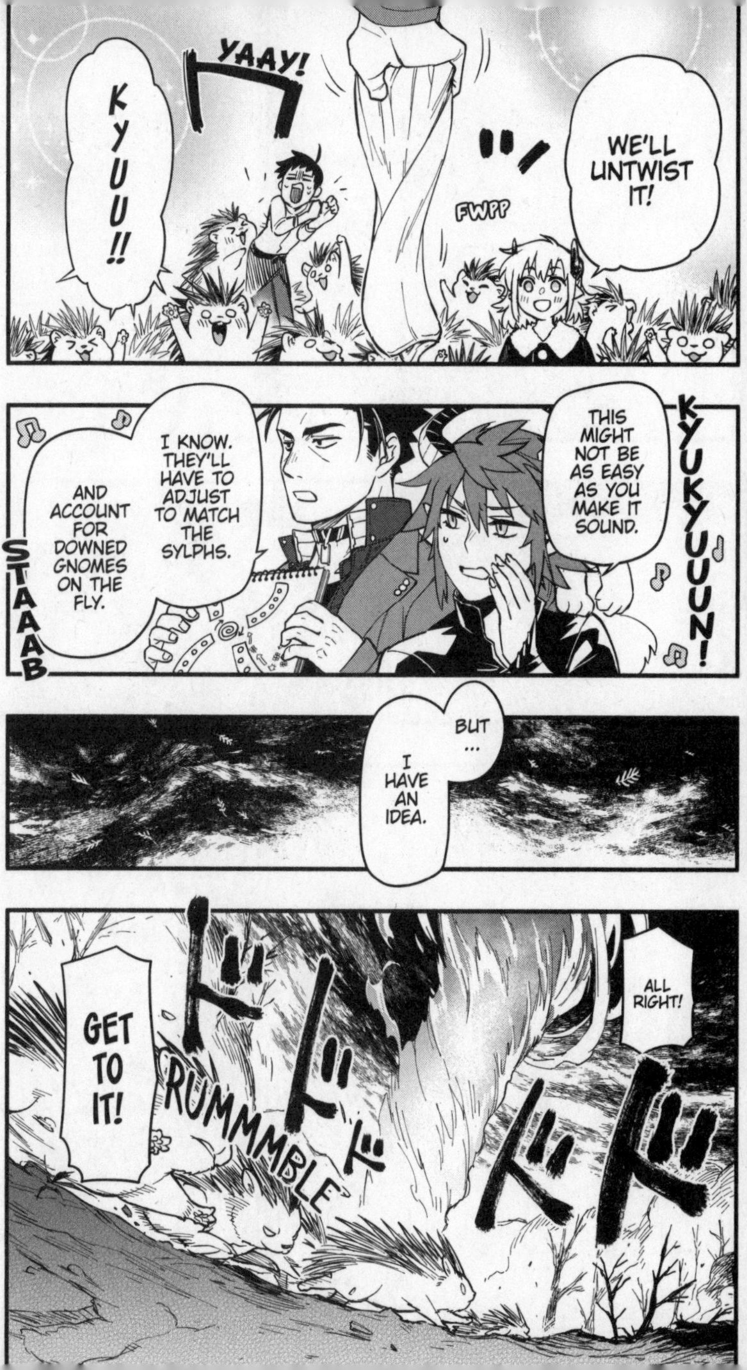
WE'LL UNTWIST IT!
FWPP
YAAY!
KYUUU!!
KYUKYUUUUN!
THIS MIGHT NOT BE AS EASY AS YOU MAKE IT SOUND.
I KNOW. THEY'LL HAVE TO ADJUST TO MATCH THE SYLPHS.
AND ACCOUNT FOR DOWNED GNOMES ON THE FLY.
STAAAAB
BUT ... I HAVE AN IDEA.
ALL RIGHT!
ドド
RUMMMBLE
ドドド
GET TO IT!

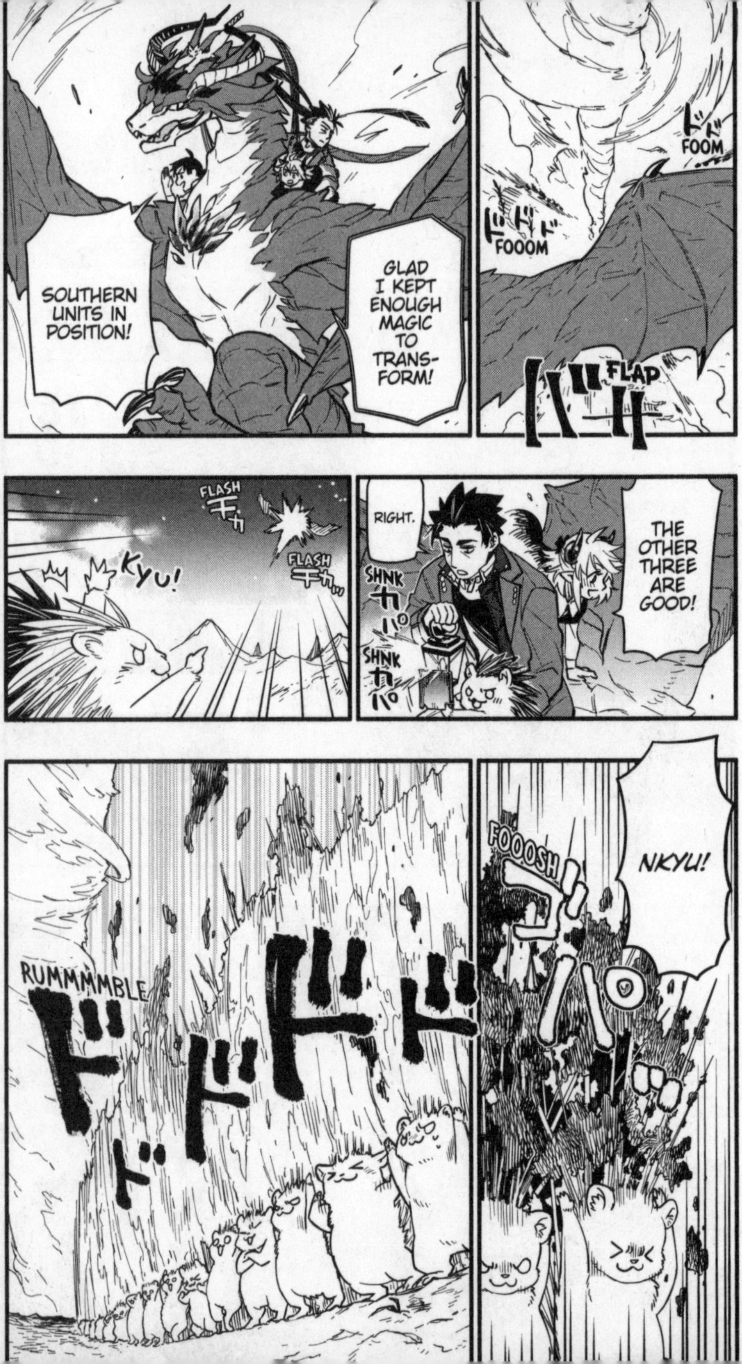
FOOM
FOOOM
FLAP
GLAD I KEPT ENOUGH MAGIC TO TRANS-FORM!
SOUTHERN UNITS IN POSITION!
THE OTHER THREE ARE GOOD!
RIGHT.
SHNK
SHNK
FLASH
FLASH
KYU!
NKYU!
FOOOSH
RUMMMMBLE

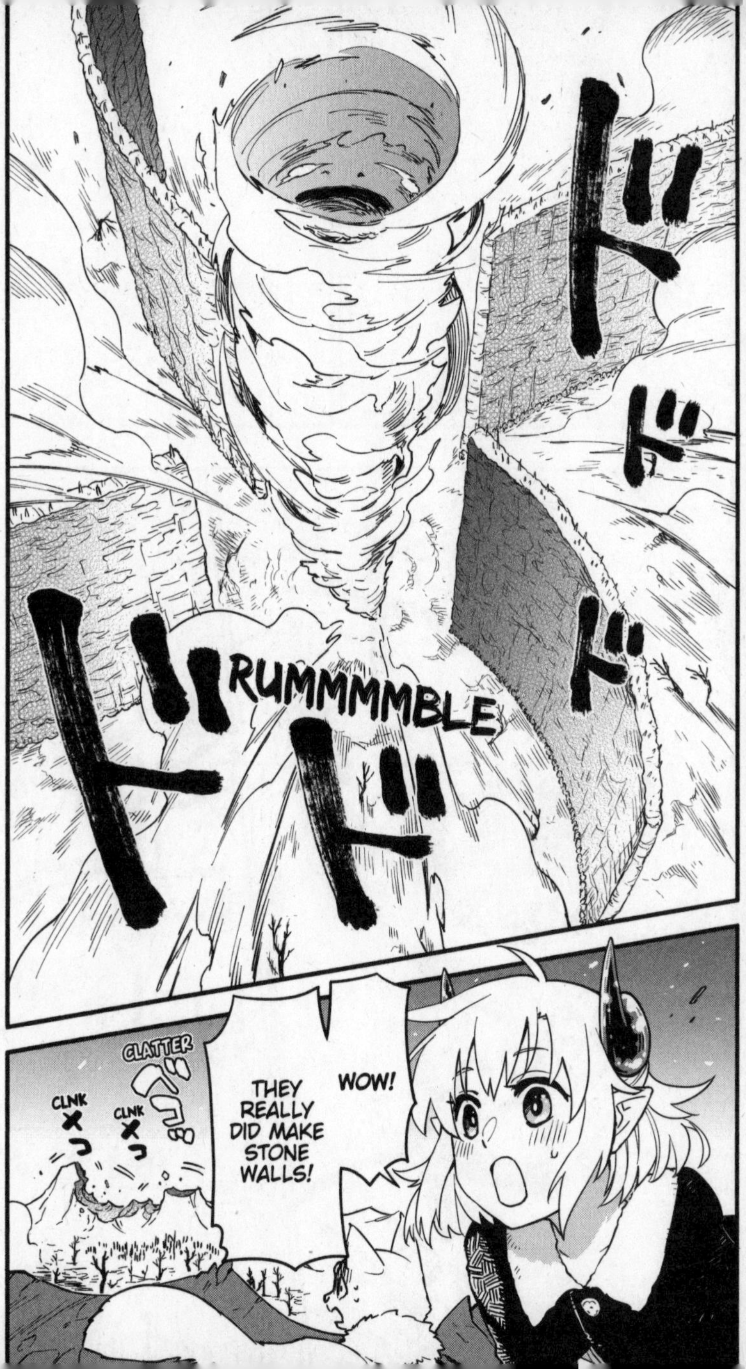
ドドド
RUMMMMBLE
ドドドドド
WOW!
THEY REALLY DID MAKE STONE WALLS!
CLATTER
ごっ
CLNK
CLNK

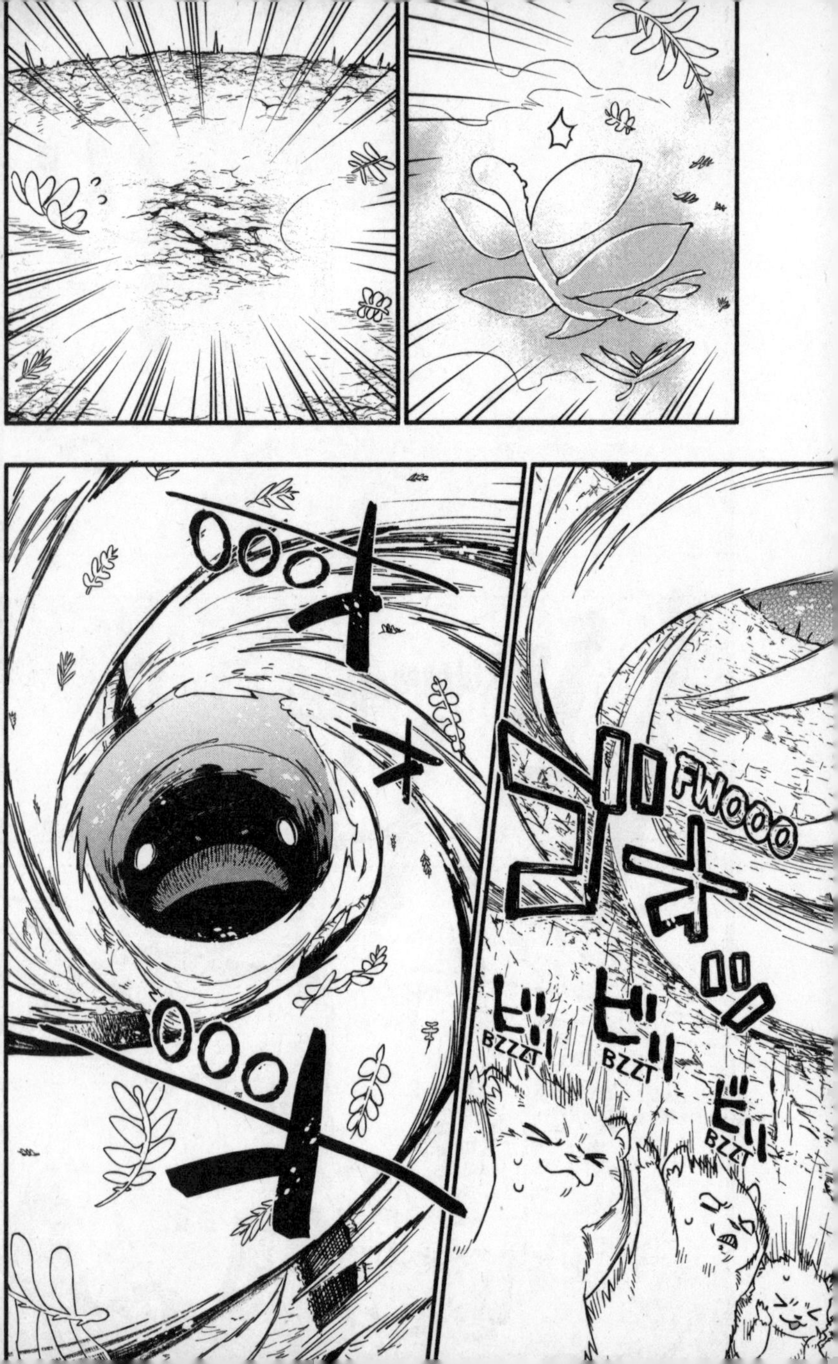
FWOOO
BZZT
BZZT
BZZT

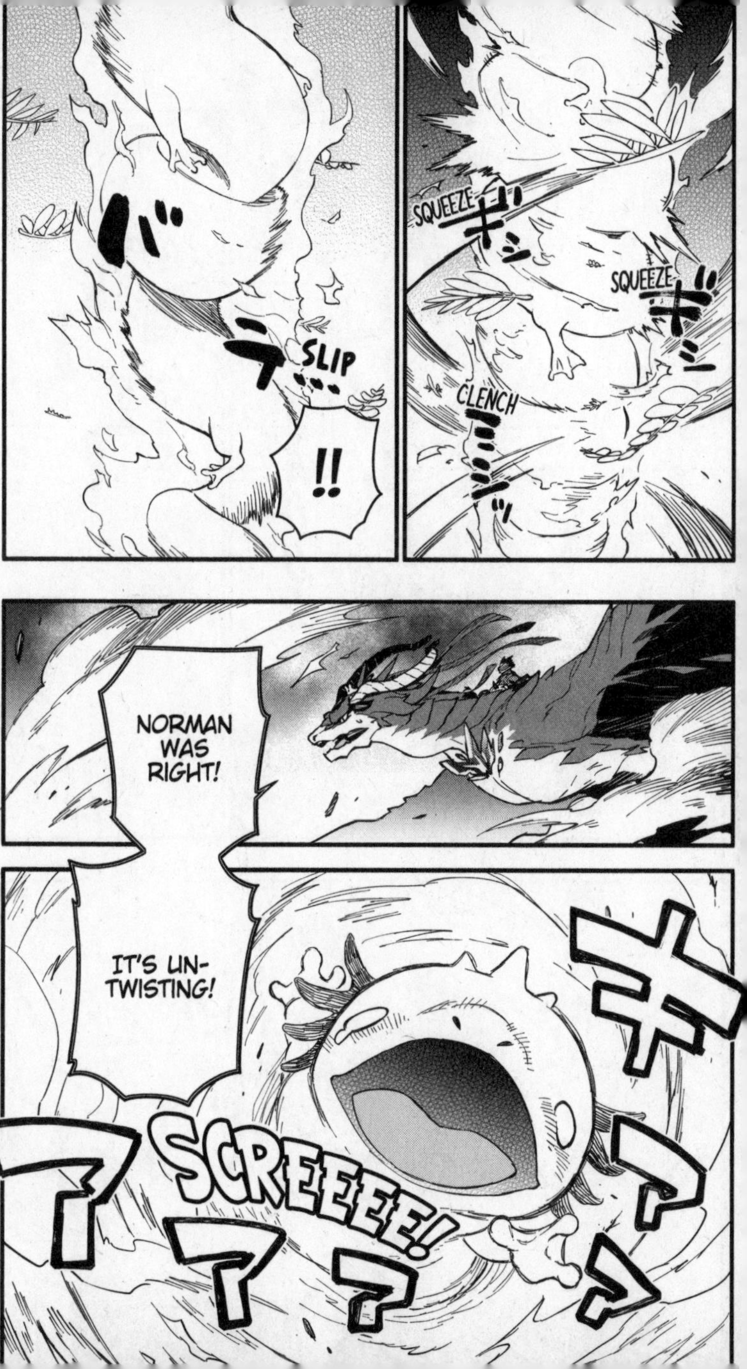
SQUEEZE
SQUEEZE
CLENCH
SLIP
!!
NORMAN WAS RIGHT!
IT'S UN-TWISTING!
SCREEEEE!

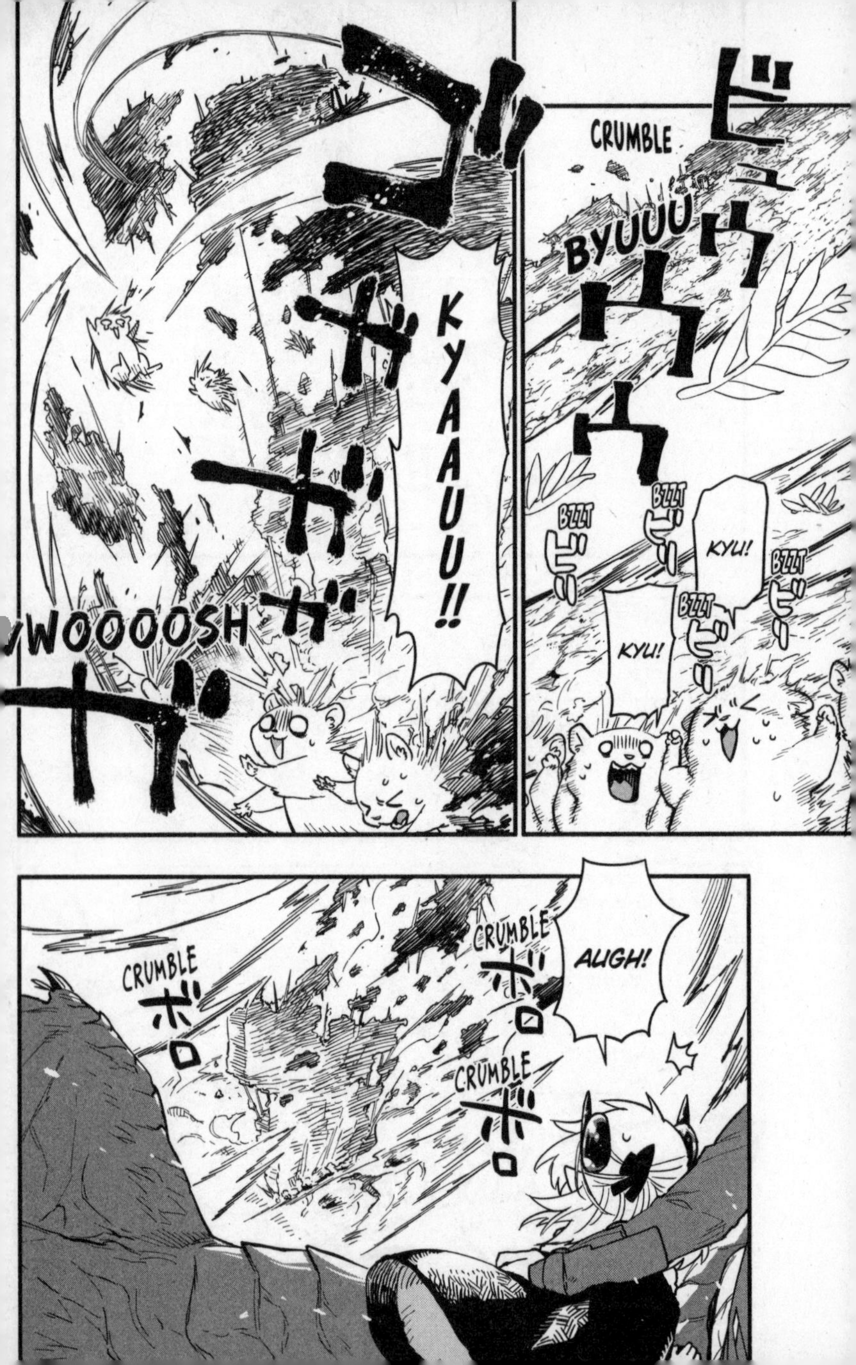
CRUMBLE
ビュウウウ
BYUUU
BZZT
ビビ
BZZT
ビビ
KYU!
BZZT
ビビ
BZZT
ビビ
KYU!
KYAAAUUU!!
WOOOOSH
AUGH!
CRUMBLE
ボロ
CRUMBLE
ボロ
CRUMBLE
ボロ

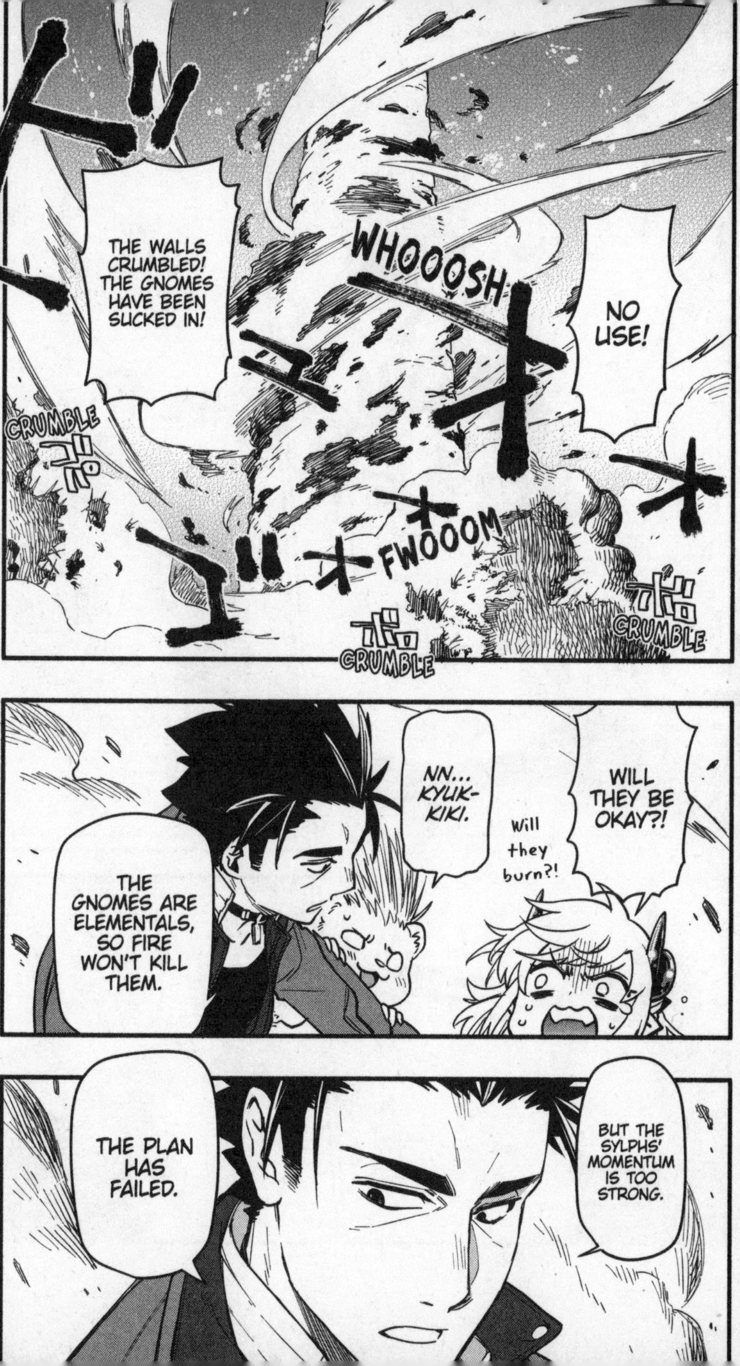
NO USE!
WHOOOSH
THE WALLS CRUMBLED! THE GNOMES HAVE BEEN SUCKED IN!
CRUMBLE
FWOOOM
CRUMBLE
CRUMBLE
WILL THEY BE OKAY?!
Will they burn?!
NN... KYUK-KIKI.
THE GNOMES ARE ELEMENTALS, SO FIRE WON'T KILL THEM.
BUT THE SYLPHS' MOMENTUM IS TOO STRONG.
THE PLAN HAS FAILED.

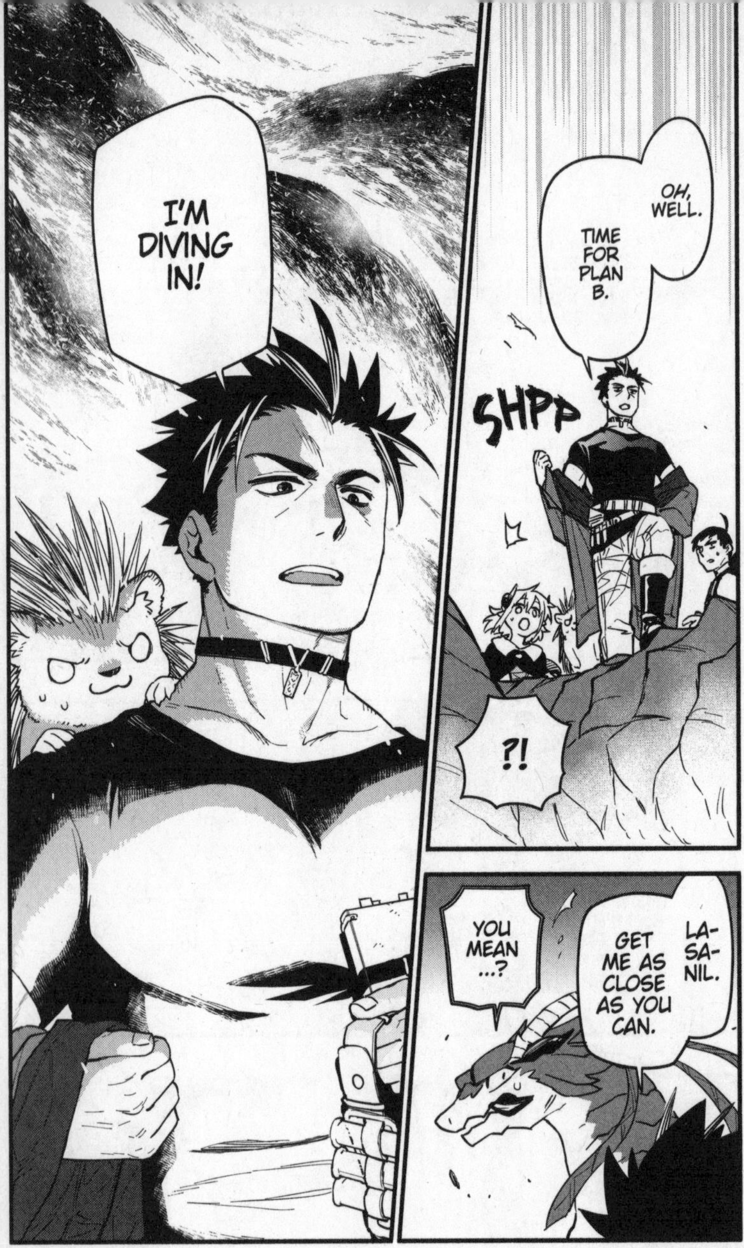
OH, WELL.
TIME FOR PLAN B.
SHPP
?!
LASANIL.
GET ME AS CLOSE AS YOU CAN.
YOU MEAN ...?
I'M DIVING IN!

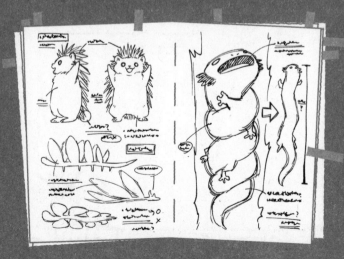

Sorry For My Familiar

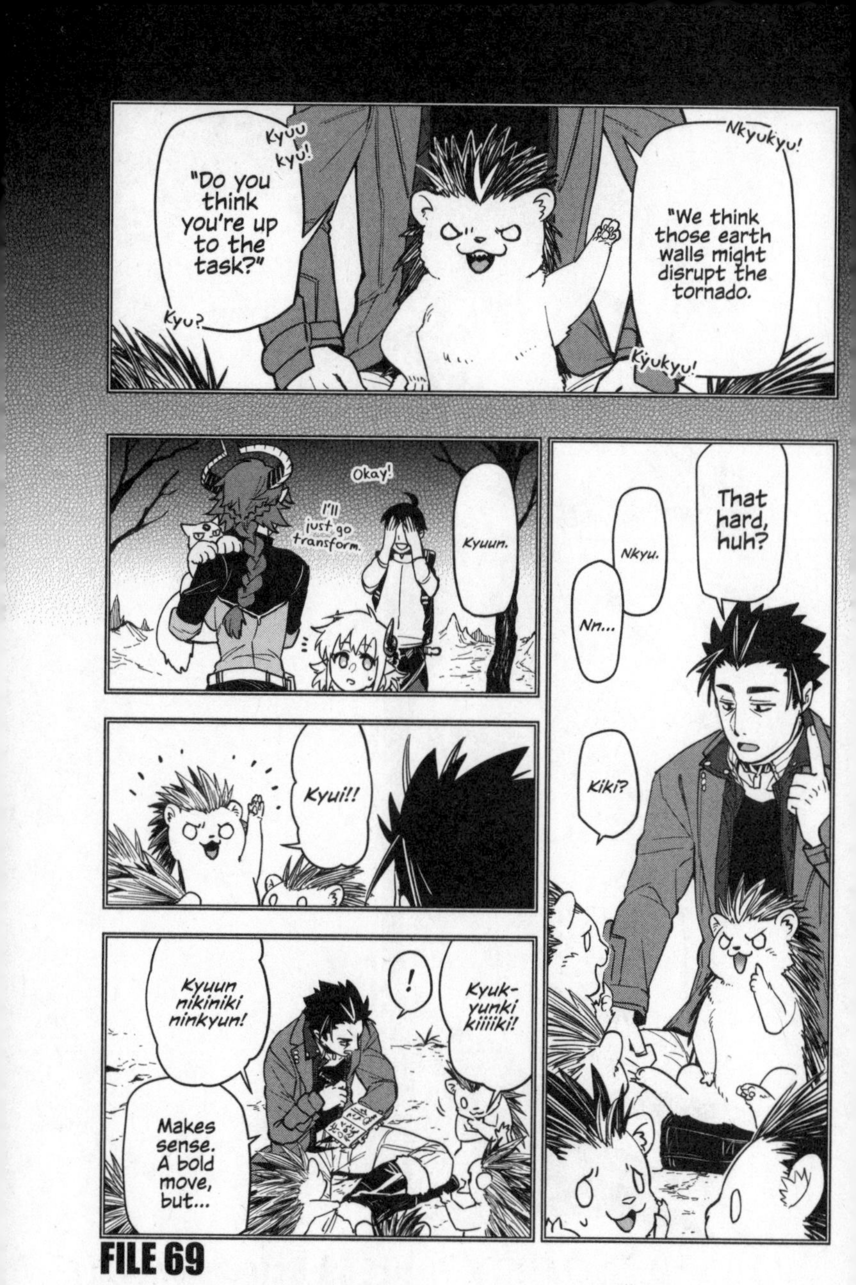
Nkyukyu!
"We think those earth walls might disrupt the tornado.
Kyukyu!
Kyuu kyu!
"Do you think you're up to the task?"
Kyu?
That hard, huh?
Nkyu.
Nn...
Kiki?
Kyuun.
Okay!
I'll just go transform.
Kyui!!
Kyuk-yunki kiiiiki!
!
Kyuun nikiniki ninkyun!
Makes sense. A bold move, but...

FILE 69

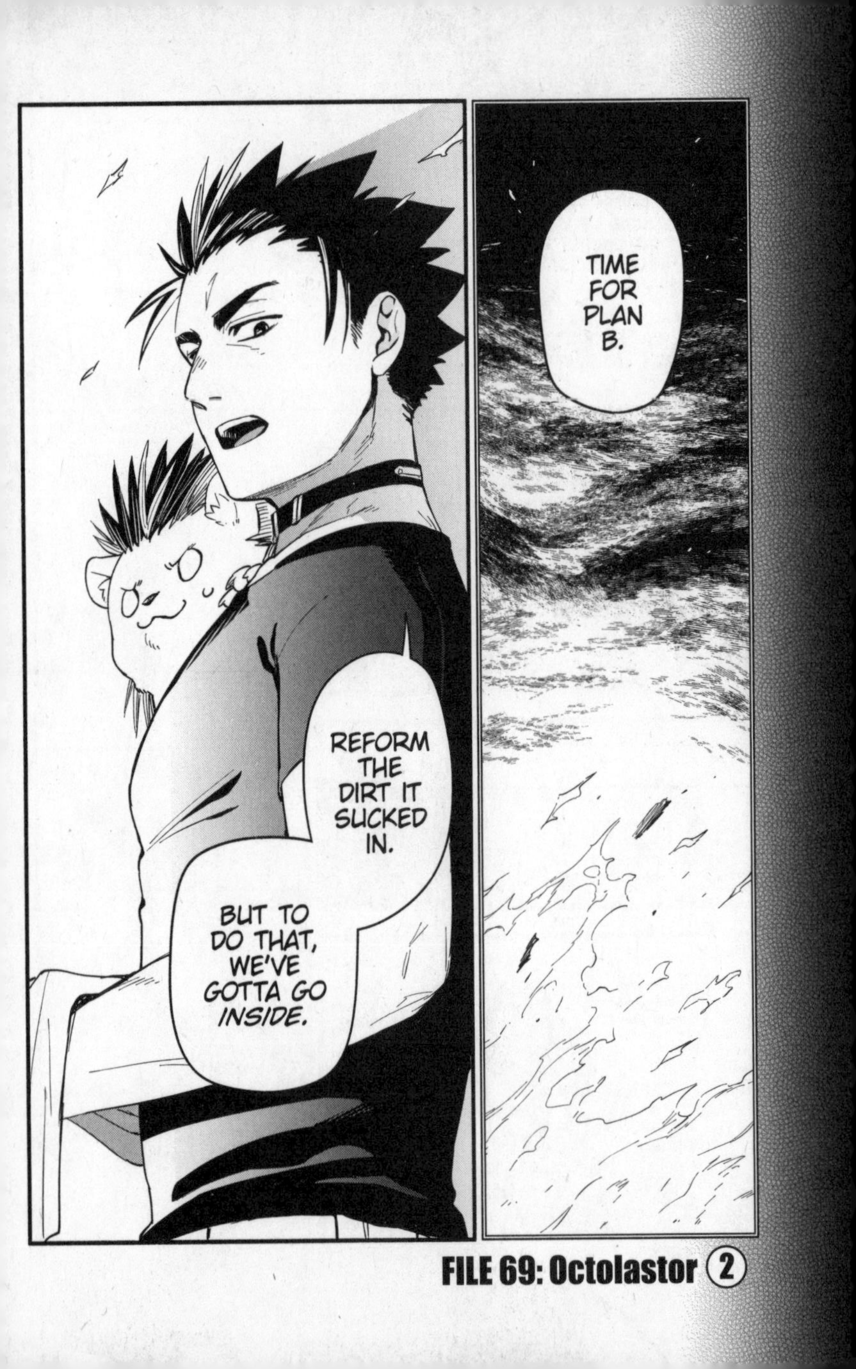
TIME FOR PLAN B.
REFORM THE DIRT IT SUCKED IN.
BUT TO DO THAT, WE'VE GOTTA GO INSIDE.

FILE 69: Octolastor ②

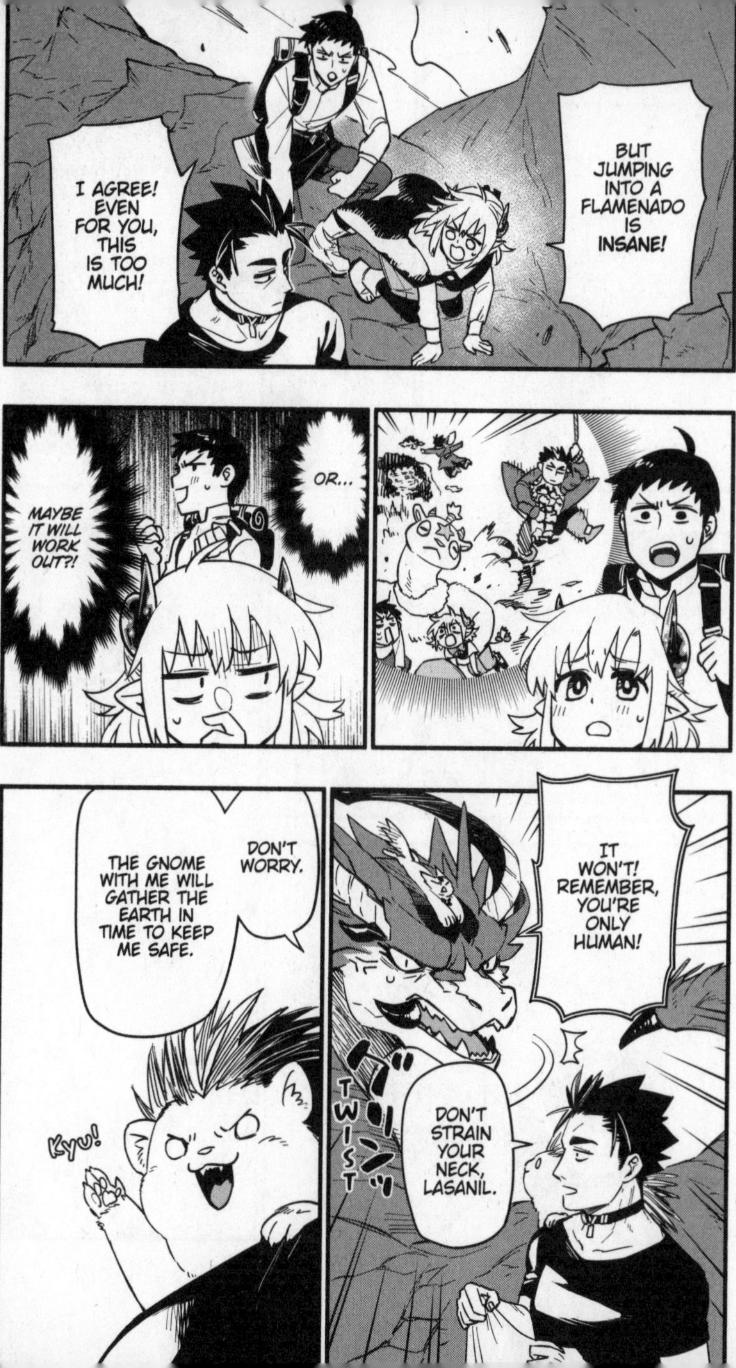
BUT JUMPING INTO A FLAMENADO IS INSANE!
I AGREE! EVEN FOR YOU, THIS IS TOO MUCH!
OR...
MAYBE IT WILL WORK OUT?!
IT WON'T! REMEMBER, YOU'RE ONLY HUMAN!
TWIST
DON'T STRAIN YOUR NECK, LASANIL.
DON'T WORRY.
THE GNOME WITH ME WILL GATHER THE EARTH IN TIME TO KEEP ME SAFE.
Kyu!

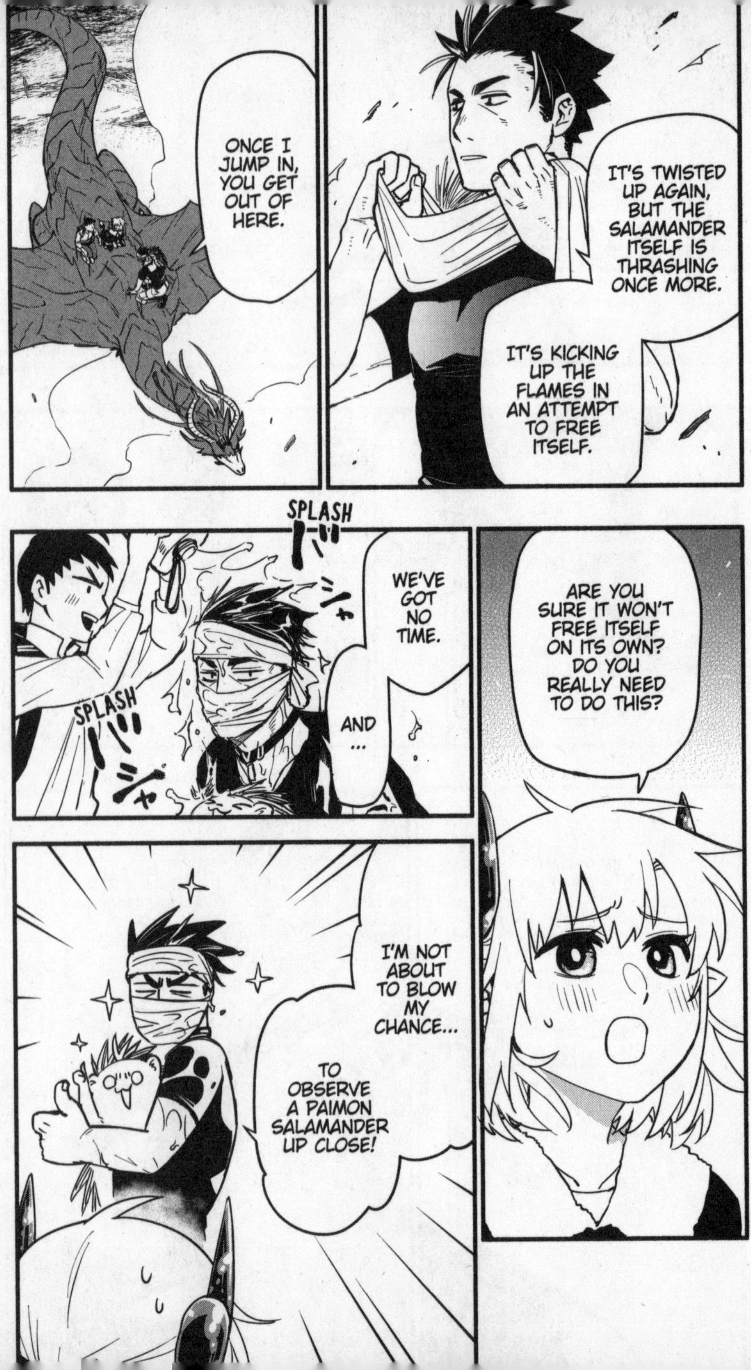
IT'S TWISTED UP AGAIN, BUT THE SALAMANDER ITSELF IS THRASHING ONCE MORE.
IT'S KICKING UP THE FLAMES IN AN ATTEMPT TO FREE ITSELF.
ONCE I JUMP IN, YOU GET OUT OF HERE.
ARE YOU SURE IT WON'T FREE ITSELF ON ITS OWN? DO YOU REALLY NEED TO DO THIS?
SPLASH
WE'VE GOT NO TIME.
AND ...
SPLASH
I'M NOT ABOUT TO BLOW MY CHANCE...
TO OBSERVE A PAIMON SALAMANDER UP CLOSE!

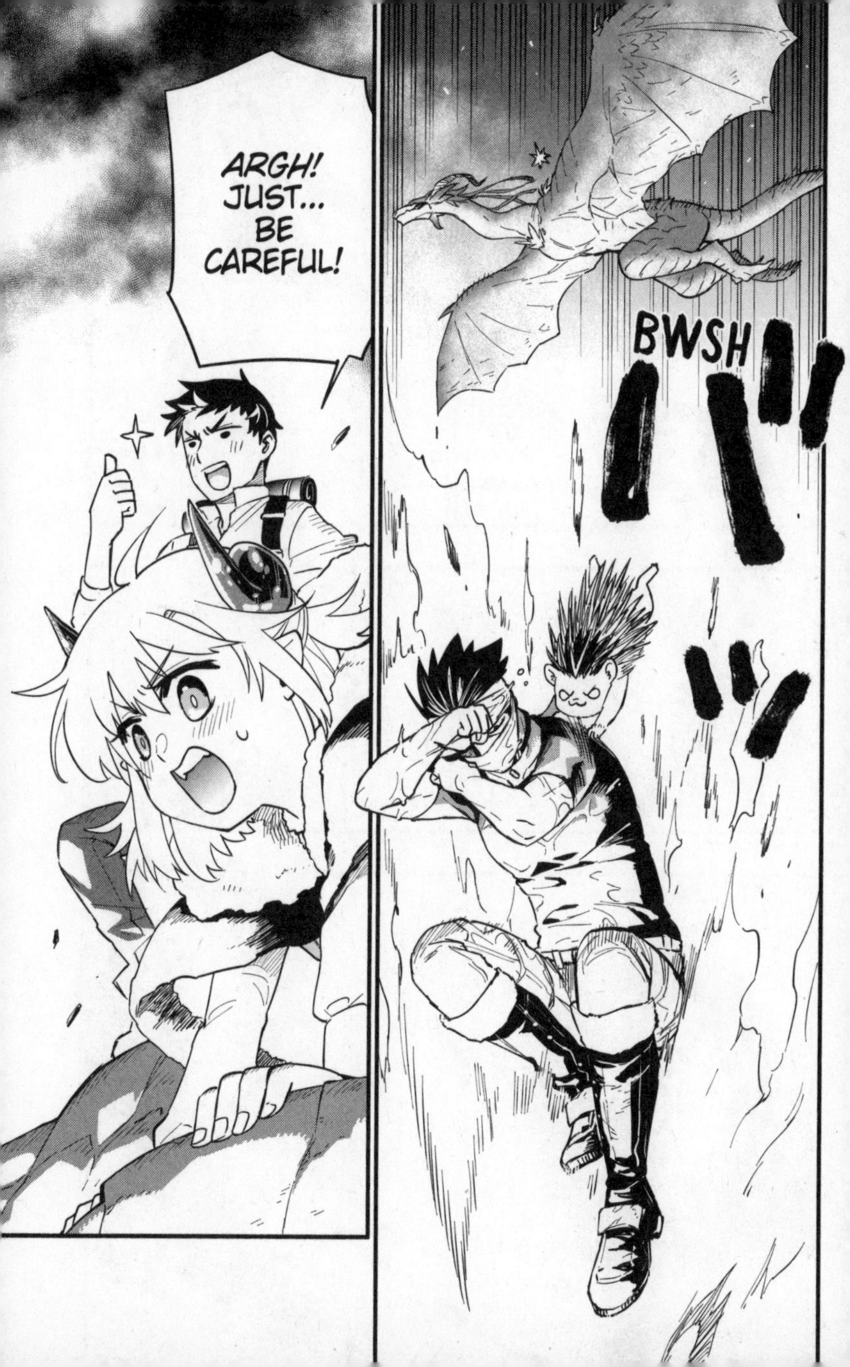
BWSH
ARGH! JUST... BE CAREFUL!

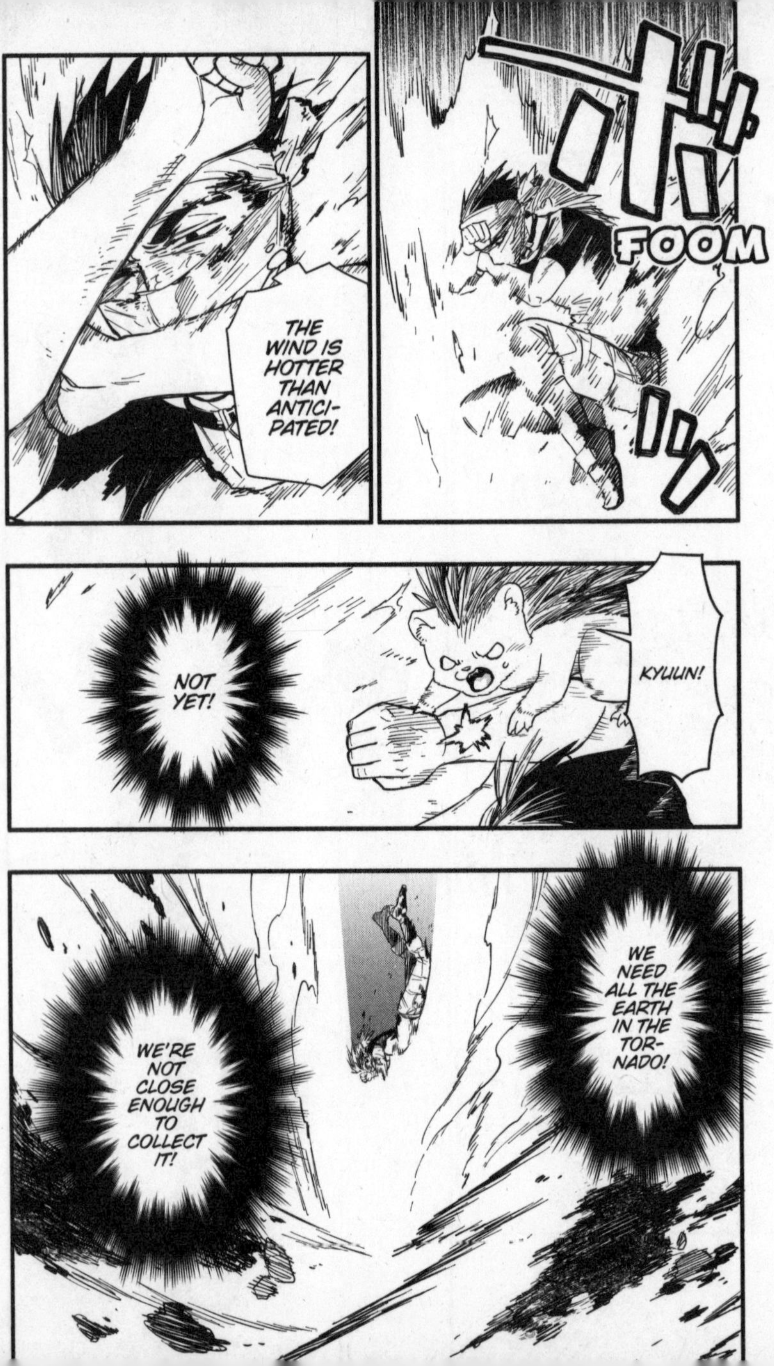
FOOM
THE WIND IS HOTTER THAN ANTICI-PATED!
KYUUN!
NOT YET!
WE NEED ALL THE EARTH IN THE TOR-NADO!
WE'RE NOT CLOSE ENOUGH TO COLLECT IT!

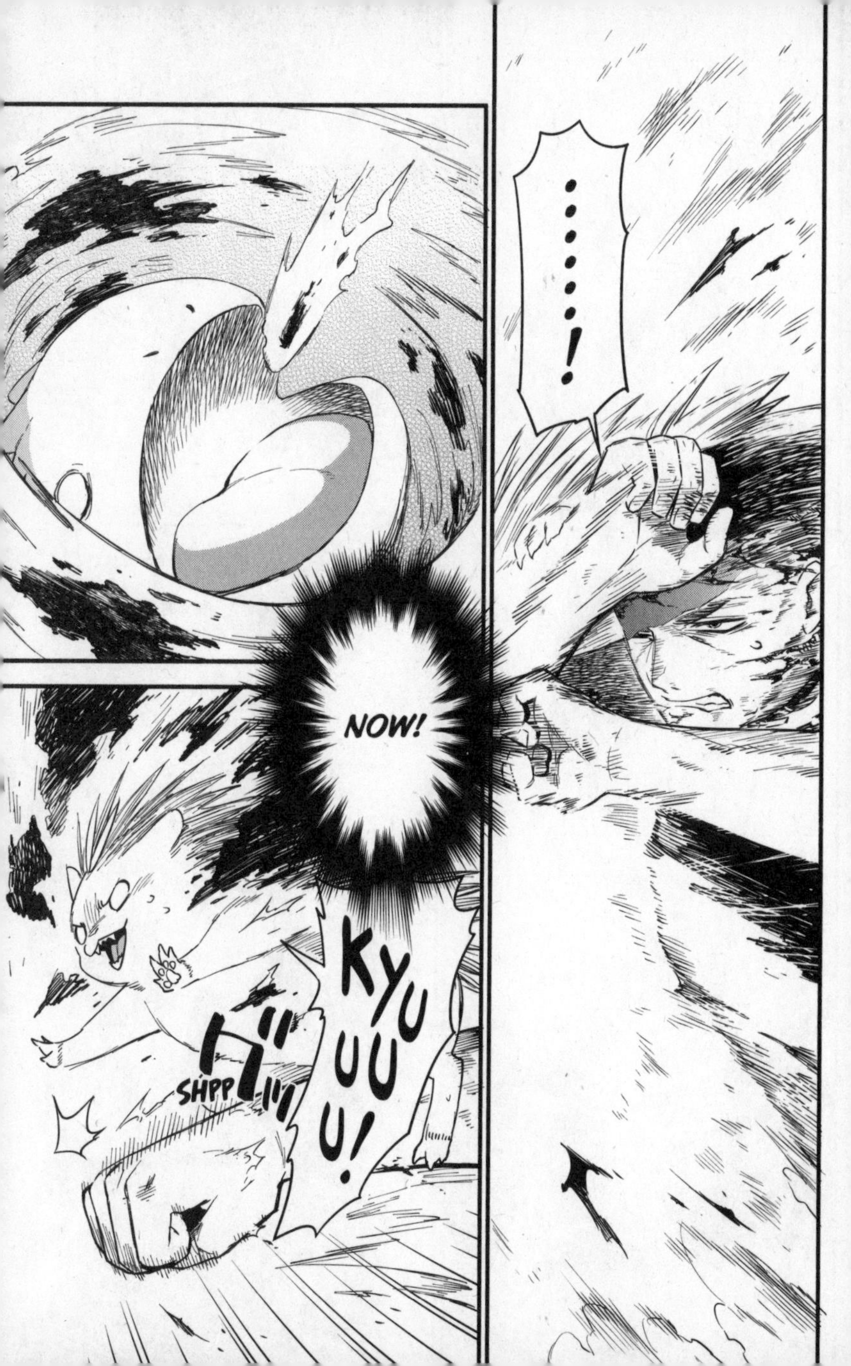
......!
NOW!
KYUUUUU!
SHPP

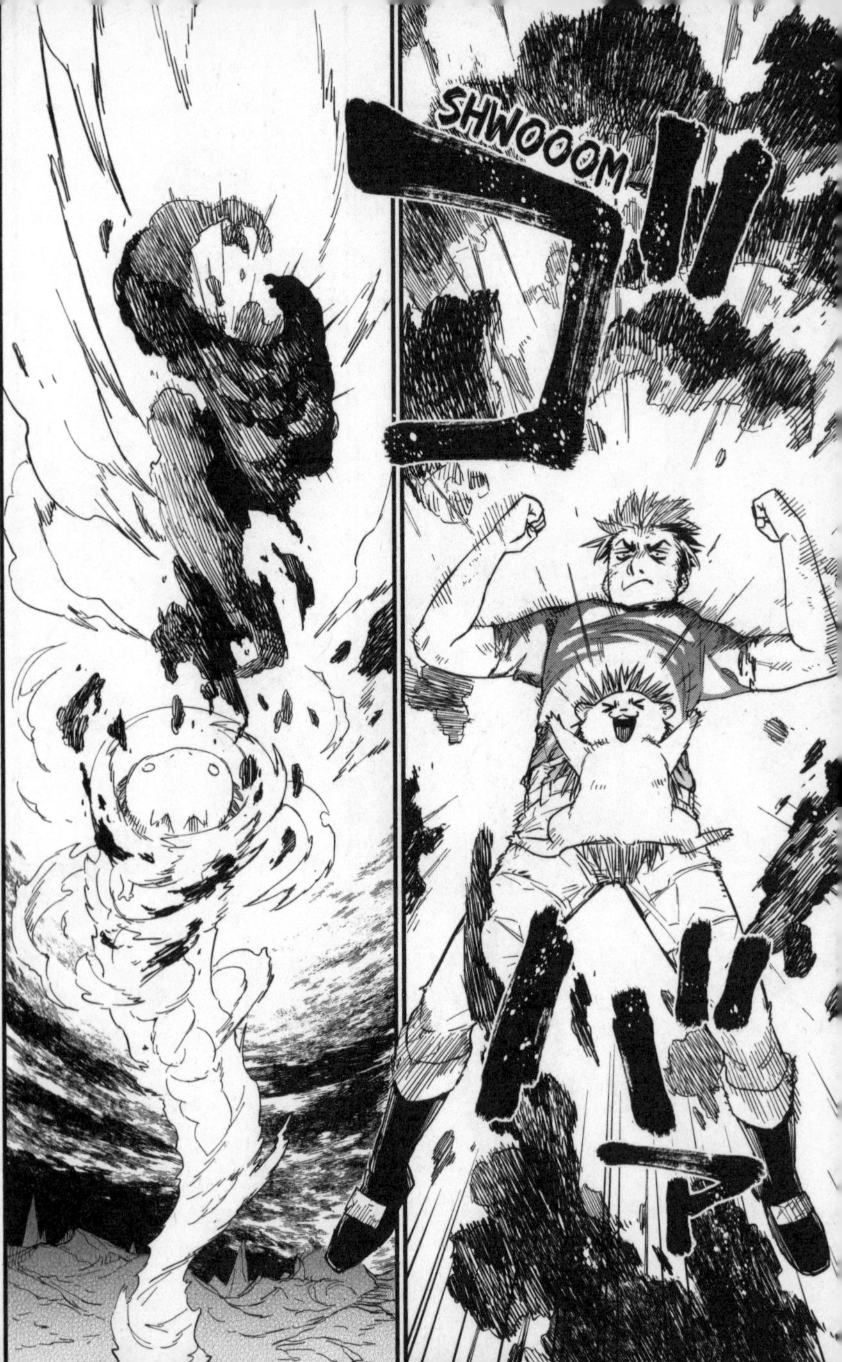
SHWOOOM

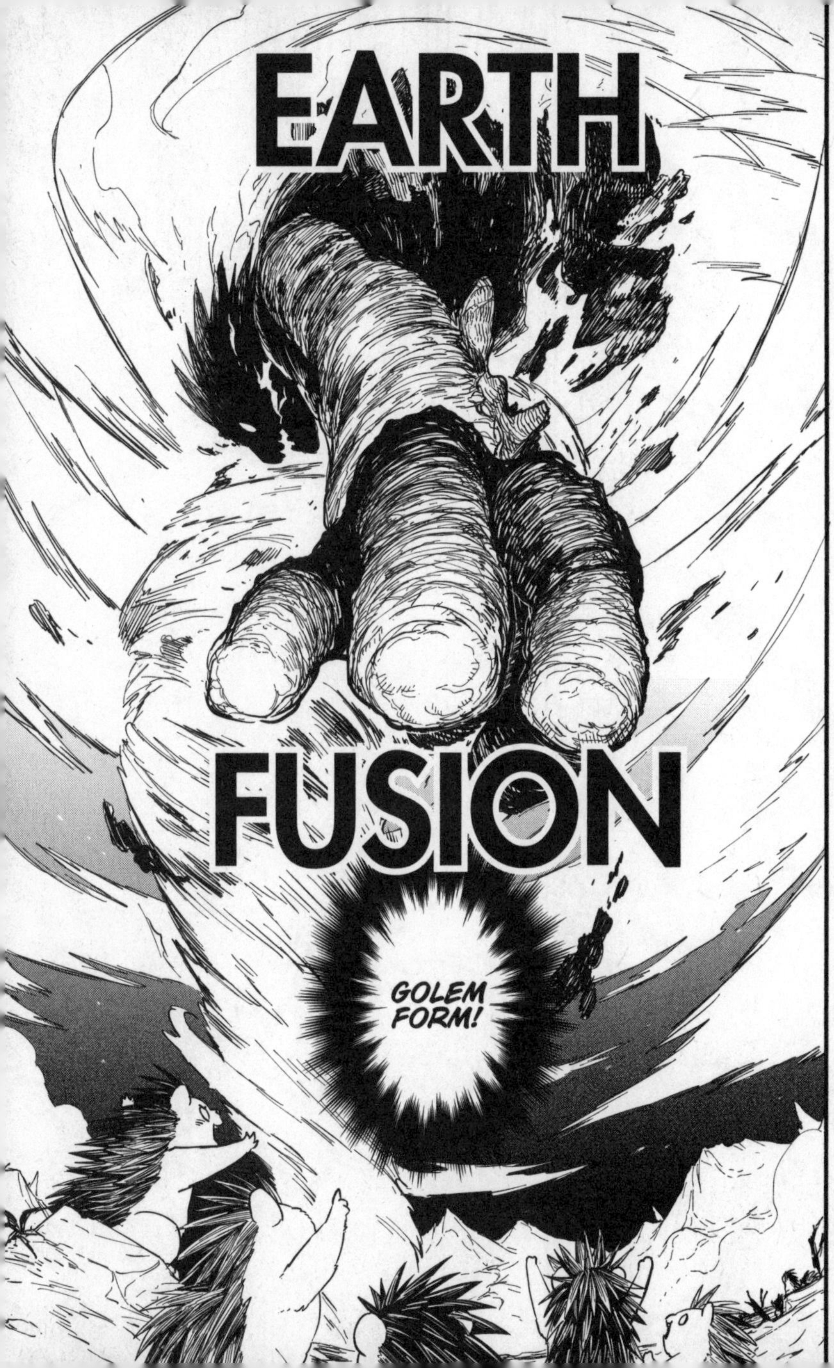
EARTH
FUSION
GOLEM FORM!

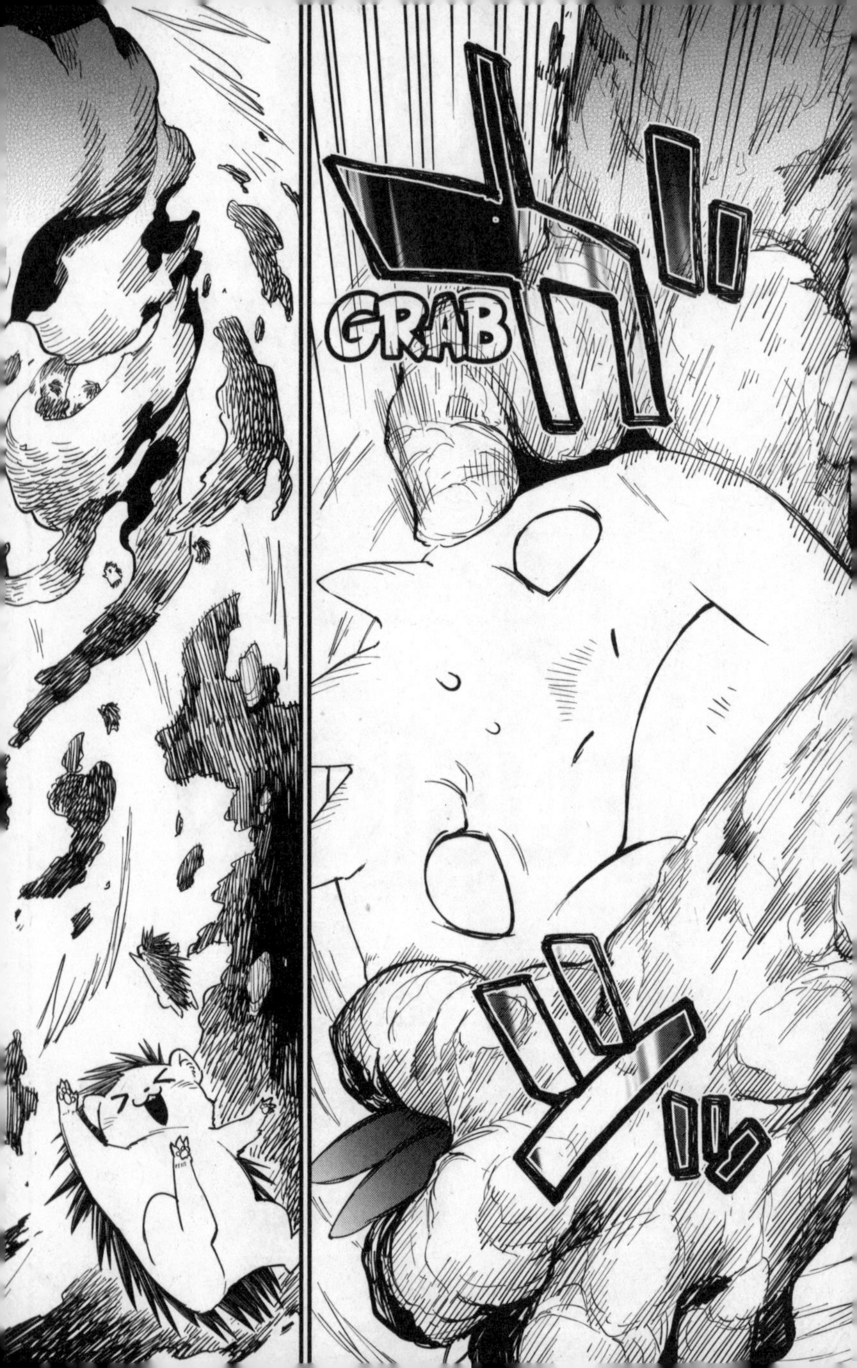
GRAB

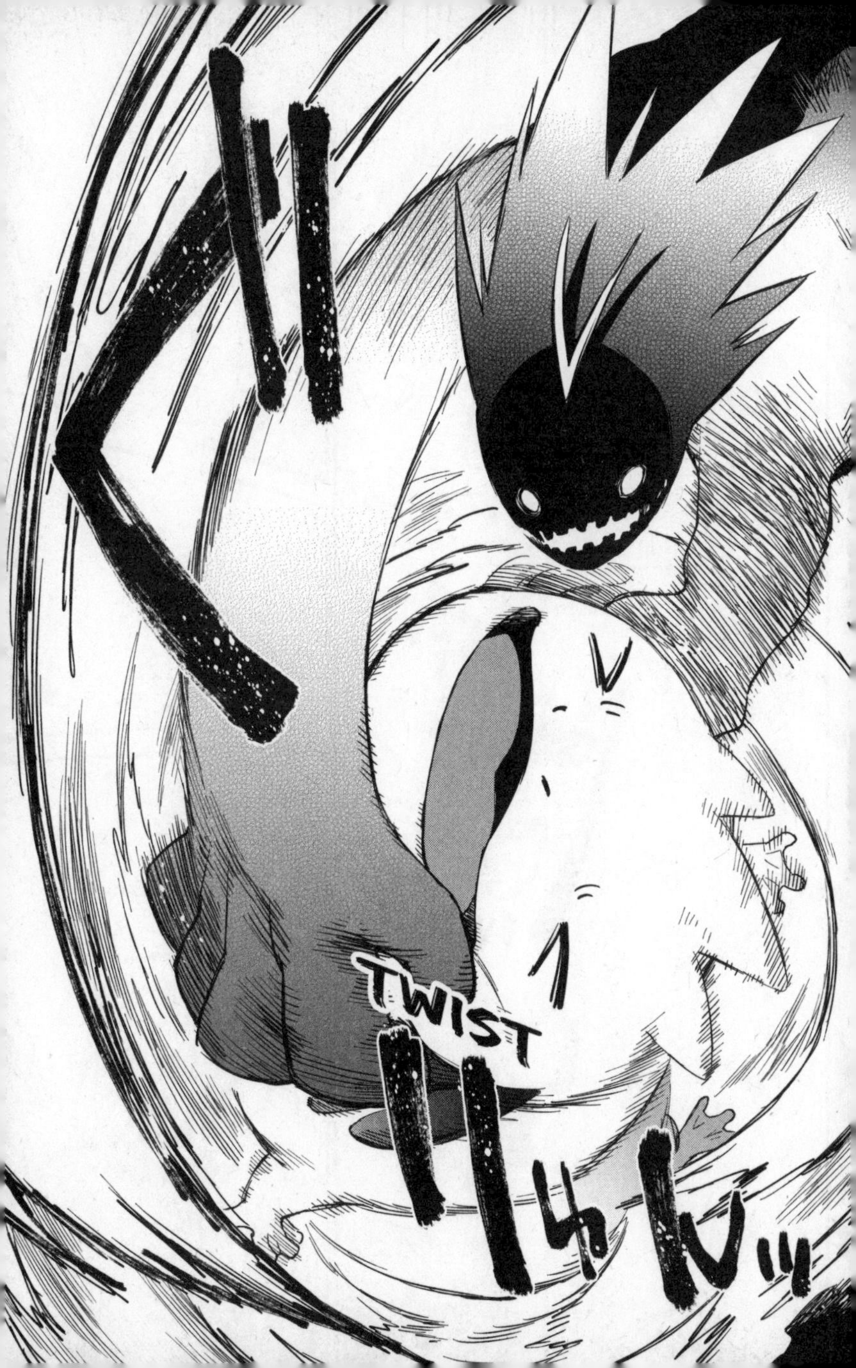
TWIST

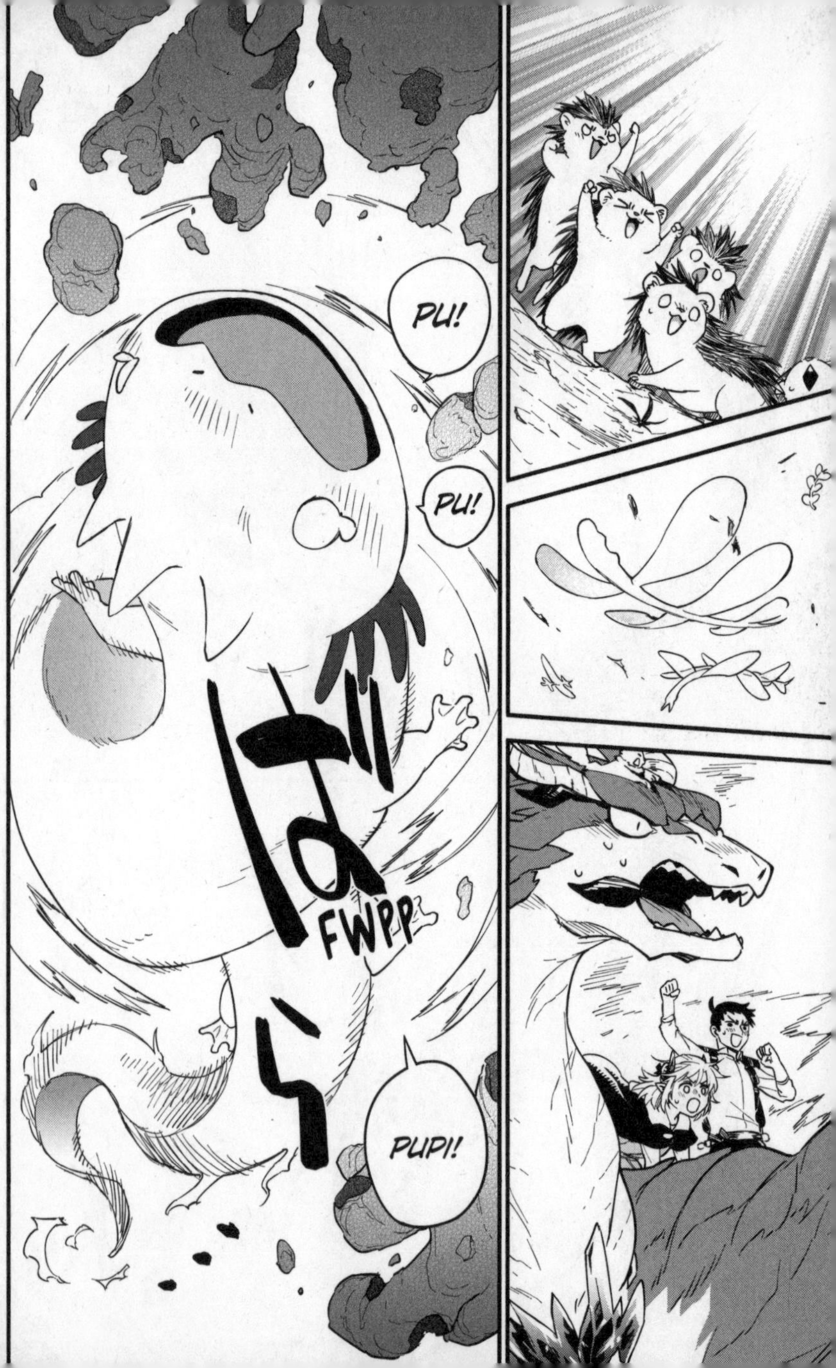
PU!
PU!
FWPP
PUPI!

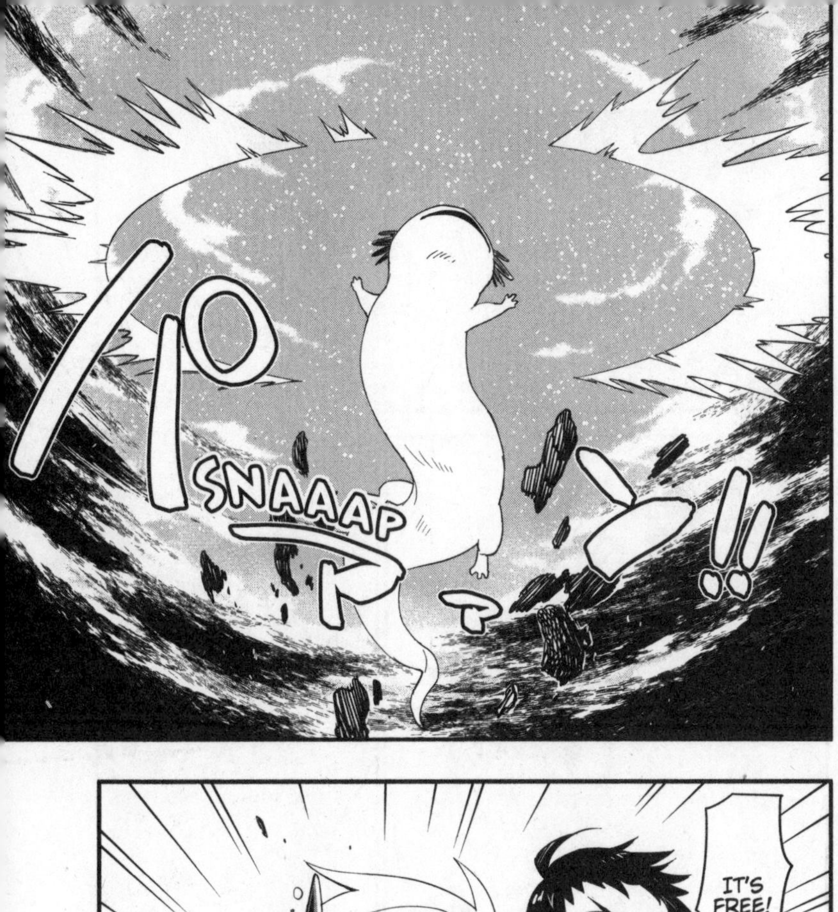
SNAAAAP

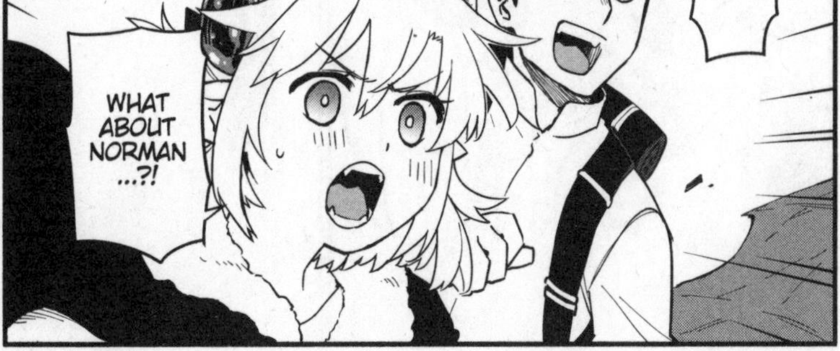
IT'S FREE!
WHAT ABOUT NORMAN ...?!

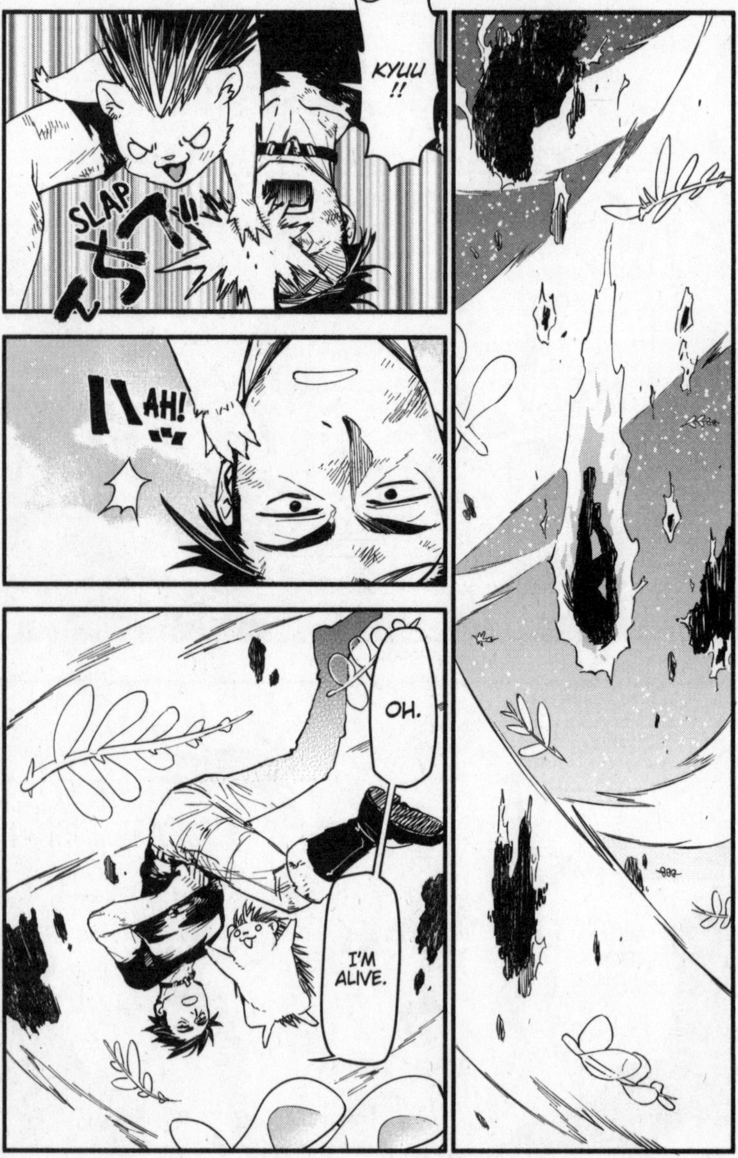
KYUU !!
SLAP
AH!
OH.
I'M ALIVE.

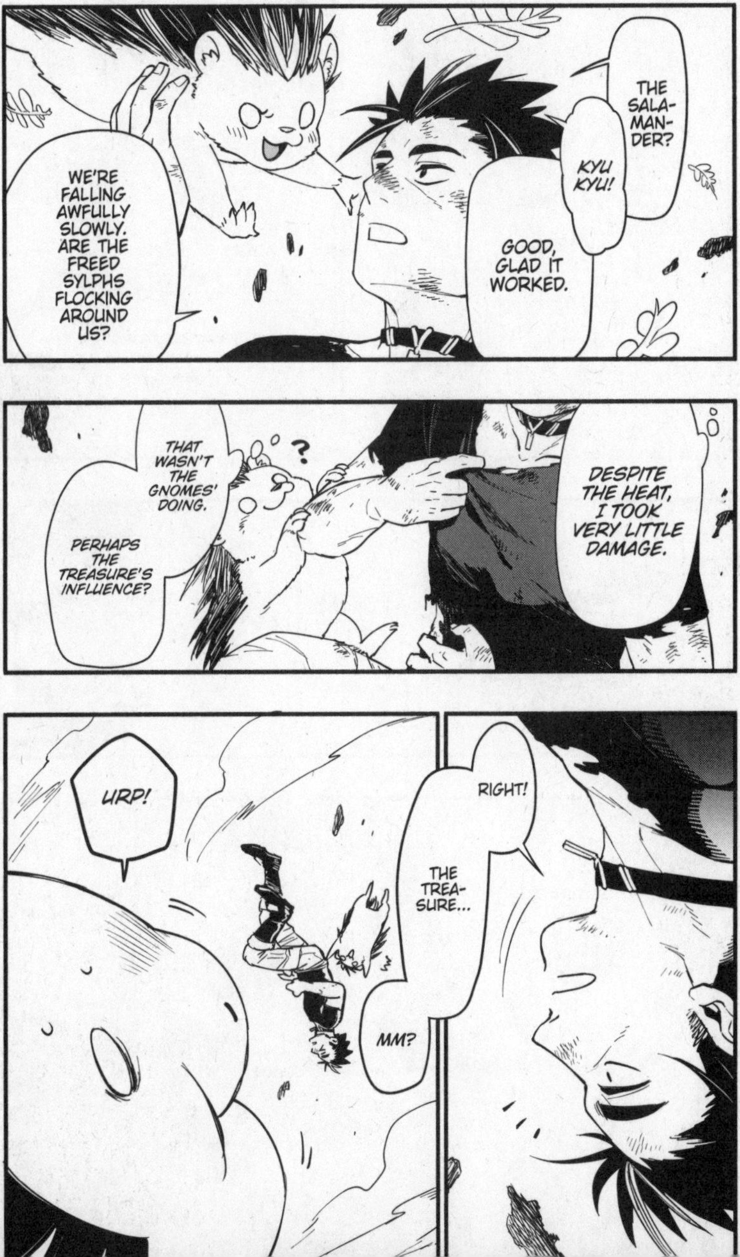
THE SALAMANDER?
KYU KYU!
GOOD, GLAD IT WORKED.
WE'RE FALLING AWFULLY SLOWLY. ARE THE FREED SYLPHS FLOCKING AROUND US?
DESPITE THE HEAT, I TOOK VERY LITTLE DAMAGE.
THAT WASN'T THE GNOMES' DOING.
PERHAPS THE TREASURE'S INFLUENCE?
RIGHT!
THE TREASURE...
MM?
URP!

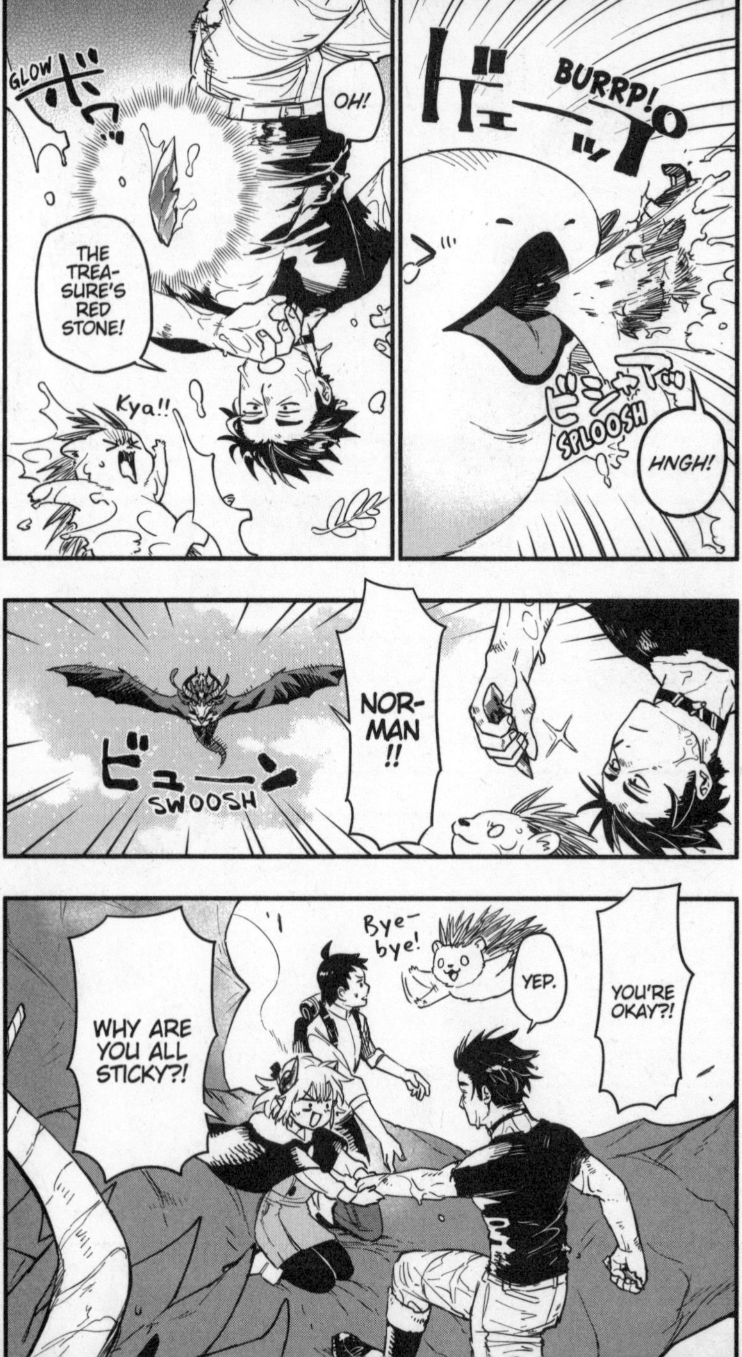
BURRP!
SPLOOSH
HNGH!
GLOW
OH!
THE TREA-SURE'S RED STONE!
Kya!!
NOR-MAN !!
ビューン
SWOOSH
YOU'RE OKAY?!
YEP.
Bye-bye!
WHY ARE YOU ALL STICKY?!

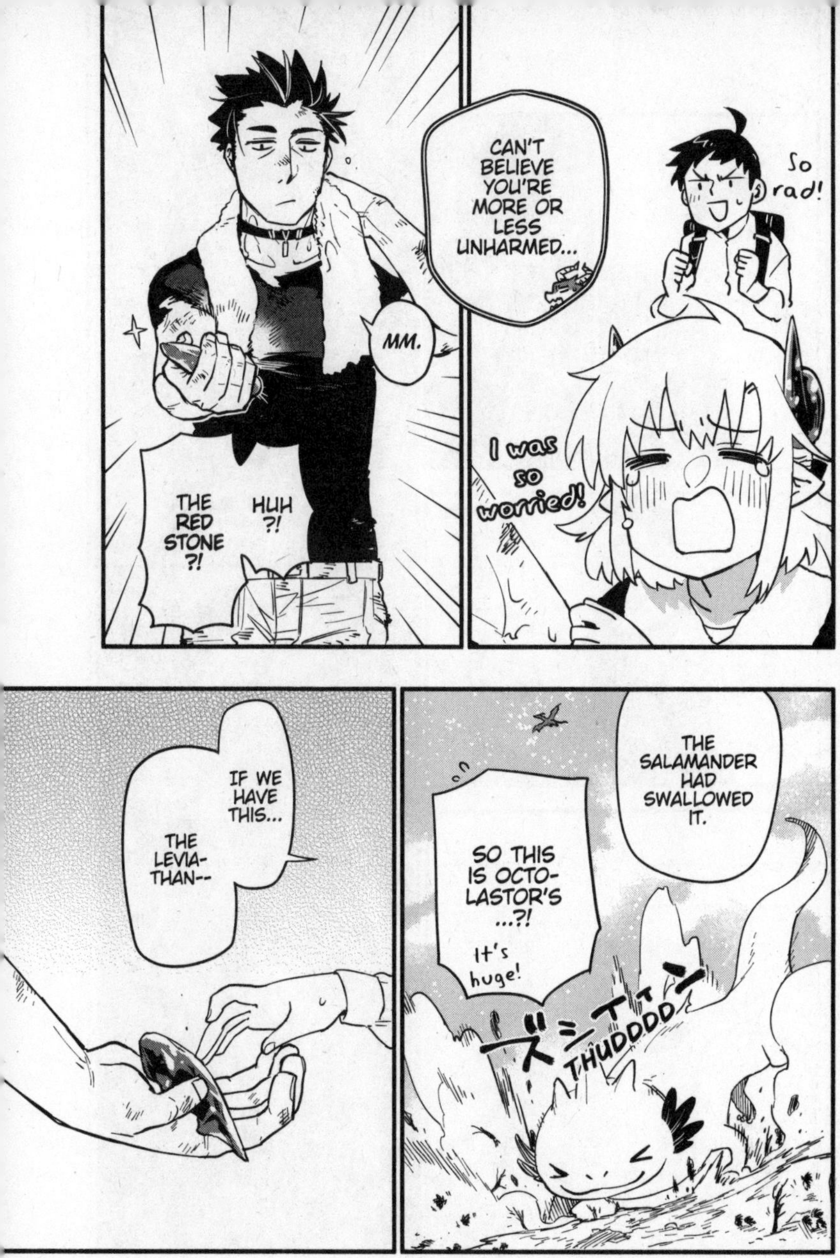
CAN'T BELIEVE YOU'RE MORE OR LESS UNHARMED...
So rad!
I was so worried!
MM.
HUH ?!
THE RED STONE ?!
THE SALAMANDER HAD SWALLOWED IT.
SO THIS IS OCTO-LASTOR'S ...?!
It's huge!
THUDDDD
IF WE HAVE THIS...
THE LEVIA-THAN--

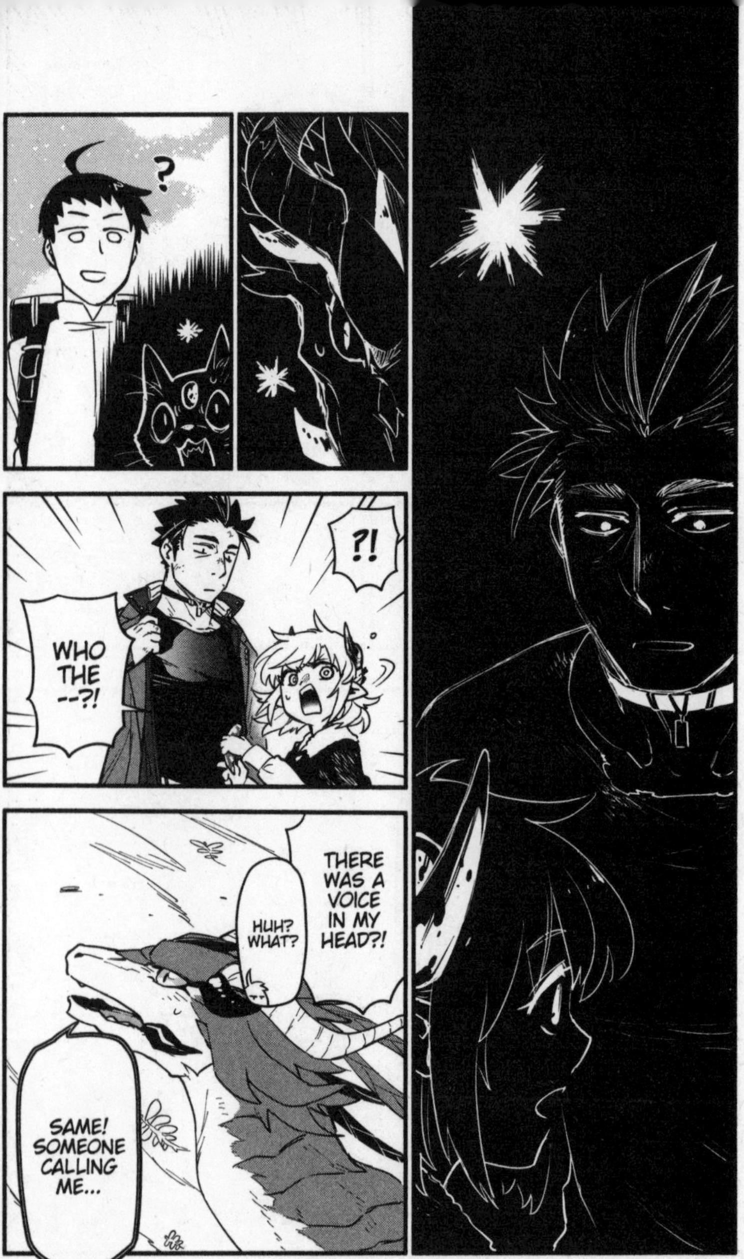
?
?!
WHO THE --?!
THERE WAS A VOICE IN MY HEAD?!
HUH? WHAT?
SAME! SOMEONE CALLING ME...

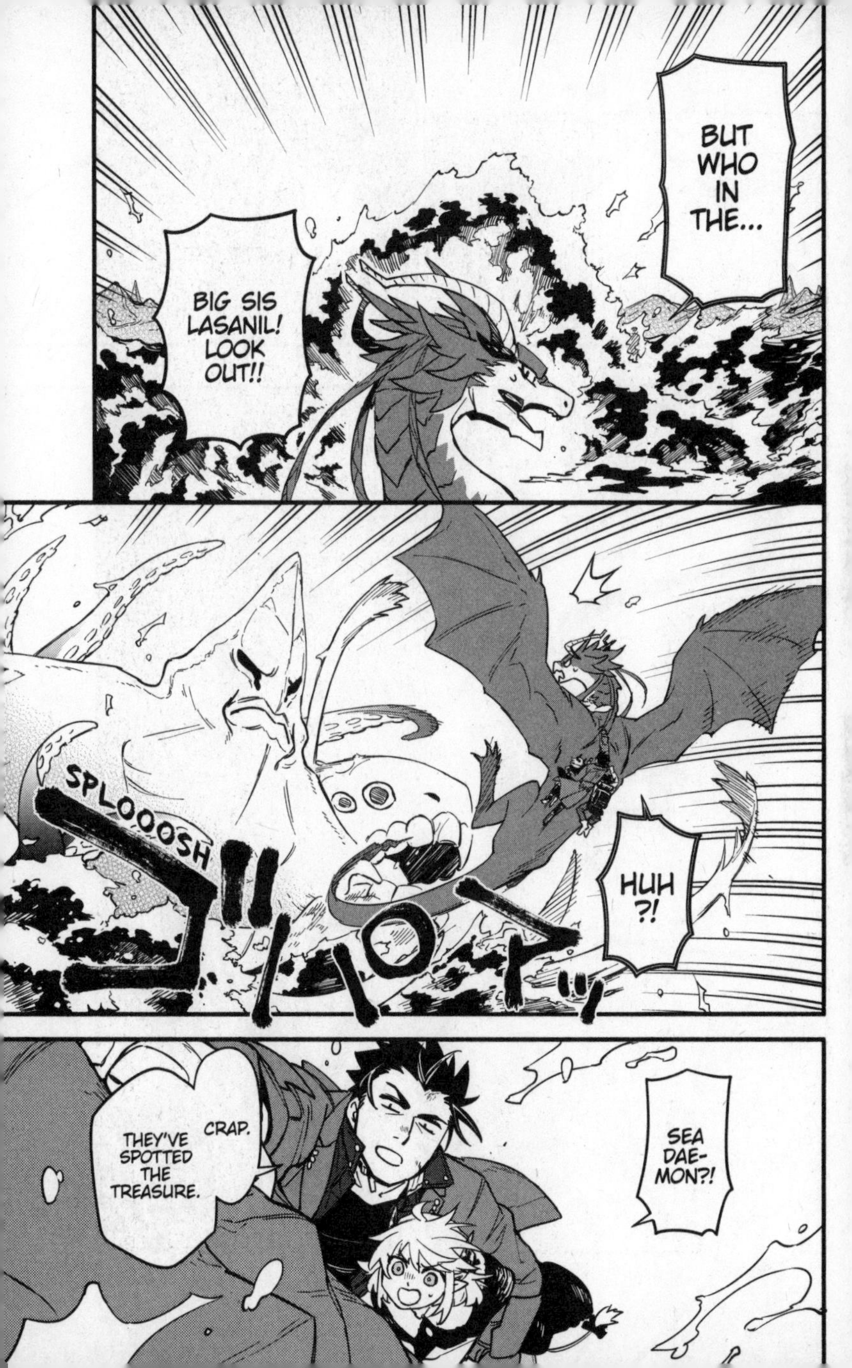
BUT WHO IN THE...
BIG SIS LASANIL! LOOK OUT!!
HUH ?!
SPLOOOSH
SEA DAE-MON?!
CRAP.
THEY'VE SPOTTED THE TREASURE.

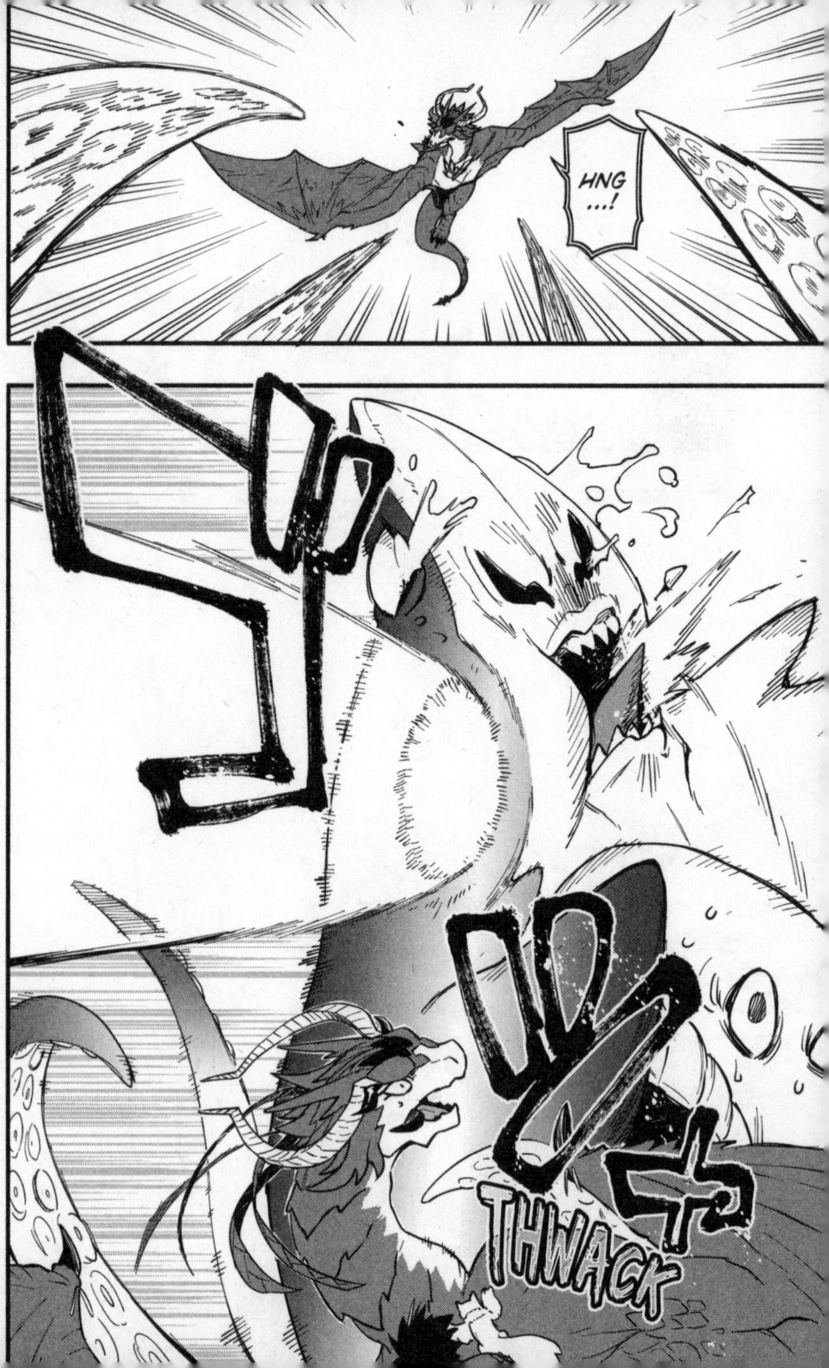
HNG ...!
THWACK

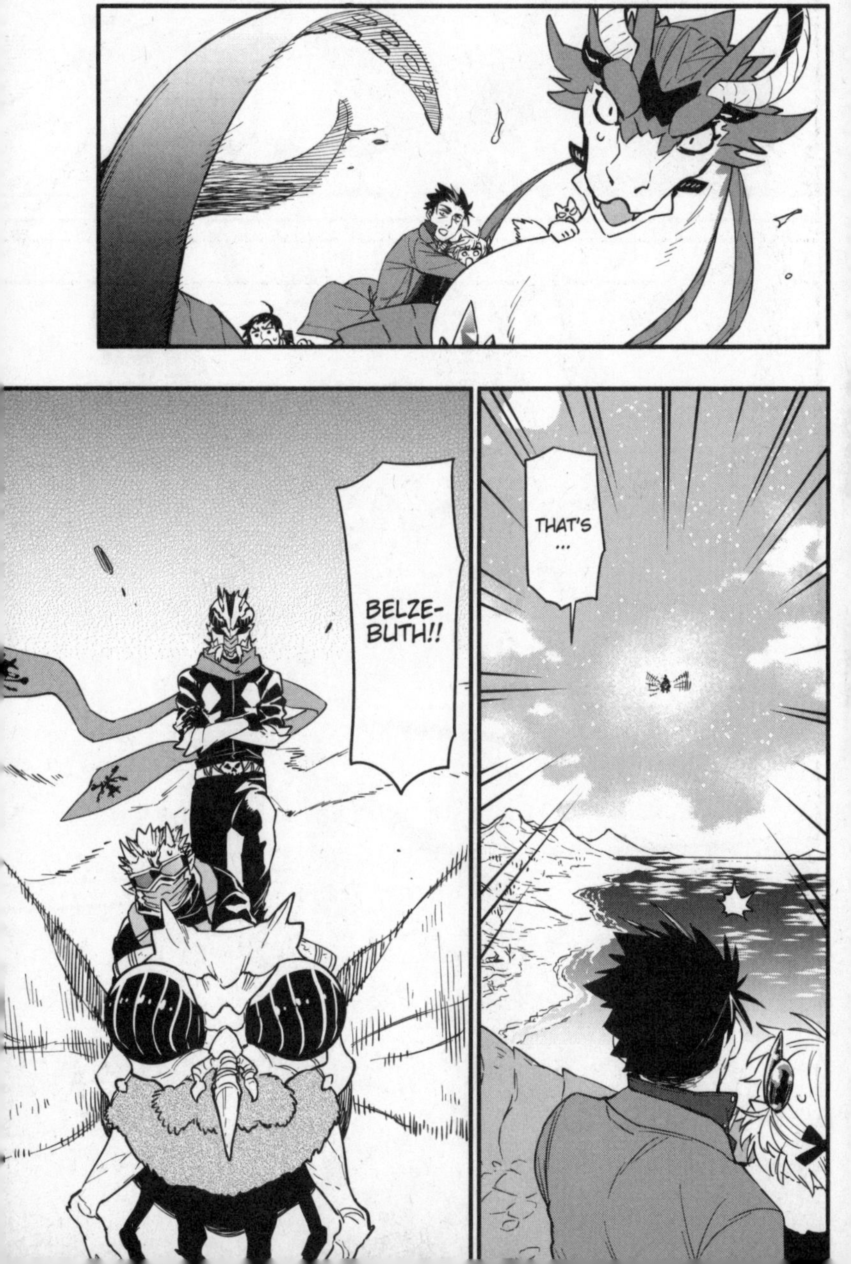
THAT'S ...
BELZE-BUTH!!

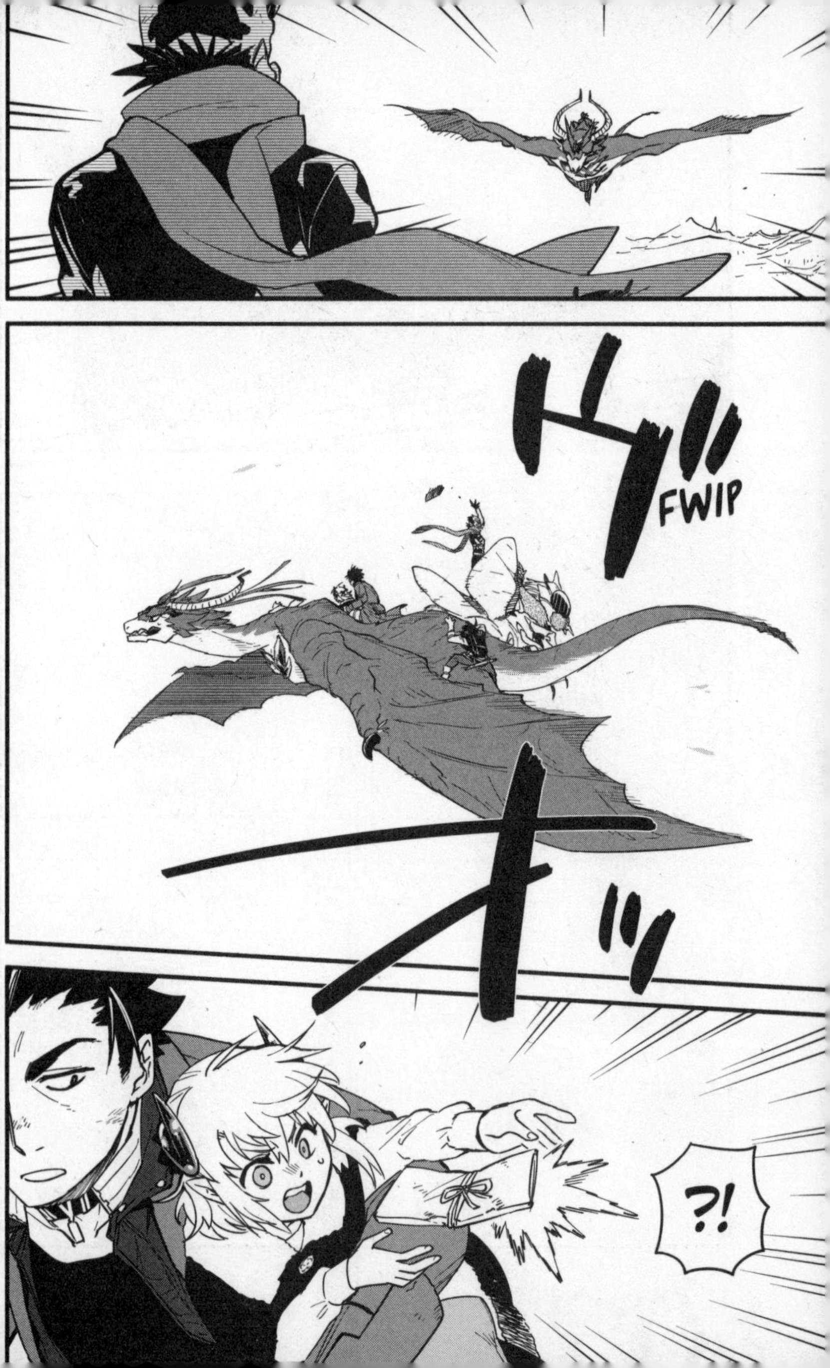
FWIP
?!

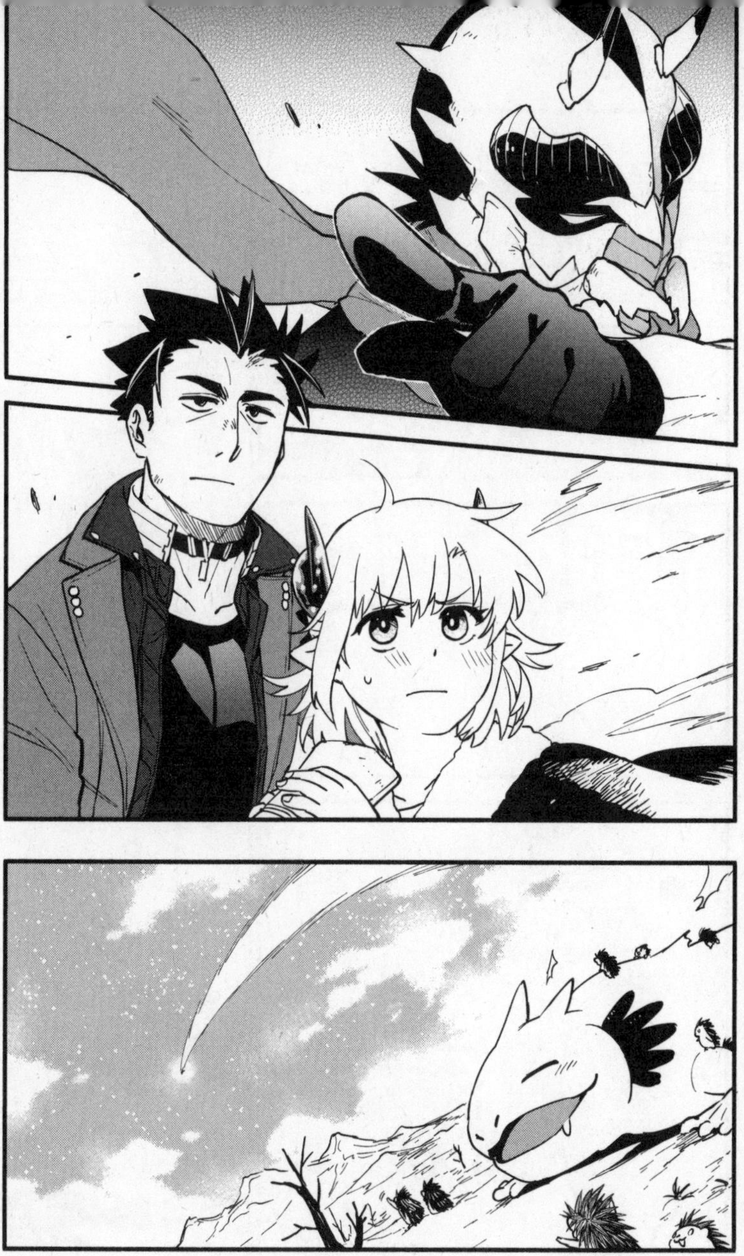

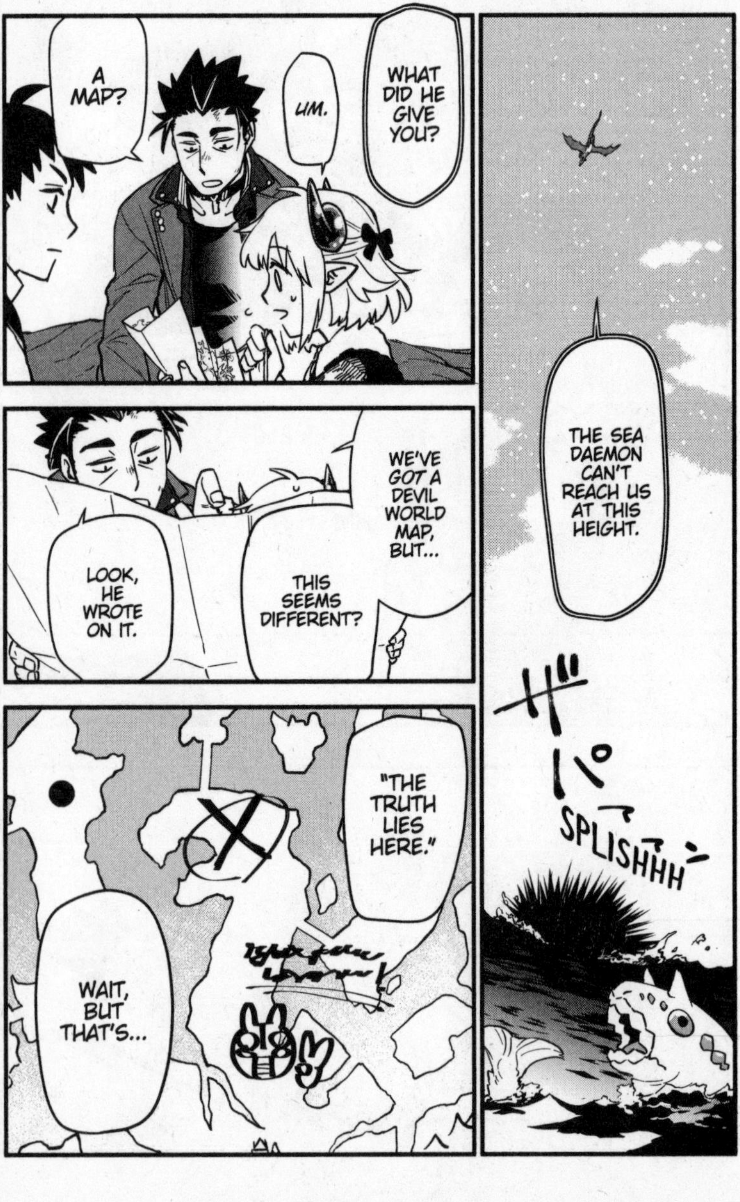
THE SEA DAEMON CAN'T REACH US AT THIS HEIGHT.
ザパッ
SPLISHHH
WHAT DID HE GIVE YOU?
UM.
A MAP?
WE'VE GOT A DEVIL WORLD MAP, BUT...
THIS SEEMS DIFFERENT?
LOOK, HE WROTE ON IT.
"THE TRUTH LIES HERE."
WAIT, BUT THAT'S...

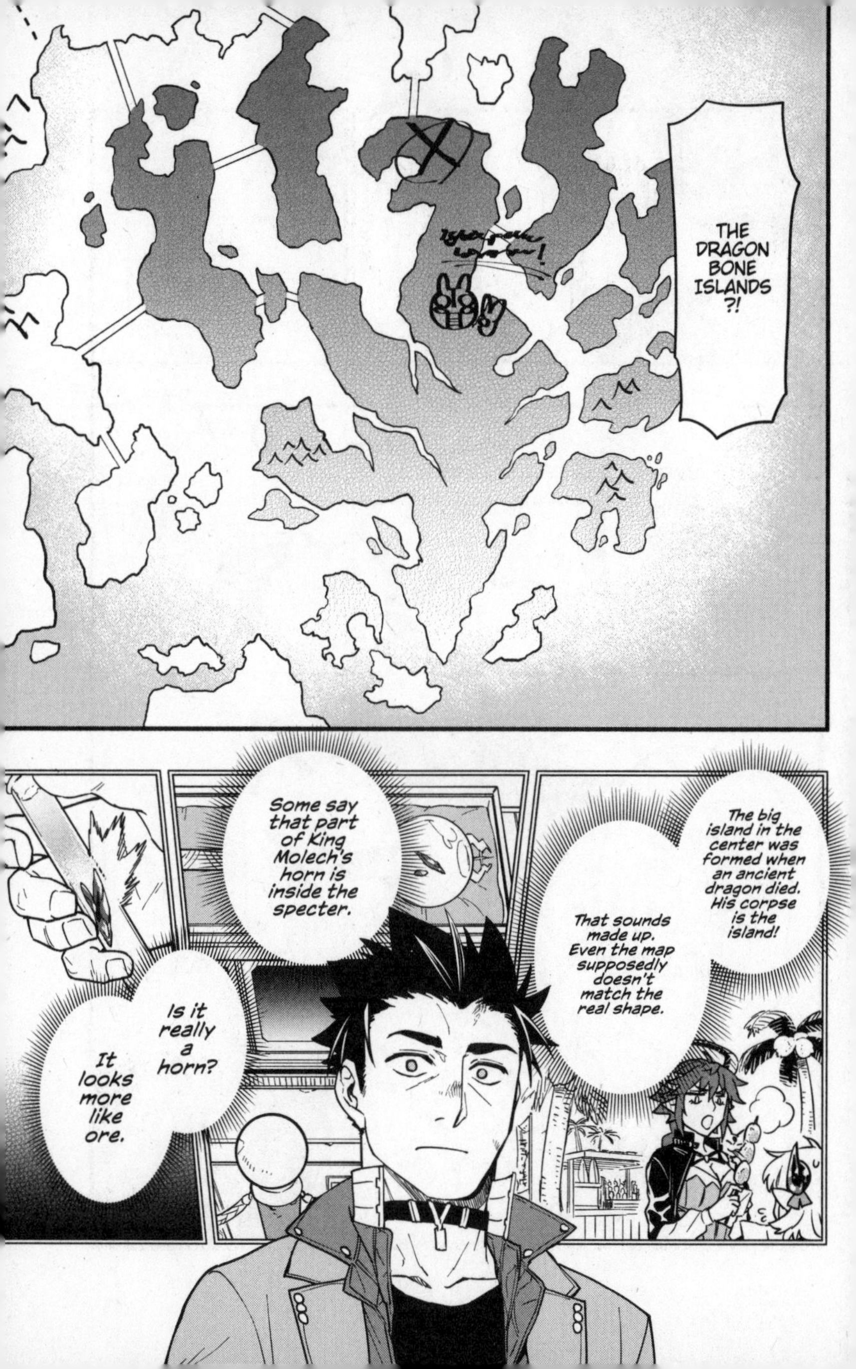
THE DRAGON BONE ISLANDS ?!
The big island in the center was formed when an ancient dragon died. His corpse is the island!
That sounds made up. Even the map supposedly doesn't match the real shape.
Some say that part of King Molech's horn is inside the specter.
Is it really a horn?
It looks more like ore.

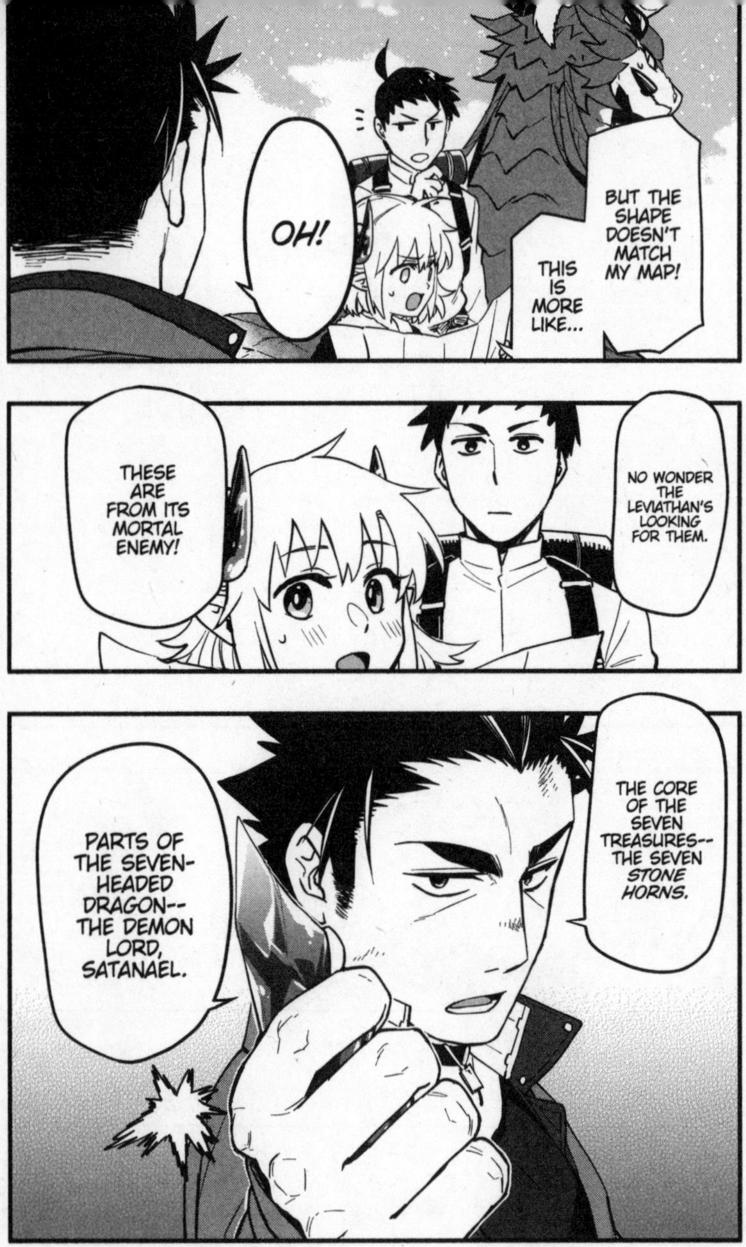
BUT THE SHAPE DOESN'T MATCH MY MAP!
THIS IS MORE LIKE...
OH!
NO WONDER THE LEVIATHAN'S LOOKING FOR THEM.
THESE ARE FROM ITS MORTAL ENEMY!
THE CORE OF THE SEVEN TREASURES-- THE SEVEN *STONE HORNS*.
PARTS OF THE SEVEN-HEADED DRAGON-- THE DEMON LORD, SATANAEL.

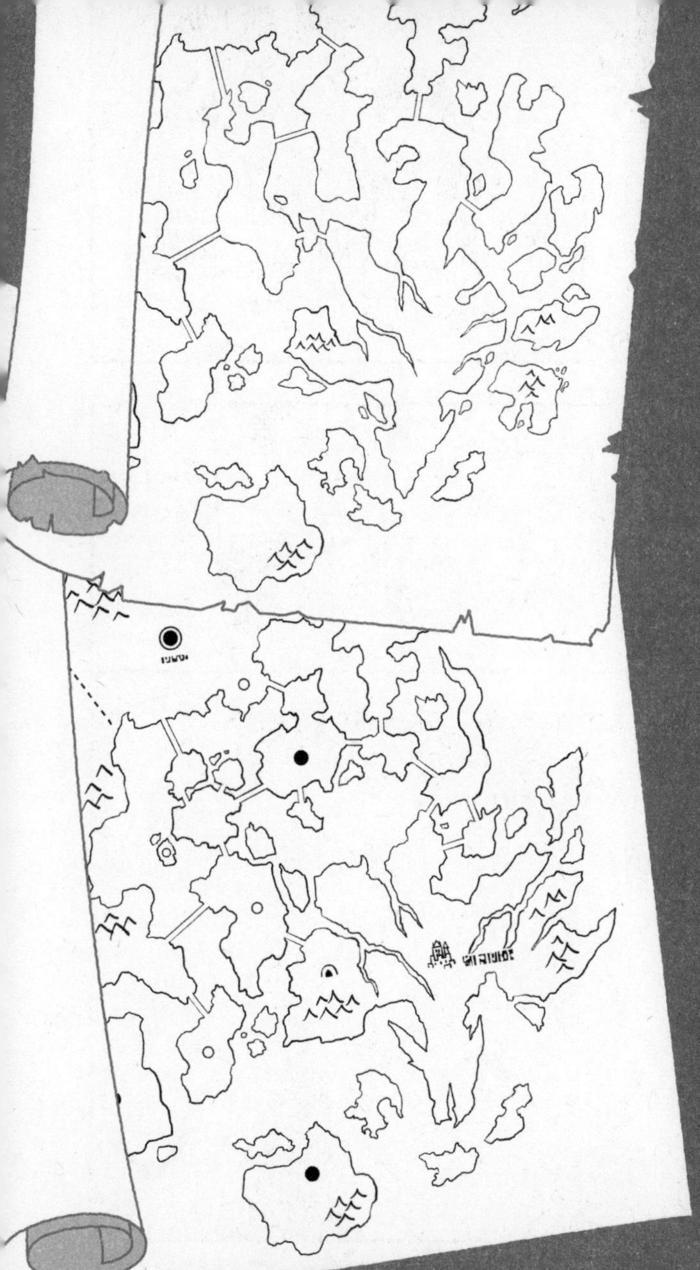

Sorry For My Familiar

FILE 70

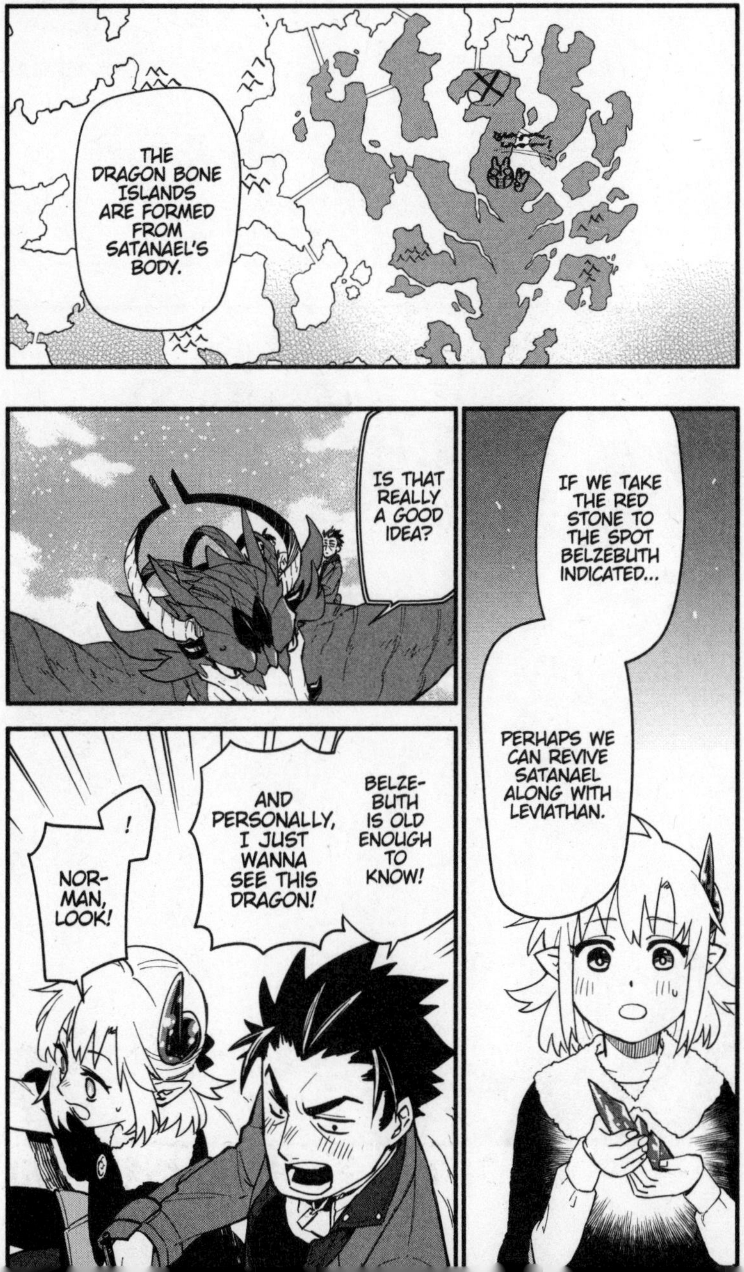
THE DRAGON BONE ISLANDS ARE FORMED FROM SATANAEL'S BODY.
IF WE TAKE THE RED STONE TO THE SPOT BELZEBUTH INDICATED...
PERHAPS WE CAN REVIVE SATANAEL ALONG WITH LEVIATHAN.
IS THAT REALLY A GOOD IDEA?
BELZE-BUTH IS OLD ENOUGH TO KNOW!
AND PERSONALLY, I JUST WANNA SEE THIS DRAGON!
!
NOR-MAN, LOOK!

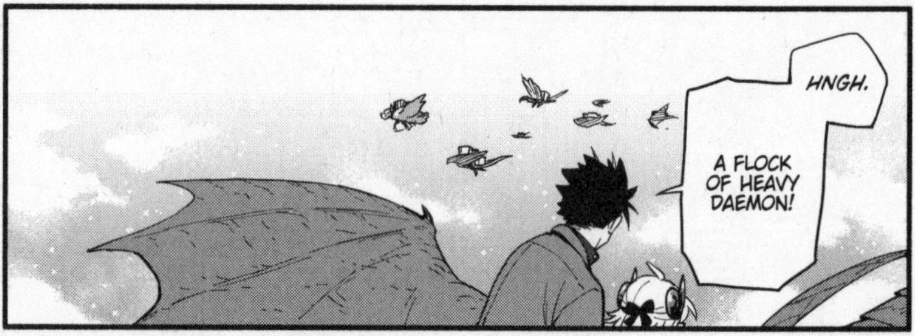
HNGH.
A FLOCK OF HEAVY DAEMON!

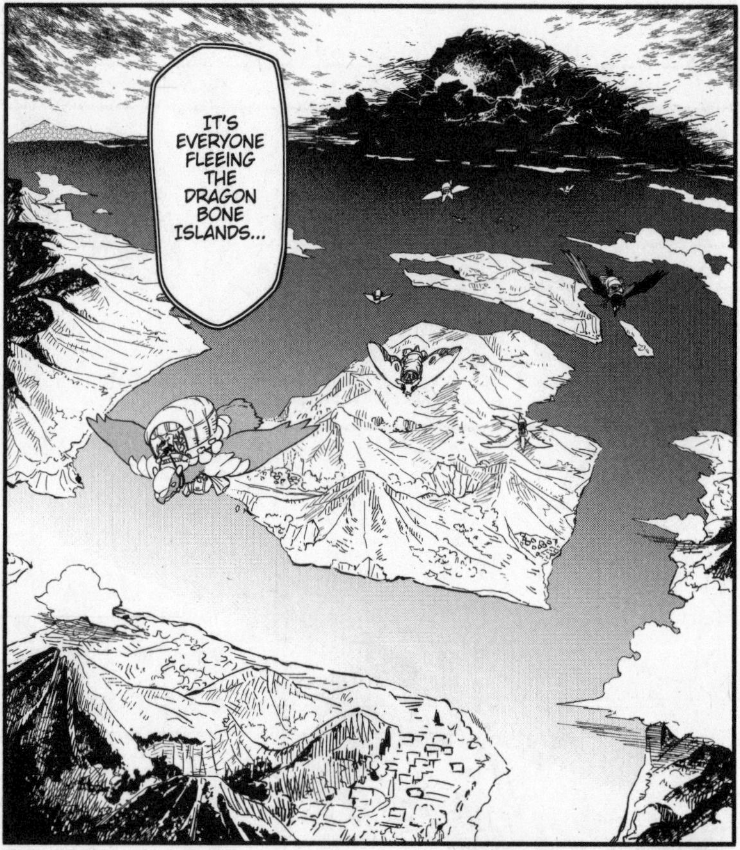
IT'S EVERYONE FLEEING THE DRAGON BONE ISLANDS...

File 70: Aval Once More

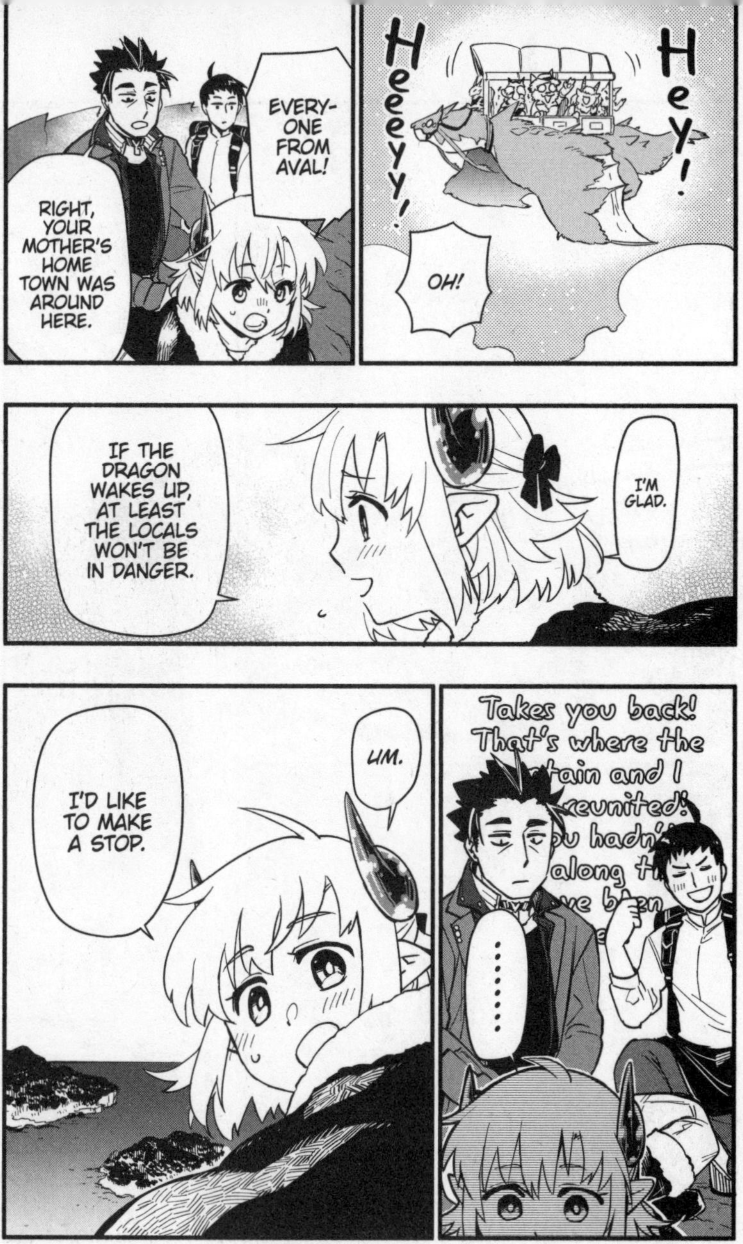
Hey!
Heeeyy!
OH!
EVERY-ONE FROM AVAL!
RIGHT, YOUR MOTHER'S HOME TOWN WAS AROUND HERE.
I'M GLAD.
IF THE DRAGON WAKES UP, AT LEAST THE LOCALS WON'T BE IN DANGER.
Takes you back! That's where the
......
UM.
I'D LIKE TO MAKE A STOP.

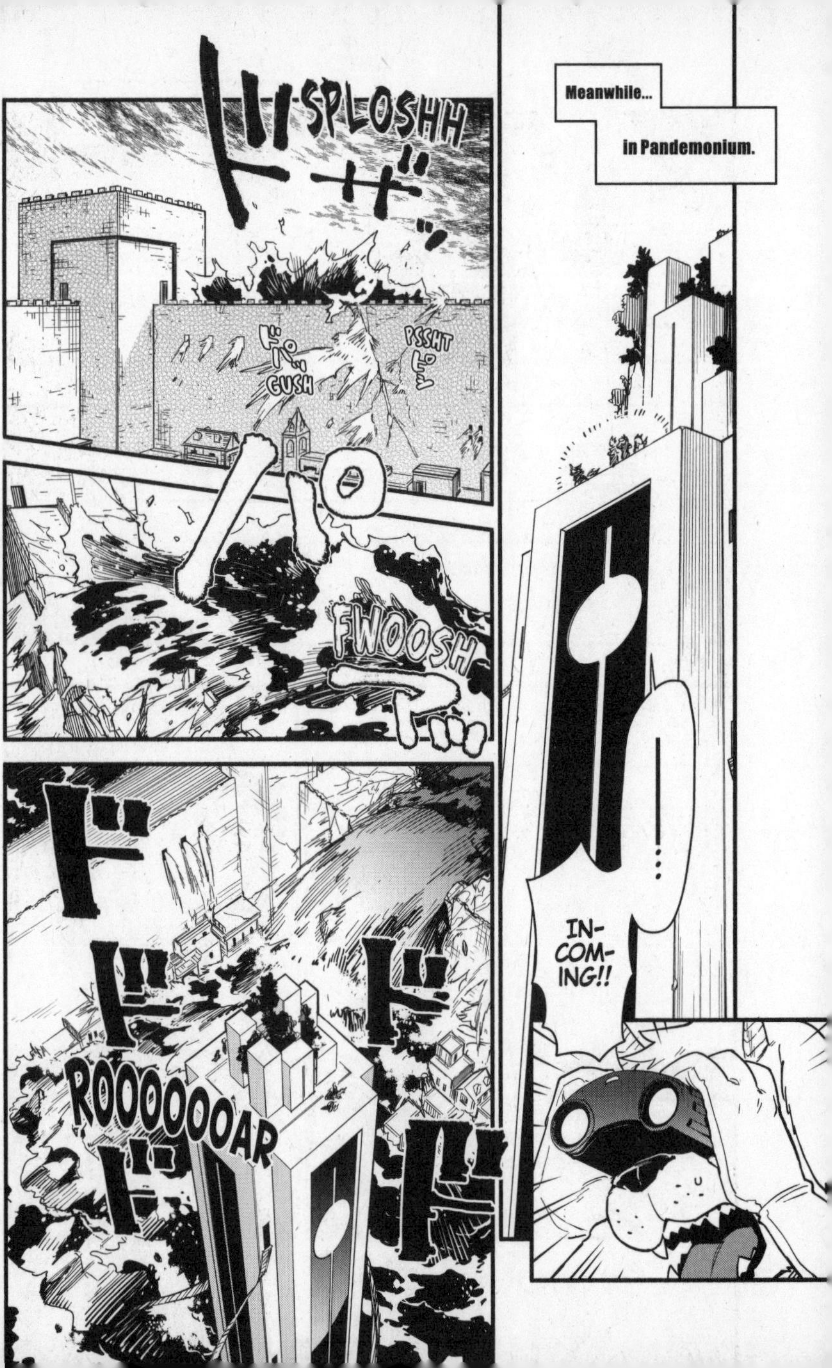

Meanwhile...
in Pandemonium.
!...
IN-COMING!!
SPLOSHH
GUSH
PSSHT
FWOOSH
ROOOOOOAR

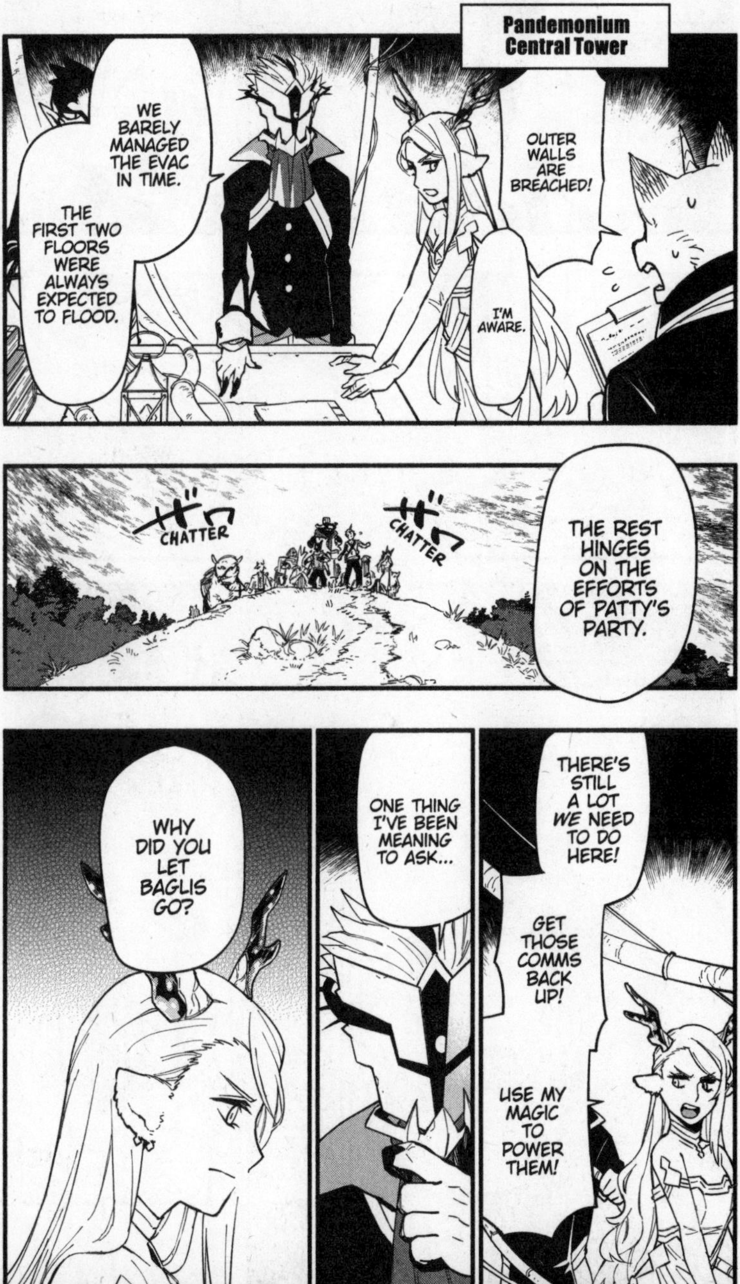
Pandemonium Central Tower
OUTER WALLS ARE BREACHED!
I'M AWARE.
WE BARELY MANAGED THE EVAC IN TIME.
THE FIRST TWO FLOORS WERE ALWAYS EXPECTED TO FLOOD.
THE REST HINGES ON THE EFFORTS OF PATTY'S PARTY.
ザワ CHATTER
ザワ CHATTER
THERE'S STILL A LOT WE NEED TO DO HERE!
GET THOSE COMMS BACK UP!
USE MY MAGIC TO POWER THEM!
ONE THING I'VE BEEN MEANING TO ASK...
WHY DID YOU LET BAGLIS GO?

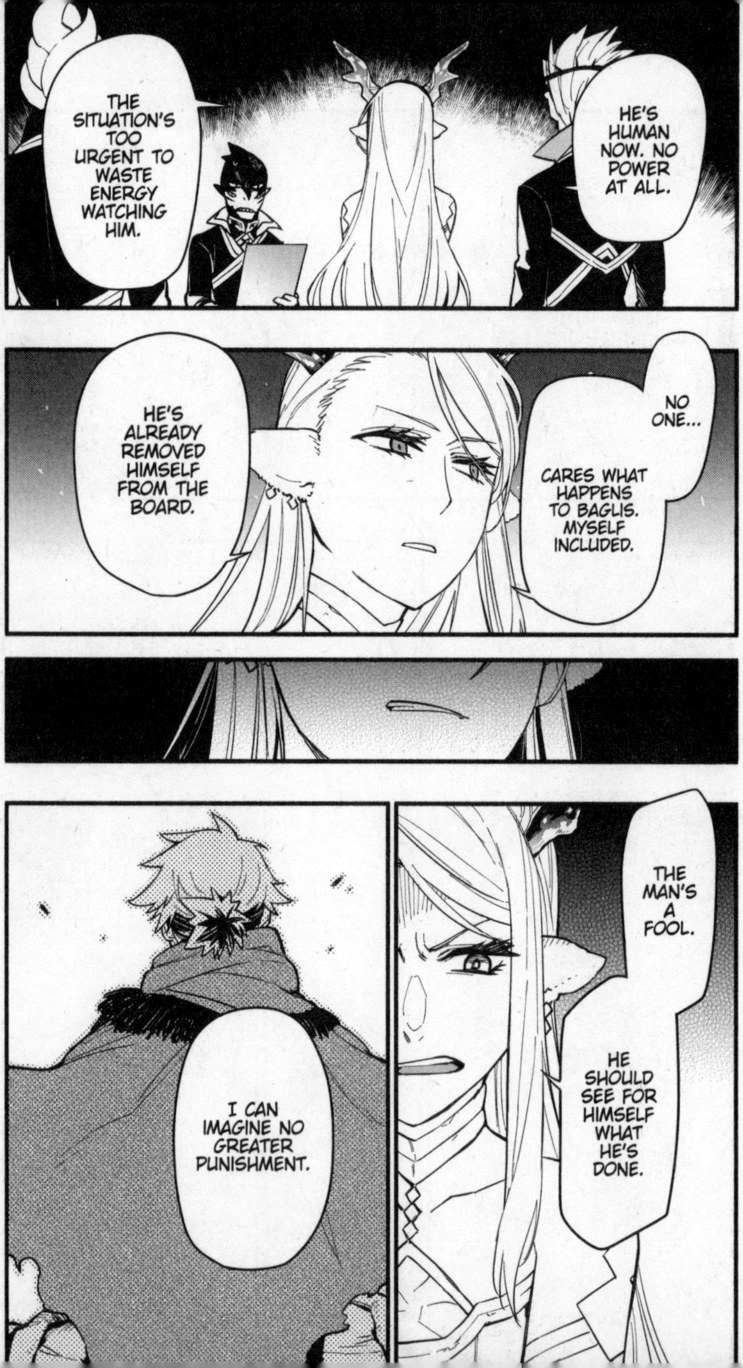
HE'S HUMAN NOW. NO POWER AT ALL.
THE SITUATION'S TOO URGENT TO WASTE ENERGY WATCHING HIM.
NO ONE...
CARES WHAT HAPPENS TO BAGLIS. MYSELF INCLUDED.
HE'S ALREADY REMOVED HIMSELF FROM THE BOARD.
THE MAN'S A FOOL.
HE SHOULD SEE FOR HIMSELF WHAT HE'S DONE.
I CAN IMAGINE NO GREATER PUNISHMENT.

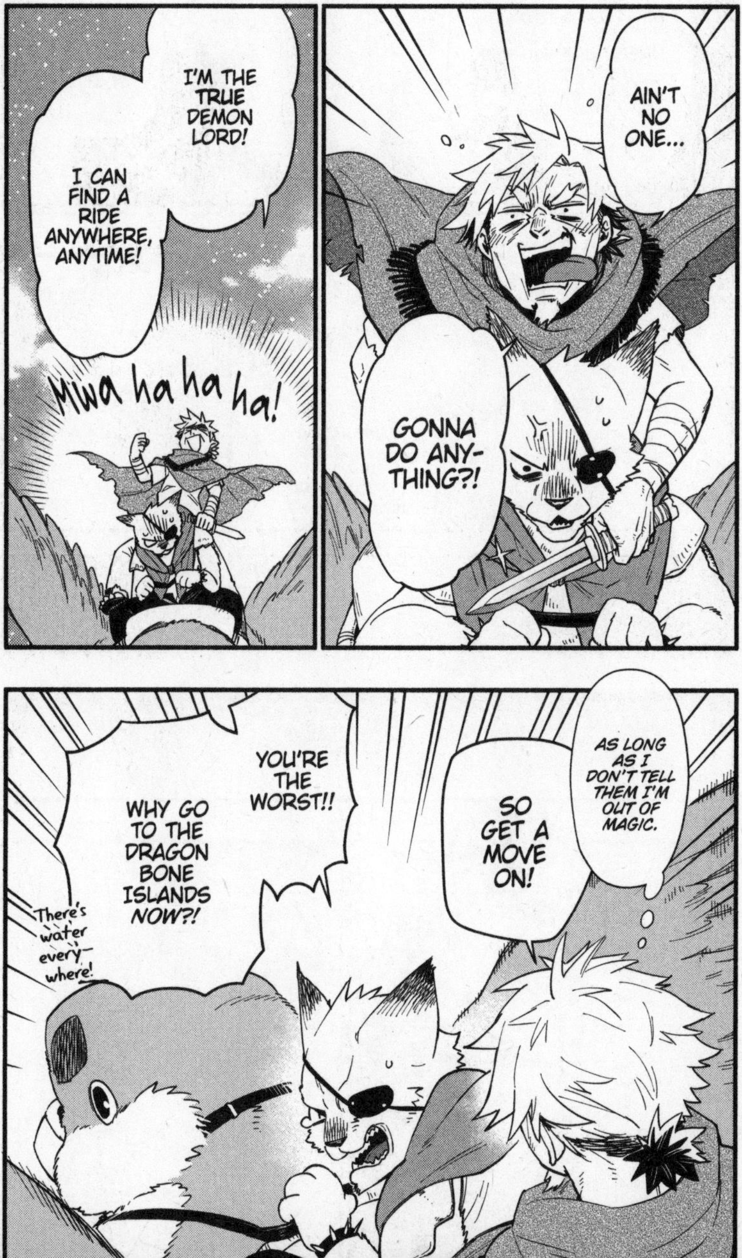
AIN'T NO ONE...
GONNA DO ANY-THING?!
I'M THE TRUE DEMON LORD!
I CAN FIND A RIDE ANYWHERE, ANYTIME!
Mwa ha ha ha ha!
AS LONG AS I DON'T TELL THEM I'M OUT OF MAGIC.
SO GET A MOVE ON!
YOU'RE THE WORST!!
WHY GO TO THE DRAGON BONE ISLANDS NOW?!
There's water every-where!

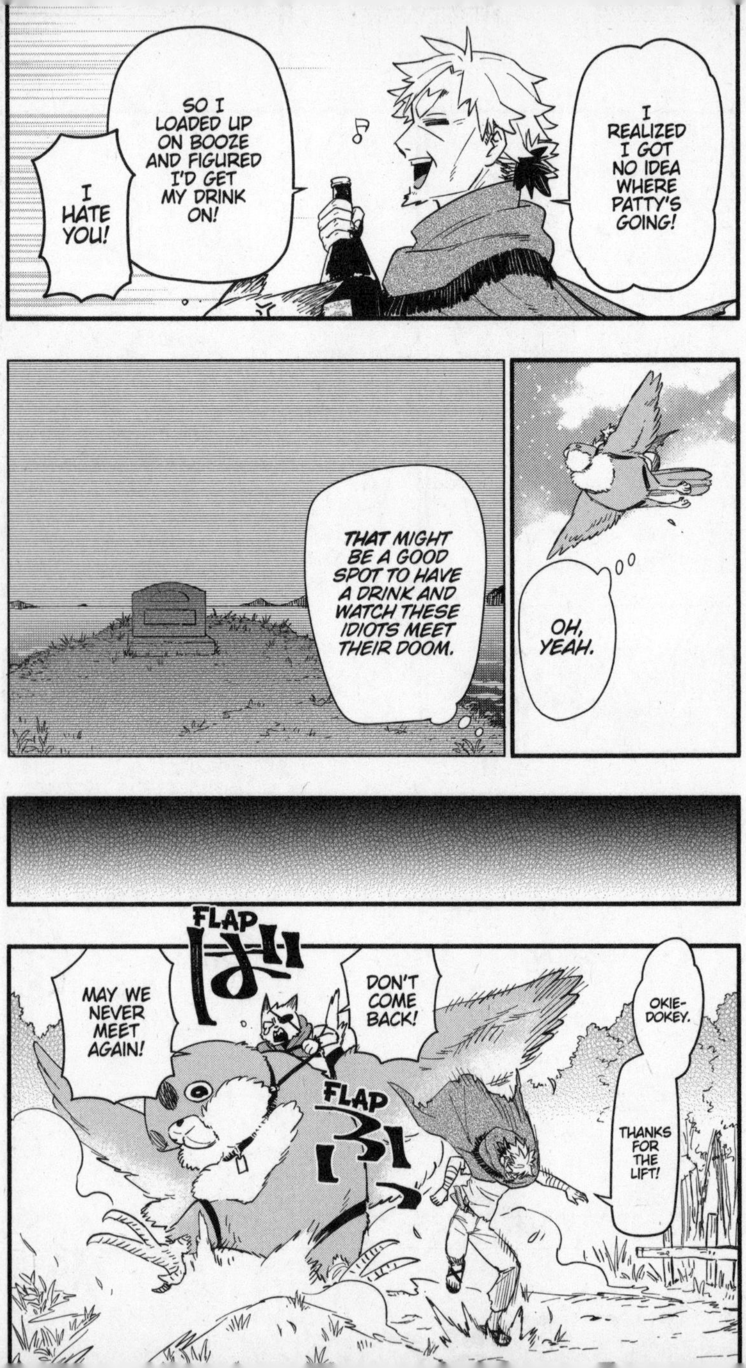
I REALIZED I GOT NO IDEA WHERE PATTY'S GOING!
SO I LOADED UP ON BOOZE AND FIGURED I'D GET MY DRINK ON!
I HATE YOU!
OH, YEAH.
THAT MIGHT BE A GOOD SPOT TO HAVE A DRINK AND WATCH THESE IDIOTS MEET THEIR DOOM.
OKIE-DOKEY.
THANKS FOR THE LIFT!
DON'T COME BACK!
FLAP
FLAP
MAY WE NEVER MEET AGAIN!

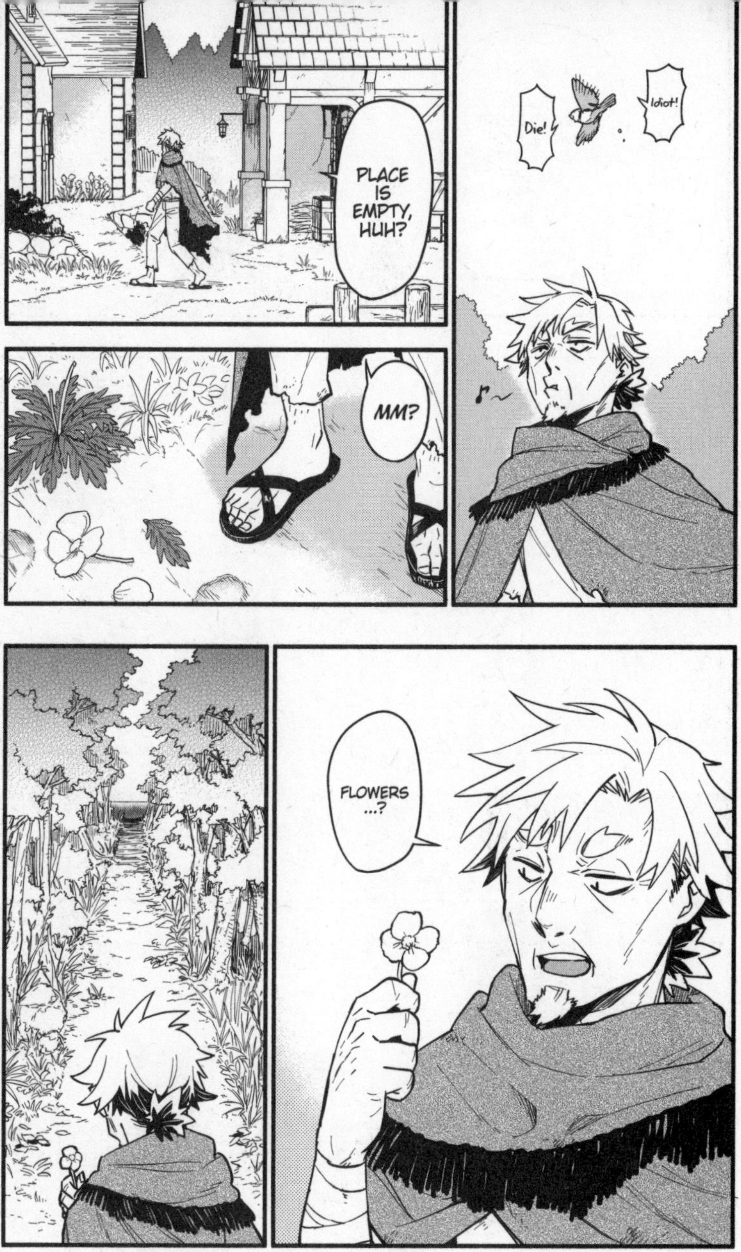
Idiot!
Die!
PLACE IS EMPTY, HUH?
MM?
FLOWERS ...?

I'M SORRY, MOM.

LAST TIME WE CAME, WE DIDN'T HAVE TIME TO VISIT.

CAUSE YOUR DAD'S MAGIC SENT US FLYING!

THAT WAS THE WORST.

THE DEVIL WORLD'S ABOUT TO END.

WE'VE BEEN TOO BUSY TO DWELL ON IT...

BUT WE MADE IT BACK.

AND I JUST DON'T KNOW WHAT TO TELL YOU.

BUT I'VE GOT NO IDEA...

WHAT TO DO ABOUT DAD.

HUH?

RUSTLE

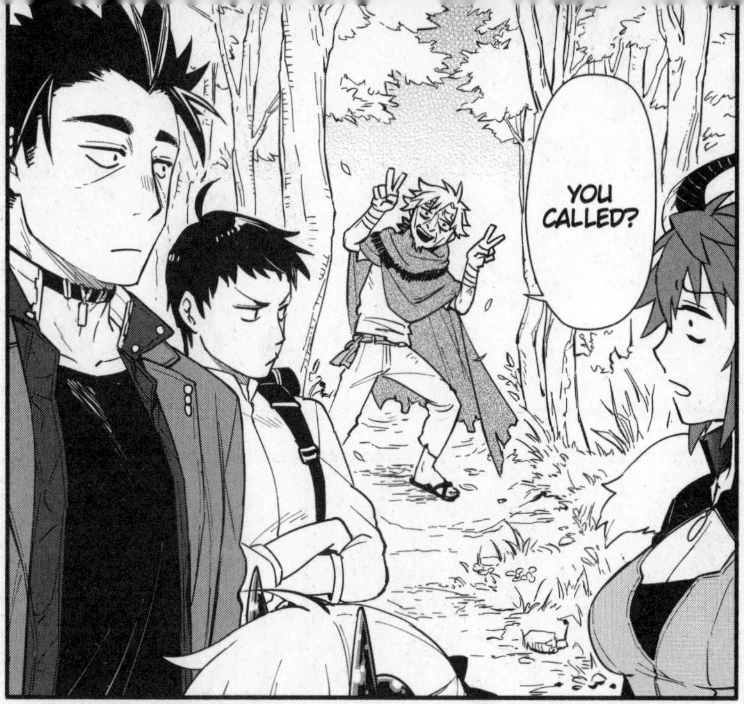
YOU CALLED?
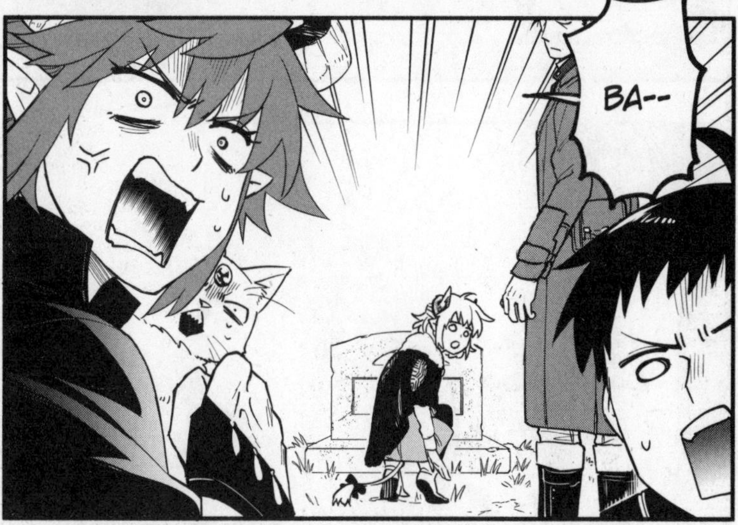
BA--

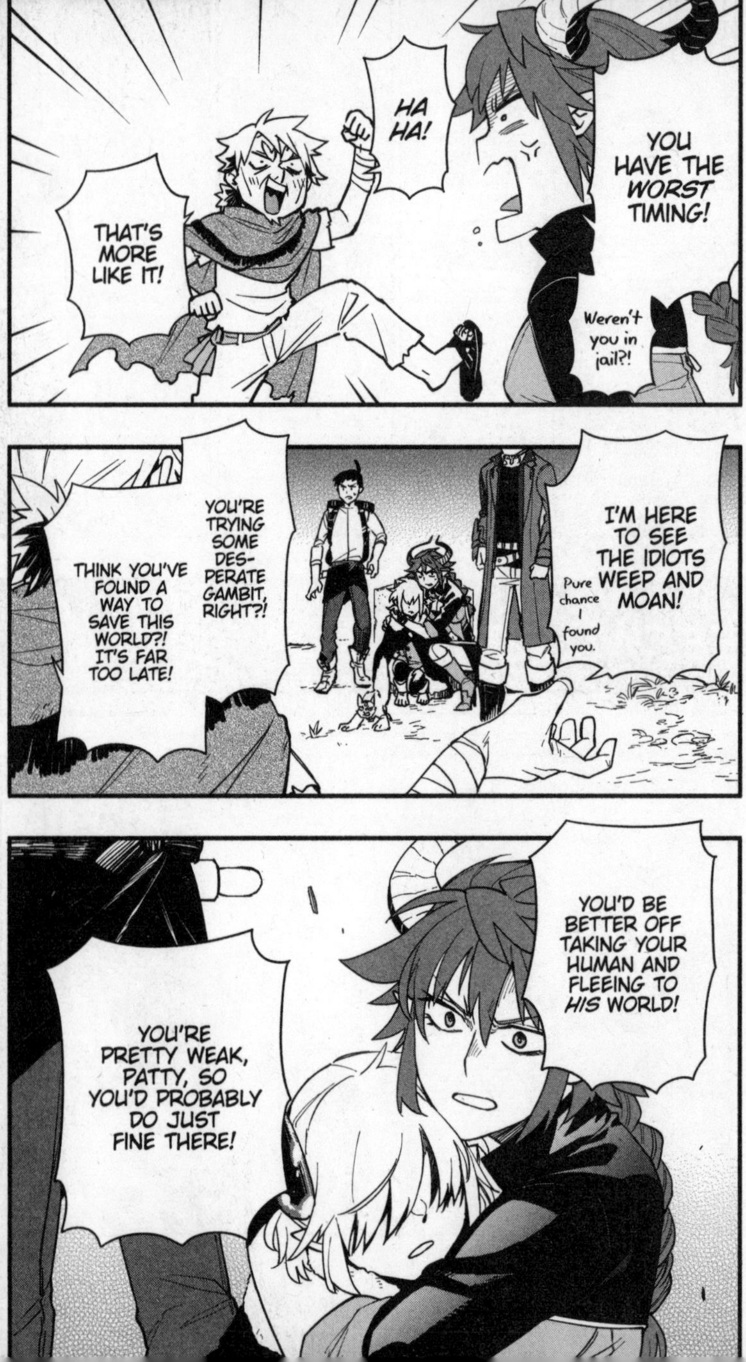
YOU HAVE THE WORST TIMING!
HA HA!
THAT'S MORE LIKE IT!
Weren't you in jail?!
I'M HERE TO SEE THE IDIOTS WEEP AND MOAN!
Pure chance I found you.
YOU'RE TRYING SOME DESPERATE GAMBIT, RIGHT?!
THINK YOU'VE FOUND A WAY TO SAVE THIS WORLD?! IT'S FAR TOO LATE!
YOU'D BE BETTER OFF TAKING YOUR HUMAN AND FLEEING TO HIS WORLD!
YOU'RE PRETTY WEAK, PATTY, SO YOU'D PROBABLY DO JUST FINE THERE!

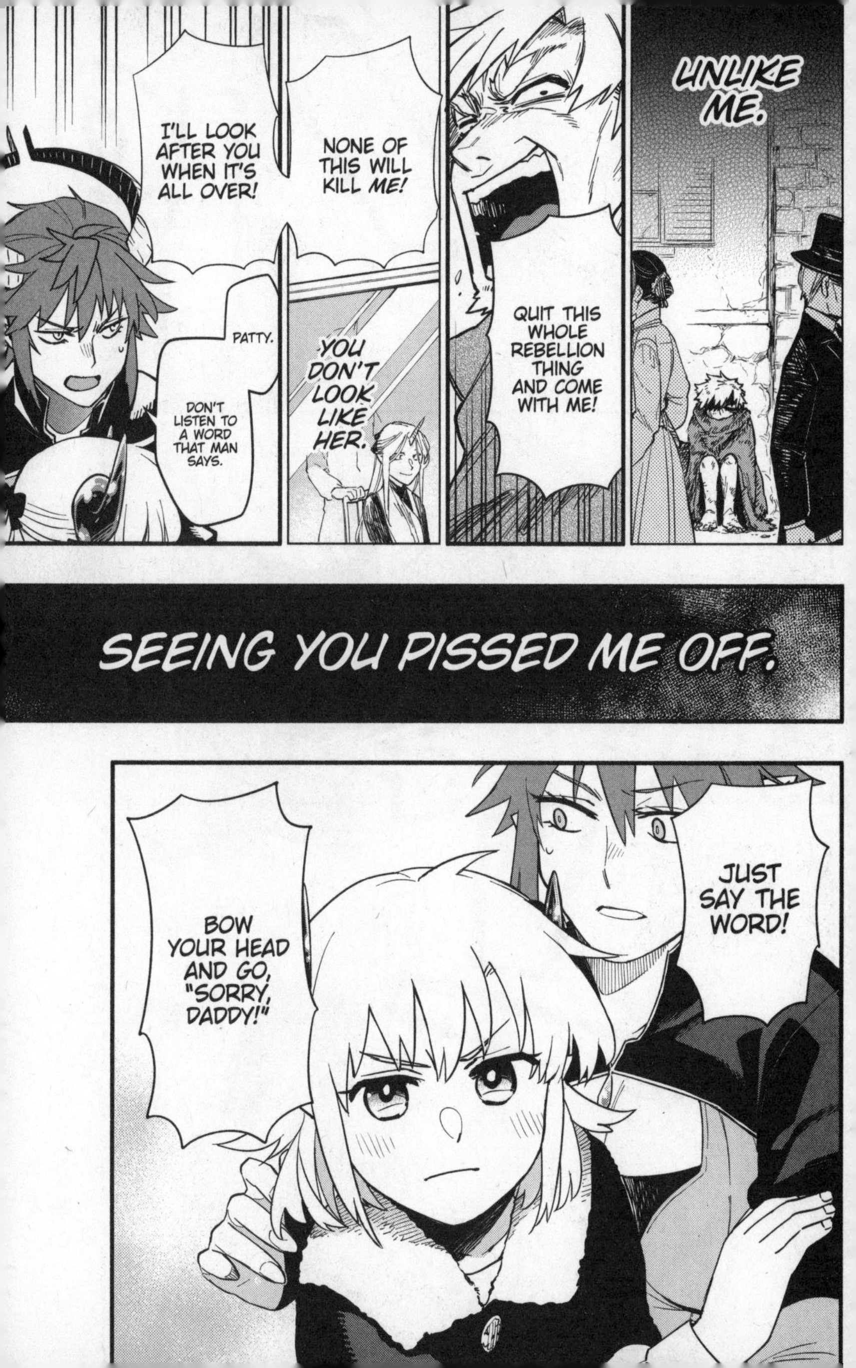
UNLIKE ME.
QUIT THIS WHOLE REBELLION THING AND COME WITH ME!
NONE OF THIS WILL KILL ME!
YOU DON'T LOOK LIKE HER.
I'LL LOOK AFTER YOU WHEN IT'S ALL OVER!
PATTY.
DON'T LISTEN TO A WORD THAT MAN SAYS.
SEEING YOU PISSED ME OFF.
JUST SAY THE WORD!
BOW YOUR HEAD AND GO, "SORRY, DADDY!"

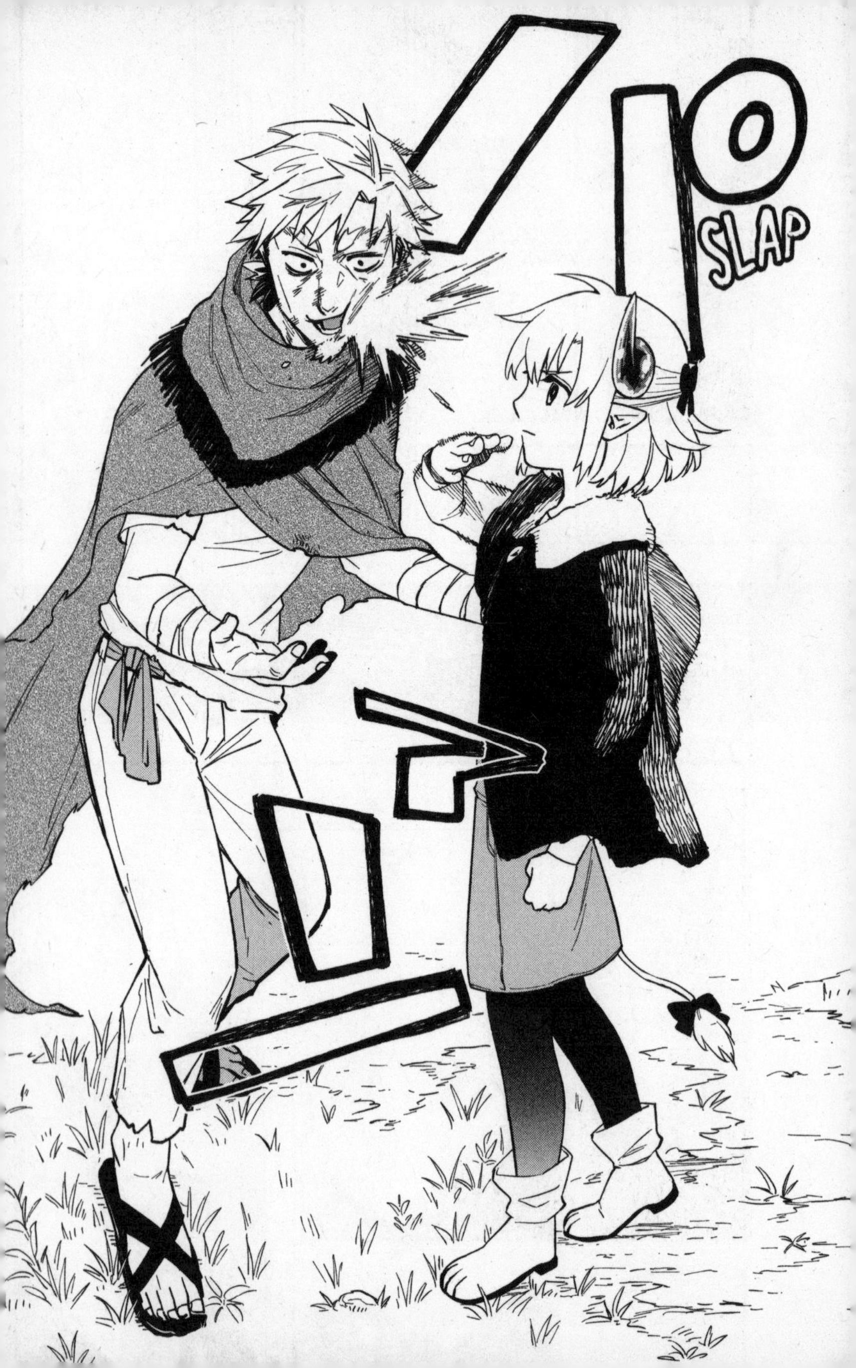
SLAP

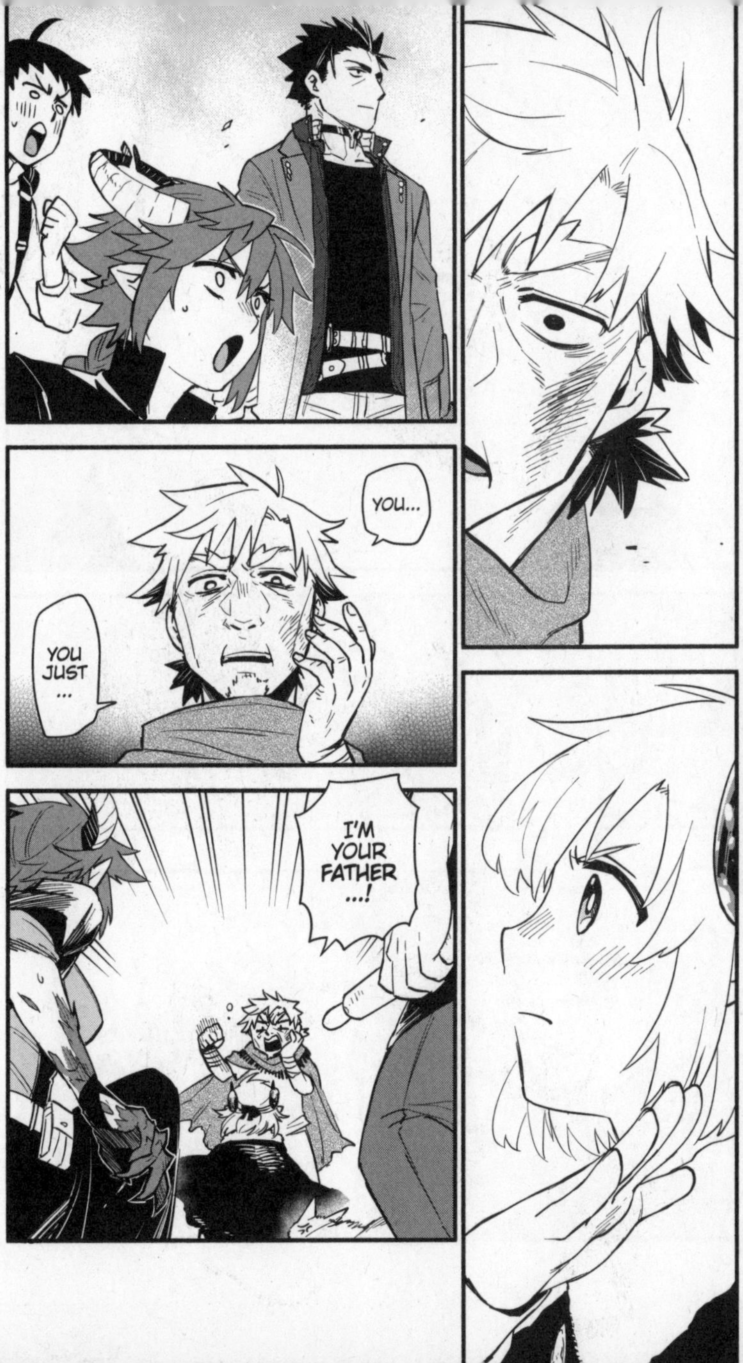
YOU...
YOU JUST ...
I'M YOUR FATHER ...!

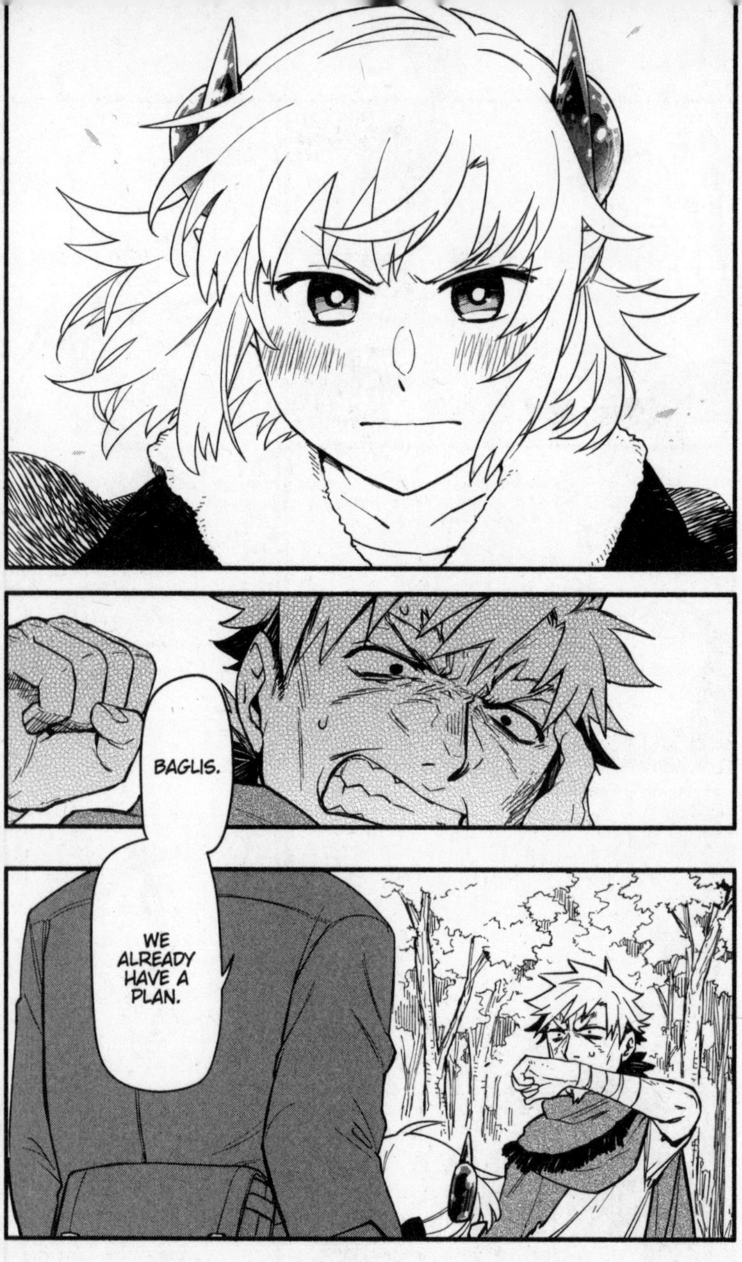
BAGLIS.
WE ALREADY HAVE A PLAN.

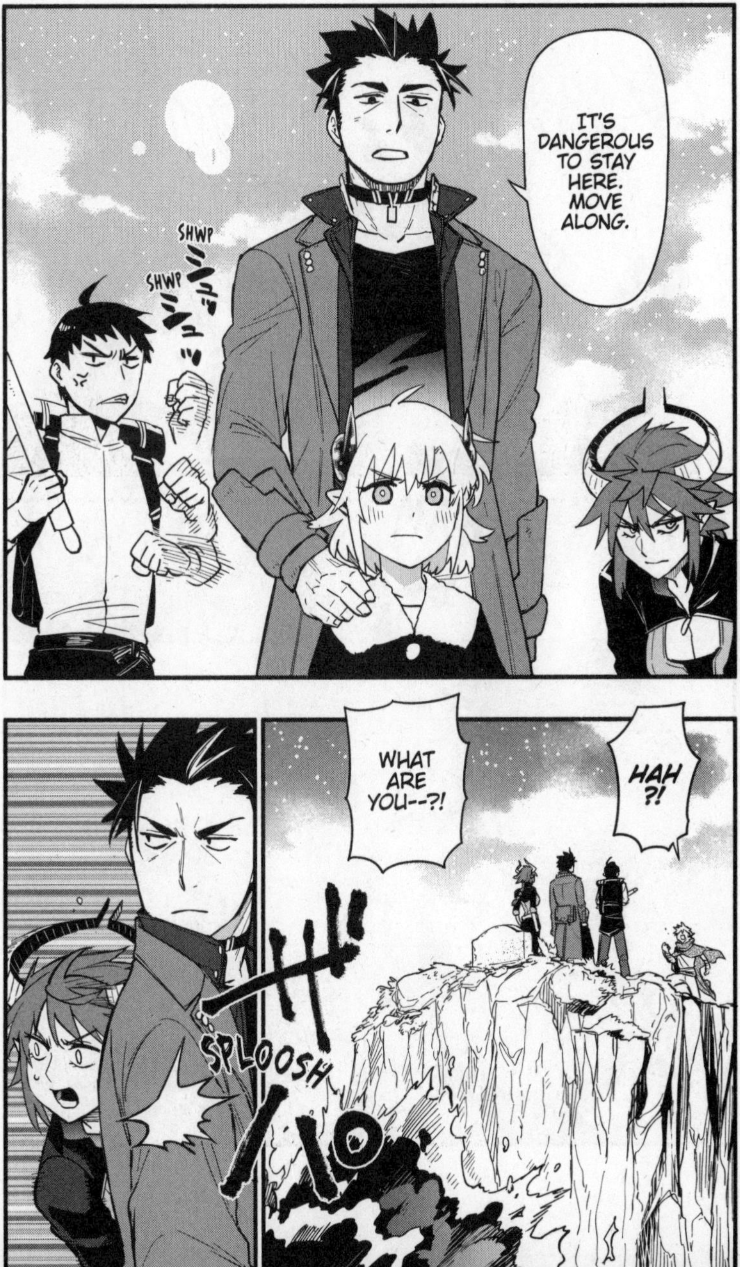
IT'S DANGEROUS TO STAY HERE. MOVE ALONG.
SHWP シュッ
SHWP シュッ
HAH?!
WHAT ARE YOU--?!
SPLOOSH

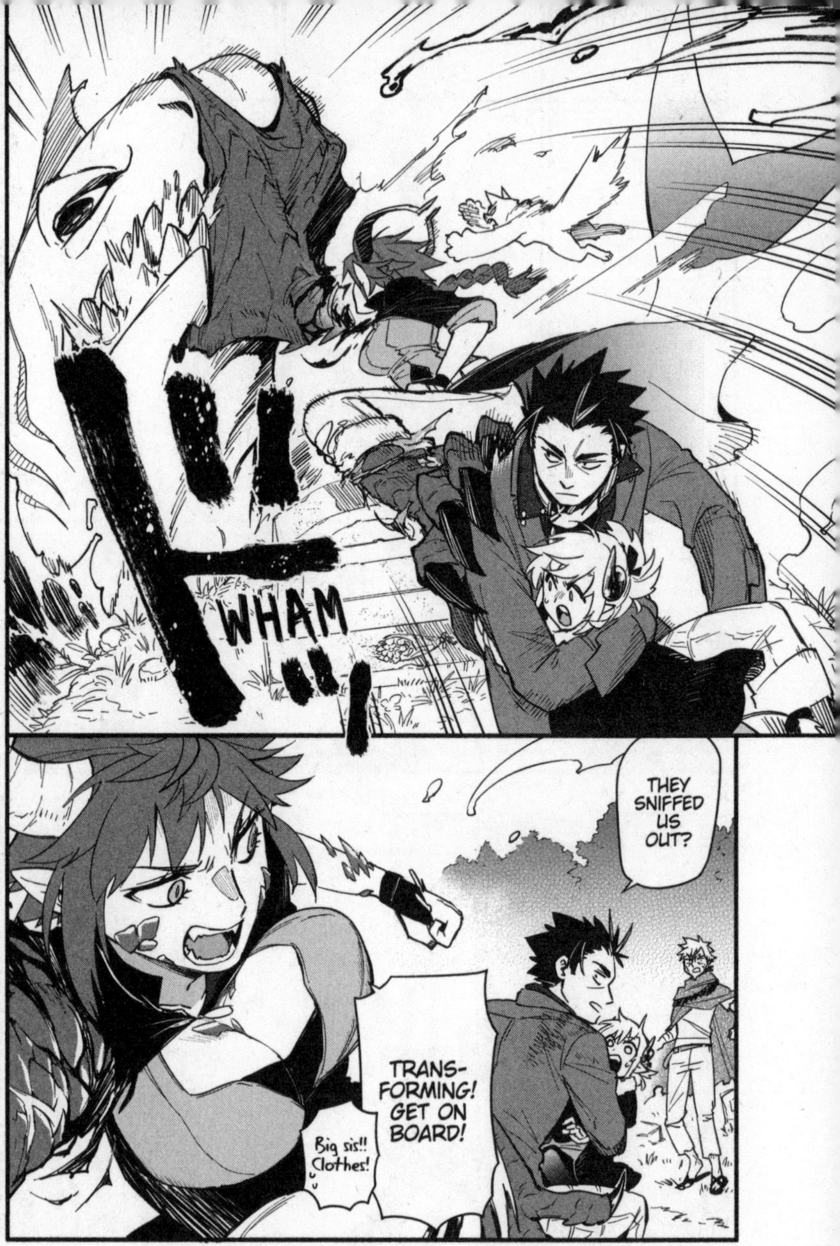
WHAM
THEY SNIFFED US OUT?
TRANS-FORMING! GET ON BOARD!
Big sis!! Clothes!

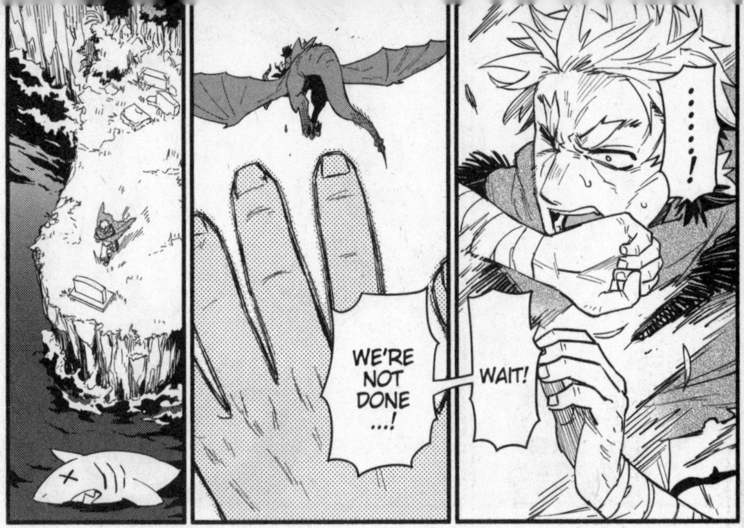
......!
WAIT!
WE'RE NOT DONE ...!

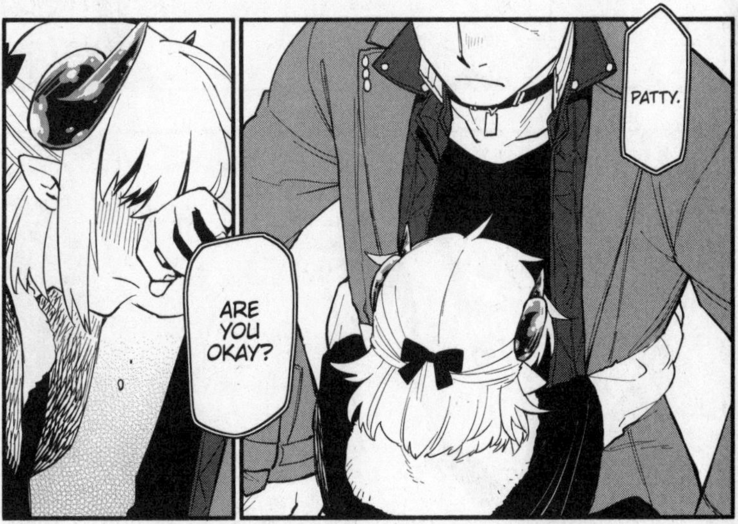
PATTY.
ARE YOU OKAY?

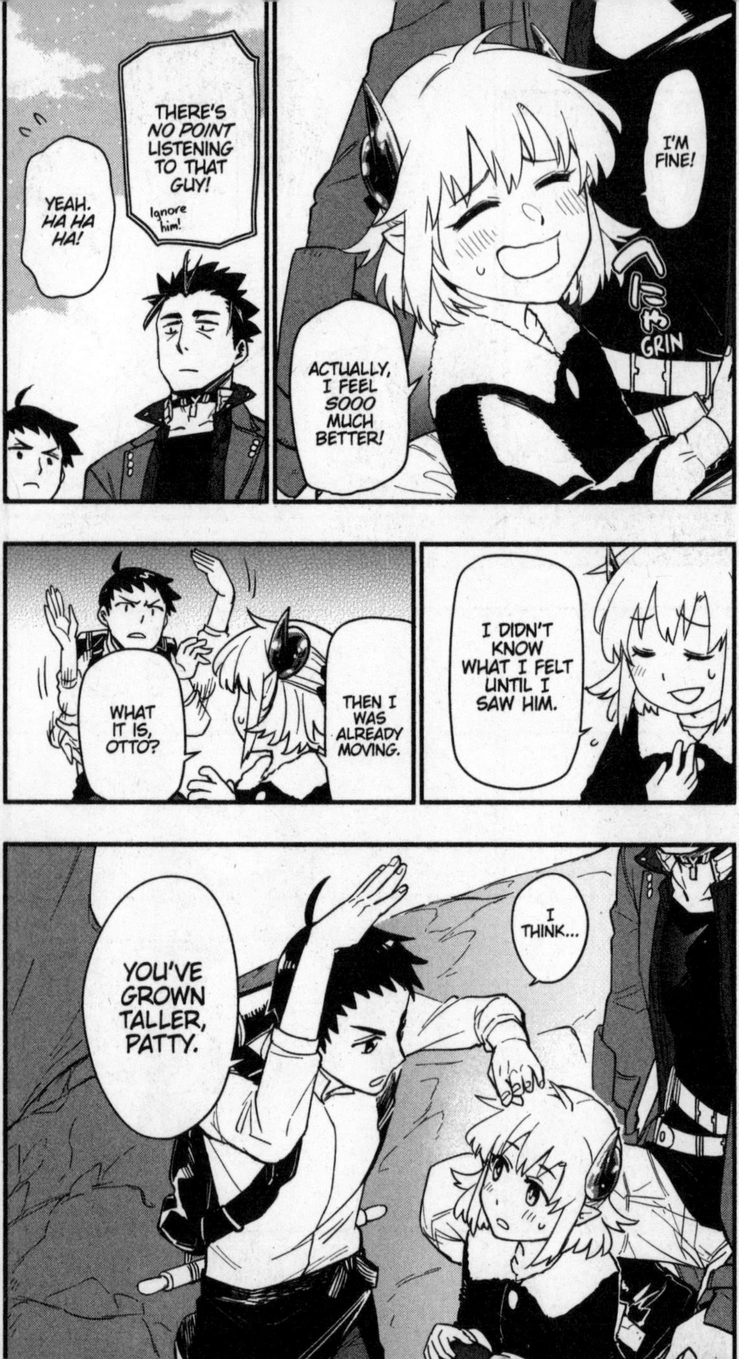
I'M FINE!
GRIN
ACTUALLY, I FEEL SOOO MUCH BETTER!
THERE'S NO POINT LISTENING TO THAT GUY!
Ignore him!
YEAH. HA HA HA!
I DIDN'T KNOW WHAT I FELT UNTIL I SAW HIM.
THEN I WAS ALREADY MOVING.
WHAT IT IS, OTTO?
I THINK...
YOU'VE GROWN TALLER, PATTY.

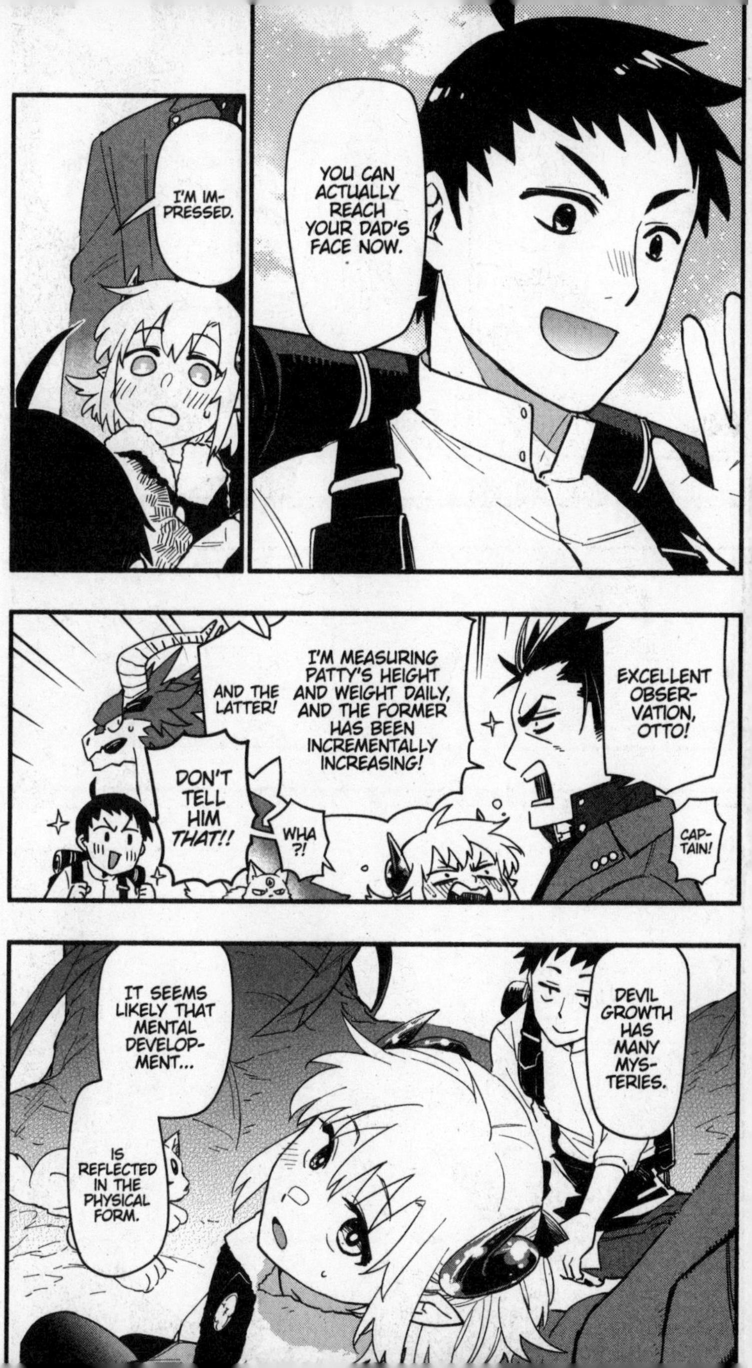
YOU CAN ACTUALLY REACH YOUR DAD'S FACE NOW.
I'M IMPRESSED.
EXCELLENT OBSERVATION, OTTO!
CAPTAIN!
I'M MEASURING PATTY'S HEIGHT AND WEIGHT DAILY, AND THE FORMER HAS BEEN INCREMENTALLY INCREASING!
AND THE LATTER!
DON'T TELL HIM *THAT!!*
WHA ?!
DEVIL GROWTH HAS MANY MYSTERIES.
IT SEEMS LIKELY THAT MENTAL DEVELOPMENT...
IS REFLECTED IN THE PHYSICAL FORM.

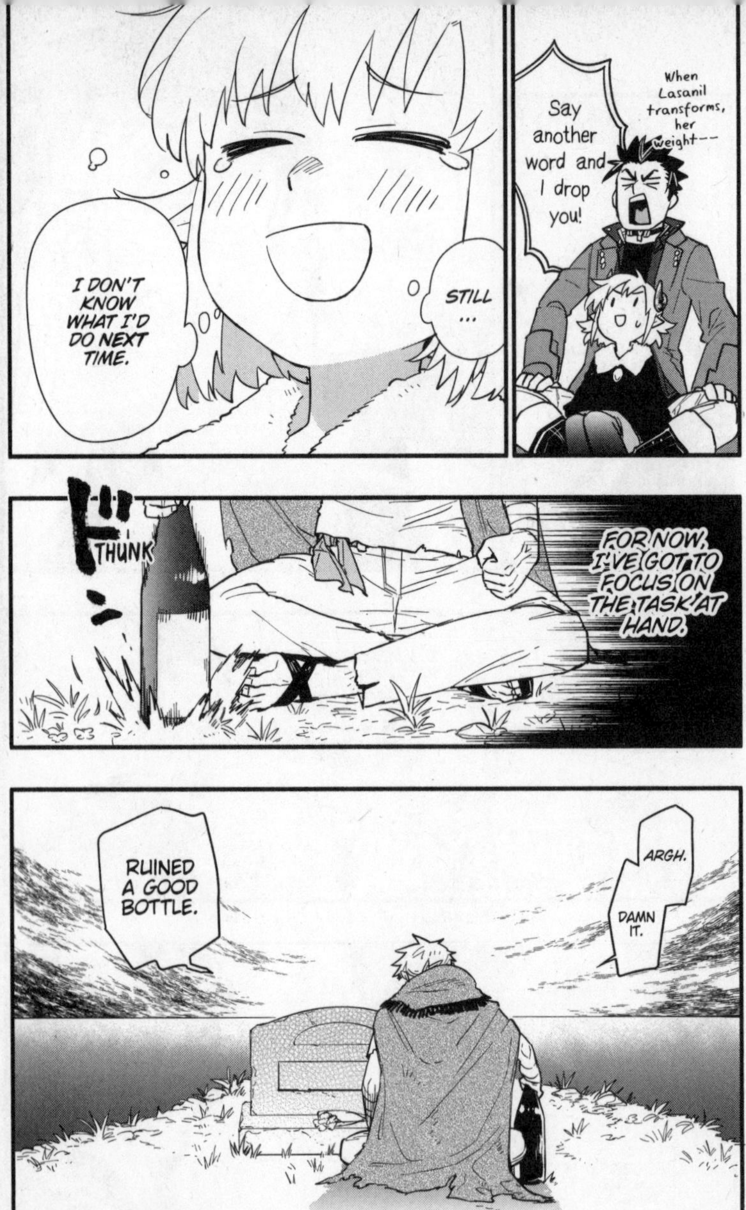
When Lasanil transforms, her weight--
Say another word and I drop you!
STILL ...
I DON'T KNOW WHAT I'D DO NEXT TIME.
FOR NOW, I'VE GOT TO FOCUS ON THE TASK AT HAND.
THUNK
ARGH.
DAMN IT.
RUINED A GOOD BOTTLE.

To be continued!

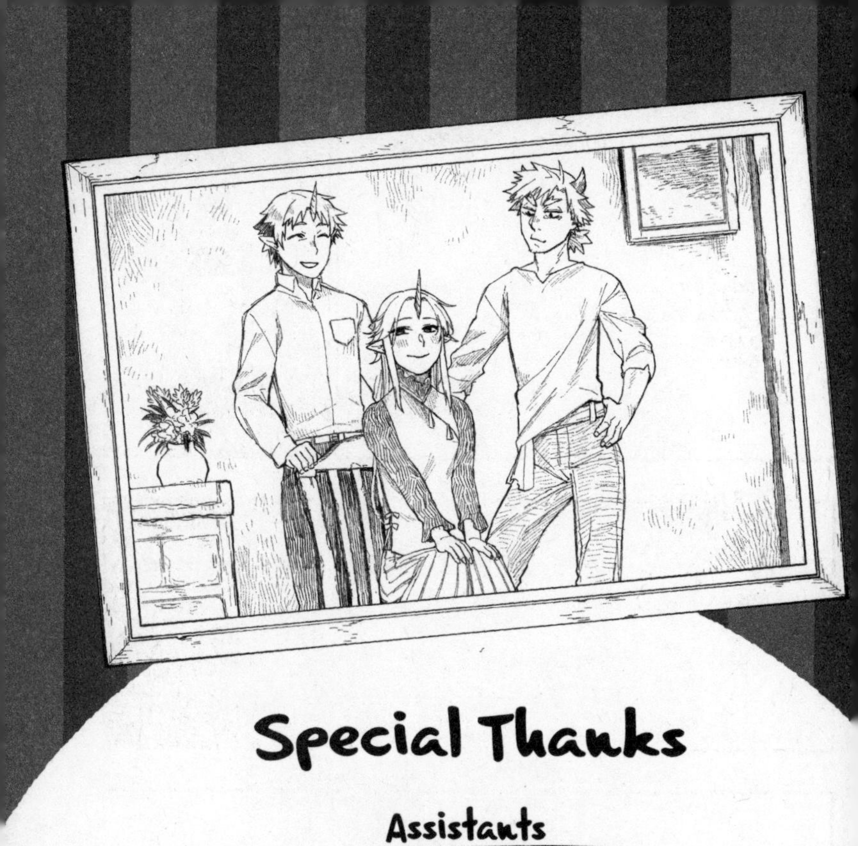

Special Thanks

Assistants

Kuroichi-san, Nanami-san,
Kaku-san, Tsukishima-san

Editor

F-san, M-san, T-san

Design/Logo

Sugita-san

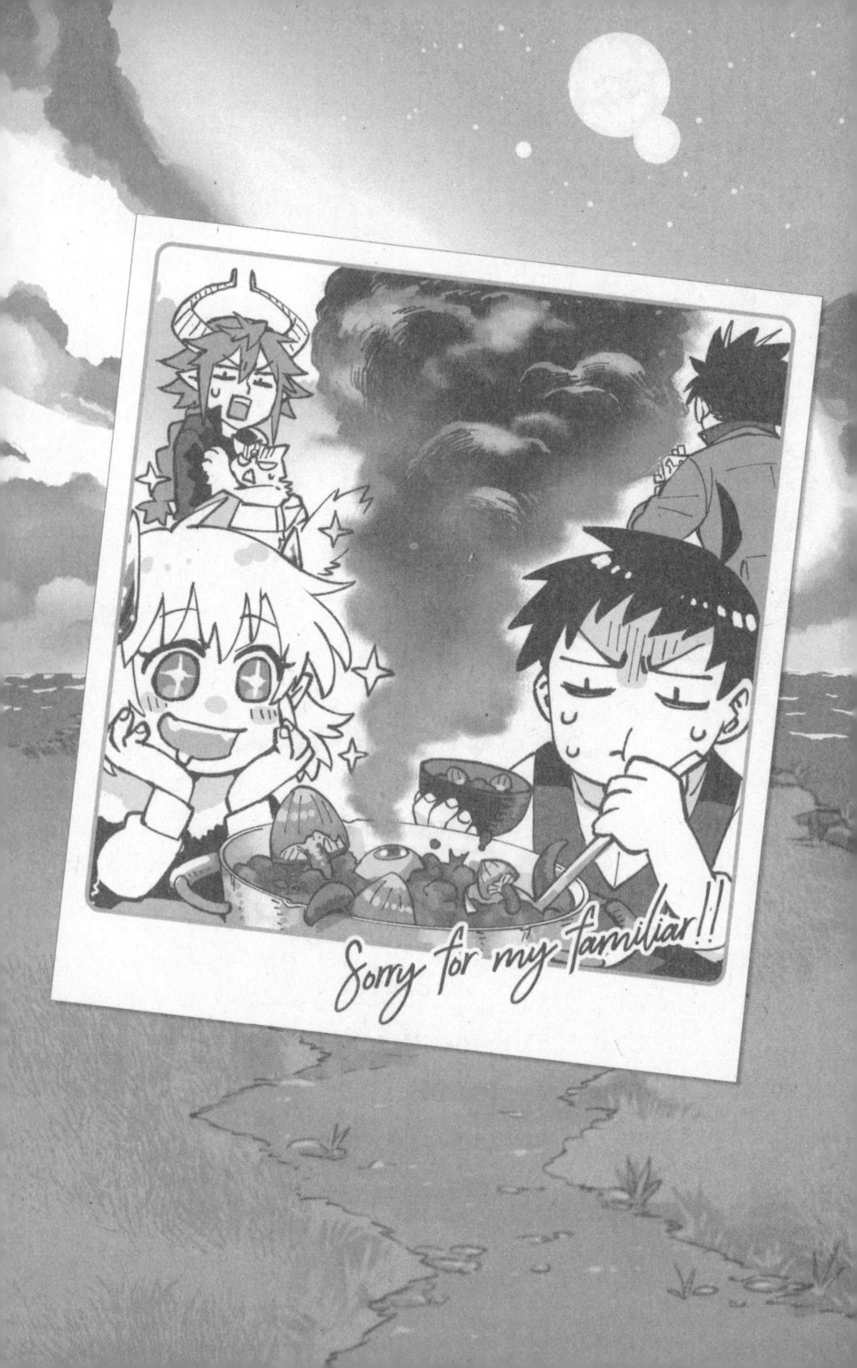
Sorry for my familiar!!

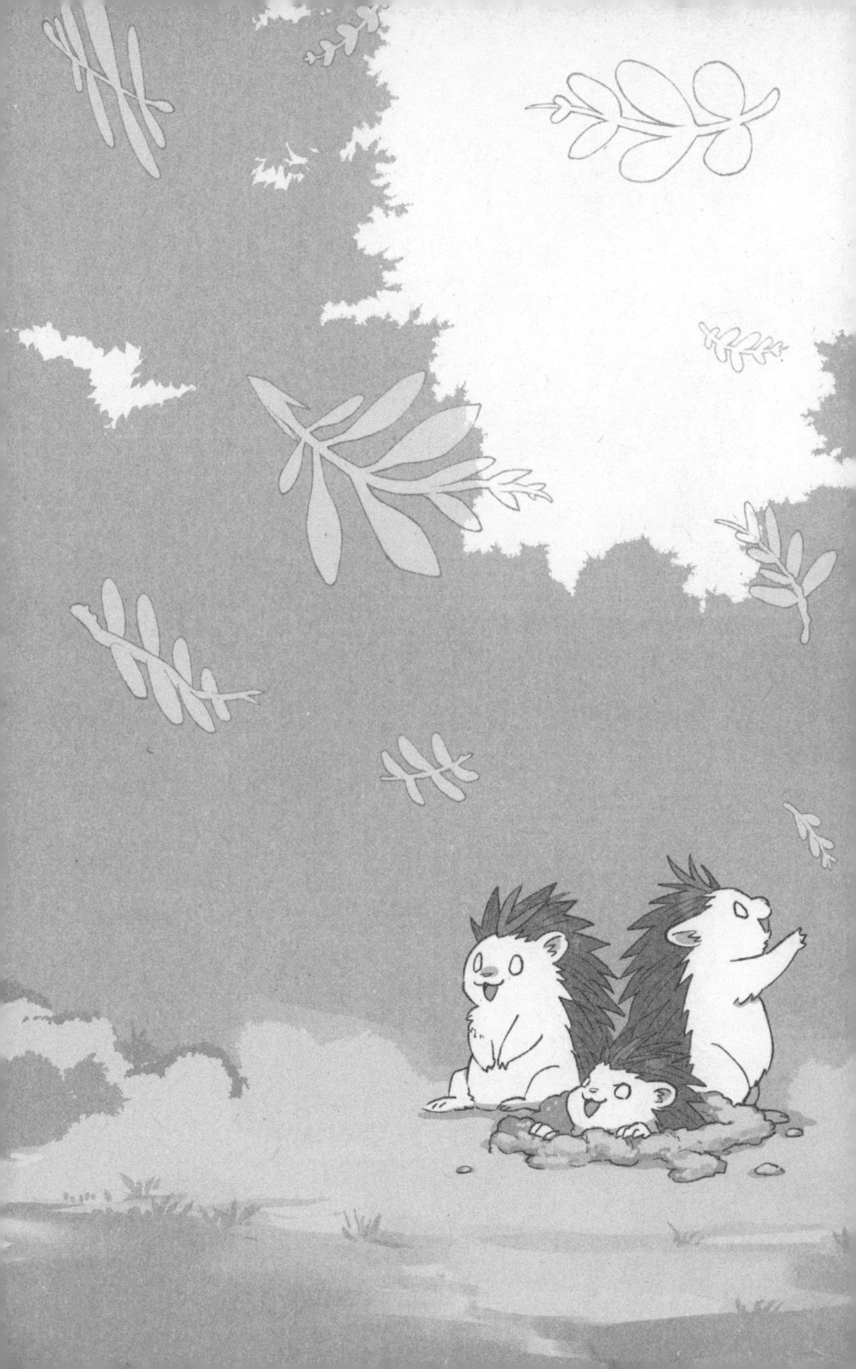

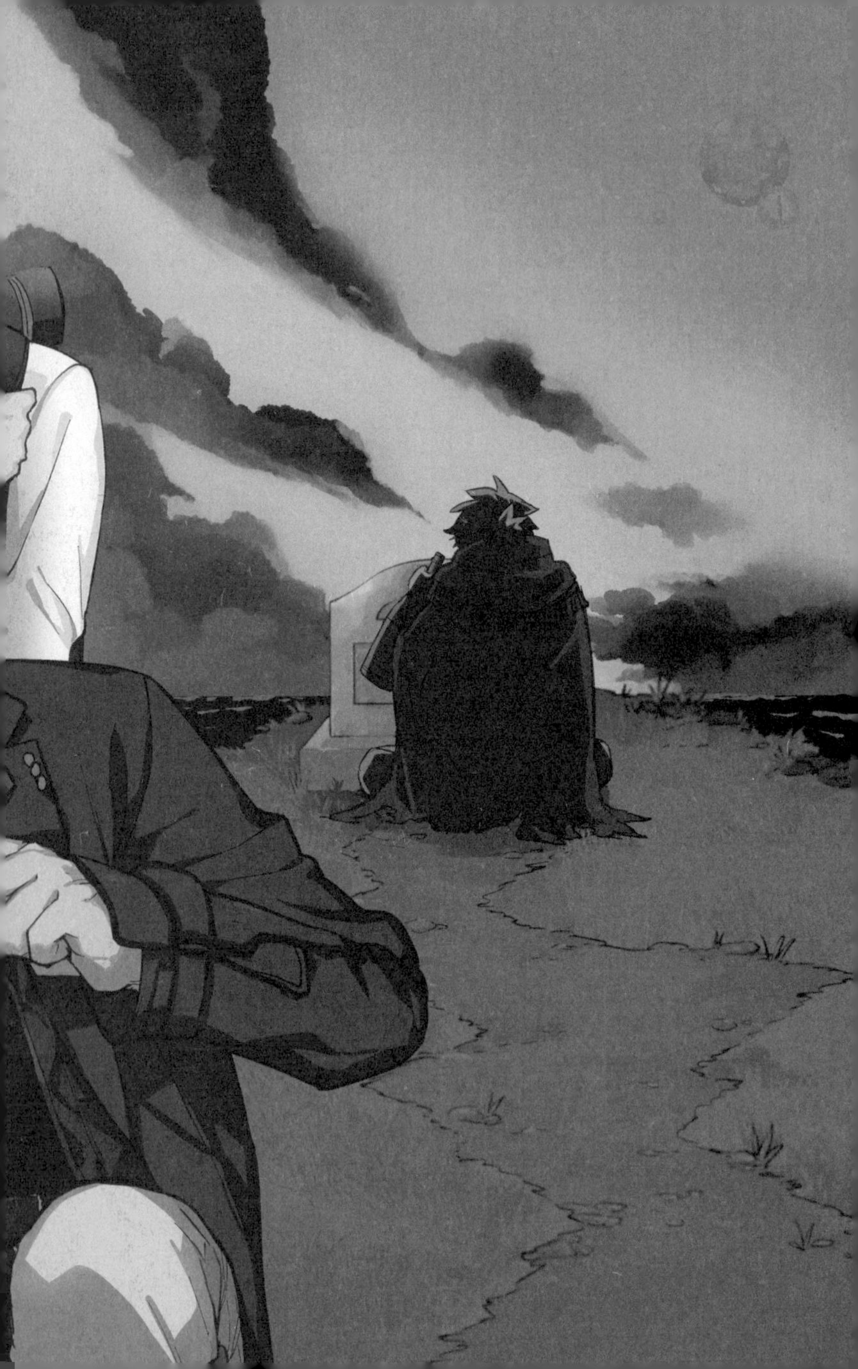

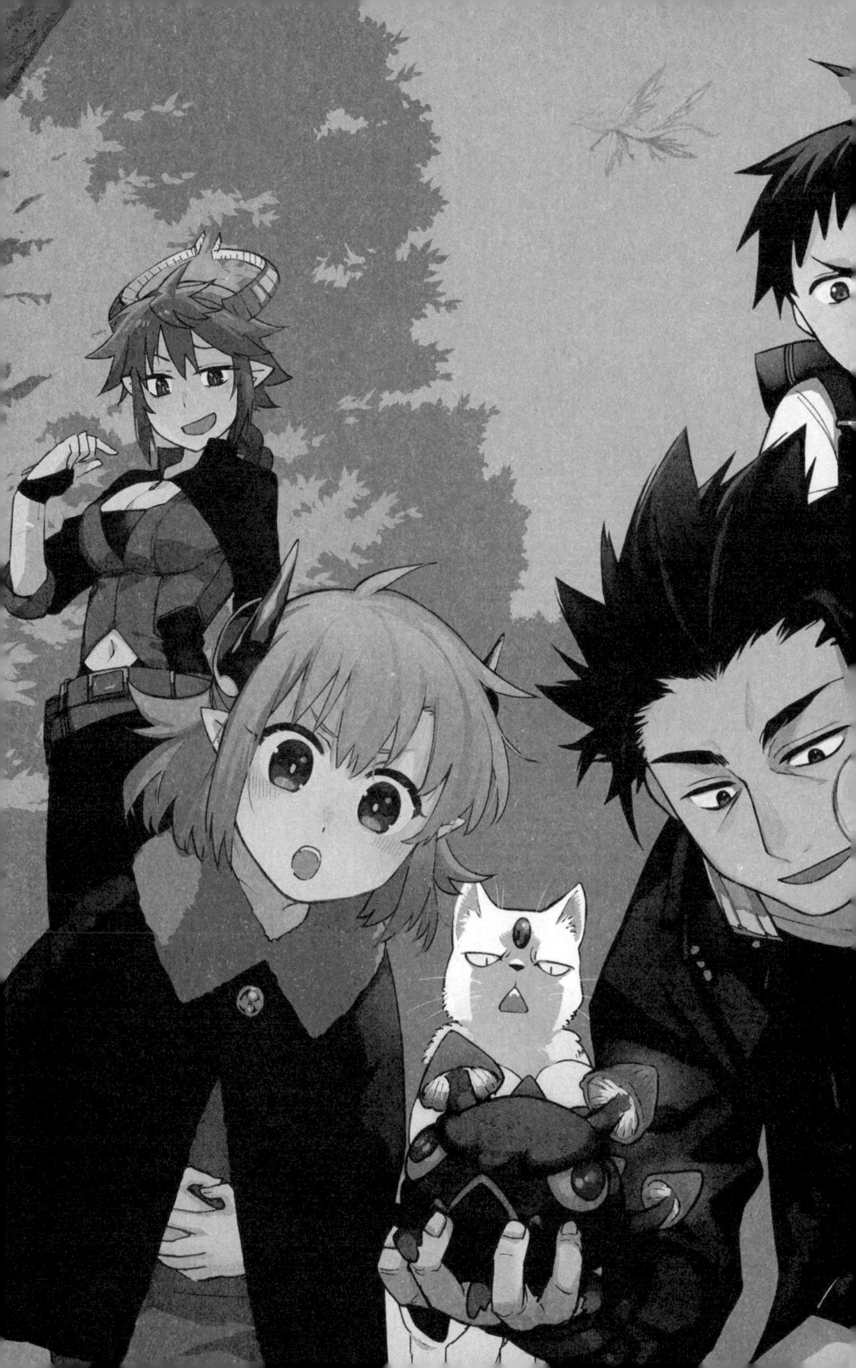

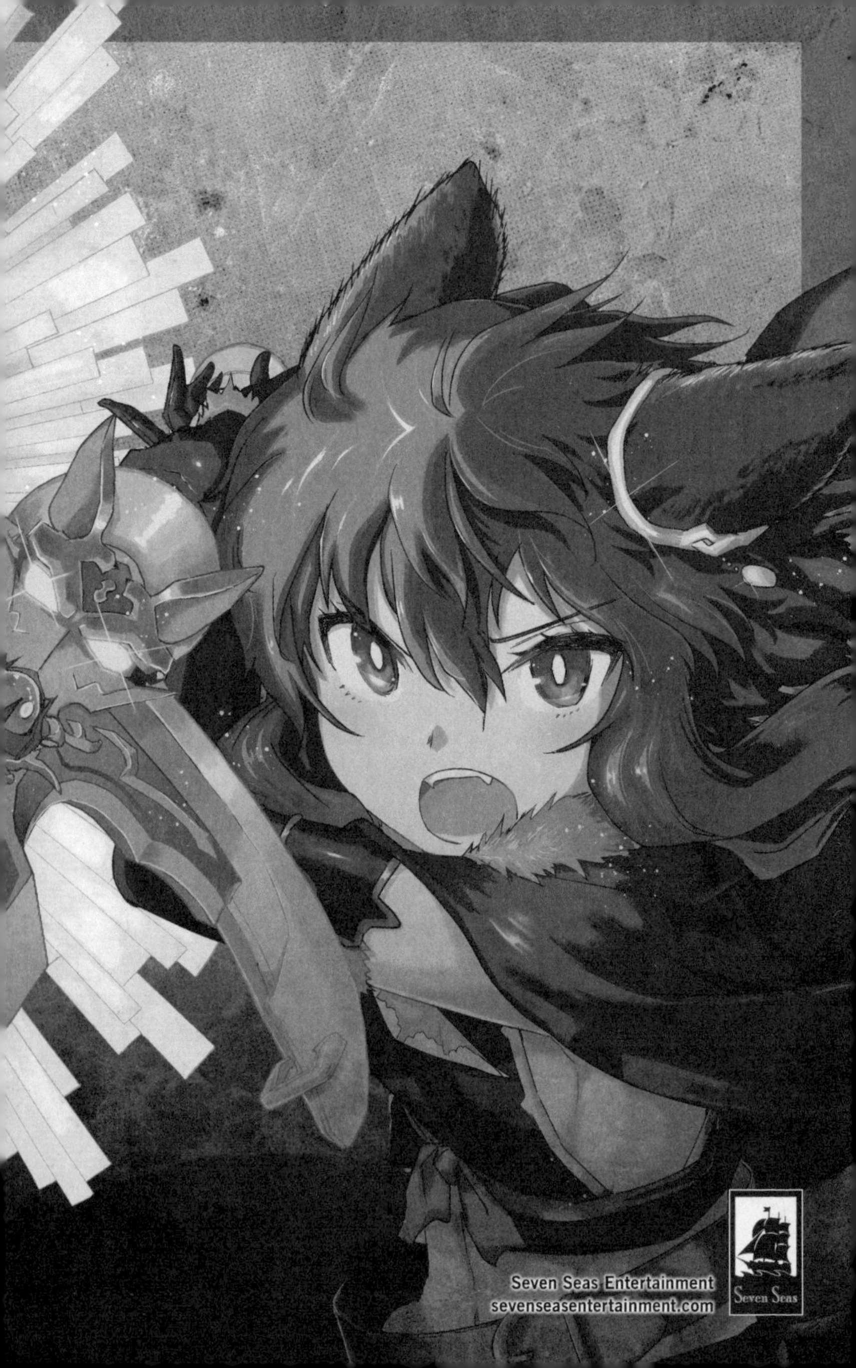
Seven Seas Entertainment
sevenseasentertainment.com
Seven Seas

Let your imagination take flight with Seven Seas Entertainment's light novel imprint

A Tale of the **Secret Saint**

NOVEL 1

Touya

NOVEL 1

I'M THE **EVIL LORD** OF AN **INTERGALACTIC EMPIRE**

WRITTEN BY Yomu Mishima
ILLUSTRATED BY Nadare Takamine

PLANET OF THE **ORCS**

Himataro Zukunashi

NOVEL 1

THE MOST **NOTORIOUS** [TALKER] RUNS THE WORLD'S GREATEST CLAN

WRITTEN BY jaki
ILLUSTRATED BY fame

THE NPCs IN THIS VILLAGE SIM GAME MUST BE REAL!

Written by HIRUKUMA
Illustrated by NAMAKO

NOVEL 01

NOVEL 1

She **Professed Herself Pupil** of the **Wise Man**

Written by Ryusen Hirotsugu
fuzichoco

SEVEN SEAS ENTERTAINMENT PRESENTS

Sorry For My Familiar

story and art by **TEKKA YAGURABA** **VOLUME 10**

TRANSLATION
Andrew Cunningham

ADAPTATION
Betsy Aoki

LETTERING AND RETOUCH
Kaitlyn Wiley

COVER DESIGN
Kris Aubin

PROOFREADER
Marykate Jasper

SENIOR EDITOR
Shannon Fay

PREPRESS TECHNICIAN
Melanie Ujimori
Jules Valera

PRODUCTION MANAGER
Lissa Pattillo

EDITOR-IN-CHIEF
Julie Davis

ASSOCIATE PUBLISHER
Adam Arnold

PUBLISHER
Jason DeAngelis

Seven Seas press and purchase enquiries can be sent to Marketing Manager Lianne Sentar at press@gomanga.com. Information regarding the distribution and purchase of digital editions is available from Digital Manager CK Russell at digital@gomanga.com.

ISBN: 978-1-63858-372-1

Printed in Canada

First Printing: December 2022

10 9 8 7 6 5 4 3 2 1

FOLLOW US ONLINE: ***www.sevenseasentertainment.com***

READING DIRECTIONS

This book reads from ***right to left***, Japanese style. If this is your first time reading manga, you start reading from the top right panel on each page and take it from there. If you get lost, just follow the numbered diagram here. It may seem backwards at first, but you'll get the hang of it! Have fun!!

1
2
3
4
5
6
7
8
9

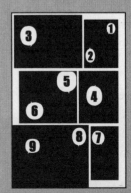